To [illegible]

Lots of Good Luck

in your [illegible] to

meet you

Love

Pat [illegible]

(2002)

THE ~~MIS~~ADVENTURES OF YIA YIA AND LUCEY

Patricia M. Linaris

outskirtspress
DENVER, COLORADO

This is a work of fiction. The events and characters described herein are imaginary and are not intended to refer to specific places or living persons. The opinions expressed in this manuscript are solely the opinions of the author and do not represent the opinions or thoughts of the publisher. The author has represented and warranted full ownership and/or legal right to publish all the materials in this book.

The Misadventures of Yia Yia and Lucey

v4.0

Outskirts Press, Inc.
http://www.outskirtspress.com

Paperback ISBN: 978-1-4787-4842-7
Hardback ISBN: 978-1-4787-4057-5

PRINTED IN THE UNITED STATES OF AMERICA

Preface

In the summer of 2007, three of my twelve grandchildren (the Dirty Dozen) headed off to Connecticut for sleep away camp. Their Mom, my daughter, strongly encouraged me to write them, even giving me stamped postcards.

After the mundane remarks on the weather, how they were and what they were doing, the dialog got stale fast.

All that changed however, when the youngest wrote and told me what she and her bunkmates did to cheer themselves up when they felt blue. Appears the cabin would put on some fast music and they all proceeded to do, Jump, Jump, and Shake your Booty. Everyone got on her bunk and jumped up and down and then, well you get the picture.

Reading that, an idea sprung to life somewhere in the deepest recesses of my mind. Oh yeah.

My imagination came to life and the wild and crazy Yia Yia emerged. A sweet, if not naïve do gooder that embarks on her many adventures. Yia Yia always thinks the best of people and that's how she views them with respect to her. These letters sent to my Grands over the years have expanded to include Lucey. A mocking know it all Cock-a-Poo that describes life from a four-legged point of view. Lucey has a more jaded outlook, especially when it comes to Yia Yia.

So now, picture yourself at mail call, waiting for the next letter from your quirky grandmother. Open it and find out what kind of mischief she gets into next.

Dedication

This book is dedicated to my most amazing grandchildren who made me amaze myself.

Se Aga Po Poli

Table of Contents

2007

July 24	Shake Your Booty	3
August 04	Knee Boarding	8
August 09	Horseback Riding	11
August 10	Skating with Shirley	16
August 12	Stars and Stripes	21
August 14	The Codester	26
August 17	Motorcycle Ride	30
August 23	Nursing Home Visit	37
August 25	Beach Day	40
November 07	Layla, Ginger &?	45
December 01	Training Days	50

2008

January 17	Good Dog/Bad Dog	55
February 20	Lucey Taking Over	58
July 21	Heelies	61
July 26	Bungee Jumping	68
August 01	BSA CAR WASH	73
August 03	Shirley's Rescue	77
August 06	Camping with the BSA	81
August 11	Go Karting	88
August 29	Visiting Pennsylvania	94
August 30	Freckles	99
August 31	Lamenting to Cody	103
September 30	Lucey's Bath	108

2009

March 15	Uncle Danny's Visit	115
April 14	Lucey's New Look	120
May 02	Escape and Torment	125
June 30	Shirley's Park Outing	128
July 01	Yia Yia's Fleas	133
July 07	Shirley's Farm Rescue	135
July 09	Lucey's Adoption Plea	142
July 14	Meeting the Doc	145
July 20	Home Coming	152
September 29	Mega What?	155
December 04	Lucey's X-Mas List	157
December 05	May Day	160
December 18	Priscilla's Visit	164
December 27	Yia Yia's New Year Resolutions	169

2010

January 19	Good News/ Bad News	173
February 20	Book Club	176
March 10	Lucey's Plea to Alicia	180
March 12	Mea Culpa Letter to Cathy	183
March 13	Lunch Disaster	185
March 21	Waiting Room Entertainment	190
April 02	Doctor Interview	193
April 04	Doctor Interview X's 2	198
May 05	Neighborhood Review	204
July 28	Cat Attack	207
August 01	Cousin Elly Mae	216
August 11	A Nun's Story	222
August 12	Chaos	233

August 13	Friday the Thirteenth	237
November 14	Vet Visit	243

2011

April 08	Rent-a-Guy	249
April 12	Decisions, Decisions	256
April 25	Official Visit	261
July 18	Sarge and the Cookie Man	268
August 06	The Prodigal Friend Returns	277
August 08	Lucey's Evaluation	282
September 29	Shades of Thelma and Louise	289

2012

February 07	The Chase	301
February 08	Ride's Over	310
February 09	Yeronna?	316
February 10	Lucey the Therapy Dog	326
February 12	Cry for Help	333
February 13	Back Again	337
March 1	Bette Bam Be Lam	343
March 2	Lucey's Nightmares	351
March 10	The Burglar	356
March 15	Dance Lessons	363
April 16	Rehearsal	370
April 20	Show Time for Lucey	377
April 24	The Show	379
October 01	Moving On	386

2014

September	Encore	395

2007

Shake Your Booty

July 24, 2007

Dear Dani,

Thanks so much for your last letter. I'm so happy you are all settled in at camp and having mucho fun. I especially like the thing you and your bunkmates do to cheer yourselves up. That Jump, Jump, Shake your Booty thing. I decided to try it out sometime.

The opportunity presented itself the other evening. I was meeting three of my girlfriends at this new fancy restaurant. The place was all right. A little stuffy and way too quiet, no life to it, if you get my drift. I thought 'perfect.' We can have some fun and liven up this dreary atmosphere.

I explained it to my friends; at first they were a bit reluctant. Finally I convinced them to at least give it a try. I told them how you and your buddies did it to raise your spirits and besides a little exercise couldn't hurt.

I went over to the ancient piano player, slipped him a couple of bucks and asked him to play something jazzy. The girls and I stood on our chairs and when the music started, I demonstrated the jump, jump, shake your booty technique. Before long they all got into it and then some of the other customers joined in the fun too!

Everything was going along fine except for the part where my friend got a little too excited during the jump phase and jumped straight into her mashed potatoes. The place was really rocking now, a few people fell off their chairs and one person collided with the busboy carrying a bucket of dishes into the kitchen. Another fell into a waiter carrying a tray full of food. It was starting to turn into a regular pileup. Dishes and food were everywhere, but we all were still having a grand old time.

I was in the middle of shaking my booty when this very cranky gentleman approached. He introduced himself as the manager of this fine establishment. Looking at him I could see immediately that his shirt was way too tight. His face was very red, his eyes were bulging, and I thought I saw the veins on his neck popping out. No wonder he was cranky.

He wanted to know who started all this and I proudly told him, my granddaughter, Dani. Then he asked where you were and I told him at camp in Connecticut. With that his face got even redder and for sure his neck veins were popping out. Maybe he could use some fiber too, couldn't hurt.

Anyway being the gracious lady that I am, I asked him to join us and cheer himself up. That's when he started shaking. I tried to explain to him as they were throwing me out that you had to do Jump, Jump first and then Shake. Some people just don't have a sense of rhythm.

Well, I guess I won't be going back there anytime soon, maybe when they give that manager a bigger shirt or some medication.

I'll just practice at home for now. So, thanks again for the suggestion and write and give me some more ideas.

Love ya,

Yia

Knee Boarding

August 04,2007

Dear Dani,

Thanks so much for your last letter. You always come up with the best suggestions. That knee boarding stuff sounded great and I decided to give it a try. Hopefully, it will turn out better than Jump, Jump, Shake your Booty.

I called my friend Shirley to come over give it a go with me. At first, she was a little reluctant. Thought we would get thrown out of another place again. I assured her we were going to do it outside, all around my townhouse complex. Okay, she said. What a good sport.

Not knowing exactly what knee boarding was, I figured you have to have a board and something to make it move. Simple. I got out my ironing board, took off the legs and voila, a knee-board. Next, I tied it to the bumper of my car and I was all set.

When Shirley arrived, I explained to her that all she had to do was to kneel on the board and I would drive her around. It was almost like sledding but without snow and kneeling instead of sitting. She was a little skeptical but I told her not to be a sissy. Seemed like a no brainer, and she was on board, so to speak.

Anyway, it started out okay except Shirley kept falling off once I got past 50MPH. I couldn't hear her too well because all my neighbors were yelling at me. I think they couldn't wait to have a turn.

I stopped and went back to get her but then the cutest policeman stopped me. He asked me what I thought I was doing. I told him knee boarding and would he like a turn?

"Do you think you're funny," he asked? "No," I said, "but my Grandkids do." "What are you doing in the yard? Don't you know you shouldn't be four wheeling around here?" was his next questions. "Listen." I told him, "The guy who sold me this car said I could four wheel this baby off road and this is off road."

Again he asked if I thought I was funny. He has to be the dumbest cop around. Didn't he ask me that already? So in case he wasn't too bright, I answered him very slowly so he could understand. "NOOOOOO, but my Grandchildren think I'm a riot."

Then he wanted to know if I was drinking. Not yet I said, but maybe he would like to go out for one later. By that time Shirley managed to find me. She had fallen off somewhere between houses. When she heard me ask him out for a drink, she told him not to go to the place that threw me out last week.

He needed to know all about that and I tried to explain how I was just teaching everybody the Jump, Jump, Shake your Booty thing and suggested we give it a try at a new place when we go for drinks. He got very flustered. Scratched his head and kept mumbling to himself, "Why me? Why me?" "Just your lucky day," I told him and wouldn't you know it, he asked me if I thought I was being funny again? What can I say? Obviously, there's no hope for him.

Well, I figured the drinks were off, so I thanked him for stopping by and if he wasn't busy would he put my ironing board back together for me. I didn't hear his answer, he kept on mumbling, however now he started to jump up and down and shake his head. When I told him he wasn't doing it right, you have to shake your booty not your head, he started crying. So cute, but box of rocks.

Keep those suggestions coming. I'm having the best times ever! Love ya,

Yia

Horseback Riding

August 09, 2007

Hi Katie,

I've been writing Dani and she's been giving me lots of ideas for having fun. That knee boarding one was terrific. My neighbors are still waving and yelling at me. They are mighty sore they didn't get a chance to try it out. I was thinking about how much you enjoy horseback riding and decided that was what I was going to do next.

Early one morning I went to the local stable to get me a horse. Walking around by the corral fence was a big lanky fellow who was wearing jeans, a checkered shirt, and cowboy boots all topped off with a big Stetson hat, a real cowboy. He saw me and meandered over. He introduced himself as Tex and asked what he could do for me.

I told him I wanted to go riding; he paused for a few seconds, pushed his hat back a bit and smiled. "Ma'am," he said, "you want to go riding on a horse? Have you ever ridden before?" "No," I told him, "but my granddaughters ride all the time and tell me how much fun it is, so yeah, I want to go riding on a horse."

Then he asked, "At your age?" I told him I thought I was old enough but if I wasn't I'd come back in a few years. With that he just looked down at his boots and kicked the dirt a little. He said,

"Ok lady if that's what you want." He told me he had the perfect horse for me and led me into the barn. I said I especially wanted one with spots because that was my granddaughter's favorite.

Not to worry, he said because this horse was loaded with spots. We got to the end of the barn and in the very last stall there was a horse leaning against the wall. Tex said his name was Slug and pointed out all the spots on him. They were a little strange looking and when I asked Tex what kind of spots they were, he answered, "age spots." "Oh Ok, and I guess Slug is short for Slugger?" "Something like that you could say, Ma'am," was his reply.

Slug seemed very tired; it was probably his naptime. Tex had some trouble getting him to get off the stall wall. Slug just wasn't in the mood.

Tex told me he was taking some people out on a trail rides in a couple of days and would I like to join them? "You betcha, count me in," I answered. Then I asked Tex if it would be all right to bring Slug some treats. He said sure, that would be okay and he would see me in a couple of days. I could hardly wait. I called some of my friends to see if they wanted to come but they all must be out of town or busy, nobody answered.

Tex phoned and let me know we were all set for a trail ride the following day. I got out all my cowgirl stuff with the fringe and went out and bought me a pair of boots with spurs. I saw that in the movies, they jingle when you walk. I was going to be looking so good!

I showed up early, all decked out and Tex was pretty amazed. He kept shaking his head. Nobody gets that booty thing around here. I told Tex I was going see Slug, I wanted to give him the treats I brought him.

Being he was so tired the other day, I got him some things to perk him up. Give him a little more pep. I was pretty sure he needed more fiber in his diet so I gave him a bottle of fiber pills and then some energy bars and let him wash it all down with a few bottles of Red Bull. Yep, that should help.

Tex saddled him up and helped me on. Then he took me to the front of the line with him. I think he liked my outfit and wanted to show me off. There were about eight other riders behind us. Everyone seemed to know Slug. They kept asking what's that Slug doing here? Gee, I was already making friends.

We set off going single file onto the trail that led deep into the woods. In a little while Slug seemed to get livelier. He started flipping and lifting his tail and next he began passing gas. I was right; he was probably all backed up and that needed fiber. My new friends were cheering us on; they were yelling, "Go, go, go on, get out of here." Tex remarked about them being downwind. Slug was certainly making progress because he began twitching and shaking his booty. Finally, someone gets it.

I said, "Giddy up," and kicked him a bit with my spurs. All of a sudden, Slug became a rocket ship; man, he was running wildly. I tried kicking him again to make him slow down, but he was having too much fun.

All my new friends and Tex were chasing after us. I sure put some life in this party. I tried to hear what they were yelling but couldn't because Slug kept passing gas too loud. I was hanging on for dear life when Slug ran out of the woods and onto the highway. We were way out in front of the other riders and we even passed a police car going at least 60 MPH.

Without any warning, Slug suddenly stopped. Must have run out of gas. Next thing, the police car reaches us and stops. Out steps the same cute policeman that I met when I was knee boarding. Boy, was he sure glad to see me. He just kept pointing and laughing. The EMT's said he was hysterical when they showed up.

By now Tex and the others caught up to us. Tex told me to take my next ride in that nice big police car and he was taking Slug to the glue factory.

All the other riders were off their horses and rubbing their booty's. Some were shaking pretty well too. Next, some EMT's put a special jacket on my cutey policeman and took him away. His partner drove me home.

He was very grouchy and I told him there were some pills for that. He asked me if I thought I was funny. All these cops use the same line. Must be taught that at the Academy.

Well, that's all for now. I'm going to visit Slug and give him some more fiber. Seems he really needed it.

Love you bunches,

Yia Yia

Skating with Shirley

August 10, 2007

Hi All,

Mom told me you were sharing my letters. I hope you are enjoying reading about my adventures. I'm having the best times ever! In fact, after my butt stopped hurting from the last one, I decided to go and check on Slug; to see how he's doing .I got to the stable early and spotted Tex walking around the corral. He saw me and came over. "What can I do for you today, Ma'am?" he asked. Geez, he's so polite. I thought I detected a little twitch, no, probably my imagination. "Oh, I thought I'd visit Slug. I brought him a few treats he likes," I said.

Tex pushed back his cowboy hat and gave me a long hard look. For sure it was a twitch. I saw it again. "Well shucks Ma'am, you won't be seeing Slug today or anytime soon. He's been taken out to pasture. If you don't mind me saying so Ma'am, maybe you should go there too."

"Oh Geez, Tex, I'd love to go but I'm going to visit my cute policeman today. I won't have time for both. I'll come back another day. Maybe I'll go riding again. The last time was so much fun." "Don't think so, Ma'am. The stable is getting closed. Too many people suing us after that last trail ride. Lots of back injuries and some folks are complaining about post traumatic stress too."

"What a bunch of wimps. Well, take care of yourself, Tex. Better check out that twitch. See ya," and off I went to visit my cutie patootie. When I got to the hospital, I went to the receptionist to get my cutie's room number. She told me he couldn't have any visitors right then because he was having a shock treatment.

I figured he must have the hiccups and they were trying to scare him. My Dad used to try to cure mine like that when I was little. He'd shock me by making scary faces and creepy weird screams. It never worked on me, but my brothers used to hide under the bed for hours.

The lady at the desk suggested I go to the garden while I waited, so I went outside and looked around at all the pretty flowers and plants. It was very relaxing and peaceful. While I was exploring, I noticed a woman sitting on a bench all alone, making noises that sounded like chipmunk chatter. I became intrigued and went over to sit by her. I couldn't believe it. It was my new friend Shirley. I hadn't seen her since I took her knee boarding. "Hey Shirl, what are you doing here?" "Oh, Yia, I had some issues and my Doctor had me come here for some rest, that's all," she told me. We started talking and I told her all the neat things I was doing. She complained that she never gets a chance to do any fun stuff.

Next thing I knew, I asked her if she would like to have some fun with me. She said, "Sure, why not? I'm crazy enough to try anything." I wanted to go right then, but she told me I had to come back tomorrow and sign her out. No problem, what are friends for?

I decided we should go skating. When I was growing up I roller-skated all the time. In fact, I used to wear my skate key around my neck like it was the Hope Diamond. My biggest treat was following the paving trucks all around the neighborhood so I could be the first one to skate on the newly paved streets.

This is going to be fantastic!

The following morning I got up early, put on my support stockings, knee brace and took my arthritis medicine. Next came my outfit. A cute blue sequin number, snug but the sequins were in good shape. I squeezed into it and put on the football helmet I borrowed from Christopher. Can't be too careful at my age. The final stop, the sporting good store. I asked the salesman for two pair of in-line skates. A jolly sort, he couldn't stop laughing, he even threw in pink fuzzy pom poms and thought that was a hoot.

I hurried back to the hospital to pick up my buddy Shirley. You would be amazed Dani at all the friends I'm making. Everywhere I went people were shouting, waving and pointing at me.

Shirley was waiting anxiously for me when I got there. She had on an electric blue body suit with a big orange lightening bolt across the chest. Said she borrowed it from her Grandson who was into scuba diving. Way to go Shirl can't miss you in that. Shirley wasn't confident about her skating, she told me she hadn't roller-skated in a long while. "Don't worry Shirl", I said, "it'll come back to you in no time, besides I'm a skating champ. You can just lean on me!"

And off we went. At first the new skates were a bit tricky. I was used to the 4-wheel kind, not these with a row of rollers going down the middle. It took a bit of getting used to. Soon though, I was up and zooming while Shirley was still struggling with her balance.

We found a new paved street and I was in my glory. As I said, Shirl was having trouble staying upright and keeping up with me. I needed a way for her to gain more confidence. Then I had a stroked of genius. We were sitting on a bench taking a break when a bus came along and stopped.

"C'mon Shirl, I have the solution." I took rope and tied us to the back bumper of the bus. We were going along fine except every time the bus stopped Shirley would smash into it. This went on for a while and finally at the crest of a hill, the bus stopped and once again, Shirley slammed into its back. "That's enough!" she yelled and untied herself. "Don't do it Shirl, don't do it here!"

But I was too late, she was already loose and when the bus pulled off she was at the top of a very steep road. I saw her flailing and trying to catch herself while I was busy getting free of the bus.

As I started back to her, I saw her begin to roll down the center of the road. She was gaining speed and drew lots of attention. All that screaming had people gawking. I estimated she had to be going at least 80 MPH, well, maybe not that fast, but boy, she was smoking!

At the end of the street was a pier with a boat ramp. As she approached, Shirley never slowed down. She shot onto ramp, hitting each bump as if they were railroad tracks. Her arms were spinning like airplane propellers and she howled bloody murder the whole way. At the end of the ramp, she flew off and soared high into the air, did two and a half flips and hit the water creating a 50-foot spray.

The huge crowd that gathered cheered and applauded. Fortunately for her, someone must have called 911.By the time I reached the scene, they had her out of the water and were giving her first aid. I didn't get chance to speak to her before an ambulance came and took her away.

Gee, I hope she'll be okay. Maybe when she feels better I could give her some pointers on how to improve her skating technique. Meanwhile, I'll go back to see my cutie patootie policeman. He should be done with his shock treatment by now. Who knows, maybe Shirley will be there too and we can all think of ways to have more fun.

Later, Big Hugs

Yia

Stars and Stripes

August 12,2007

Dear Shirley,

I hope you're feeling better and have cut down on your caffeine. The Doctor told me they only had to pump your stomach once to get rid of all that river water. Next time you should wear a floatation device if you want to go near the water.

While I've been waiting for you to recover, I've been thinking about all the fun I've been having. It's only right that I should share it with my neighbors. They are such a quiet bunch and I never see them having a good time. Of course, the exception was when I was knee boarding and they all came out to cheer. Suddenly, I got an inspiration. I was going to organize a parade around my complex for everyone to enjoy, something to raise the community's spirit.

First, I needed a band. Nothing special, just some people to enhance the Sousa marching music. My kids and I used to march around the house clanging pot lids and beating pans with wooden spoons all to the music of Stars and Stripes Forever. Not much on talent, but the noise cracked the plaster and knocked the pictures off the walls.

The plan was beginning to take shape. Next, I needed marchers. I had to look for people who weren't too busy. I drove up the Avenue and there on a corner was a group of young fellows hanging out. I pulled over to talk to them and asked them to join my band. They were probably all related; they kept calling each other Bro.

Had to be a family nickname. The oldest Bro and spokesman wasn't too sure. He must have been worried about the other's safety because he kept asking me about security at my complex. I told him my place is so safe that people don't even lock their doors. That reassured him and he said, "Count us in."

Further up the Avenue, I saw some nice ladies at a bus stop. I could tell they were collecting donations because they had shopping carts full of stuff. I told them my plan and said there were plenty of items in the clubhouse that could probably use. They volunteered right away.

Just a few more and I'm all set. As luck would have it, I spotted two older gents sitting on a porch. They were playing a game of passing a brown paper sack back and forth between them. I could tell those two could use some exercise. One of the men had on a most interesting necklace. I asked him what it was and he told me it was a flea collar. When I inquired if it came indifferent colors he took a real long look into the sack. Finally, they both agreed it could be cool and joined.

Eventually, the big day arrived. I donned my Drum Majorette outfit, tied my orthopedic shoes real tight and collected my band. I distributed the pots and pans, the pot lids, some cow bells, wooden spoons and pumped the music on my portable stereo to the max. I proudly stood in front with my American flag and led the way. The others fell in step behind me.

On my first turn round the complex not too many neighbors came out, but boy, on the second sweep, they showed up in force. All of them were cheering and shouting, mostly doing that one finger salute. My group got into the spirit and yelled right back and did that salute too! Talk about bringing people together.

We proceeded to the clubhouse where I encouraged my group to take a dip in the pool. I didn't have to tell them twice because with no hesitation, they jumped in at once. My neighbors, who were already swimming were good sports; they all got out to give them room.

Unfortunately, it didn't last long. The lifeguard tested the water and claimed it was polluted. He ordered the pool emptied. Sure hope my new friends don't get sick. But not to worry, all was not lost. I invited my band into the clubhouse to have some pizza and relax. I was disappointed though, none of my neighbors joined us, but they were yelling and cheering outside.

The ladies, Bless them, started looking for donations right away. I found some hefty bags to give them and that clubhouse was empty in no time.

Meanwhile, the gents with the brown sack got everyone into that passing game. I didn't realize how popular it was, it certainly brought a smile to all their faces.

Things were going along just swell. Even that cranky policeman showed up. Seems a few of the Bros got lost and wandered into some of the houses. The neighbors were nice enough to call to get them help. Soon, a paddy wagon arrived and the policeman insisted my new friends take a ride.

As my paraders got into the wagon, all my neighbors cheered even louder and kept doing that one finger salute. And lo and behold, before you knew it, the paraders were banging on the windows giving that finger right back to everyone, including me. I was so moved. What else could I do? I returned the salute.

Well, it just keeps getting better. As if thanks weren't enough, I was told not to attend the next homeowner's meeting. I think they are planning to surprise me with a plaque or something. How lucky can you get?

So, that's about it for now, Shirl. I'll see you on next visitor's day. I'll bring some music and pot lids so we can do some entertaining.

Love,

Yia

The Codester

August 14, 2007

Hi Kids,

Hope everyone is well and getting ready for the new school year. I'm thinking of going back myself. I haven't decided what courses to take yet. I just want it to be something fun.

Early last week, Aunt Mimi asked me to come over and watch her children and Cody. Cody, aka the Codester, or the Prince is their buff colored Cock-a-Poo with a haughty attitude. I swear if he could talk there would be people to whom he wouldn't even speak. Anyway, she had some errands to run and I said, "Sure. no prob."

Early the next day I went to her house. Uncle Steven was in the garage. I could tell he was having a bad moment. He was headed out to play a few rounds golf and couldn't decide what car to take. He just stood there paralyzed, waiting for Aunt Mimi. She breezed into the garage, let the air out of one of the car's tires and then Uncle Steven didn't have a choice. He was mightily relieved and went merrily on his way.

I found the kids at the table eating breakfast. Sal was having his lightly toasted bagel with butter and Nesquik. Katie was eating the middle out of her M&M pancakes and Dani was wolfing down her third bowl of pasta. Everyone was glad to see me.

As she was leaving, Aunt Mimi gave me some instructions, the girls were to practice the piano and Sal had 6 hours of studying. He was allowed a 20-minute break after every 2 hours. Then she gave me 2 pages of typed instructions for Cody. When to walk him, when and what to feed him, how to cut his meat, when to give him a nap and what radio station he like to listen to and more. Much more. I had to read all of it and sign off on the bottom that I understood. Feeling confident that I could do it, she waved good-bye to the kids and kissed the dog.

As soon as she left, I told the kids that I was now in charge and they had to listen to me. They said, "Of course, Yia Yia." Then Sal went downstairs to play his drums, Katie went upstairs to go under her covers and read her latest book and Dani settled down to watch her 345th episode of Animal Planet. I tidied up the kitchen, let Cody out and went upstairs to attack the Vesuvius Mountain of laundry on the guest bed.

Time slipped away from me and when all the laundry was folded, I went back downstairs. Dani was on the 367th episode of Animal Planet, Sal was lifting weights and Katie was still in her room. I didn't see Cody anywhere and asked Sal and Dani if they let him in. They both said, "No!" I went out on the deck to look and call for him. No Cody. I looked in the yard, no Cody. Sheer terror was gripping me. I threw the kids in the car, drove out and scoured the neighborhood for the dog. We stopped at all his doggie friends' houses but no one saw him. We canvassed block after block looking for him. I was trying to remember where I left my will in case Aunt Mimi murdered me.

Going down one of the blocks, I spotted three huge black dogs outside. On the front steps of their house, lay a fluffy little bundle. Might it be? Oh No! We got out of the car, I praying hard while I made it to the steps, grabbed it and ran as fast as I could. I didn't get far before I realized it was a stuffed fluffy animal.

Rats! I wasted 4 Hail Mary's and 6 Our Fathers. Well, maybe not wasted because when those three giant dogs sensed intruders were in their yard, they started barking and chasing us. I threw that stuffed animal as far as I could and we all high tailed it back to the car. Whew! Boy, that was close.

With heavy hearts, we headed back home. Pulling into the driveway, Katie exclaimed, "Look, Yia Yia, it's the Codester!"

There he was, sitting smugly at the front door. I forgot, Cody is a very superstitious dog. He always goes in and out of the same door, never walks under ladders and throws split salt over his left shoulder with his right paw. All's well in the world again.

As soon as things settled down, Aunt Mimi came home. She had gone to the spa for a facial and Mani, Pedi. After that she headed to the mall and saved Uncle Steven a bundle with all the stuff she bought on sale. She was bringing in the last shopping bag when Uncle Steven came home.

First thing he said was, "What's to eat?" Aunt Mimi stopped in her tracks and stared at him, "I can't believe you, Steven. I'm exhausted from doing all my chores today and all you can think about is food?" Uncle Steven begged her forgiveness and told her to go take a nap, he would fix supper. She said fine and went upstairs after kissing Cody, Hell-o.

Uncle Steven then proceeded to take out three or four pots, fill them with water and put them on the stove to boil. Next, he pulled out some take-out menus and called an Italian restaurant. He made me swear not to tell Aunt Mimi with threats of cutting off my knee injections. What could I do? I'm a Novocain junkie.

Supper was great. Aunt Mimi said Uncle Steven sauced the chicken too much but it was tasty. He smiled and kicked me under the table. I'm going to need that shot a lot sooner than I thought.

As soon as the table was cleared, I decided to head home. I told everyone, "Good Night," and waved good-bye. Then I kissed Cody and left.

Lot's of hugs and kisses,

Yia

Motorcycle Ride

August 17,2007

Hi Again,

Just wanted you to know the most amazing thing that happened. I was busy making my famous chicken soup for you guys, when the phone rang. I didn't recognize the number and when I picked up a raspy voice on the other end asked if I was the Grannie who organized parades.

"It's Yia Yia to you," I said and wanted to know who was calling and how did he get my number? Well, of all things he said his name was Turk and that the Bros told him to get in touch with me. I was elated. I asked where the Bros were and what they were doing?

Turk said they were doing 10 to 15 at the Big House. "Awesome," I told him. They finally got off that street corner. Nice that they are in big house, there was such a bunch of them. I advised Turk to get a hold of the donation ladies to help them decorate with the stuff they got from the clubhouse. Turk said he'd look into it.

Meanwhile he told me the Bros asked him to take me for a ride. How thoughtful, aren't they sweet? Of course, I had to know how to dress for this special occasion. Turk said he'd pick me up at 10 A.M. the next day on his hog and to wear something in leather.

Oh my goodness. I had just ridden a horse for the first time and now I got to ride a hog. Geez, this is so exciting, life is good. I searched my closet and came across my old lederhosen outfit. It had the nicest suspenders and the Alpine hat with the feathers was so fashionable, I found a pair of big wooly socks and some mountain shoes that completed the outfit.

Next day found me all decked out and anxiously waiting for Turk. He came riding up the street on a very loud motorbike with a bunch of his friends. I figured that the hog had to be much too slow for traffic. Oh well.

The group pulled into my driveway and he introduced all the fellows. He began with The Hun, Frenchy, The Greek, Polack and finally, himself, Turk. All the boys had on the cutest little helmets with spikes and leather jackets that said, Hell's Angels. I imagined they belonged to an international church group.

Before got on the road, Turk asked me to do him a little favor and stop by some banks. Seemed he needed some withdrawals. "Sure, happy to," I told him. With that he put me into this side-car next to him and off we went. Strangest thing, none of my neighbors were out. Lately they had been keeping tabs on me. Guess they're all asleep or away.

We proceeded down Passaic Avenue until we reached a bank. Turk handed me a note that he wanted me to give to a girl teller, any cute young teller. Well, Bless his heart, I believed Turk was shy and needed someone to break the ice for him. The Big Softie!

I got into line and gave the note to the cutest young teller I could find. She read it and got a little pale. She handed me a package and when I told her what Turk said, "Turk has his eyes on you," she passed out.

Well, Turk must be very fickle or desperate because he had me do that at two more banks. After the last one, Turk yelled, "Let's Go! We gotta make our get away!" I thought, about time, I finally get to have my ride.

We headed to Route 80 and started traveling very fast. They don't call it Route 80 for nothing. A few miles later, the boys all shouted it was time for me to buy the farm and Turk reached down to the sidecar's handle. Next thing I knew, I was zig zaging across the highway. By myself!

Cars were blowing their horns, lots of tires screeching, a sound or two of metal crunching, but I kept sailing all over the place. I headed straight for an 18-wheeler in the right lane and flew under it. Amazing all the stuff beneath that thing. I didn't stay long because I zoomed right out the other side and down a hill. At the bottom was a ramp and I became airborne.

I flew for a little while and then made the most perfect three-point landing in soft sand. I looked up, and there was that nice Doctor from the Asylum with three of his friends, they all had golf clubs in their hands.

He asked me what was going on and I explained to him that the Bros arranged for some church club members to give me a ride on a hog but they showed up to motorbikes instead. They all were members of a group called the Hell's Angels, I think and then, Turk, he's the leader, had me hit up a few banks for them so Turk could get some money to buy me a farm.

I don't think he was paying attention because all of his twitching had him distracted. Meanwhile that cranky policeman showed up and told me I had to go downtown with him. Don't these guys ever go uptown?

When we arrived all those cute tellers from the banks were huddled together in hard plastic chairs in the hallway. I was happy to see them so I could remind them that Turk still had his eyes on them, wink; wink. Can you believe that none of them had the foggiest idea who I was? So cute but such a bunch of rocks.

Officer Cranky spoke to them inside his office. I couldn't hear anything but I saw a lot of gesturing. He pointed to me a few times and all the girls just shrugged their shoulders and shook their heads, no. After a while he told them they could leave and then said he would drive me home. I asked him if he's like to come in for a bowl of my famous chicken soup. Couldn't hurt to cheer him up. "No Thanks," he replied. "I have to work overtime tonight. Route 80 is back up for miles and they need help filling out all the police reports."

Whatever, I sure do hope those boys made it to the farm.

Later,

Love you bunches,

Yia

Nursing Home Visit

August 23,2007

Hi Kids,

Glad you are all home from camp now, can't wait to see you so you can tell me all about your adventures. I'm still doing my thing and plan to expand my horizons. I've been having so much fun; I decided to share myself with those less fortunate.

What better place than a nursing home? Bet those folks would sure like someone to put a little sunshine in their lives. So, one fine day, I put on my cheerleader's outfit, tied my new fuzzy pink pom poms onto my orthopedic shoes and ventured out.

I walked into the nursing home and the lady at the front desk told me to sign in and someone would take me back to my room. "Oh no, Miss," I told her. "I'm not a patient, I came to make the folks happy. "With that she called to another woman and when she came over she said, "Get a load of this," then they both started laughing. See, it was working already.

She directed me to the Day Room and wished me good luck. I don't know why they call it a Day Room because most of the people there were sleeping or about to nod off. I'll have to fix that! I began arranging the wheelchairs in a semi circle around a makeshift stage I set up for myself. One man kept rolling away. I kept bringing him back. He kept rolling away. I kept bringing him back. After the third or fourth time, he asked me what I wanted. I told him I wanted to make him happy. He said, "Lady, I'll be happy when I get to the bathroom!" Then he revved up that wheelchair to warp speed and took off. Talk about a man on a mission. Well, at least he's getting his fiber.

Now I had to get my little group conscious. I looked around and saw a mop up against a wall. I borrowed it, took a big swing and hit a pail pretty hard. The pail rolled over with a big clank that even woke up the janitor. A couple of patient's defibrillators went off and they woke up in a hurry. The rest came around little by little.

I chose to begin with a medley of smiley songs, so everyone could sing along, that's always fun. We did, Let a Smile be Your Umbrella, When you're Smiling, and finished up with Put on a Happy Face. I told them to give me some really big smiles and show me some teeth. That's when they all threw their dentures at me. Now they're catching the spirit!

Next came the exercise portion of my program. I moved the furniture against the walls and lined up the wheelchairs in the back of the room. I explained we were to play 1-2-3 Red Light. One little old lady asked me if the were any prizes for the winners. I didn't have much but I offered to share some shots of Red Bull with them. That gave them incentive and we were off.

All was going fine except for some of the contestants running into each other. Eventually 1-2-3 Red Light turned into Bumper Cars, wheelchair style. It was unbelievable how they were really getting into it, especially the ones with a few shots of Red Bull in them. Two chairs ran into each other and got locked together. I tried to separate them and found a mop handle to try to pry them loose. I almost did it when I lost my balance, flew backwards, and the mop hit the little red box on the wall. Its glass broke and before you knew it, loud alarms were going off. The doors to room shut and then the sprinklers came on.

Everyone became nervous until I broke into, Splish, Splash I was Taking a Bath. That broke the tension and those folks really got into it. They stripped down to their underwear and shook their bootys the best they could. Now clearly, we were having some good clean fun.

In a little while, the sprinklers stopped, the Day Room door opened and in came firemen. I couldn't believe my eyes! That cute policeman changed jobs. He was now a cute fireman. He took one look at me and said, "You again?" I was so glad he remembered me especially after all those shock treatments. I said, "In the flesh." With that he took off his fire helmet and started jumping up and down on it. He finally got the jump, jump, jump part. Some of the other firemen came and took him away. He did the shaking part perfectly as he was being carried out.

All my new friends waved at me and gave me the best gummy smiles ever as they were being wheeled out. Clearly, my job is done here.

As I was leaving I asked the receptionist when she would like me to come back. She said she didn't know how long it would be to repair the day room. I offered to volunteer in the dining hall but she didn't think they would use it until all the dentures got sorted out She said, "Don't call us, we'll call you."

Okay, at least now I'll have time to visit Mr. Cute Fireman.

Later,

Luv ya,

Yia

Beach Day

August 25,2007

Hi Guys,

So great to hear all your voices, I can't wait to see you tomorrow. I know it's sad that camp is over, but just think of the great adventures awaiting you. A whole new school year begins with new classes and so much to learn. I can hardly believe that Sal will be starting High School.

With summer winding down, I wanted to go to the beach just one more time. I overheard Georgia say her family was planning to go, so I thought I'd just tag along .By the time I got to their house, Uncle Chris had the car already packed. There was no room left for me. No problem, I told him. I saw this movie on TV about The Griswold Vacation where the grandmother rides on the roof of the car.

At first Uncle Chris said, "No way!" but I convinced him it would be fine, a piece of cake. All he had to do was put my beach chair and me onto the roof rack of the car then tie me up with some bungee cords. It would like riding in a double decker bus.

He wasn't really thrilled with the idea but did it anyway and soon we were on our way. From the top of the car one had a bird's eye view and plenty of strong wind gusts. I had to be careful of low-lying tree limbs and small under passes. It was pretty exciting.

Of course, a few people on the Parkway were surprised to see me. I just waved and smiled at them. One thing really got to be annoying though; the little bugs that stick to the windshields when you're driving, were now sticking to my sunglasses and teeth. I couldn't give out big toothy smiles. No matter. Soon I got tired and lowered the back of my beach chair and took a nap.

When woke up, I found I was under a canopy. Oh yeah, it had to be Burger King. Christopher was getting his daily fix of chicken fingers and French fries and orange soda, no ice.

From there it wasn't far to the beach. We arrived and Uncle Chris helped me down from my perch. It took only about ten minutes for the feeling to come back into my legs and about twenty minutes to floss the bugs from my teeth. We found a nice spot, opened the umbrellas and set out the chairs. Aunt Pat got right into hers, put down her jug of Margarita's and opened a book.

Annie stripped down to teensy-weensy bikini and spread her blanket as far away from her parents as she possibly could. She then proceeded to look totally bored. Christopher finished off his Burger King meal and played with the toy. His collection is getting so large that Uncle Chris is thinking about an extension to the house to be able to store them all.

Georgia, ever the Fashionista, was prancing around the beach in a pair of high-heeled flip-flops and matching purse, wherever does she find them? She sure can accessorize.

As for Uncle Chris, he got tired sitting around just staring at any boy that came within 50 feet of the girls and decided to play Frisbee with himself. He's in amazing shape. You should have seen him running back and forth, throwing and catching to himself. He managed to scare off any boys that were brave enough to hang around and after fifteen minutes he was exhausted. He jogged over, then plopped down next to Aunt Pat and helped her polish off the stuff in the jug.

Meanwhile, I slathered myself with Panama Jack sunscreen and topped it off with some olive oil. It's very good for your skin. One can never be too careful. I started getting weary of sitting, actually my butt was a little sore from the car ride; I needed some exercise.

High tide began coming in strong and lots of kids took advantage of the waves. I asked the girls to teach me how to boogey board and they said, "Sure Yia." First, I had to borrow Christopher's board. He drove a hard bargain. He said, "Alwright, it'll cost you two trips to Burger Kings and a bag of Milanos for the goggles." He's turning into a pint size Donald Twump.

I put on my rubber swim cap, Christopher's goggles, and oiled myself down again. All prepared, Annie and Georgia and I paddled out to where the waves broke. We did a couple of runs and I was having the best time ever.

On our next trip out, we couldn't believe our eyes. It looked like the giant tidal wave that swallowed Manhattan was coming straight at us. We brace ourselves and hoped for the best. As the wave crested, the girls rode it in like champs. I was holding on for dear life but overdid it with the olive oil. I slipped off the board and into the water, tumbling over and over until I landed on the beach feet first. I started being sucked back into the water when someone grabbed my ankles and dragged me to shore. I couldn't have been easy with all that oil.

Finally, he stopped and rolled me over. I was sputtering and coughing, but eternally grateful. I took of my goggles and swim cap to thank my rescuer. There is something to be said of Fate, because right in front of me was that cute fireman/policeman. He saved my life. Seems they gave him a few days off after the nursing home incident. Talk about being at the right place at the right time!

He was even more surprised than me. You could say he was speechless. He was so overcome; he started to cry. I told him since he had saved my life, I would be his forever and ever. With that he cried even harder, actually, he howled.

Everyone came to make sure I was okay and in the excitement, my rescuer slipped away. He's so modest, but I'll track him down when I get home.

Soon, it was time to go home. Christopher was weally, weally mad at me for losing his board. He's suing me for a replacement and a year's worth of kid's meals. Uncle Chris volunteered to ride home on the top of the car. He said he could use the peace and quiet. I warned him about getting bugs in his mouth and he said he wasn't planning on doing much smiling in the near future.

I guess he was ok up there except that his long legs hung over the wind shield and Aunt Pat kept turning on the wipers.

I'm sorry to see the summer go, I was just getting into the swing of things and making new friends. I guess I'll have to take up winter sports. Anyone interested?

Later,

Lot's of Hugs,

Yia

Layla, Ginger &?

November 07,2007

Hi All,

I finally did it!! All of you have been encouraging me to get a puppy. I wasn't too sure. With all my adventures, I thought having a dog would cut into my escapades. However, your Moms all volunteered to take care of one if I required free time. So I took the plunge.

Actually, the circumstances presented themselves. I was visiting with Aunt Sophia in Pennsylvania, and having a grand old time with your cousins. On one especially bleak and dreary November morning, she announces we were going to Country Junction. What's that you ask? Country Junction is an old fashion general store on steroids. It has everything. Its motto is, "If we don't have it, you don't need it."

We gathered up Trisha and put Abbie in her baby car seat. RJ was in pre-school that morning. I wasn't even thinking about getting a pup that day. No, I was planning to wait for spring when the weather would be better. So much for plans.

Once there, I was amazed at the size of the place. Short on frills, no ambience to speak of, but lots of merchandise. It was then Aunt Sophia told me that her friend ran the pet department. Immediately hearing that, the kids pleaded to go see the puppies. I was doomed.

After walking what seemed to be miles, though a gazillion mazes, we came into an area with the distinct aroma of pets. You know what I mean? Aunt Sophia introduced me to her friend, Marge, and proceeded to tell her that I was thinking of getting a Cock-a-Poo. I settled on that breed because of knowing Cody for two years, he's the calmest and smartest little dog with a lot of attitude. He's low maintenance, no shedding, no bad habits, and so laid back he's almost a non-dog. Perfect for me, a Cock-a-Poo was my choice.

Marge said she just got in a litter of them and took us over to a pen. There laid six little buff-colored Cock-a-Poos, all huddled together in the straw keeping warm. As we neared them, they stirred, shook themselves off and ran over to the side of the pen where they began yipping and yapping and looking for attention.

The litter contained four females and two males. They were eight weeks old and the biggest probably weighed in at only five pounds. They were tiny but very energetic and friendly. The kids were so excited and wanted to hold them. Marge picked out three pups and brought them to a gated area to play.

After a while, Aunt Sophia checked the time and said we had to go pick up RJ. We thanked Marge, who gathered up the pups and returned them to the pen. On the way out, I stopped to take a second look at them, my heart melting already.

Driving to the preschool, I had a great thought. Aunt Pat and Aunt Sara both were eager to get a dog. I called Aunt Pat and offered to buy the family a puppy for X-Mas. She jumped at the chance. She too, knew the Codester and was impressed by him and the breed. Uncle Chris was reluctant but she said, "He would get over it. So, Yes, Yes, Yes!!!"In fact, she had a name already chosen, Layla. Pup number one was it's way to a new family.

Next, Uncle Tom, he's been hesitant about getting a dog, although Aunt Sara has been pleading for one, like forever. I reached him at work and he had forty questions for me and also requested a photo. Really? So we pick up RJ and went back to see the pups again. Same deal to make our way to the pet department. Now RJ joins in playing with the pups and I watch the interaction.

The kids are having a blast, and the puppies doing what puppies do. Licking faces, tugging on shoestrings, trying to shake and losing their balance and squeaky woofing acting tough, all trying to get adopted. (They know.)

I sent Uncle T some photos and after more interrogation than the F.B.I., he agrees to the deal. "Get the pup, but don't let anyone in my family know." I chose the bigger female of the bunch, calling her Ginger. Okay, pup number two has a new home.

Now comes decision time. Do I or don't I? Oh, but that littlest female really took a liking to me. Goodness knows she so tiny and sweet. How can I turn away? I don't know. Hmmm. Oh, all right. She's mine.

We get the pups, sadly leaving the other three behind. The pups ride out of the store in their own grocery cart like a parade. Into a cardboard box they go for the ride to Aunt Sophia's house. After some play time and water the pups are put into my car for the journey to New Jersey. They settle down after a while and I feel like Santa Claus. Make that Mrs. Claus on my way with very special presents.

First stop, Aunt Pat's where she is anxiously waiting by the door. Layla is handed over to her new family and it's love at first site. (Uncle Chris eventually comes around.)Next day takes me to Uncle T's house. He told me to call when I reached his block. Okay. I do as I'm told. Next I'm instructed to pull up to house and wait. Okay. I'm waiting. Out he comes. Big broad smile. He takes Ginger from me, (she has on a big red bow), and tells me go in the house and call everyone into the kitchen so he can make an entrance. OKAY! Already. Geez.

I do so; Allie, John and Thomas come quickly, Aunt Sara lagging behind. All in place, Uncle T struts in holding Ginger and everyone is hooting and hollering. Everyone except Aunt Sara, she is crying, truly surprised and overwhelmed. In spite of himself, Uncle T is smitten with the pup too.

So now it's just me and? She needs a name. Gosh, she's so dainty, such a little princess. So, Princess? No. Queenie? No. Let see. Little, delicate, sweet, I got it. Her name will be Lacey. Yeah, that's it. Perfect.

Next few days are filled with getting her a crate, puppy proofing the house and taking her to the vet. So much to do for one small dog, she weighs in at three and a half pounds and is proclaimed healthy.

Trying to housebreak her is another story. I take her outside every couple of hours where she looks all around at the birds, the trees and what ever strikes her fancy. No idea that this is where she is to do her business. No, this is fun time. I scoop her up and bring her inside where she pees immediately. "No, no, no Lacey. Outside, you do it outside."

I get a quizzical look and she's off attacking a new pair of my shoes. Oops, have to put them away. Okay, back outside. "Com'on Lacey, Make! I'll give you a treat. Hurry up, make already." Now I'm hopping from one foot to the other and I have to go. Back inside, I do the cross-legged walk to the bathroom and she pees on the carpet. ARRGGHH!!!Why did I get a pup in the fall? It's so hard to train them. I just have to keep trying.

"Hold on Lacey, don't chew that wire." Drat! Off to the store I went and bought baby gates. Now my house looked like a maze with all the blockades.

She's really good at night. I put her in the crate in the laundry room and she's quiet most of the night. I convinced myself to be more patient and it'll work out.

If I only knew.

Love.

Yia

Training Days

December 01,2007

Hi Kids,

Getting ready for Christmas yet? Make sure I get your list early. I've been slowing down a bit. Nothing to worry about, no, it's the puppy. Forgot how much work they are, I'm exhausted by noon. I've been taking her out every two hours for house breaking. So far she hasn't gotten the idea.

Should have stuck to my guns about getting a pup in the spring; too late now. The weather hasn't helped much either. She hates the cold and runs back towards the house. It's not making me any happier either.

I have been putting gates all over but somehow she manages to get through them and get into areas where she does her mischief. The other day she was in the den behind the couch chewing on the lamp wire. It was almost bitten in half before I reached her. I couldn't get over the gates. I'm amazed she didn't get a shock from it. I know I did when I picked it up.

Also, she has begun jumping and climbing. Cat like, I find her on furniture and steps, I have no idea how she got there. I'm beginning to think she's possessed. On the plus side, she's good at night in her crate. She can hold her business until morning without an accident, but she pees every half hour in the house during the day. Go figure.

Mornings are the worse time for me. I don't even have coffee in me when I'm outside in my pajamas pleading with her to make. The rest of the day is spent keeping her out of trouble. Well, it won't last forever. It just can't!

Anyway, send those lists, it will get my mind on something else.

Thanks,

Yia

2008

Good Dog/Bad Dog

January17, 2008

Hi All,

The holidays are all finished and now we settle down and wait for the end of winter. It can't come quick enough for me. I never realized how much I don't enjoy the cold weather. Never thought too much about it before. Nowadays, I stand shivering and sniffling every morning trying to get Lucey to do her business.

Oh yeah. I changed her name. She is definitely not a Lacey, far from dainty. Quite the opposite I have no idea how she manages to get on things. For instance, the kitchen island, the kitchen table, the dining room table, top of the couch. And that's just the beginning. She has springs on her feet; I swear she's 50% kangaroo.

She has been getting into stuff I've never even had dreamed she could. But in her defense, she has infinite patience with kids. Over Christmas the little ones were dragging her around, teasing her, dressing her up in doll clothes, sticking her in boxes. You name it; they did it. Lucey never once tried to get away or growled or showed anything but tolerance. In fact, once a few of them were in the Jacuzzi having a bubble bath. Lucey, managed to get up on the tub's edge and from there she jumped right in and joined them.

She truly loves kids. How bad could she be? One good quality, friendly; don't even go there, she loves everyone, doesn't matter who there are. Anyone who comes to the door or she meets on the street, is greeted like a long lost friend.

That's the good stuff. The other side of the coin is her constant need for attention. So needy, she's always in your face, literally. Climbs all over you, there's no getting away from her.

And talk about Houdini. I don't know how she gets past all the gates I set up, but I'm the one locked in the kitchen area. I have rolled up the rugs, unplugged anything at floor level and stripped the house of anything she might chew.

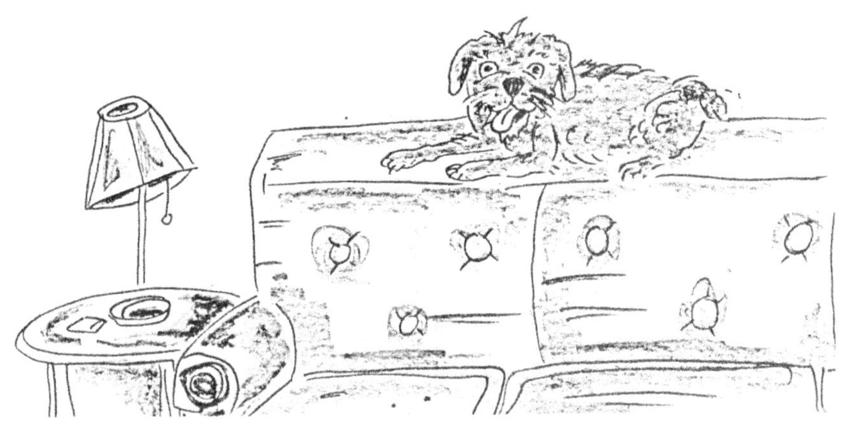

Like I said, I forgot all the things a pup can get into, time will settle her down. I hope.

Stay warm.

Love,

Yia

Lucey Taking Over

February 20,2008

Hi,

What I really mean is HELP!! I'm cracking! The dog has me on the ropes. Like I told you before, she has some good qualities. That's what's making me crazed. She's so over the top friendly and sweet. It's sickening.

It's like when you're in school and there's one girl that's perky and wants to be everybody's pal. You know the kind. A real suck up to the teacher and always volunteering to help with whatever. The one that comes into the cafeteria when you hanging with your friends getting the latest gossip. In she strolls, greets everyone and says, "Mind if I join you?" Then down she sits. My group gathers up their lunch debris, roll their eyes and says, "See ya later," leaving me with Miss Sugar.

I'm trying hard to swallow the last of my peanut butter sandwich, which is stuck to the roof of my mouth. Meanwhile, she's telling me how nice my hair looks today. Really? It was one of my worst hair days. LIAR! I manage to leave and she goes right over to another unsuspecting table.

But that's not the worst of it. Oh no. I'm at my locker and the cutest guy that I have a crush on, comes over to talk to me. We're hitting it off and guess who just happens to stop by. Yeah!

He says, HI to her and then tells me he'll see me later. I want to strangle her.

The following day before the morning bell, he was at my locker as I went to get my books. Yea! We start talking and I think he was about to ask for a date. Well, it was short lived. Right at that critical moment, Miss Friendly pops by. Before I know it, they're discussing about last Saturday's football game. Oh, did I mention she's a cheerleader too? Next thing, he's walking down the hall with her, arm in arm.

I'm dreaming of revenge and thinking how I can get away with lobbing off her cute blonde ponytail. How can anyone be so upbeat and smiley all the time? You see? That's the effect Lucey is having on me. I can't stand all that sweetness and happy. It's not natural.

But that's not all. Remember I told you I thought the dog was possessed? Well, I'm sure of it now. When she isn't following me around or is under foot, she disappears. I mean, gone. I have everything blocked off. Everything! I erected the Berlin Wall in my house. I can't even escape. Yet she's gone. I find her in the weirdest places. In the bathtub, under the covers in the bed upstairs, behind the TV set in the basement. Doing what? I think she's contacting her other worldly friends. And jumping, it's totally freaky. She is on the counter tops, the tables the dresser. It's like she levitates.

I brought her to the Vet and told him about her hyperactivity. I asked, actually begged for him to put her on Ritalin. He shook his head and told me that it was just puppyhood. All puppies have a lot of energy. Give her a little time and she'll be fine. She'll be fine, sure, but what about me? I'm becoming a nervous wreck. I can't go out any longer than two hours because I have to be home to walk her. (I won't even talk about her house breaking or lack of) Or that my social life has all but dried up because my friends think I'm rounding the bend.

What I want to ask is that maybe she can spend a little time at one of your houses? You know, just a mental health weekend for your poor old Yia Yia. It's either you Guys or the Bide-a-Wee home. Not really, only kidding, I'm too old for the Bide-a-Wee home.

Maybe the Vet is right. I just forgot how demanding a puppy could be. I'm just being cranky. Forget what I told you about my school nemesis. I'm just hoping she 300 lbs. and toothless.

Love,

Yia

Heelies

July 21,2008

Hi Happy Campers,

At least I hope you're happy. Are all you friends from last year there? Ready to have a great time? Okay! Just write your old Yia Yia a postcard when you can and let me know that you're doing fine. For me, you know how bored I can get, always looking for some new adventure. Well, last week, I got an inspiration from your cousin, Christopher.

As I was visiting Aunt Pat, Christopher came gliding across the kitchen floor like he was on air. I looked down and realized that he was wearing some kind of special sneaker. When he got done terrorizing the dog, he showed me his "heelies." Awesome! Sneakers with built in wheels. Definitely something I could do.

It's always more fun doing things with a friend, so I decided to see if Shirley wanted to join me. At first she wasn't into it, but I explained it was not at all like line skates and I promised I wouldn't tie her to the back of a bus. It took a little convincing, that plus doubling her medication, but finally she said, "Yes."

Off we went to the mall to get our heelies. Shirley had this goofy grin on her face, but hey, she's hasn't been let out in a while. We got to the store and I asked the salesman for a pair of heelies in flamingo pink, size 10 and a pair in passion purple, size 8. He looked a little confused and asked, "Are these for you, Grandma?" I replied, "That's Yia Yia to you, Sonny." Unfortunately, they didn't come in fashion colors so we had to settle on yucky camouflage brown. Shirley then started winking and making kissy, kissy sounds at the salesman, maybe doubling her medication wasn't such a good idea.

I got her out of the store and we proceed back to my place. I still had our spiked helmets and protective gear from our last outing. Shirley's stuff was a little moldy from that river water, but a little spray deodorant should knock out much of the stink.

Shirley had on the body surfing suit she borrowed from her grandson. Remember? It was the blue number with a lighting bolt across the chest. She decided to put her protective gear under the suit to hold them in place. Wow! That spandex sure can stretch. I, on the other hand wore my favorite skating outfit, my pink polka dot sweat suit.

Wondering about a place to try out our new heelies, I decided on ShopRite. Think about it, big aisles, and lots of flat space plus we can hold on to the carts for support until we get the hang of it. Shirley sort of agreed; actually, she was just grinning and bobbing her head. I took that for a yes.

Not to draw too much attention to Shirl, we decided to wear raincoats over our outfits. I thought the lighting bolts might be a bit much for the Shop-Rite crowd. And we were off! Shirl was still grinning and bobbing when we got there, just as happy as a clam.

We grabbed two carts and started "heeling" down the produce aisle. Man...what a rush! I was whizzing past people like crazy. Too bad those carts didn't come with horns.

Shirley was having a bit of a problem getting started, I think it was all that head bobbing keeping her off balance; that plus glazed over crossed eyes. I guided her into the frozen food section. The aisles are much wider there. Sweating badly, she decided to take off her raincoat. Now that was quite a sight.

"Well, it's now or never," I yelled, "hold on tight." and gave her a big shove. In truth, she was never very graceful. She just careened off one display case after another and then she let go of the cart and was totally out of control. Startled customers took notice of her blood curdling screams (didn't I tell you she's quite the drama Queen) and they began gathering and watching.

Trying to catch up to her, I had a hard time getting through the crowd that formed. When I finally did, I realized that Shirley managed to go head first into one of those small ice cream freezers that were placed in the middle of the aisle. All you could see was her legs sticking straight up with the camouflage sneakers and those extra knobby knees. Unfortunately, her spiked helmet pierced the freezer pipes giving off a loud bang, after which a heavy fog began filling the store.

I admit; it was a very eerie scene. Somehow, Shirley got herself out of the freezer. She stood up, helmet gone, hair all askew, her face and hands totally blue and covered with frost. Bug eyed, she began yelling at the top of her lungs, threatening to kill someone. A hysterical customer screamed, "Alien!" Another shouted, "Terrorist!" Before you knew it, everybody was stampeding to the exits.

I rushed over to a raging Shirley, to try to calm her down. I told her even though she took a little tumble, she was progressing nicely. I said with a little more practice she could be a star. Being we had the whole place to ourselves, now was the perfect time for her to hone her skills.

The thought of being a star stroked her ego and with that influx of confidence, she tried again. Amazingly, she really did seem to get the hang of it. Before I knew it, she was gliding all around. It sure warmed this old heart to see her enjoying herself. You know, that's what friends are for.

Unselfishly, I took off my helmet and gave it to her; hers was still impaled in the ice chest. I figured while she was doing her thing, I would pick up a few items I needed. I wish you could have seen Shirley, she was coasting up and down the aisles with the beat of the piped in elevator music .She actually looked like she was floating, sort of antigravitational.

While passing the storefront window, she noticed a crowd of onlookers outside. She had herself so hyped up, that on the next pass, she pulled down her pants and mooned everybody. Now, she was totally out of control.

Suddenly, the music stopped. A gruff voice came over the loud speaker. He introduced himself as Captain Dudley of the State SWAT team. He said to surrender immediately and to come out of the store with your hands up. Hey, this is serious stuff. I looked around but didn't see anyone. Then I got it; there must be robbers in the store. No wonder everyone left.

I needed to get Shirley out of there in a hurry. I caught up to her in the bakery aisle. She was getting pretty fast on those heelies. I told her we had to leave. Wouldn't you know it? She shouted, "No! I'm having too much fun!" Then she started throwing a big hissy fit. That's when I grabbed her and pulled her towards the door. Her meds must have worn off because she was wild eyed and screaming.

When I got to the exit, two big cops took Shirley, who by that time was ranting, saying she was going to kill me over and over. She was kicking and fighting and downright scary. I addition, she smelled like swamp thing. I guess that deodorant didn't work after all.

Anyway, Captain Dudley approached me and said it was a very brave thing that I did. I said, "Wasn't anything really, just another ordinary day." Then he told me I was being too modest. I asked if they caught the robbers? "Oh, I get it, you told Shirley there were robbers in the store. Good ploy, Yia Yia."

Huh?

He told me not to worry about Shirley; they were going to take her downtown for observation. She'll love that once she calms down. She can show off her new skating skills.

Next week, I'm supposed to get a Good Citizen's Award, plus I'm being named Shop-Rite's Customer of the Week. Ain't that great? I sure hope Shirley finishes her shock treatments in time to be there when I accept. It just won't be the same without her.

So, that's about it for now kids. I'll keep you posted about my adventures. I have to take Lucey for her walk now, I'm checking into whether they make heelies for dogs. I bet she would love them.

Be good and hug each other for me.

Love,

Yia

Bungee Jumping

July 26,2008

Hi Kids,

How's it going? Things are busy here; thought you'd like to keep up to date with what I'm doing, I received my Good Citizen's Award. Very nice. I might even get my picture in the paper soon. However, my Customer of the Week award is delayed.

Seems, when they removed Shirley's helmet from the freezer, it punctured the pipe even more and sent a cloud of Freon gas throughout the store. The Environmental Protection Agency team was called in and they closed Shop-Rite. Everything had to be either discarded or decontaminated, including all the people, customers and employees alike.

If you thought Shirley looked weird, you should have seen all the guys in orange Haz-Mat suits running around spraying people with the cleansing solution. Lots of unhappy disgruntled people, especially the employees. They are picketing Shop-Rite already and are threatening a class action lawsuit, all this over some little gas leak.

Word on the street is the store is going to be closed for about a month. You would think the staff would enjoy having some time off. Oh well.

I decided while I had the chance, I'd go over and pay Shirley a visit. I found her in the library, engrossed in a book. She looked up and gave me one of her big goofy grins. No head bobbing as yet.

I asked her, "What's up?" She answered, "Doing some research. "That's great, she's trying to improve her mind, whatever is left. Looking down, I read the title '101Murder Mysteries.'

She asked me what I've been doing and I told her, "Not much." With that she said she had the greatest idea for a new adventure. That's amazing coming from Shirley. She's usually a follower and not a leader. Those heelie lessons really boosted her self-confidence. How good am I?

"What do you have in mind?" I asked. Bungee jumping was the answer. I couldn't believe my ears. I asked her if she talked to my Santini grandchildren. You guys have been suggesting I try that. She said she didn't, but I bet you kids did. Didn't you?

First, I wanted her to tell me all about it. "Simple, nothing to it," she says, "First, I will get all our gear, then you'll drive us to Fort Lee and park the car close to the bridge. We will wear our heelies and use the walkway until we get to the middle, then we'll jump off."

Darn those heelies, I should have never taught her how to use them. I made a monster out of her.

I'm trying to be a good sport about this, so Saturday, she gets a weekend pass. I pick her up and take her home to get the supplies ready. Sunday morning, I go back to her place and she's wearing her blue body surfer suit, you know, the one with the lighting bolt. She has on her heelies and carrying two backpacks. She was so upbeat and giddy, sort of euphoric. Me, on the other hand, I'm full of dread. Jump off a bridge?

ME?

But then, I couldn't disappoint her, she was so happy, she kept looking over at me with that goofy grin and saying, "It won't be long now." Yeah, I want to get it over with soon too, I thought. Well, I parked the car and started heeling over the bridge walkway. Even that's scary. Shirley is humming and chattering to herself, totally lost in Shirley land.

We get to about the center of bridge, and I look down….. Yowee! That's a long way to the river. Shirley meanwhile is busy tying one end of the rope to a rail. Next, she takes out what looks like parachute harness and proceeds to put it on then helps me with mine.

At this point I tell her I can't do it. She says, "Oh, but you have to! You just have to!" "Okay," I tell her, "you go first." " NO! NO! No! "She screams, "That's not the plan!" Trying to be the reasonable person that I am, I tell her I want to watch her technique. She starts laughing hysterically and a maniacal look comes over her.

Now, I figure if I can get her to go first, maybe it will get out of her system and she'll leave me alone. I slip the end of the rope into her harness in the back and give it a good knot. She turns around asks what I'm doing? I say she's all set and do me a favor, go first. Immediately, she becomes belligerent and starts shoving me towards the railing. I'm struggling with her, when she starts slipping. Before I knew it, Shirley's up and over the rail, heading for the river.

Hey, she said it was safe; perhaps this will calm her down. I look and expect her to come bouncing back up, but Shirley didn't use a bungee cord. Nope, just a plain all rope. Who knew?

I see her hanging there, at the end of the rope. She's looking up and shaking her fists at me. With all her kicking and squirming, she starts swinging like a pendulum, back and forth, back and forth.

Going under the bridge, about the same time is an empty oil tanker from a foreign country. On the upswing, Shirley goes up over the deck and some swarthy sailor grabs her and cuts her down. Shirley gives him a big kiss and I can tell she's in love already. Strange thing, looked like the sailor was too.

As the tanker passed underneath the GW, sailing down the river, I saw Shirley standing on the deck waving at me and hugging this guy. I think the ship was headed for somewhere in the Middle East. I'm at the railing, screaming at the top of my lungs, "Shirley, come back, Shirley come back." At the same moment, a young man leaves his car and approaches me.

Oh, did I mention that traffic started backing up in both directions to watch the Shirley and Yia Yia show? I draw crowds wherever I go.

The young man looks down and sees the empty rope, and tells me he witnessed everything. Said how he saw me trying to save her life that how I even tied a rope on her to prevent her from jumping.

I tried to explain that wasn't exactly right, but he kept calling me a hero. When the cops arrived, the nicest policeman told me they were going to do their best to find Shirley. "Do you think you can?" I asked. He said most people wash up in a few weeks. What kind of answer was that? Next, he said I was a brave little lady and all the witnesses told him how gallantly I tried to stop Shirley.

Not exactly the truth, but close enough. When I tried telling him she's out there somewhere, he just patted my hand and said, "There, there, little lady, I understand." "You do?" I asked. "Sure, we have a couple of jumpers a month," he replied.

Okay, I guess this bungee thing is more popular than I thought. No biggee.

All I can say is, I sure hope Shirley's happy out there with her sailorman and she has a supply of her meds. As for me, I get another Good Citizens Award.

Every one of the people I tell that Shirley is on the big blue Atlantic Ocean, look at me sadly and tell me I'll get over it soon. What's to get over? I'm not jealous, who wants a sweaty sailorman? That cop was pretty cute though. Maybe I'll see him next week, at the Good Citizen's Award ceremony.

Meanwhile, Shirley has a friend. Marsha. She introduced me to her at the library. I think I'll go visit her; she might need cheering up and some adventures.

Be good kids, and remember, don't jump off any bridges.

Love ya,

Yia

BSA CAR WASH

August 01,2008

Hi Kids,

Can you believe August is here; one of my favorite months of the year. Besides it being summer, it is also my birthday month along with Christopher, Dani and Abigail. So here's to all us August Babies

To keep you up to date with Shirley, she finally called her family. Said she was fine and happy. Now at least they can stop dredging the river for her.

Moving on, last weekend I was called to duty. The Boy Scouts of Ridgewood were having a fundraiser for the Red Cross. They needed a nurse to supervise and do first aid if necessary. So happily, off I went.

When I got there, a make shift car wash set up in a parking lot. There were bunches of buckets, hoses and ten very enthusiastic Boy Scouts. I introduced myself and told them to call me Yia Yia. I said how proud I was to be with them.

We were off to a busy start. A line of cars was waiting and the boys got right to their tasks. Some were washing, some were wiping and one studious entrepreneur was collecting the cash. Good team work. They must have washed every car in Ridgewood, because after a few hours we ran out of customers.

The boys got bored and before long they were squirting each other and acting rowdy. I went to stop them and that's when the serious one (?) picked up a hose and sprayed me. The scouts all thought that was the funniest thing ever. Not one to be out done, I took the hose and proceeded to give each of them a good dousing.

They were hooting, hollering and having a blast, so much so that I never saw or heard someone come up behind me. He tapped me on my shoulder and in my surprise, I turned around, hose in hand, and sprayed him full force. He was drenched and sputtering. I immediately dropped the hose and it began dancing and wiggling all over the ground. Unfortunately, there was a lady standing behind him and the hose squirted water right up her skirt. She shrieked and took off like a big bird, leaving me with this soggy, angry man.

The cold water did nothing to calm him down, his face was red and he was in a rage. He demanded to know who was in charge of the group. "That Sir, would be me, Yia Yia Linaris and who wants to know?" I asked. He introduced himself as Mr. Smedley, the Middle School Principal. No wonder all the boys got quiet.

Next, he wanted to know just what I thought I was doing. "Very simple, Mr. Smedley," I replied. "I was just demonstrating the field technique of decontamination." "The what?" "The field technique of decontamination. Surely, you must have read or heard about the incident in the Shop-Rite a few weeks ago?" I replied.

He looked momentarily puzzled, and then he sputtered, "Oh yes, of course, right." "I was just preparing these fine scouts in case such an emergency arose here." I watched him think this over. It was obvious that all the lights were not on in his attic.

"I see, why yes, good job. My, my, you sure seem to know a lot about scouting, Yia Yia Linaris." he said. I proudly told him that I was a Brownie and Cadet leader and had my very own Cub Scout Den in my younger days. What I didn't tell him was that the only badges my Cub Scouts worked on was making fires and eating me out of house and home.

"Well, carry on," he said. I convinced him that it would be very community minded if he would patronize our car wash. "Certainly." he replied. "Let me get the car and the Missus and I'll be right back."

The boys, bless their hearts were at the ready when he pulled up, they all hosed down the car at once. Unfortunately, they didn't notice that Mrs. Smedley had her window open. Now her top half matched her bottom. When Mr. Smedley got out to complain, my little financial genius charged him for a full service. "WHAT'S THIS?" he demanded. The entrepreneur scout told him he had an interior and exterior wash.

As I said, he wasn't too bright. He snorted and paid.

As he drove off, the boys all cheered… "Yia Yia, Yia Yia." My old heart swelled. I announced for a treat, I was taking them to the ice cream parlor. They all followed me as if I was the Pied Piper.

Settling into a large booth, someone started shooting spitballs. I can't imagine whom? Almost at once, the owner came over looking not happy." What's going on here?" he growled.

"They are practicing sending encrypted messages," I said. "Say what Lady? It looks like spit balls to me. "I answered, "Exactly, that's what we want it to look like." "We, who?"

Very quietly, I took him aside and whispered, "These men are in training to become agents with the CIA. "He gave me the most incredulous stare. "They don't look like spies to me," he said. I told him they were undercover in disguise.

"Disguise? You're telling me they're not Boy Scouts?" he retorted. "Pretty amazing isn't it? It even fooled a bright man like yourself. "He glanced over at the boys, who by this time were sitting up at attention, giving him a smart, snappy salute.

"Well, I'll be," he muttered, turning his attention towards me. "So you're their leader? Who are you?" he wanted to know. I stood up as straight as I could and looked him right in the eyes. "I'm Lieutenant Buzz Lightyear at your service." "Buzz Lightyear, you? Can't be." I responded by telling him, "Sir, that's my code name, I'm under cover too!" "Well, well," he said, scratching his head. "That's amazing, you look like an old Yia Yia."

DUH!!!

He started walking away, but I wasn't done, not quite yet. As the boys began sending their messages again, I stopped the owner. I told him it would be very patriotic gesture to give each of the agents gift cards for a year so they can continue their training at his fine establishment.

He said he was happy to, and then asked if I could show him how to do those disguises. Sorry, I told him that would be impossible; it was highly classified information. He reluctantly said he understood.

When we left, the boys gave me another rousing cheer and made me promise to come back and visit them. I told them I would try, but there is just so much Yia Yia to around.

Well, my job was done there, now to infinity and beyond.

Love and take care. I'll write soon as I find another adventure.

Yia

Shirley's Rescue

August 03,2008

Hi Campers,

Well, it happened. Shirley called and she's so upset. Seems her wonderful Sailorman already has two wives He's planning to add Shirley to his harem and have her help raise his eleven children. The policy in the Middle East is a man can have as many wives as four, if he can afford them.

Shirley's freaking out, I told her to go to the ship's Captain but being she's a stowaway, she would get tossed in the brig. What to do? What to do? I came up with an idea. I told her to find out the name of the ship and if it was making any stops on the way to its homeport.

She had to do it quickly because her battery was low on her cell phone and she had no way to charge it. Calling me back in an hour, she told me the tanker's name was, 'Shazamititi.' Interpreted it means, 'High oil prices to Americans,' also she found out that the ship planned to refuel in Greece.

I drove to Ridgewood to see the owner of the ice cream parlor; he looked Greek to me. I was hoping I was right. Luckily, he was there when I arrived. I pulled him aside and told him I had a problem of the utmost urgency and might need his help. First, I asked if he was Greek. "Yes," he said, "how did I know?"

"Classified info," I told him. He nodded.

He let me know that he came from Athens. Many of his relatives were still there. This is working out better than I expected. I explained to him that there was an undercover agent aboard a foreign tanker and her identity was about to be exposed. I needed to get her safely off the ship.

"Anything for you Lt. Lightyear," he said. "Oh Nick, please call me Buzz."

He asked why I didn't go? I said, "I have another assignment and would be away for a few weeks." "You see Nick, it seems there's some hanky panky going on at the gorilla exhibition at the National Zoo in D.C. I'm going undercover as a monkey's uncle to check it out."

He nodded his head enthusiastically, "Of course, of course." I told him, "Besides this operation calls for people they would never suspect; native citizens." "I see your point, count me in," he was beaming.

First, I told him I had to set him up with a contact person while I was gone. "I'll put you in touch with my Yia Yia." "You have a Yia Yia? You're Greek?" I stammered, "Sort of, my Popou's family came from the Island of Chios." "OPA ! OPA! That's wonderful. You know, I thought you looked Greek," he exclaimed. (Really?)

I informed him that I fashioned my disguise after my Yia Yia. I also said what an extraordinary person she was, courageous, smart, a great cook and she was even better looking than me. "Thank goodness for that," he said.

DUH!!!

Together, we formulated a plan. Fortunately, Nick had a cousin Nick that worked the docks. He would hire a couple of his friends. While the friends distracted the sailors, Nick the Cousin would whisk Shirley away. The idea was to hide her at Nick's, Uncle Nick's house until the ship left port.

So far so good, he asked how they would recognize her. I said it wouldn't be hard. She's wearing a blue body surfer suit with a lightning bolt going across the chest.

I think this will work; I saluted Nick and told him if he was in D.C. in the next few weeks to come and see me at the zoo. I told him not to be upset if I don't talk to him. Undercover and all that, you know.

He was smiling broadly, "You're a good man Yia Yia, I mean Buzz."

Whatever.

"You are too, Nick, you are a great American. Your country owes you." "NO! NO! It is me, Nick Seagapopolis, that owes this great country." "Keep that thought Nick," I said and left.

Well, now I had to reach Shirley and give her the details. Her phone was nearly dead just as I was finishing. I told her everything and told her to pretend she was an agent. "Pretend I'm aging?" she asked.

"NO! You're an agent."

"I'm ancient?"

"NO! AN AGENT, AN AGENT, AN AGENT!"

"Oh, I'm an aging, ancient agent."

"Yeah, Shirl," and that's when her phone died.

Nick called Yia Yia (me) around midnight. He said mission accomplished. Nick, his cousin brought Shirley to his Uncle Nick's house, where his Popou Nick greeted them. Nick told me his cousin Nick said Shirley smelled like a swamp thing and she was grinning and bobbing her head. I told him they got the right one.

After a bath, Nick's wife Nicki gave her some fresh clothes to wear. Now all I have to do is send her passport and some money and she can get home. What would she do without me?

A couple of weeks went by, and no sign of Shirl. I called ice cream parlor and asked Nick if he knew anything. He told me that Shirley was in love with his other cousin Nick (on his mother's side) and intended to stay in Greece.

He also told me he went to Washington to visit the zoo and saw Buzz. He knew it was him, because Buzz kept looking at him and winking.

And I think Shirley's strange.

Well, at least Shirley's safe and in love again. Maybe I'll take Dani's suggestion and try Go Karting. Wish me luck.

Take care of yourself and each other.

Lotsa of kisses,

Yia, aka Buzz

Camping with the BSA

August 06,2008

Hi Guys,

What's up? From the pictures I've seen it looks like you are having the best times ever. Good for you. I must admit, I'm a wee bit jealous. But really, I can't complain, I went camping too.

The Boys Scout from Ridgewood called me and asked me to go with them on their camp weekend. How nice was that? I said "Sure, you betcha," and started getting ready right away. I packed all the essentials and a few things to make my tent more home like.

Lucey and I met up with the boys at the bus around 10 AM last Friday. The scouts were loading my 4 suitcases and a few cartons of snacks, when I was approached by what looked like an overage Boy Scout with a moustache. He was dressed in a scout uniform. Shirt with insignia, a bandana and a pair walking shorts exposing two very hairy legs wearing rolled down gym socks with work boots finishing the outfit.

He introduced himself to me as Scout Master Bob and asked where I thought I was going? "To the woods with my boys, of course." "Not possible! Not Possible! This outing is for Scouts and their leaders only. No Grandmas or dogs allowed!"

I was stymied, but only for a minute.

"Scout Master Bob" I said, "are you telling me I can't go because I'm old, I'm female and I have a dog?" "You could say that," was his brusque reply. "AHA! Scout Master Bob, that's prejudicial I am going to sue you for age, sex and animal discrimination." "Don't be ridiculous, there isn't any animal discrimination," he shouted back.

"Oh yeah," I answered, "you'll be sorry when I sic the ASPCA and PETA on you. You heard of them, haven't you? And while I'm at it I'm going to call the ACLU, the AARP and the YWCA. What do you think about that?" Flustered, he shouted, "Alright, already, you can go, but you can't ride the bus and you can't take that dog."

I wanted to press the point more, but I was holding up the boarding and a small crowd was forming to see the commotion. I didn't know what I was going to do with Lucey. If I took her home, I wouldn't be able to follow the bus.

It was my lucky day; I spotted Mr. Seagapopolis, the owner of the ice cream shop and waved to him. He came over and gave me a big hug. He told me that his grandson Nick joined the scouts and was going camping. I said I was supposed to go too, but the Scout Master Bob won't let me on the bus and I can't take Lucey. He said, not to worry, he would watch her. He asked me what kind of dog she was? "A Rottweiler in disguise," I told him. He was impressed and gave me a knowing wink.

I trailed behind the bus in my rocket ship. The boys were waving at me out the back window. Bless them. We reached Maine, just before suppertime. Everyone ate in the huge mess tent. Scout Master Bob kept looking over at me, glaring. Maybe I should call the FBI too!

We were assigned the campsites; ours was very picturesque.

Situated right on the lakefront surrounded by a forest of thick bushes and giant trees; Mother Nature at her finest.

My scouts pitched my tent and I got right to work unpacking and making the place cozy. I put out the pictures of all you grands, (the Dirty Dozen) and hung my favorite poster of my dream man, Brad Pitt. What he sees in that scrawny, blubber lipped Angelina when he could have a real woman, like me, I'll never know.

Night was fast approaching, the campsite was secured, sleeping bags all put out and of course, the boys started the campfire.

It sure does get dark in the woods. The sky turned inky black, and one by one little points of light came out. The frogs were doing their ribbit thing and the crickets were making a racket. Fireflies blinked on and off and the air was filled with the scent of pine and burning logs. I tell you, it doesn't get better than this.

Soon everyone was sitting around the fire, I broke out the S'Mores makings and we started telling ghost stories. Some were funny and some were scary, but the one that had the boys shaking the most, was the one about Mel the Maine Monster. He is as elusive as Big Foot, whom they say he resembles, only uglier, and he stalks this very forest. Seems he waits for night and when everyone is asleep, he sneaks into camp and carries somebody off. Supposedly, they are never seen again.

While they were scaring themselves pretty well, little Nick came over to me. He said he heard noises in the woods. I said, "Oh Nick, don't worry, it's probably only a bear or a wildcat." He said no, it had to be Mel. I figured if I were ever going to get these boys to bed down, I would have to check it out.

Feeding into the spirit of the moment, I told Nick to get the biggest scout and meet me in my tent. "Don't tell the rest of the troop. We don't want to panic them." Once inside I hatched a plan. I've seen a lot of war movies and know just how to capture someone. I told Nick to take a big blanket, George to grab some rope and I would carry my bat.

"We have to spread out in separate directions, then we circle around, converge on the subject and at the signal, we attack." "What will be the signal, YiaYia?" I told them, I will hoot like an owl three times, and then we close in on him very quietly." When we are close enough, you Nick, throw the blanket over him and George, you move in quickly and tie him up with the rope. If he gives us any trouble I'll hit him with the bat," I instructed them.

Never expecting anyone out there, I led my soldiers into unknown territory. At least if they see its all clear, they can report to the rest of the boys and I can get some sleep.

We circled the area where Nick thought he heard the noise and I actually thought I saw something move. Oh no! Could it really be true? There was some kind of figure lurking behind a tree, spying on our camp.

Time for action, I hooted three times, Nick rushed in, threw the blanket over whatever it was, and George had it tied up in second. There were a lot of squirming and guttural sounds coming from our prey. For good measure, I whopped it with the bat. I must have knocked it out because it became still and quiet.

My cell phone wasn't working; so we lugged it back to camp for the scouts to guard. I told them to just sit on it bop it if necessary until I came back with the police.

I ran to the mess tent, but no one was there. Luckily, I got a signal and called 911.The Maine State troopers answered. I told them we captured Mel the Maine Monster. The cop asked laughed and told me to try lying off the sauce. I insisted he come,

I told him my boys were sitting on it. "Your boys? How many do you have?" "I think there's about 10," I said. He said, " You don't know how many children you have?" "Don't be ridiculous, of course I know. There's my 4 plus their spouses and then there's the Dirty Dozen." Why he was asking me about my family when this was an emergency, I don't know. Finally, he said," Hey lady, I'm going to come just to check you out, where are you?"

I told him I'm in the woods, but actually now I'm in a mess tent. "A messy tent," he asked? "No, actually my tent's pretty neat, it's very homey with pictures and posters," I started to tell him.

Say, wait a minute. First, he asks me about my family, now he's asking me about my tent. Doesn't he realize the danger we're in? I yelled, "What's wrong with you? I'm in a mess tent at a camp in the middle of the woods. My scouts are in mortal danger and you want to chitchat? Are you coming or not?"

"Why didn't you say so in the first place, Lady? We're on our way!"

When I got back to the campsite, all the other units were there. Word spread that we captured, Mel. My scouts were still sitting on him and every time he started to stir, he got bopped.

In a few minutes, a very cute State trooper arrived with his men. "Let's see what you have here," he said.

Mel started to move, very strange, low guttural sounds with coming from beneath the blanket. Slowly, they began to untie the rope and uncover him. That's when I saw it! The work boots, the rolled down socks, the very hairy legs.

Oh no! Scout Master Bob!

I was so doomed.

He staggered to his feet, dazed but able to point an accusing finger right at me. "Arrest her! She's a menace! She kidnapped and assaulted me and...and..."

"Hold on just a minute," interrupted my cute Trooper. "What were you doing hiding in the woods?" "I was not hiding. I was checking the camp site inconspicuously as to not disturb the boys or the moment," Scout Master Bob tried to explain.

"Sure seems like stalking and spying to me," the Trooper shot back. "And come to think of it, this fine lady here did a brave thing. She protected her boys when she thought they were in danger. From what I can tell, she did a great job. You're lucky I don't run you in for stalking."

Scout Master Bob sputtered. For once he was at a loss for words. Finally he said, "Yia Yia, he's right. You did do a brave thing and you set a good example for these boys. I'm going to make you an honorary Boy Scout."

Cheers of Yia Yia rang out. Once again, my old heart swelled.

Scout Master Bob was taken to the hospital to check him out for a concussion. Seems he got a lot of head bops.

The rest of the weekend was great. We all had a terrific time but no ghost stories were allowed at the campfire. I just told them my adventures with Shirley. They were scary enough.

We arrived back in Ridgewood on Sunday evening. Nick, the new scout ran and told his Popou Nick all about our adventures. Big Nick came over to me and in a low voice he said, "Buzz, I know that's you."

"How's that," I asked?

"Because, first of all, your Yia Yia is much cuter and I suspect that was an undercover exercise for the men, right?" "Can't fool you, Nick Seagapopolis."

Then, I took my Rottweiler and went home.

Big hugs all around,

Love,

Yia

Go Karting

August 11,2008

Hi Kids,

I can't believe how fast summer is passing. Enjoy each day even though I can't wait to see your smiling faces. I'm glad you're having a good time. As you can tell, I've been keeping busy this summer too, so many new things to try.

Guess what? Shirley's back; seems she couldn't keep all the Nick's straight. She got very confused, plus the fact she couldn't stand feta cheese. She told me she left some unfinished business here and decided to come home.

I met her at the airport; she actually looked good. Guess the sea air was beneficial for her. She asked what I've been doing. I sort of filled her in and then told her about Dani's suggestion that I try Go-Karting. She said she never heard of it. I told her neither did I, but I looked it up and it definitely is for MOI (me).

"I already took a few lessons and I'm in the process of getting my very own Kart. It's a Formula 125, has 35 HP with 6 gears and I'm having it painted metallic silver with bright flame decals on the sides. I'm getting a driver's suit and helmet to match," I told her, excitedly. I said, "Shirl, I think I was born for this. You know how much I love to drive the Rocket Ship, with this kart

I can zoom around legally." That didn't impress her. She hasn't driven since they revoked her license for 50 years.

To encourage her I told her to come with me to my first meet. "There's a track near my daughter's, Sophia's house. It's Pocono Race Way and I'm entered this weekend." "What will I do while you're racing?" she whined. "You can be my Pit Man, I mean, Pit Woman. When I pull in for refueling, you can help check out the Kart, plus you can hang out in the pit with the rest of the crew. Some very cute guys, Shirl!" "You've got my attention," she said.

"Maybe I will. I'll have to study up on it so I can look smart." I doubt that could ever happen, but she might look cute in pit overalls. They might even have lighting bolts on them.

When I dropped her off, I made her promise to think about it and let me know soon. After a couple of days, I went to see her. She was reading an auto manual and gave me her big toothy grin when she looked up.

I figured I should clear the air between us. "I'm sorry the bungee jumping didn't work out as planned, Shirl." She gave me a quizzical look and said, '"Don't you worry, I'm going to fix that." I thought I heard a little chuckle after that remark, but I wasn't sure. She's still strange as ever, but she is a good sport. She agreed to be my pit person and we were soon off to the races.

When we arrived, I had to do a qualifying race. A lot of the youngsters were giving me the once over. One smarty said, "Shouldn't you be home baking cookies or knitting, Grannie?" "That's Yia Yia to you, Butt Face. You just get out of my way and eat my dust," I hollered back.

Shirley was in the pit, her head was bobbing and she was mumbling to her self. "Are you all set, Shirl," I asked? "More than you know, heh heh." was the answer.

Good! She's into it.

I was psyched. Suited up, strapped in, my engine started waiting for the red blinking lights to turn green. BINGO!!! GREEN!!! I gunned the gas and the kart and took off. I made it around the track with time to spare.

I qualified. Dani was right. This is so me!

Back at the pit, Shirley looked preoccupied. "Are you okay Shirl?" "Oh, I'm just dandy. I'm saying some prayers for you, you're going to need them," she said. I thought I heard that chuckle again.

Guess she added another eccentricity to her list.

My race was next. I got strapped in again, gave my last minute instructions to Shirley and the crew. Before I knew it, it was show time! I drove onto the track with all the other Karts. Then the sequence started, Red Light, Red light, Red Light, Red Light, Red Light,.... GREEN!!!!

I put the metal to the pedal and sped off. I was zooming and zig -zagging all over the place. What a rush! After the 5th lap, I pulled in for gas. While the boys refueled, Shirl opened the hood and tinkered around.

"Everything alright in there, Shirl?" "It is now, heh heh," she chuckled. A push and I was off again. I picked up speed and got back into the thick of the Karts.

Then, that Butt Face cut me off. I swerved to miss him and pumped my brakes. Uh oh, they weren't catching. Next, my steering wheel started to come loose in my hand. Now what?

I headed for the stockade fence at the end of the track. I hit it hard and went though, splinters flying all around me. I was going downhill towards a cornfield, picking up speed. I plowed across that field mowing down everything in my path.

Once out of the cornfield, I came into an opening. Great, a pasture, oh, no! Cows! They were everywhere. I closed my eyes and waited for the collision. Those cows must have moved fast because when I opened my eyes again, they were gone. Next, I saw a farm looming up in front of me.

A large barn was coming up quick, a man in a pair of overalls slid open the barn doors. I flew in one side and out the other. I barreled through a barnyard full of chicken and a big one landed on my windshield. There were feathers all over the place.

How am I ever going to stop? Fifty feet later, I drove straight into a pond. The engine was killed and I was sitting in the middle of the water. There were frogs jumping and dead fish floating all around me.

The man in the overalls came running over. He was holding a pitchfork and didn't look too happy. He said he was a farmer and this was his farm I just wrecked.

He started yelling at me, telling me that I scared the cows so bad that they're giving sour milk and the chickens are now laying scrambled eggs. Next he waded over and removed the chicken from my windshield. He said it was his prize rooster. Was, being the operative word here.

"What do you have to say for yourself?" he growled, his eyes bulging.

"Thanks for opening the barn doors?" I answered meekly.

That didn't go over too well.

Luckily, Mrs. Farmer came running down. She said, "Oh, Edgar, don't be such a grump, this here lady needs our help." Oh, Bless her. Bless her. I was saved.

She helped get me out of my poor ruined Kart and took me back to the farmhouse. She gave me a big glass of lemonade and called the Sheriff. They were already looking for me and they were there in no time.

The police proceeded to remove my Kart from the pond. They said they were going to examine it for tampering. "What do you mean tampering," I asked? The Sheriff replied, "Seems like there may be some foul play here, Granny." "That's Yia Yia, and how's that possible?" "Looks like your brake line might have been cut and the bolt on your steering column loosened. We'll have to check it out."

No, that can't be possible. The only one that was under the hood was my best bud, Shirl. Could it be? Shirl? No way. No way!!! There must be a mistake.

They took me back to the track. I looked for Shirl, but she was gone. Someone said she left with one of the pit crew.

That's so Shirl.

The Sheriff told me he was going to put an APB out on her. He wanted to know how I knew her. I told him I met her about a year ago "Where exactly did you two meet?" "At Blackstone Hospital, we had some adventures together." "Like what?" he asked.

"Oh, let's see. Well, first we went knee boarding on my ironing board around my complex until the cops came, and next we did in-line skating until Shirl let go of the bus and went into the river. She was okay once they pumped her stomach. Lately we did heelies in Shop-Rite until Shirl fumigated the place out and then there was our bungee jumping off the GW Bridge and…"

"Hold it, hold it," he screamed. "Where exactly did you two meet?" "The hospital, I met her at the hospital," I answered, "at Blackstone."

"Blackstone? Are you sure? "Of course I am. It was my lucky day, I told him. "Listen, Yia Yia, Blackstone is a hospital for the criminally insane."

"You're sure met Shirley at Blackstone Hospital?" he asked again." Yes, I am sure," I answered. "What was she doing there?" his next question. "My goodness is he ever nosy; I told him she was a patient.

With that he just gave me a sad look and shook his head. I know Shirley's quirky, but insane?

What do you think, Kids? It can't be possible, can it?

Nah! She's my BFF. Best buds could tell those things. Right?

Bunches of hugs and kisses,

Yia

Visiting Pennsylvania

August 29,2008

Hi Kids,

I'm back. How's it going? Having lots and lots of fun I hope. I had an interesting weekend too. Lucey and I went to visit the Derrick family in what Uncle Tom calls, Pennslytucky. Don't ask me why, he just does.

Lucey loves going for a ride and before long we were there. Lucey got out and started greeting everybody, greeting everybody and greeting everybody. You know how friendly she is.

Abigail, just turning two is a perfect playmate for Lucey. She's the right size and she has plenty of toys. Abbie was having a ball and also added lots of new words to her vocabulary. "Stop Woocey, no Woocey, down Woocey, mine Woocey, not nice Woocey." Trisha and RJ took turns taking Lucey for walks. After about 15 or more, Trisha and RJ got tired but Lucey was all revved up, still eager to go.

She's always so happy and has an incredible abundance of energy. If I could harness all that power it would solve the world energy crises. She is actually an engineering marvel, too. You have to ask yourself, how a 20 lb. dog has 200 lbs. of pull? She yanks her leash so hard that my right arm is actually 3 inches longer than my left since I got her. She also has managed to break 4 retractable leashes so far and I am trying to buy one that's made out of steel cable.

You see Lucey has this game she plays when we go outside. She starts from a standstill position, takes off at warp speed and runs the leash out to the end. Her head snaps back and she is airborne for a few seconds, pretty similar to bungee jumping but without the bridge. I don't know how she doesn't get whiplash, but it sure explains why my arm is getting longer.

However, I digress, while RJ and Trish were walking Lucey, Aunt Sophia and I was pulling Abbie around in her wagon. Aunt Sophia went in the house to start supper and I continued to pull Abbie. I got tired, and then had a brainstorm. Why don't I let Lucey do it? She would be great.

Just as I attached Lucey's leash to the wagon's handle and it was set to go, wouldn't you know it, Freckles the cat came walking towards the house. Lucey spots her and takes off like a rocket, pulling the wagon with Abbie behind her. She was tearing down the back yard chasing the cat when Aunt Sophia looks out her kitchen window and sees the whole thing. She runs out the door, flies over the steps and races down the yard.

Man, was she smoking, seems to me she must chase the cat a lot. Midway, Lucey and the wagon hit a bump and Abbie is jettisoned. Aunt Sophia reaches up and makes a one arm midair catch. Wow! That girl should play for the Giants; she's unbelievable.

Well, Lucey gave up the chase and we all returned to the house. Aunt Sophia fed the kids supper and began getting them ready for bed. In a little while Abbie went into her crib, nite nite. RJ passed out cold on he couch and Trisha and I settled down to watch a movie.

Aunt Sophia wanted to go out and visit Uncle Steve, who was working that night. He works in a restaurant sometimes on the weekends. I said, "Sure, go ahead, I'll watch the kids." She told me she would walk Lucey and lock her up when she got back. Lucey usually sleeps in the laundry room in my house, so I told Aunt Sophia just to put her in her laundry room too.

Trish and I finished watching the Sound of Music for the 35th time and off we went to bed taking Lucey with us. Lucey wiggled and squirmed around a bit, but eventually we all were asleep.

Aunt Sophia came home around midnight, of course Lucey greeted her and greeted her and greeted her some more. She took Lucey, closed my door and proceeded to put Lucey in the laundry room. Then she went bed herself; Lucey, however had other plans and scratched incessantly at the laundry room door. Aunt Sophia tried to ignore her but after 20 minutes, she thought she was under attack by an army of rats.

She got up and let Lucey out, turned her loose in the hallway and went back to get some rest. It was not to be. Lucey just proceed to scratch on every door looking to play with someone. She finally succeeded in annoying Aunt Sophia enough that she got up and brought her into her bed. Lucey finally quieted down and they both feel off to dream land.

Well, the peace and quiet didn't last too long.

Uncle Steve came home from work about 2AM. When he opened the bedroom door, he was greeted by Lucey, greeted by Lucey, etc. He kissed Aunt Sophia, 'Hell-o,' and headed to the bathroom to take a shower.

He didn't shut the door tight enough and Lucey with her exceptional door scratching skills managed to open it. She joined Uncle Steve in the shower as he was lathering up. At first, he didn't realize she was there until she started licking the soap off his legs. He freaked out, dropped the soap and started hooting and hollering. Lucey grabbed the soap, took off running and jumped onto Aunt Sophia's bed.

Soaking wet, face full of soap bubbles, she woke Aunt Sophia with quite a shock. Aunt Sophia jumped out of bed, told Uncle Steve to stay in the shower and took a waterlogged Lucey downstairs.

After drying Lucey, she tried putting her in her puppy crate. Unfortunately, Lucey outgrew it. Then she decided to make Lucey stay in the kitchen/den area, which she proceeded to tightly barricaded.

Meanwhile, back upstairs, Uncle Steve finishes his shower, gets out and starts for the closet. Never seeing the bar of soap that Lucey dropped, he steps on it. He slides across the wet floor unable to catch himself, heading for the open closet door. He hits it dead on, right between the eyes. The impact propels him backwards; he loses his footing, falls and knocks himself out.

That's how Aunt Sophia found him when she returned upstairs. She managed to get him to come to and put him to bed. He was groaning and moaning, with a giant goose egg appearing on his forehead along with two black eyes.

In the meantime, while she was tending to Uncle Steve, Aunt Sophia didn't hear the commotion that was going on downstairs. Seems that Freckles was asleep on a chair and Lucey spotted her. She went over to greet her and maybe to get her to play. Freckles was in no mind for that and all hell broke loose.

Lucey started chasing her and Freckles couldn't escape, due to Aunt Sophia's superior barricading of the room. All the lamps got knocked over every cushion thrown around, magazines and books shredded, the kids toys strewn all about. It looked like a tornado ripped through the place.

Aunt Sophia probably wouldn't have noticed until morning, but she went to get Uncle Steve some ice for his eyes and head bumps.

On her way down the stairs, she heard horrible hissing and screaming emitting from the kitchen. When she turned on the lights she saw that Lucey had chased Freckles up onto the kitchen table. From there, Freckles leaped up onto the ceiling fan and was slowly rotating around and around. Lucey was on the table too, jumping up at Freckles on every revolution, trying to grab her tail.

Next morning, I got up from a great night's sleep and went to get Lucey. When she wasn't in the laundry room, I went down stairs to find her. What I found was Aunt Sophia sitting at the kitchen table holding Lucey very tight. Talk about bed head, I told her she could win a prize.

Man, was she cranky, I guessed she didn't have her coffee yet. I asked if she had a good time last night and that's when she started twitching and mumbling. Reminded me a little of Shirley. Maybe she should try some of Shirl's medication.

I gathered up Lucey and asked if there was anything Aunt Sophia wanted me to do before I left. I couldn't quite make out what she said, but her head just kept shaking so I took that for a no. I kissed her good-bye and told her I'd visit soon. She just kept shaking her head, no. I swear, so many twitches going around.

So that was our weekend adventure, kids.

I'm thinking I might visit your Mom with Lucey while you are away. She could use the company and Lucey needs more fun.

Take good care of yourselves.

Love you lots,

Yia

Freckles

August 30,2008

Hi Cody's Kids,

Just a short note to straighten out the record, seems I'm getting some bad press. Just don't believe everything you read or hear for that matter.

There's a nasty rumor going around that I wrecked Aunt Sophia's house. NOT TRUE! It was that sneaky, no good cat, Freckles; and she put the blame on me, its no wonder dogs don't like cats.

When I got to the Derrick's abode, I played with all the kids, even tried to go swimming with them. For reasons not known to me, I wasn't allowed in the pool. Already discrimination. Then they strap a harness on me like I'm some kind of pony and expect me to pull this wagon around with Abbie in it. So okay, I'm game. They are almost finished when strutting up the lawn comes that snooty cat Freckles. I bark at her to come help me, but she takes off. How fair is that? It's her family.

I run after her to talk to her, and then I spot Aunt Sophia chasing her too. She was probably trying to help me catch her.

Anyway, we didn't get her, so we all went back to the house. Aunt Sophia was making supper telling Yia Yia that she was hare-brained. The kids wolfed down their meals, even tried to sneak some off to me. Yuck!!! Why would I eat string beans??

Next, they all were off to bed. I'm not tired, why should I go? The evening is young. Everybody starts passing out. Aunt Sophia leaves and I'm stuck watching The Sound of Music with Yia Yia and Trisha. Do you know that there is not even one dog in that whole movie? How boring.

There's nothing to do, so I give up and try to go to sleep. It's not easy, I'm suffering I' m listening to Yia Yia's snore when Aunt Sophia came home. She opens the door and lets me out. She's being real nice to me but then she sticks me in this smelly dark room. No bed, no toys, no treats, nada.

Hey, I want out. I try digging my way through the door and suddenly it opens. Aunt Sophia is standing there, eyes bulging, hands on hips looking mean and puts me in the hallway. Say, there were lots of doors there; maybe someone wanted to play. I tried them all and the one that opened was Aunt Sophia's. Now she's looking meaner than a rattlesnake.

She grabs me and drags me into her bed then orders me to lie down. Guess there's no fun for me tonight.

Luckily it wasn't long before Uncle Steve came home. I was so happy to see him. He's always so nice to me. After I greeted him, he says "Hi," to Aunt Sophia and heads to the bathroom. I hear the shower running so I thought I'd go and give him some help.

I was washing his legs when he had some kinds of a seizure. He started yelling and jumping around. I darted out of the shower to get help, dropping the soap I used on him. I leaped on the bed to alert Aunt Sophia.

Instead of going to aid Uncle Steve, she takes me down to the kitchen. Why? Anyway, I did my duty; she must be use to his fits. She goes into the garage and gets my puppy crate. Next, she tried shoving me into it; did I mention she's getting mean? Thankfully I was too big for it. Then, she proceeds to turn the place into a mini prison, barricading all the exits. She's mumbling incoherently under her breath, finishes and leaves.

In the meantime I, due to my extra sensitive ears, heard a thud. It sounded as if a large tree fell down. Always something.

So here I am, I look around and guess what? There's that uppity cat all curled up asleep on a chair. Well, lah-de-dah. I go over to talk to her and she gets all freaked out. She starts hissing at me and running amok.

She knocks over lamps, pillows and toys; next she rips up magazine and books. Finally, she turns over my water bowl and jumps up onto the kitchen table.

I had enough of that; I can jump too. So I get on the table but she one-ups me. She leaps to the ceiling fan and it starts rotating. So stay there I tell her, and when you want to be nice, I'll let you down.

While I was guarding her, Aunt Sophia comes back to the kitchen. Why this woman can't sleep, I don't know. But guess what, she's upset about the cat. THE CAT? After the mess she made, she upset about THE CAT? Is there no justice?

She grabs hold of me puts me in a strangle hold, opens the door and let's the cat out. Freckles proceeded to sashay past me; looks backs, flips her tail and leaves. Meanwhile I have to sit there in this death grip and take it.

When Yia Yia came down in the morning she said something about Aunt Sophia's hairdo and that's when the twitching started. And I thought Shirley was strange. Yia Yia kissed Aunt Sophia, Good-bye and we started home. I never got to make that cat pay. Next time I won't be so nice.

So kids, that's my story and I'm sticking to it! Remember, have fun but never ever trust cats!

Your pal,

Lucey

Lamenting to Cody

August 31,2008

Hi Cody's Kids,

It's me Lucy. Hope you're having lots of fun. Me? I'm truly living a dog's life.

Saw the Codester the other day, I tried to talk to him about it, but he kept falling asleep. I must bore him. He finally did tell me that if I wrote to say 'Hell-o' and to tell you that he misses you all terribly. I said, "Why don't you write and tell them yourself?" and he just nodded off. Coma Cody.

I'll be so glad when you guys get home. Maybe you can calm your Yia Yia down a little. She's all over the place. Last week, she goes camping with a bunch of boys and hands me over to this strange man. He kept looking at me peculiarly and showing me off to everyone saying I'm a Rottweiler, an attack dog. Who me? Loveable me?

The only thing I attacked was the big bowls of ice cream he kept feeding me.

I tell you, your Yia Yia is running with a weird crowd. Even when she's home, there are some issues. Let me give you some for examples. I'm going to start not at my waking up, no; it's more interesting at my bedtime.

When I was a wee pup, I had my very own room. I had this cool crate, almost like a cave. The room had two big machines. That's another story, your Yia Yia is forever putting clothes in one then takes them out and puts them into the other. Some kind of hobby, I guess. Anyway, at night she would put me in my little crate, with my blankie, a treat and lights out till morning.

Soon I graduated to a cozy bed, same room, not too big but all mine. Same deal, my cushy bed and blankie, I get a treat and lights out, nobody, nothing until morning. I stretched, rolled around, slept; my own pad.

One night, not so long ago, a storm came rolling in, lots of thunder and lighting and howling wind. Well, it must have scared Yia Yia, because she decided to take me into her room for the night. I guess she needed some comforting.

Hey? What could I do? She feeds me. So okay, storm's over back to my room. But NO! Now she wants me to sleep with her every night. PA-LEEZEE!!! The woman snores like a lumberjack. The paint is peeling off the walls. How does a dog get any rest? I'm embarrassed to mention the 'hiney burps'. The covers get lifted a foot in the air after one of those stingers.

I try to escape but the bedroom door is closed. She needs me so much. I suffer through most of the night.

Come morning, I have to go out. She takes her time; I'm doing the crossed legged dance while she's brushing her teeth. Finally I get my leash on, and I'm outside. Whew, I barely made it. Next comes the most interesting thing of all. Excuse me, but I have to poop. Yeah, you read it right. Poop, yucky, smelly, right?

Not to her, she picks it up and packages it. Like it's some kind of gift. Then, she sticks it in a flowerpot. What does she expect? A poopy tree? Humans!

Now the day begins, I never know where she's going to drag me. Some time I go and visit my sister Layla at Aunt Pat's. She's a wimp, like Cody, way too calm. When the humans go out, we climb over the gates into the mudroom. There we rip up all the plastic bags we can find. Someone has to save the environment. Layla's proud that I taught her how to climb over the gates. She's happy now that she can have fun by herself.

Once in a while, I go visit your Mom and Cody. Man talk about laid back. He's this side of rigor mortis. I try to get him going the best I can. It's not easy. He shows me all his hideouts. Katie's room, the bed, mostly Dani's room once in a while and now and then Sal steals him away. As long as he gets his cheese, he's cool.

Aunt Sophia's place is one of my favorites. They have this cat that I can almost catch except that Aunt Sophia tries to get her first. One thing that does annoy me is that baby. She insists on calling me Woocey. I can barely stand Lucey. What kind of name is that anyway for a dog like me?

I started out Lacey, then Lucey, Lucey? A dog of my stature should have a regal name like Queenie, or Princess or Duchess. Lucey! What an indignity!

I digress. Another great place to visit is Aunt Sara's. She's neat. Hardly any rules apply. Ginger and I run all over, even outside without a leash. Aunt Sara always has the best yummy treats and Ginger tells me she sleeps in the big bed with her and Uncle Tom. Ginger's happy when Uncle Tom gets up and goes to work. Seems he has the same problems as his Mom with the snoring and hiney burping.

Their kids are fun too. Allie Girl, she's the boys pick for favorite girl cousin, she does this trick with me. It's terrific. I run straight at her and leap and she catches me mid air. We do it a few times and then Allie gets tired. I could do it forever.

John and Thomas are always going to the park. Sometimes I go along with them. They have this gang of boys they hook up with then, they go about trying to terrorize any other kids that try to use the park; sort of like vigilantes.

Enough about my sisters, I have to tell you about your Yia Yia. She has this friend Shirley, nice lady, not exactly Fruit Loops but definitely a few fries short of a Happy Meal. Yia Yia and she get into some pretty peculiar situations. Shirley always gets the worst of it for some reason.

They think they are 20, no, make that 13, they do all kind of mischief and when things don't work out, they start all over again.

Poor Shirley, she's always nice to me, even shares her milk bones. Yia Yia told her they had a lot of calcium and Shirl's been eating them ever since. I hope she gets hooked on Greenies soon; they're my favorite.

I have to go now, just a little note to let you in on what's going on.

Poor Yia Yia can't accept getting old; she's fighting it all the way. Aunt Sophia could be an Olympian in track, she runs like the wind.

Aunt Sara's the bird lady of Westwood, knows all the birds and feeds them. She puts lots of little houses all over too. Have to say though, there's sure a lot of bird poop in that yard. Aunt Pat is still trying to manage Layla in between trips to Burger King with Christopher.

Your Mom's busy cooking for the Codester, she's totally controlled by him. Please don't narc him out, she clueless.

So okay, kids let's just keep all this little information amongst ourselves. No sense annoying the adults. You know how cranky they can get.

See you when you get home.

Your four-legged friend,

Lucey

Lucey's Bath

September 30,2008

Dear Dani and All,

Hi guys thought I'd say Hell-o and vent a little. Well, maybe not vent, more like protest. Hey, don't stop reading, this is important. Has to do with canine behavior, all dogs and a smidge of me in particular.

I base my complaint on a happening the other morning. Yia Yia was putting out the garbage cans and I got a chance to sneak out and roam around by myself. As I was perusing the neighborhood I happened upon a fresh pile of rabbit poo. My instincts took over and before you'd know it, I was rolling around in it, having a grand old time. It was awesome.

I was totally proud and riding high until I returned home and ran in the door. At first Yia Yia said, "Oh there you are, I was just going to look for you." Then the next words were, "Oh my Lord, what did you get into? You stink!"

You know I never complain about how she smells, I mean let's face it, why would a grown (in this case, over grown) woman want to smell like Chanel Number 5 or Musk Oil or Old Spice? The very same reason we canines do, to disguise out scent, to say where we've been and whom we met. It's nature, the way of the wild, Moi at my primitive best.

I couldn't believe the commotion she was making over a little rabbit essence. It wasn't like I came home reeking of cow dung or horse manure or even dead fish Those are the best, strong and aromatic. Rabbit poo is minor league compare to them.

Next thing I knew the laundry room sink was filling up. Uh oh, that meant bath time. No way, I wanted to live in the moment for a while. I went under the dining room table, also known as my fort and took cover in one of the chair rungs. It's hard to get at me in there.

Meanwhile Yia was playing nonchalant, trying her best to act like nothing was happening. She ignored me as she carried towels and bottles of shampoo into my torture chamber getting ready for her dastardly deed.

Well, I wasn't moving. I tried taking a bath one time when I was a pup. A couple of the Grandkids were in the Jacuzzi having a grand old time and I decided to join them. Darn near drowned and got water in my ears and eyes and the Jacuzzi jets pinned me to the side of the tub. If it wasn't for one of the kids getting mad because the tub wasn't working right I might not have made it. I still got nightmares over my near death experience. Baths are dangerous, and in my case, interfere with the basic canine behavior. So there!

As I dug myself in, Yia started her ploys to get me out. "Come Lucey, waving the leash, it's time for your walk, let's go."

Er, no, don't want to.

Next was, "Oh Lucey, let's go take a ride in the car," she even jingled the keys for effect.

Er, no, don't think so.

Then she goes out the garage door, making believe she's leaving. Really? She's in her ratty PJ's and her bed head has hair sticking out in all the points of the compass. Yeah, right, she might drive off like that. Wait, I take that back, it's possible.

I didn't hear the garage door go up or the car start, so I stayed put. I'm making a stand for all my canine species that have a right to smell as bad as they want. Someone has to carry the torch. I appoint myself.

She comes back in with a huff and a snort, stomping around trying to intimidate me. Ha, I know all the tricks, can't fool me.

Now came the hard part, she opened the refrigerator door and got out some cheese. It's like water to a dying man, or in this case, dog, my Achilles Heel. I had to be strong. The wrapping crinkled and she swung the refrigerator door back and forth, sending the scent of cheese wafting my way. I could feel my resistance slipping. My mouth watered, I tried and tried to be strong, I knew what was at stake. I couldn't be weak. I was determined to resist.

Then it happened, she shut the door and walked away. When I peeked out again, I saw it, a piece of cheese on the floor, just lying there.

I had to think...what to do? The cheese was calling me, Lucey, Lucey, Lucey, ARRGGHH!

All righty, I decided to run out and snatch the cheese and run back under the table. I'm fast and she's; well let's just say her marathon days have passed. I darted out from my hideout, full speed ahead, grabbed the cheese and raced back to my den.

Can you believe she was there already and blocked my path? How was that possible? She hadn't moved that fast since she slipped on a piece of dog food that I dropped and dove head first into the floor. Utterly amazing!

So now I'm held tight, trying to wiggle free but before I can, I am unceremoniously dumped into the sink and scrubbed from tail to snout. This time I smell like a pine tree. Well, better than roses, I guess.

I'm toweled off and then I run around the house doing rooster tails to try to air dry. Next I rub myself all over the furniture for good measure. I hate being a damp dog.

There's no justice, bathed against my will, denied the simple pleasure of a roll in poop. Who knew domestication carried such a high price tag?

So at least I feel a little better getting this off my chest. Thanks kids. But before I sign off let me give you a little warning. Be careful when you visit; don't step in any rabbit poo unless you want to get thrown in the laundry room sink. If you do however, make sure you get a piece of cheese first.

Your four-legged friend,

Lucey

2009

Uncle Danny's Visit

March 15,2009

Hi Kids,

Lucey here. I know I haven't written in a while. Your Yia Yia keeps me on the go. Speaking of whom, I hate to complain, but lately I can't figure her out. I'm getting to feel like the Rodney Dangerfield of dogdom. I get no respect. Even on top of that, I'm unappreciated too! Why you ask? The list is long but I'll try to give you the Reader's Digest version.

Last week Uncle Danny comes to visit. He usually brings his goofy yellow Lab. Yia Yia lets him in and I go over to greet him. Hi, Uncle Dan. Hi, Uncle Dan. Hi, Uncle Dan. Where's Flash? Where's Flash? Where's Flash? Finally Yia Yia asks, "Did you bring Flash?" Dan says, "Not today, too much to do." Shucks, I was looking for some four-legged company. Oh well, I'll just have to amuse myself with Uncle Dan.

Uncle Dan and Yia Yia had their heads together talking and I heard him say, "No, that's Okay, you can leave her, she'll calm down soon." She, who? In a little while, Yia Yia leaves and it's just good old Uncle Danny and me.

He goes into her bedroom and before I know it, he's moving all her stuff. "Hey Dan, you better cut that out, Yia Yia isn't going to like that." Then he starts taking the pictures off the wall. Boy, is he going to be in trouble. I tried telling him, "She's gonna come home, see what you've done and yell, Bad! Bad! Bad! Grab you by the collar and throw you in the laundry room."

He doesn't pay any attention to me, and begins to spread some big sheets all over the floor. I tried to help him by grabbing onto one of the corners and pulling, but he just chased me away. Hey, what's this on the floor? Some small sticks with hair on the end. I'm going to take some for my collection. I have about three or four, when Dan comes and snatches them all away from me. Boy, he's really Mr. Cranky Pants today.

Next, he goes out and comes back carting in a big ladder. He takes it into the bedroom and starts to climb. I see my chance to really impress him. I start climbing right up behind him. "Betcha your fleabag, Flash can't do this."

When he reaches the top, I decide to show him my feat. I tug on his pant leg. He turns and freaks out; the ladder starts shaking and begins to fall. Uncle Dan is whooping and hollering and next thing I know, we're toppling off together. He lands on his butt, almost crushing me. Wow, is he clumsy or what? He gets up, brushes himself off and turns towards me. Immediately, he grabs me, throws me out of the room and slams the door. Did I mention he's cranky?

Yia Yia returns; Danny comes out of the bedroom and tells her that he has to leave. He wants to start Happy Hour early. Boy, that's a good idea. He sure needs happy. Before he goes, I hear him complain to Yia Yia about me. Hey, I didn't take all her stuff, move it around and rearrange her furniture. Wait until she gets a load of that. We'll see who gets in trouble, Narc!!!

The following day, Uncle Dan comes back. Again, no Flash, I could really use a play date. However, he brings a friend, Jimmy.

He says Jimmy going to help him. Help him? He already made a giant mess.

After talking with Uncle Dan, Yia Yia straps on my leash and drags me out to do her chores. Chores, those are chores? All she does is drive that rocket ship around, park it, go into a store, come out with some bags and then goes and does it again a few more times. You call this work? Try being a St. Bernard in a blinding snowstorm, or a Burmese herding a bunch of dumb sheep all over the mountains, now that's work.

Sorry, I digress, tasks over, we head back home. She pops her head into the bedroom where Uncle Dan and Jimmy have barricaded themselves. "Coffee, soda or some sandwiches?" she asks. Uncle Dan says, "Great, give us five." Five what? Coffees? Sodas? Sandwiches? There are only two of them.

They come out and while they're busy eating, I see my chance. I sneak my way into the bedroom and look around. Aha! They are painting. That's painting? Where's the picture? The art? The drama? Boring!

If she wants painting, I'll show her painting. I spy a pan on the floor with blue paint. I have a moment of genius. This will put me into the Dog Hall of Fame. I'll be right along side of Lassie, Rin Tin Tin and Tramp. They'll have nothing on me. I'm going to be the Picasso of the dog world, Me, Lucey, or should I say, Lu C.

While they are all in the kitchen, I spring into action. I go over to the paint tray and with great personal sacrifice, lower my bottom half into the blue paint. Yikes, it's really cold and gooey. Oh, the things I do for love. Fully loaded, I peruse the area for a place to best express myself. Rembrandt has nothing on the Lu C. "Voila! *" The living room rug could use a dab of color. N'cest pas*? (I'm really in the groove)

Mais oui* that looks belle*, next, the gold damask couch. That will be my masterpiece. I rub my butt side to side along the back, imprints of paws on the bottom cushion. This is looking better than I expected.

Onwards, I might as well do the den couch too! Plain leather is so drab, n'cest pas*? Oh, I'm too, too amazing! Wait until she sees this, doggie treats, spa treatments, a trip to Dog Disney. I'm so worth it.

Soon I hear a scream. I've just been discovered. "Oh my! What have you done?" She's overwhelmed. She comes and grabs me, hugs me tight. Where are we going? Hey, what's this, a bath? Okay, this stuff is beginning to itch. Into the sink I go and she starts scrubbing. "Just a sec, Yia, take it easy. That's my private parts, you know." She keeps asking over and over, "How could you? How is this possible?" I shrug, "Nothing really, I'm glad you like it. Now maybe I'll get a little respect around here. No ordinary dog, Moi! *"

Danny is screaming now, too, says he's never seen anything like this. Gee, thanks, Dan. It's about time I got your attention. Sorry old Flash hasn't got any talent. Danny, Yia Yia and Jimmy are all oohing and aahing, loudly in concert. How proud am I?

Wait a minute! What's going on? They are washing away my Mona Lisa. No! Stop! Stop! What are you doing? Would you destroy Whistler's Mother? The Last Supper? The Tomato Soup Can?

Quick! I need a milk bone, some comfort food. How could they? I told you, no respect and even less appreciation.

Danny keeps saying something about drop kicking me. What the heck is that? Yia Yia keeps saying, I didn't know what I was doing. Of course I did, you morons, silly me trying to put a little culture into your dreary human lives. All my efforts erased, I'm looked at as some kind of menace. Me! I'm so crushed. Nothing but a T-bone steak is going to snap me out of my despair. No picture on the Alpo can, no Dog Disney. Nada.

Like I said kids, no respect.

Finally, Uncle Danny and Jimmy finished their job, gathered up their stuff and left. The bedroom is all blue and boring.

Days passed and I must have been acting sad because Yia Yia took me over to Aunt Pat's to visit my sister, Layla. While the humans were busy talking, we went down to play in the basement.

How drab and dreary! I convinced Layla that we could spiff it up with a little decorating. We ripped up some papers, made confetti and spread it around with a box of dry cereal we found. You know what we got as a reward? We got yelled at, that's what. No thanks for all our efforts. Layla got locked in her crate and I got sent home. Yia Yia kept asking what she was going to do with me? Some appreciation for one thing and then, how about that Dog Disney trip?

So kids, when you visit make sure to bring the Codester. I want him to help me to shred some pillows. That might dress up that boring bedroom.

Your furry friend,

El Lu-C

* Voila,	French for-There it is
* Moi,	French for-Me
* N'cest pas	French for-Is it not?
*Mais oui	French for- But yes
*Belle	French for- Beautiful

Lucey's New Look

April 14,2009

Bon Matin Mon Cheri's,

Lu C ici!* That's French for Good Morning, My Dears, Lu C here. As you can see I am really getting a hang of this French stuff. I guess it's all those genes coming to the forefront. What can I say? Either you have it or you don't. I am so excited today. Yia Yia is taking me to the groomer and now my transformation will be complete. OOO, La, La. I will be magnifique!*

Spring too, has me all a twitter, so to speak. I've been watching Mr. & Mrs. Robin pecking at the ground outside and all the rabbits are hopping in and out of the brush; lots of activity going on. Yesterday, when we went for a walk there was a great big fat earthworm lying on the sidewalk sunning itself. Well, not for long because Big Foot, (aka Yia Yia) who never watches where she going, squashed that thing into a great big blob. Yuck, what a mess. Nothing left for the poor thing to cell divide, complete annihilation.

With all the snow and ice gone, it's a lot easier for me to pick up my messages. There was a couple from that German Shepherd, Bruno, I don't like him. He's always barking orders and acting superior. I sniffed a few at the hydrant from Roscoe, he's a brown and white Boxer. I think he has eyes for me. Wait until he sees me in my new do. Speaking of which, I picked up a message from Fifi, my role model. She just got back from Florida. That's where we Poodles go in winter, you know.

I'm planning to look just like her. No more of this silly moustache, no I'll be trimmed so that you can see my pointy snout with my long alluring eyelashes and pouty lips. I hope they'll be pouty; maybe YiaYia can buy me that lipstick that plumps them up. Then, I'll have a big puff on top of my head with a cute bow, one puff for my stumpy tail and big fluffy legs. I'm hoping the groomer paints my nails. Fifi tells me it's all the rage in Florida. Yes! I will be sooo adorable. Roscoe won't be able to take his paws off me. Too bad I'll have to tell him I'm fixed.

Well, back to our walk. You know, Yia Yia should be more grateful to me. I'm her very own personal trainer. I tug her real hard to walk briskly for cardio and all that pulling helps with her upper body strength. Do I get appreciated? No! Just take it easy Lucey. Stop pulling Lucey. How am I going to get her in shape? Then when it's time for me to make a deposit, she tells me to hurry up? What are you kidding? This coming from a woman who sits on the bowl with two magazines for hours while I'm doing the crossed legs jig at the front door. No, this stuff takes time.

I have to find the perfect spot. Okay, over here, No, that's not it, Okay, how about here? No, wait that spot looks right, nah, too wet, how about this clump of grass? Maybe. I'll circle around a few more times. Yeah, this seems right. Ok, deposit time.

I hardly finished before Big Foot has her plastic bag out and took away my monument. Can you believe she's still collecting that stuff? I have no idea what she's doing with it; as I said, anything to keep her happy.

Now it's time to board the rocket ship and go to the groomer. Yes, my lucky day. I hope they have some French perfume to finish the job. Some Chanel #5 would do.

We're parking now, leash on and into the store. I greet the lady at the desk; she says how cute I am. You ain't seen nothing yet lady. Get ready for some eye candy.

Now the moment I've been waiting for. The groomer comes out and she and Yia Yia talk about my do. I can't believe my ears. What is she saying? You! You Judas! How can you do this to me? She tells the groomer to give me a cut that is more like a Cocker Spaniel. No puffs, no nail polish, no pouty lips. Nada! Arghh!!!

I had to get out of there. I made a break for the door, I almost get there when my leash ran out and I'm snapped back. Yia Yia is saying "I don't what's come over her, she's usually so happy to get groomed."

What's wrong with me? Haven't you paid any attention to all the studying I've been doing? My French accent bark? My prancing? My cravings for French Fries and French toast, how can you ask what's wrong with me?

How can fate be so cruel? First, no Dog Disney and now this!

My life is over. I was going to be the model for my sisters Layla and Ginger. I was going to encourage them to follow my lead. Oh, woe is me. Now I know what they mean when they say all great artists must suffer. This must be my agony.

I submit to my fate and before long I emerge clean and cute. Yeah, yeah, big deal, so at least I got two bows for my ears, some consolation prize.

Yia Yia shows up to take me home, she oohs and ahhs. I just sulk. She pays the lady. She paid for this desecration of mind and body? I'll teach her. When I get home I'm going to shred her newspaper or those magazines she has stashed in the bathroom. Maybe even chew a few shoes. I'll rip the stuffing out of my toys like Cody does. I'll start to bark incessantly just to annoy her. How would you like that, Yia Yia? No more Miss Nice Dog, this is war.

Well, we get home; she takes me for a walk. I'm so embarrassed. I don't want to be seen. That night I have recurring nightmares of the grooming parlor. They are chasing me around with the clippers and a blow drier. When I get up I can't even eat my Mighty Dog. It's a sad, sad day.

Another walk, this time I get a new message from Roscoe. I bet he's disappointed too. What's this? He loves my look. Can you believe? He says he I'm the cutest thing, not like that stuck up Fifi, who's too full of herself. I'm the real deal. Who knew?

Now, some neighbor stops to say how adorable I am. She wants to know my breed. Yia Yia tells her I'm an expensive Mutt, a Cock-a-Poo. Yep, that's me, a good old American mixture. Cute and tough! Maybe the Obama's will want me for First Dog, I can even tell them I bark in French.

Viva la difference!

Your 4-legged pal,

Lucey

*Magnifique	French for- Magnificent
*Ici	French for- Here

Escape and Torment

May 02, 2009

Hi Kids,

It was so great seeing everyone at Greek Easter, all the humans and canines. My sisters and I had so much fun; Cody played it Mr. Cool as usual. I really look up to him, I wanted him to go around with me and get some messages, but we didn't have time.

Although there were a lot of people, I was hoping that Shirley would have showed up. She's always so nice to me and she's lots of fun, in a sort of peculiar way. Yia Yia said she had to go back to the sanatorium. Seems Shirley was watching TV and fell in love with that Frank Perdue guy. You know, the one in the chicken business. Shirley thought if she morphed herself into a chicken she would get his attention.

Went out and bought herself a chicken suit and started strutting around the neighborhood. She flapped her arms like wings and scratched and pecked at the ground. Nobody got too upset. They all know Shirl. It wasn't until she tried to hatch the eggs in the dairy case in Shop Rite, that the authorities hauled her away. She made the evening news, so maybe that Frank guy will get to see her.

Meanwhile, with the warm weather, I've been in contact with a lot of my friends. There's mucho gossip going around. Bruno the German Sheppard bit the UPS man. Bruno says it's a misunderstanding. The man's pants leg was riding up and he was just trying to straighten it out. It was an accident his ankle got in the way. You know these Krauts, always fascinated by uniforms.

Next, Fifi is so jealous, Roscoe is so gaga over my new look and not paying any attention to her. To think she used to be my role model. That was during my French period. I'm all American now. Yep, Hot dogs, hamburgers and Alpo.

There's a new dog in the complex, Chi Chi, a Mexican hairless something. She got out the other day and drove her owners nuts trying to catch her.

You know that's my favorite game. I call it Escape and Torment. I manage to get out of the house without my leash and take off. I run around like crazy. I hear Yia Yia calling me and I play deaf. Then she goes and gets my leash. I stand as still as I can, making believe I don't notice her creeping up on me. Like you could ignore Big Foot. Just as she bends down to snap on my lead, I bound off again.

I do this a few times, and then I run around the back of the house, out of sight and just listen to her calling for me. Lucey, Lucey, where are you? I have a treat for you. Oh Yeah! Right! Some treat. Bet it's not a pork chop, or a hunk of liver. No, it's probably a stale milk bone. I'm not coming back for that, Yia Yia. Raise the ante.

Next thing I know she goes back in the house. What? Leave me out here? All by myself, don't you care? I'll see about that. I run to the front door to check it out and she opens it with a, "Gotcha!" Well, okay that's one for you.

Devious, isn't she? I was getting bored anyway. Next time, I won't fall for that trick.

We go out for a walk and Yia Yia gets into conversation with one of the neighbors. The lady is telling her how cute I am. What exactly is her breed? Oh no! Here we go again. She's an expensive mutt. A Cock-a-Poo. She's half French Poodle and half Cocker Spaniel.

Always the same line, I'm all American I want to scream! Then I get an idea. Now that my artistic and French periods are over, I need to focus on something else. I'm going to do research on all the dogs' genealogy. I'll trace our roots. There may be a Nobel Prize for that. Yes, me awarded the Nobel Prize.

For what? I'll figure that out later. I hear there's a monetary prize to go along with the honor. Dog Disney is back in my sights.

I start with myself. My Dad was a French Poodle, so he was from France. My Mom was a Cocker Spaniel; she's from Cocker.

Oh, this is going to be fun. I already know where Bruno is from and Chi Chi's from Mexico. I have to ask Roscoe where Boxers are from. I left him a message and he replied that Boxers are from the Gym.

This is going swell. I'm going to Aunt Sophia's next week. I'll ask Shatzi where Airedales originate and then interrogate that goofy Lab next store.

I have to go now, lots of work to do. I'll be busy squirting out messages to get my data. I'm knocking the water bowl for the third time around and Yia Yia can't understand why I'm so thirsty. The things we scientist do for our craft.

Have fun kids,

Your future Nobel Laureate,

Lucey

Shirley's Park Outing

June 30, 2009

Hi Happy Campers,

Hope this finds you all settled in and having lots of fun. I'm so jealous. I even thought of hiding myself in your duffle bags and surprising you. I managed to squeeze into Katie's bag but when I tried to get Lucey in with me, she just wanted out; wouldn't lie still. You know Lucey, always moving, so I gave up the idea and decided to visit Shirley instead.

She's been locked up ever since spring when she thought she was a chicken and tried to hatch the eggs in Shop-Rite. Figured it was time to see how she was doing.

When I got there, she was so glad to see me. "Hey Shirl, I missed you too." I asked how it was going; did she still think she was a chicken? "Heavens no," she said, "only if I'm hungry for a worm or when I see a carton of eggs. Other than that, I'm fine."

"Glad to hear it Shirl. You look great." She asked if I would take her out for an afternoon. She wanted to check on her apartment and have some fun. "Sure, just let me make arrangements with the nurse." Least I could do for old Shirley.

The nurse said okay, but I was to stick very close to Shirl and not let her out of my sight. She suggested I take her someplace quiet, not too much stimuli, if you know what I mean. No prob,

I'll take her for a hike in the park. Lots of fresh air and exercise. I'll have to find a way to keep her close to me. I got it, I'll get a pair of handcuffs and then I'll be sure not to lose her. Good thinking.

The following Sunday I signed her out and headed for the park. Shirl asked me to stop at her place first. "Er, okay but just for a few minutes." While I doubled park, she ran in and quickly returned, carrying a box.

"What's in there, Shirl?" " My chicken suit," she said. "Your chicken suit? Why?" "Oh," she replied, "I'm bringing it back with me for show and tell at my group therapy session. You know, acting out my problems." That made sense. See, she is getting better.

Next stop, the park. I didn't tell Shirley about the handcuffs yet. Thought it would be better to get to our destination first. As we got out and approached the gate, I pulled them out and said, "Hey Shirl, one little thing, I need us to wear these while we're here so I don't lose you. You know, like being together like Hansel and Gretel, or Thelma and Louise or Bonnie and Clyde."

"What a great idea," she said. And I thought she would give me trouble. "Let me see them." I handed them over and told her not to close them. I left the keys in the car. "Oh, alright," then she said, "Give me your wrist." I held out my hand and she snapped on one cuff. I expected her to put the other one on herself, when she suddenly reached over and snapped it onto the chain link fence. "What are you doing Shirl? Where are you going?" She headed back to the car, I assumed she was getting the keys, but instead she came out wearing her chicken suit and strutting. "No Shirley, no!" This can't be happening!

Off she went, happy as a clam or should I say chicken? She was clucking loudly as she disappeared into the woods. Now what? I spied a group of Boy Scouts heading towards the entrance. "Hey Guys, get me some help," I cried. "What's the matter Granny?" they yelled back. "It's Yia Yia, and my friend bolted me to this fence. Hurry, I need to find her." "Okay, wait here we'll get somebody," they said and left. Wait here? What part of I'm bolted to this fence didn't they understand?

It seemed like an eternity, I thought they forgot about me, but slowly up the path came the Park Ranger. I'm sure glad I wasn't in imminent danger; this guy was no speed demon. "Quick, get these cuffs off me, I need to find my friend."

"Just a darn minute, Lady. What are you, some kind of protestor?" He wants conversation. "Do I look like a tree hugger to you, Sonny? I'm locked onto this fence and my friend is in danger. Put some juice in your caboose and cut me loose."

"Well, as I see it," he said, "I'm the one who is giving the orders around here and first, I have some questions." Do you believe this? I found me a junior G-man. Must be watching too many cop shows.

Okay, I'll have to play along, all right, "What you do need to know?" "The usual," he said, "name, address, phone number, where did you get the cuffs and why are you locked on the fence?" This is torture. I gave him the basics and told him I borrowed the cuffs from a cop I knew. I told him I was going to use them to keep my friend from wandering off.

"Heh, heh, heh, seems she turned the tables on you," he chuckled. Boy, was he being smug. "Well, Mr. Smug, she's an outpatient from the mental hospital and now she's running around amok here because you won't free me, Heh, Heh, Heh!"

That set a fire under him. He got on his cell phone and called for back up. Now maybe, I'll get loose.

In the mean time while waiting for the cavalry to arrive, he asked me for Shirley's description. "Oh, she's about 5'7 and looks like a chicken." "What is she young and cute?" "No, genius, she looks like a chicken, she is probably wearing her chicken suit." How hard could it be to find a 5'7 chicken? This Park Ranger is impossible.

I'm still attached to the fence when a patrol car pulls up. Out comes, would you believe, my old nemesis, Mr. Cranky Policeman. He takes one look at me and twitches. "Please, please take these cuffs off me I have to find Shirley," I begged.

"Shirley, Shirley. Oh no! It's all coming back to me," he says. "Is this the same Shirley you tied to the back of a bus?" "Yes, Yes!" " Is this the same Shirley that shut down the Shop-Rite because people thought she was an alien?" " Yes, Yes!!" "Is this the same Shirley that you helped bungee jump off the George Washington Bridge?" " Yes, Yes!!" " Is this the same Shirley that was having a grand old time in Greece while we dredged the Hudson River for her body?" "Yes, yes!!" "And is this the same Shirley who tried to kill you by sabotaging your go-Kart?" " Yes. Yes!" "This is the same homicidal maniac Shirley that is running around loose in these woods now?" "Well if you put it that way ...Yes, Yes!"

"Okay, next what is she wearing?" " Oh my gosh, I don't know how to tell you this, but Shirley now thinks she's a chicken and she is running around here in her chicken suit," I was trying to be gentle with him.

When the twitching calmed down, he told the Park Ranger to send out a search party for her. I interrupted him," Excuse me, excuse me, I have an idea!" With an exasperated sigh, he turned to me and asked, "WHAT?"

I suggested that instead of just calling out her name, they make like a rooster and yell, 'Cock- a Doodle-Do'. Shirley always had a soft spot for sweet talk.

Mr. Cranky Pants said he was just weeks away from retiring and now this. He kept muttering, "Why? Why?" I guess he's just lucky.

With all that was going on, I was still attached to the fence. Finally, Mr. Cranky asked me where were the handcuff keys? "Oh, there in my rocket ship." " Your what?" "You know my Rocket Ship, I mean my car." "You think your car is a Rocket Ship," he asked? "Well, yeah, because it's so faa... faa ... fab... fabulous, yeah that's it, it's fabulous."

That was close. No need for him to know about my Rocket Ship adventures.

Checking the car, no keys were found. Shirley must have taken them with her. When will this nightmare end? Now I have to wait for a locksmith to come and get the cuffs open. While I'm waiting I hear the woods alive with calls of, 'Cock-a-Doodle-Do', then someone yelled, "I found her!" Shirl had found some duck eggs and was sitting on them, trying to get them to hatch.

As they led her out of the park, I tried to talk to her. "Shirley, please give me the keys, Shirley. Shirley." She just gave me a vacant stare and said, "Who's Shirley? My name is Henrietta, and my close friends call me Henny Penny."

"Yeah," said Mr. Cranky Pants, "and I'm Chicken Little."

Yeah, and I'm still latched to this fence.

Later,

Love,

Yia

Yia Yia's Fleas

July 01, 2009

Hey, Hey Kids,

Guess what? I'm on vacation too! Not exactly Dog Disney, I'm with the Linaris clan and my sister Ginger. The kids have been great to me; I've been going to the park, fetching, sleeping with Thomas, and playing with Ginger. Yep, I'm having a grand old time. I'm even getting that two-timer Roscoe out of my system; meeting lots of other dogs at the park. That'll teach him.

My trip was kind of unexpected. As usual, there's something going on with your Yia Yia, probably fleas. She's always scratching and slathering something all over herself. I think its Advantage. She kept throwing me in the sink and washing me with this horrible smelling soap. Then she'd jump in the shower, lather up with the same stuff and come out with all those suds all over her and let it dry. Try not to picture that, it's not a pretty sight.

Maybe you kids can take up a collection and buy her a flea collar. Just don't go to close to her. Those little buggers can jump.

Hopefully while I'm on vay-kay she'll get the house exterminated. The German Shepherd, Bruno, told me all about that. He's big into exterminating.

As you can see, I'm in much better spirits, even with YiaYia's bug problem. I just hope she doesn't get worms.

Have a good summer,

Lucey

Shirley's Farm Rescue

July 07,2009

Hi Campers,

I hope you are having a grand old time and meeting lots of new friends.

Me, I'm kind of stuck with the old ones. Why you ask? Well, let me tell you. Last week while I was cooking my famous chicken soup, my phone rang. When I answered it, I heard some peculiar noises. I couldn't quite make them out, it sounded like, Oh my gosh, it was. It was clucking.

"Shirley, Shirley is that you?" Some loud BUC-BUC- BUC's followed the clucking. "Shirley," I screamed, "stop speaking chicken and speak English."

The phone was dropped and then someone else began to talk. "Hell-o, hell-o is anyone there?" "YES, YES," I shouted! "Okay lady, calm down," he said. "Who is this," I asked? "Is Shirley with you? Is she alright?"

"Listen, Ma'am, I have some question of my own, I found your phone number in one of her pockets, I haven't been able to get her to talk except for that terrible clucking. She's wearing a chicken suit and strutting all around here. She's got most of my animals spooked except for my rooster, who is madly in love with her. I want someone to come and get her off my farm."

"Your farm? Where is it?" He told me his farm was right near the Go-Kart track. Oh, no. That's the farm I wrecked when Shirley sabotaged my kart. If the farmer knew who we were, he would probably shoot Shirley or worse yet, pluck her feathers. I was totally freaked out. I hadn't a clue what to do. I told the farmer I would be there as fast as I could and asked where he had Shirley. " I have her sitting on some eggs right now, seems all the other chickens ran off and I need her to hatch them for me," he growled. I figured that should keep her happy for a while until I got there.

I had to have a plan. Last I saw Shirley; she locked me on to a fence and ran off. How she managed to get loose again, I have no idea. For sure, she's a sly one. I was straining my brain; I certainly didn't want the farmer to know it was me. He was not too happy about my careening through his barn and into the pond last time we met. What to do? What to do?

Aha! I got an inspiration. He never really met Shirley, so he wouldn't recognize her. Me, well that's another story; I'll have to go in disguise.

The more I thought about it, the bigger headache I got. Let me think. Obviously, Shirley is still in chicken mode, I have to be something barnyard friendly to gain her trust and get her out of there.

How about camouflaging myself as a pig? No, that's not it. Okay, how about a goat? Nah, I don't think so. Wait a minute, I got it! I'll be a cow. Yes, that's it. A cow. Shirley loves cows, not as much as chickens, but she has a soft spot for them. Actually, everybody likes cows, what's not to like about cows?

I'm a genius, off to the costume store and back in a flash with my cow outfit. I was all set to go then realized, I hadn't walked Lucey. She was staring at me all the while I was getting dressed; I even think I might have heard her growl. No, couldn't be, like I said, everybody likes cows. I took her for a fast walk and I think she was a little reluctant to be outside with me. "Hey Lucey, what's the problem?"

I didn't have time to worry about Lucey right then, I had to get going to rescue Shirley.

Driving was a little bit difficult. My hooves kept sliding off the pedals and the steering wheel was poking my udders. The things I do for friends.

I reached the farm in a flash, the Rocket Ship, you know. The farmer came running out to meet me. He was a bit taken back to see a cow driving.

"What's going on here," he yelled? I could see the veins in his neck popping. "I'm here to pick up my chicken friend," I mooed.

"First a chicken and now a cow? I think I'll call the cops, I have a bad feeling about this," and he turned and headed for his house. I untangled the seat belt that was wrapped around that darn udder part and ran after him. Not too fast, cows can't move all that fast.

"Wait a minute, let me explain, my friend and I are doing research and needed some real life farm experience. Yours, being the best farm around here, we naturally chose you." Flattery gets them every time. He stopped in his tracks and turned around. "Really, hmm, what kind of research did you say?" Darn, I found me a smart aleck. I couldn't think too quickly, my brain was being fried in that cow head. Those things are hot. Finally, an inspiration, "A Halloween study to determine the realism and the genuiness of their product," I told him. There, didn't that sound like official gobbly gook? Man, am I good or what?

He stood, scratching his head, turned it from side to side and then nodded, yes. He understood. Great!! Houston, we have take off!!

He led me to the chicken coop and said, "I don't know what kind of program you're doing, but just get her out of here." "MOO, I mean yes." I answered. As I approached Shirley, I saw how contented she was, just roosting there, clucking away. I almost hated to disturb this Kodak moment for her, but, hey how long could my luck hold out? Besides, it was getting close to milking time and I had to get the heck out of there.

"Hi Shirley," no response. "Hi Shirley, It's me, your best friend." again, no response. "Come on Shirl, we got to leave." No response. All right, my ace in the hole. "Henny Penny, there's a handsome rooster at the next farm that heard all about you and wants a date." With that she jumped off the nest and covered it up tenderly with straw, looked at me and clucked, "Let's go." Shirl can't resist a good-looking male.

I got her out of the coop, and we headed for the car, when behind me I saw what looked like the biggest bull I ever seen. "Run for it Shir, eh Henny Penny, run fast as you can," I yelled. The bull was closing fast. Why do I have to be so darn good looking? A curse, I guess. We made it to the car just in time. I had to stuff Shirley in the seat, with those darn feathers getting all over. I squeezed behind the wheel and sped off.

I took Shirley back to the sanatorium and pulled up to the front door. All kind of people came running out. One grabbed Shirley, who by then realized what I had done. She was clucking some horrible threats, vowing to pluck my eyes out with her beak. She's scary at times.

Next thing I know, someone comes over to my side of the car opens the door and yanks me out. "What's going on here?" I demanded. "I brought Shirley back and now you hustling me?" "Okay, okay now, just stay calm. We're going to take you inside for a while and you can tell the good Doctor why you think you are a cow," the Guard told me.

Oh no, they think I'm delusional too! "Wait, don't I get one phone call?" I pleaded.

"Just one," and they handed me a phone. I dialed my daughter, Pat. "Mom, where have you been?" I didn't want to tell her right then what I was up to, so I started to tell her I went to see a show. A what?" she asked. "Speak louder I can't hear you." I shouted, "a MOOvie, a MOOvie." With that they carried me off.

I might be a while,

Love,

Yia

Lucey's Adoption Plea

July 09,2009

Hi Cody's Kids,

How's camp? I sure wish I were with you. Things are going from bad to worse around here.

First the good news, I'm pretty sure Yia Yia is over her fleas. No more scratching. Boy, that was driving me crazy. Also, I don't think she has any worms. She's not licking herself or doing any butt rubs on the carpet.

Here's the not so good news. I hate to keep narcing on her, but someone has got to get her under control. I don't understand why she can't be a regular old lady. Do some knitting, get a rocker, play canasta or something. No, she's always doing weird stuff.

Get ready for this. Now she thinks she's a cow. That's right. A cow! Not that she thinks she fat, oh no, she thinks she a real, live MOO COW! Four legs, udder, cowbell, the works. Scary!

She's been acting weird, weirder than usual ever since Shirley became a chicken. Yesterday she comes home with a box, opens it and puts on a cow outfit. Black with white spots or white with black spots, I can't tell. She has four legs and a tail longer than mine with a bow on the end of it. I won't mention the udder part. Gross!

Then she tells me it's time for a walk. Are you kidding me? I don't want to be seen in public with a cow! What will all my friends say? How embarrassing. I make it quick. I go out do my business real fast and tug to back to the house. "Oh no," she says," We need a big walk because I have to go out for a while." Where is she going? To hang out with the girls in the pasture, I'm so mortified. What with Roscoe think? I'll die if Fifi sees me. Of all the people that could have adopted me, why her? Guess it's my penance for being so darn cute.

Walk over; she pats my head with her hooves and leaves. How she can drive in that outfit, beats me. I really think she has snapped this time.

What if she wants to live on a farm? What will I do? I'm not a rural kind of dog. Getting up early in the morning, all that fresh air and sunshine, it's unhealthy. You have watch where you walk in a barnyard. No one picks up after those animals. They leave deposits all over. It's like walking through a minefield. Yuck! Give me my cozy room, air conditioning, carpeting, grooming parlor and pawdecures. Now that's living.

If she wanted to do an animal thing, why couldn't she become Lassie or Lady as in Lady and the Tramp? Then she could get a job in Dog Disney and I could go with her. What a waste.

So kids, here's the deal. I think I have to run away from home. It's becoming intolerable. I wouldn't be much trouble for your Mom and your Dad is already crazy about me. The Codester could become my main squeeze and I won't even take his greenies anymore. I promise. Please come rescue me. I'll even bring some paints and spruce up the house a bit. I can bark French and give French kisses. Besides I'm so adorable.

I really think I'm in danger. Who knows, next she might come down with rabies or distemper or worse yet, mad cow disease? To think I was worried I might catch fleas. Those were the good old days.

Your friend,

Lucey

Meeting the Doc

July 14, 2009

Hell-o Again Kids,

It's Yia Yia, writing from the sanatorium. I thought I'd be out of here by now, but that Doctor insists on keeping me a few more days. Says he finds my conversations intriguing. I guess if it's for the cause of science, I can spare a little time.

After I arrived, the nurse who took me to see the Doctor told me he was the headman around here. I thought she meant he was the boss, but no, she said he dealt with head cases. Well, I suppose he needed some advice about Shirley. He's a quiet kind of guy with a hint of smug superiority. He sat back in his big black leather chair with his pad and his ballpoint pen, ready to take notes. He suggested I make myself comfortable on the couch. If I liked, I could recline. I said, "No thanks," I wanted to watch him, watch me.

Every now and then I heard the click of his pen and I was sure I detected a twitch or two. He was pretty interested in my relationship with Shirl and the things we do together. Our conversation went like this:

Doctor: So Mrs. L, tell me how you came to be here?

Me: Oh, you can call me Yia Yia and I came in my Rocket Ship.

Doctor: Yia Yia, is that your given name?

Me: No, that's what my Grands call me; it's Greek for Grandmother.

Doctor: Oh, so you are Greek?

Me: No, I'm German.

Doctor: Hmm. Interesting, (click) and you say you arrived in your Rocket Ship?

Me: Yes, I didn't have my crew with me this time; I soloed to bring Shirley back.

Doctor: You have a crew?

Me: Yes, some of the Book Club Ladies. Let's see, there's Cathy, she's my co-pilot, Jo, she's the navigator and Linda. Linda's our newest crewmember and she's on light assignments until we get her evaluated for duty.

Doctor: You say all these grown women believe that they are traveling around in a Rocket Ship? (Click)

Me: Of course, they look forward to our Rocket Ship adventures.

Doctor: And do you have many adventures?

Me: Well, not a lot with them right now, I'm busy with the Grandkids. Summer vay-kay time, you know.

Doctor: Your grandchildren travel in your Rocket Ship?

Me: They love it; we just had a trip to Washington DC.

Doctor: How many grandchildren do you have?

Me; Twelve homemade, I call them my Dirty Dozen and some honorary ones too!

Doctor: And they all went to Washington in your Rocket Ship? (click)

Me: Oh, no. Just a few of them, my Rocket Ship only holds four passengers and me, their Captain.

Doctor: Do all your grandchildren believe your vehicle is a Rocket Ship?

Me: Certainly, they all cheer when they see me. Rocket ship, Rocket ship! They can't wait for a blast off, all but one. My eight-year-old grandson, Christopher was skeptical. He thought it was a regular SUV, but I cleared it up for him right quick.

Doctor: (click) How so?

Me: I explained to him that although it looked like a regular car, that it was a Rocket Ship really in disguise. That under that hood beat the heart of a 20 cylinder; jet fuel injected, 800 horsepower dual turbo engine. It has forward thrusters, reverse thrusters, side thrusters and the all-important, hip thrusters. Besides after burners, it has a navigational, communication and environmental system. There's an oversized celestial window for observing the constellations and looking for extra-terrestrials. Oh yeah, he was impressed. No ordinary Yia Yia, am I.

Doctor: Ok. (click,click) Let's move on. Tell me how you know Shirley.

Me: Let me think. I went to dinner with her a few times with some mutual friends. Once, I called her to come over and do knee boarding. That's when you take your ironing board apart. You tie it to the bumper of your car, kneel on it and get towed around. You should try it. It's a hoot.

Doctor: Maybe, sometime. (click, click, click) That's how you know Shirley?

Me: Well, yes but I didn't see her for a while and one day, I bumped into her here. Actually, I was waiting to see my cutey patootie policeman and met her in the garden. We started talking and I told her all about my adventures. She asked me if I would sign her out so she could have some fun too.

Doctor: And you did that?

Me: Sure, we had lots of fun. I found some exciting things for us to do.

Doctor: Like what?

Me: First, she made me promise not to do the knee-boarding thing again. Seems she didn't care for it. That was no problem. I had a better idea. I was a roller skating champ as a kid, so I thought we try that. I got some skates, signed her out and gave her some lessons. Every thing was going fine until she untied herself from the bus and went into the river. After they pumped her stomach, she was okay. Our next adventure was in Shop Rite. We got heelie's and she was having a blast until the cops came and hauled her away. It's really a long story.

Doctor: That's okay; (click) I see a picture emerging here. (click, click)

Me: Hey, Doc, you should have somebody check out that twitch.

Doctor: Maybe, I will. (click) It's stress related. (click, click) Now how did all this wind up with you thinking you're a cow?

Me: C'mon Doc, I never thought I was a cow. I needed some camouflage to go rescue Shirley from the farmer.

Doctor: Why (click) did you (click) need a disguise? (click, click, click)

Me: It's like this, Doc. When the farmer called me to come and get Shirley out of his chicken coop, I realized it was the same farmer whose farm I nearly wrecked with my Go-Kart

Doctor: You wrecked a farm with your (click) Go-Kart?

Me: Not exactly totaling it. I took out the pasture fence and some cows escaped. I barreled through the barn and into the barnyard scattering the chicken and bumping off the prize rooster. Next, I landed in the farmer's Koi pond, all but eliminating anything swimming. The farmer was pretty grumpy about that.

Doctor: What (click) happened to the Rocket Ship, (click) why a Go- Kart?

Me: Actually, it was my Grandkid's idea, Shirley volunteered to be a pit crewmember and then she sabotaged the kart.

Doctor: Why do you think she did that? (click, click)

Me: I think it was payback for me tossing her off the George Washington Bridge. You really ought to get that twitching checked, Doc. It seems to be getting worse.

Doctor: Oh yes, soon. (click, click. click) Oh, excuse me a second. I just dropped my pen. Now, where were we? You tossed Shirley off a bridge.

Me: It was in self-defense, she wanted me to bungee jump and she was going to cut my rope. I just turned the tables on her.

Doctor: So, happened next? Er, wait a second, I lost my pen again. Where is it?

Me: Doc, aren't you holding it?

Doctor: Oh, of course, silly me. Sorry. Please continue.

Me: Some swarthy seaman on an oil tanker headed for the Middle East cut her down. He planned to make her part of his harem. I had to get my Greek friends to save her and return her to the good old US of A.

Doctor: (click, click) How did you manage that? (click, click, click)

Me: I reached out for my friend, Nick Seagapopoulos. He thinks I'm an undercover CIA agent, Buzz Lightyear. Nick then contacted his relatives in Athens to rescue her. It was going along fine until Shirley, with her big libido, fell in love with Nick's cousin Nick, whose wife Nicky, didn't like that idea too much. At that point, Shirley decided to come home, plus she didn't like feta cheese.

Doctor: What makes you think Shirley has a libido problem?

Me: Really Doc, if it breathes, has a moustache and wears pants, she picks any two out of three and bingo, she's in love.

Doctor: I'll take that under advisement, excuse me a minute, (click, click) I need to get some medication. We'll talk again tomorrow. I think that's about all I can take for today.

Me: I can't tomorrow. I need to get home to Lucey.

Doctor: Lucey?

Me: Yes, my dog. Right now she's probably writing some of my Grandkids about me.

Doctor: Your dog writes your Grandkids? (click, click, click, click)

Me: Mostly while they are at camp. She's trying for a Nobel Prize so she can go to Dog Disney. Doc, Doc you better sit down. You're twitching all over now. I'll go get the nurse.

Doctor: Please do and Yia Yia, you better go now. (Click, click, click, click, click, click, click)

Me: Sure thing. I'm closing the door so you can rest. Goodbye.

Doctor: HELP!

See you at home kids,

Love,

Yia

Home Coming

July 20, 2009

Hi Guys,

I'm home! Finished conferring with that Doctor on Shirley's case. It took a little time but I'm sure I gave him some insight into her personality. Hey, what are friends for? It's nice to know that I've still got it and even nicer that someone still wants it. What can I say? Just so much Yia Yia that can go around.

I picked up Lucey; Aunt Pat took her for a few days while I was in conference. She was having so much fun that it seemed she didn't want to come home. Kept tugging on her leash to go back into Aunt Pat's house. I told her we would visit or Layla could come over to our house for a play date, but you know Lucey, she wants instant gratification. She'll be okay once she sees Roscoe.

I sure hope that that Doctor gets some help for his nervous condition. The man was a wreck when I left him. Perhaps I could help him. I think he never has any fun. He seems to be the repressed type. You know, he only speaks in short sentences or questions. Never really contributes to the conversation, seems to get jumpy and twitchy. He probably has some kind of anal retention syndrome.

I could ask the Book Club members if he could be our medical director for our Rocket ship adventures. He seemed very interested in them. What the heck, maybe we could make him a member of our club, get him to read some fun stuff instead of those stuffy medical journals. Maybe not, it actually a girl's only society. If he was really interested he could dress up in drag. That might be fun for him too. I don't know, I'll have to ask the girls. They're very choosy about our members.

I'll have to start slow; first I'll try to get him to loosen up by teaching him that Jump, Jump, Shake your booty thing and then move on to knee boarding. Afterwards, I could introduce him to some guy stuff like bungee jumping or Go-Kart racing. Of course, not the tracks near the farm. Yeah, he will have such a good time his hair could even start to grow back. I can hardly wait to talk to him again. If Shirley's better perhaps she could join us. Sort of like curing two birds with one stone, or something like that.

The things I do for people, I just can't help it. It's in my nature. I know folks appreciate it. They all wave and point at me wherever I go. Some even shout but I can't make out what they are saying. It's probably a ground swell for me to run for Governor or Senator. I would if I had the time. I'm so busy on all my other projects.

Take for instance; just the other day when I was doing my volunteer duty at the Red Cross, I had the opportunity to redirect a confused contributor. A very nice man came in and introduced himself to me; I was working the reception desk. He said he had just won the lottery and planned to give the Red Cross a big donation. I told him I thought we had all the money we needed and that he should take his money and go out and have some fun. He said great and left happy as a clam. I should have given him that doctor's card; he could show him a good time too.

I look forward to seeing you girls soon. Camp is nearing the end and it's almost time for school again. I'm thinking about going back too! Last week I went with your Mom and Sal and Annie to look at some colleges. I need some astronomy courses to take the Rocket Ship on more intergalactic missions. What do you think?

Have to run off now, poor Rocket Ship has sat in the bay, idle for a few days and it needs the dust blown off its engines. I plan to do a few orbits around town and take Lucey over to Aunt Pat's. She's been moping around and acting strange since I got home. I think she has the idea I went to Dog Disney without her. Oh, well. I'll dress up in a Lassie costume and take her to the park. Maybe she'll think its Dog Disney. I'll see you soon.

Love,

Yia

Mega What?

September 29, 2010

Dear Alicia,

It's me Lucey. I have to tell you the most amazing thing. First, however, I think you should hold up on our custody case, at least for now. There has been a new development that I need to understand. Ever since the Book Club meeting when all the ladies were so enraptured by me, Yia Yia has done a complete turnaround. Oh Yeah Alish, she's worried. Finally she is coming to understand she has a rare and incredible dog; at long last an appreciation for Moi.

Wondering why I'm hedging? Well, I'm softening a bit; I don't want to break Yia Yia's old heart. At her age you never know. At least not until I find out what's behind her change of attitude.

Now in the morning when she comes to let me out of my room, she coos, "Oh Lucey, how's my Mega Hemorrhoid this morning?" Then she refers to me by that sweet nothing all day long. Isn't that adorable? She never called me by an endearing name before. She must be really scared I might leave.

Incidentally, do you have any idea what language is mega hemorrhoid? I think maybe its German or Swedish or something like that. Could you interpret it and let me know? I'm anxious to find out what it means.

I'm almost feeling bad for being so tough on her. After all, she's, you know, not so spry anymore, and I'm so vibrant and effervescent. It must be difficult accepting her limitations. Well enough about her, let's get back to me. I'll be waiting for your answer and I'll reconsider those adoption papers for now. Okay? Don't feel bad, I'm just being my charitable self during this Christmas season.

Thanks,

El Lu-C

Lucey's X-Mas List

December 04, 2009

Hi Kids,

Merry, Merry. Are you getting in the X-Mas spirit yet? I sure hope so. There's a small favor I need to ask.

Would one of you take my list to Santa? I would go but last year Yia Yia and I got thrown out of the mall and told not to come back, just a simple misunderstanding. Actually, it was just a small chain of events that got totally blown out of control.

You see, Yia Yia decided it would be cute if we got our picture taken together with Santa. So off we went; I even had to wear a big red bow around my neck. Cute eh?

We lined up with a whole bunch of kids and Moms, all waiting to see the fat old geezer and have our picture taken. You with me so far? Well, YiaYia got to talking with some women and not paying any attention to me and I had to go. You know, relieve myself? I tugged on my leash, tried to pull her away, but no, Yak, Yak, Yak.

I spied what looked like a piece of grass in the Santa village and quickly made my deposit. Nobody seemed to notice. Unfortunately, some little boy not watching where he was going stepped in it.

All was okay until he sat on Santa's lap. Santa started twitching his nose, looking at the kid suspiciously, and then he discovered that the kid's shoes had wiped dog doo all over his Santa suit.

Santa abruptly stood up; the boy fell to the floor and started howling. The Moms started screaming, all the rest of the kids on line started crying and shoppers all ran over to see what was going on. Soon, mall security arrived at the scene.

Santa was all huffing and puffing about his suit being soiled. Are you kidding me? Is this the same guy that gets filthy going up and down those chimneys? And what about those reindeer? Don't tell me they're house broken and I bet their deposits are monumental. Please, the guy needs a chill pill.

Next, all the Moms ganged up on Yia Yia and me. "It was your dog, your dog," they all shouted at her. "You ruined our kids visit with Santa!" That's when the mall cops came over and started giving Yia Yia a hard time, one said, "You and your dog caused this entire ruckus, now you have to leave." Of course Yia Yia being Yia Yia stood her ground and asked what proof they had, "Did you do DNA on the poop? How do you know it was my dog and not one of these lovely children?"

With that Rent a Cop grabbed Yia Yia by the sleeve and started to tug her along. Well, I couldn't let that happen, so I bit him in the ankle. He hooted, hollered and jumped around. Soon, we were swarmed by what looked like a swat team. We were escorted to the exit door, but before we left, they took Yia Yia's picture and mine. (No Santa in it unfortunately) Said they were posting it at all the malls in the area and we were never to see Santa at any of them

Talk about the Christmas spirit. Geez! So you see I can't go myself so I'm asking one of you to bring him my list. Hopefully, he has a short memory and doesn't know my name.

So first, on my list:

A trip to Dog Disney, I've been trying to get there with my paintings and writings but no luck so far. I really need to see Hootch, and Benji and Tramp before I lose my looks. Right now, I'm irresistible but in a couple of dog years, who knows?

Next, some gift certificates for pawdecures, one must always look their best.

An autographed picture of any of the aforementioned heart throbs; Hootch, Benji or Tramp for my bedroom/ laundry room wall.

A subscription to Dog World to keep me informed of the latest fashions and events

A new Coach collar with genuine leather, no knock offs.

Some real pork chops, not a plastic mutant that smells like dog bones and vinyl.

That's all I can think of for now. Thanks, you're real pals. I'll send some post cards from Disney and I'll share if I get enough chops.

Love ya,

Lucey

May Day

December 05, 2009

Kids and All,

May Day, May Day, S.O.S., Code Red, in other words HELP! When are you guys going to believe me and come to my rescue?

Why you ask? You know why or better yet, you know, who! It's Yia Yia, of course. Once again, she's off the deep end. There's no controlling her. She's an embarrassment to my dog world. I keep asking you to either let me move in with you or rein her in. But NO! My warnings go unheeded, so now you all will have to pay the price.

Just wait and see what she's up to now. It started when your Mom took her to that school fundraiser. Remember that she won a raffle basket? Do you remember what it was? Well, it was an electric guitar and amplifier, that's what.

At first, she was puzzled to whom to give it, then thought she would sell it, then maybe grab bag it with the grandkids. All sensible solutions. So what happened? Dani did! I got sabotaged by my pal, Dani. Seems when she and Yia Yia were together; Yia Yia told Dani about her dilemma, Dani's solution? "Why don't you learn to play it yourself, Yia Yia?" And then, the monster was born.

Yia Yia came home, opened the case, took out the instruction book and decided to become a rock star.

Now she gets up in the morning and puts on these costumes. Usually black leggings or maybe fish net stockings, with a mini skirt or hot pants. She tops them with a sequin blouse or Grateful Dead tee shirt. With me so far? Now visualize it with orthopedic shoes and a leg brace and ergo, her outfit. I want to gouge my eyes out.

But that's not even the half of it. Next, she proceeds to take the equipment into her bathroom; says acoustics are better in there. The noise is unbearable and that's just her singing. Then she hooks up the amplifier to the guitar, ratchets up the amps and starts to practice. You know she's deaf, so she keeps upping the volume until the tiles start cracking. I have to cover my ears with my paws and even that doesn't stop my eardrums from exploding.

Next on the rehearsal list, is standing in front of the mirror, playing air guitar, gyrating and singing,' Wake up a Little Susie, Wake up.' Believe me, if Susie was dead and six feet under for 20 years, that racket would wake her up.

When Shirley gets released from the sanatorium; Yia is going to buy her a set of drums. Then Yia, Shirley and me are going to go on a road trip. Plans are to tour all the nursing homes and entertain at them. The last time she entertained at a nursing home it took months to repair the dayroom and everybody wore everybody else's dentures. Remember the cute fireman who came to the rescue? Well, his therapy was set back three months.

So what are you guys going to do about this? No way am I going with her. My nervous system is shot. I'm having night terrors just dreaming about her outfits and how I have to walk down the street with her in those get-ups. Paa-Leeze, take this seriously. Think about her out there representing your families, how could the kids go to school? How could you show your faces in the neighborhood? Don't you have any sense of embarrassment? Why must I always have to deal with her eccentricities? I need your help. At least if you won't or can't contain her, get me out of here!

Why can't she knit or play Bingo like other grandmothers? I thought I'd be spending my life in a peaceful suburban setting, chasing rabbits now and then for excitement. How could this have happened? She seemed so old and tranquil when I first met her. I licked her face and played sweet so she would pick me. Oh, if I could only turn back the clock. An axe murderer leads a calmer life.

I'm going to my room now, I'm putting my head under my pillow to drown out another chorus of YMCA and trying not to think of how she's in there boogying.

Wait a minute someone's at the door, Oh forget it, it's just the guy to install the disco ball in the bathroom.

HELP!

Lu-C

Priscilla's Visit

December 18, 2009

Good Morning All,

Sorry to report that my worst nightmare came true. A veritable dooms day. I tried to warn you all to rein Yia Yia in before it was too late. Did you listen? No! I don't know what's going to happen, just my doggie instincts telling me that we have a situation here that needs attention.

It all started first thing this morning. Yia Yia was up early, dressed in one of her band outfits and raring to go. She brings me into her bathroom, sits me on the closed toilet lid and tells me to stay. Then she grabs a hairbrush, makes believe it's a microphone and starts singing, 'You are the sunshine of my life, that's why I'll always be around.' I'm shaking all over from the sight and sound when the bell saves me, literally, the doorbell. I jumped off the commode and hurried to the door. Yia Yia followed close behind me, telling me to come back. She never heard the bell. Now, I'm sorry I did too.

Standing outside was the complex's main busybody, Priscilla. Yia Yia opens the door and here's what follows:

Yia Yia: Hi, Priscilla, what brings you out so early?

Priscilla: Oh, Good Morning Pat, I'm collecting for the Fireman's Fund today.

Y.Y.: Please step in and I'll get my checkbook. Don't mind Lucey, she's a very exuberant greeter.

Pris.: Really? Don't worry, I like dogs. Say Pat, isn't Halloween over?

Me, Lucey: *Uh oh, - here it begins!*

Y.Y.: Oh, my outfit? Do you like it? I am rehearsing for my Rock Band. Lucey, stop jumping.

Pris.: Really? You have a rock band?

Y.Y.: Oh, yes, I'm forming one now. Just waiting for my friend Shirley to get out of the sanatorium and get her charges dismissed, then we're off.

Pris.: Really. Your friend is in a sanatorium? Why?

Y.Y.: It's a long story. She fell in love with Frank Perdue and thought if she morphed into a chicken, she would get his attention. Lucey, stop that jumping, now!

Pris.: Really? How did that turn out?

Y.Y.: Not too well. He never gave her a tumble and she just got more delusional. Started trying to eat worms and hatch eggs.

Pries. Really? You said she had charges?

Y.Y.: Just some minor ones. She made a commotion in Shop-Rite when she nested on the eggs in the dairy case. Then she resisted arrest and pecked at a forest ranger when she escaped from the hospital. I'm sure they will be dropped. Lucey, I'm not telling you again. Stop jumping.

Pris.: Really? She sounds like a very disturbed person. Aren't you concerned?

Y.Y.: About Shirley? Nah. She's a good soul. She just has a very overactive libido and has problems saying no. She's a real people pleaser. That's why she'll be great for my band. Lucey, one more time, stop that jumping. Sorry Priscilla.

Pris.: Really. And you said you're going on a tour?

Y.Y.: Some nursing homes, maybe Veteran's hospitals. I can't wait. I've been rehearsing day and night. You want to hear something?

Lucey: *Oh, No!*

Pris.: Really, not right now. So, what else do you do for fun?

Lucey*: Oh, NO, NO, NO!*

Y.Y.: Well, some of my book club buddies and I get in my Rocket Ship and have we some adventures. Lucey, for the last time. Stop that jumping!

Pris.: Really? Rocket Ship? Pat, do you mind if I sit down?

Y.Y.: Where are my manners. By all means, can I get you something?

Pris.: Really, I'm fine. Well yes, maybe a little something. Do you have any Vodka?

Y.Y.: No, sorry. How about a cup of coffee? Just made it. Lucey, get off her lap.

Pris.: Really, well, actually I must be going. You know Herb; my husband is a psychiatrist, if you ever need to talk to anyone.

Y.Y.: Oh, I speak to one at the sanatorium. I met him after my cow incidence. Nice man. A bit twitchy. I give him my best advice.

Pris.: Really, I don't think I'll ask about that. I'm starting to feel twitchy myself.

Y.Y.: It's probably because Lucey is licking your face. Lucey cut that out!

Pris.: Pat, I really, really must be going. This has been a most interesting visit.

Y.Y.: Sure you won't stay for just one song? I'll get my guitar. Lucey and I have been rehearsing all morning. Lucey, stop licking.

Pris.: Really, I think I better leave now.

Y.Y.: Oh, sorry about Lucey, she can be annoying at times. I'll put her in her room. I just hung some of her favorite posters she wanted in there. She'll be occupied for a while and then I'll try out my new number on you.

Pris.: Really? Lucey has her own room with posters? How quaint. What else does Lucey want?

Y.Y.: She wants her own computer so she can write without waiting for me to finish. She is pretty good at it and sends letters to my Grandkids all the time. That's it Lucey. You're going in your room.

Lucey: *Shoot me now*!

Pris. I really, really, really have to run along. I forgot I left a cake in the oven or something.

Y.Y.: Don't you want to wipe off all that dog slime first? What about your check?

Pris.: Check? What check? I'm out of here.

Y.Y.: Well, okay. See ya around. Come on, Lucey. Back to work.

Lucey. ***REALLY, REALLY, REALLY! Send in the marines!***

Yia Yia's New Year Resolutions

December 27,2009

Hi, All My Two and Four Legged Pals,

Checking in to wish all of you a Doggone Happy New Year. Hope you had a great Christmas, too. Yia Yia had the whole gang here, the whole fam damily, my sisters and even the Codester. Boy, what a fun day. No pork chop but Aunt Mimi, bless her, snapped up a piece of prime rib when Uncle T was carving and divided it up amongst us pooches. Uncle T protested a bit, but Aunt Mimi said it was our Christmas too and he stood down. Is she something or what?

Not that I was snooping or prying, but I just happened upon Yia Yia's 2010 resolutions. I thought maybe you would like to see them. Mostly, if you notice there is no mention of going to DD (Dog Disney) or any porcine additions to my diet. Just so you know and would like to rectify my situation.

Yia Yia's Resolutions for 2010

1: Join a gym. Exercise is an option; one thing at a time.

2: No smoking in 2010, never smoked but plan not to start in the New Year.

3: Keep the 5 o'clock wine hour going. According to Doctors, wine has health benefits and it is also holy. Even Jesus knocked back a few with His boys, so I can be healthy and holy at the same time.

4: Plan to eat at least one unhealthy thing a day; I have my gym membership, that plus the wine.

5: More rocket ship adventures. Plan to explore more uncharted places in search for those pesky Eyetrailians.

6: Take zumba lessons, maybe at the gym. Will help with my show biz career.

I so resolve,

Yia Yia

That's it guys, not even a mention of me. It's a heavy burden I carry. Hope one of your takes pity on my hardship and rescues me SOON!

Your pal,

Lu-C

2010

Good News/ Bad News

January 19, 2010

Hi all,

I'm back and what a BULLETIN I have for you! It's sort of a good news, bad news, good news all wrapped up in one. It's like finding a pork chop in my dog dish every morning. Well, not quite that good, but you get the picture.

First, the good news, Yia Yia has given up her Rock and Roll career. Yep, yep, yep it's over. No more dragging me into the bathroom, (her sound studio) no more locking the door so I can't escape, no more covering my eyes with my ears and trying to keep my paws on them. Life is sweet again. Honestly, I don't know how much more I could have taken; I was even picking up messages from my friends. Roscoe wanted to know if we were skinning cats, he heard the horrible screeching emanating from our house.

Come to think of it, I should have contacted the military. Perhaps they could have used Yia Yia to break the detainees. Getting locked up with her doing her thing would have been better than water boarding and even more inhumane. Ten minutes of that torture and they would have been singing like canaries. Lost opportunity, oh well.

Now, on to the bad news, the guitar and equipment are demolished and the house nearly burned down. This happened about a week ago. Yia Yia was ready to rehearse, all gussied up in one of her outfits. Don't ask, way too painful to describe. Drags me into the bathroom, and places me on my perch, the toilet seat. I try escaping but she has the door shut tight, so back to my seat of honor to await the show.

The amplifier is plugged in and ratcheted up to max, strobe light rotating, guitar strapped on, everything is and ready and she's off. Oh yeah, her theme song is 'Stayin Alive,' thought it would be the rallying cry for the nursing homes. Me, I want to off myself when I hear it. Sorry, I digress.

And so it starts; Uh, Uh, Uh, Uh, Staying Alive, Staying Alive, Uh, Uh, Uh, Uh, Staying Aliiiiiive, she's strutting around ala John Travolta, having herself a grand old time. When suddenly, without any warning comes the loudest Pop I ever heard!

The strobe light starts vibrating, ready to fall out of the ceiling, the amp hisses and crackles then sends a spark of electricity up the guitar.

Yia Yia drops the thing like a hot rock and that's when all the lights go off. Nothing but the glow from the amplifier and the sound of guitar strings snapping. Yia Yia tries to find her way to the door in the darkness and manages to step on the dying guitar, another loud crunch, some more hissing and next, the smell of smoke. Yikes, I had to get out of there. With my keen sense of direction I make it to the door, scratching on it for dear life. Yia Yia follows my lead and we get the blazes out of there. Whew, almost incinerated in the John. What an epitaph!

The damage could have been worse and I could have easily become a real Hot Dog. So that's it. No more guitar, outfits donated to Good Will and the bathroom is getting remolded.

The insurance adjuster had a hard time trying to determine

how to settle the claim. Yia Yia offered to demonstrate how it happened and sing him a few bars, but he declined and left ASAP. Smart man.

Yia Yia was a little saddened, her aspirations of show biz shot down in flames so to speak. But here is the next part of the news.

The Red Cross called and asked her to come back to desk duty. I guess they forgot the last time she was there. Remember? Some man came in and wanted to give a big donation and Yia Yia told him the Red Cross had enough money and he should go out, spend it and have a good time. They must have forgotten or they are desperate. Either way, she agreed to return and I'm free again.

Now I have time to hunt down the candy I hid from Christmas. I put some in seat cushions and under furniture. There was a big bowl of caramels on the table and I took some for emergencies. I would have taken more, but Yia Yia came home and saw my paw prints all over the glass kitchen table and moved the bowl. I just hope she didn't find the rest of my stash.

So that's the latest. Hopefully, she will become a real old lady from now on and do her rocking in a chair. One could only pray.

Your pal,

Lucey

Book Club

February 20, 2010

Bon Jour 'Mesdames,'

Merci, merci, merci beaucoup. * Je t'adore tout. * Oh, pardon moi. * I get so excited that I revert back to my heritage and start parlaying Francaise. *I wonder if I'll ever speak Cocker? It must be my recessive gene.

It was just too divine seeing all the Book Club ladies the other night. It was Yia Yia's turn to host and I got to stay and greet all her friends. They just simply adore me, can't get enough of my affection. Actually, two of the members are competing for me. If I play my cards right, they will fight for me and I'll be adopted by the winner. Surely, that will be my lucky day.

Cathy gave me a Valentine card with canine heartthrobs. I'm going to hang it in my room as soon as Yia Yia reads me the enclosed article. And Alicia was the tops! Finally, pork chops! I can't believe my bon chance. Oops, there I go again.

I don't know how to tell Alicia, but I had to share the chops with my cousin. His family is on Vay-Kay and we're dog sitting him. That's why I couldn't go out and see all my canine friends. His name is Cody, we call him, ' the Codester' for short. A Cock-a-Poo like me and he thinks he's really cool. He acts so laid back that I swear he wouldn't move in a convulsion. Maybe, Alicia has some extra chops… I don't want to seem greedy… but hey, I had to share.

Yia Yia made herself busy putting out treats and offering wine, and then the meeting began. Jo positioned herself right in front of the cashew bowl and had Frannie on her right to block any assault on the nuts. Linda was not wearing her Hootchie boots. Hope she's okay; she's the resident fashionista. Joan, Sharon, Jo-Anne and Debbie settled in and Alicia took the seat near the only light source in the room.

Cathy proceeded to give Alicia the list of questions to review the book. After some bizarre queries, Alicia wanted to know if Cathy got the list from some Marxist Social group. There was definitely tension between them. Probably competing for my affection caused them stress. Right now Alicia has the edge, but Cathy shouldn't stop trying.

Anyway, everyone said how sad the book was, but they enjoyed it. Huh? Next, they discussed the choice for their next read; again, more sad stories. I had a great suggestion. Why not pick a book about us canines? We are very inspiring and uplifting. Did you ever hear of dogs knocking over a Pet food convenience store on a Saturday night or losing all their milk bones on a crap table? No! We are motivated by pure loyalty and devotion. We are on constant vigilance to protect your homes, inspecting your foods, testing your waters. Do we ever give up? Never! Not even when you tell us to, "Stop that infernal barking! Stop begging at the table!" Not even when you slam the toilet lid on us as we are checking the water reservoir. We press on and continue doing our duty. Regular four legged Semper Fi's! That's us.

Now wasn't that better than some depressing human narrative? You betcha!

Well, I said my piece. What would they do without me? For appreciation they might want to consider contributing to my Dog Disney fund. These brainwaves don't come easy.

Finally, I got Yia Yia to read the enclosed article in Cathy's card after everyone left. It was about a beauty contest at the Westminster Kennel dog show. Oh My Gosh! Cathy found the way for me to get to Dog Dis… I'm a shoo-in; I'll be a star. Wow, the solution. And to think I doubted her just because of the silly pictures of pork chops and that plastic thingy thing. No need for her to redeem herself now. To think, my moment has arrived!

Wait a minute… what did you say? Yia Yia told me that the show is for pure breeds. So what am I? Chopped Liver? No, she said, you're an expensive Mutt. Mutt? Ain't I special? What's with this purebred stuff? My parents were cool. Yes, but they weren't the same kind. You have to be the same kind if you're purebred. Next, she tells me not to feel bad. Most people in the United States are mutts.

Yeah, that explains why there aren't any people shows at that fancy Westminster.

My hopes for Dog Disney shot down in flames, so close and yet …oh I can't even talk about it... I'm so depressed. I'm going to ask the Codester what he knows about this. Hopefully I can wake him up. He's taking his morning nap. Sleeping all night wears him out.

"Hey, Codester, get up. I need to talk to you. Come on Cody. I'm in pain here. Don't make me get physical, I can nip your tail in an instant." Finally he opens one big brown eye and asks me, "What's your problem?"

"Not just my prob Codester, yours too. I just found out we are ordinary Mutts because of some breeding defect." No says

Cody, he is not a Mutt; he refers to himself as a hybrid. I told you he thinks he's cool.

"So Cody," I say, " what do you know about this breeding stuff?" He opens the other eye, "You mean as in boinking?"

"Boinking? Oh, Boinking! Yeah, I guess so. So Code what's the deal?"

"Did you ever. You know, Boink?"

"No, I tried making love to somebody's leg once, but Aunt Mimi took me to get fixed so no, no boinking for me."

"What about you," he asks. "Ever?"

"Oh my goodness, no. I got fixed too."

How depressing. No Dog Disney and no Boinking.

So there we lay side-by-side, the Codester and me, two un-boinking mutts.

Au revoir, * mon amis, *

La* Lucey

Mesdames	French for madams
Merci beaucoup	French for thank you very much
Je t'adore	French for I adore you
Pardon moi	French for excuse me
Au revoir	French for Good-bye/ till we meet again
Mon amis	French for my friends
La	French for the (female gender)

Lucey's Plea to Alicia

March 10, 2010

Hi Alicia,

It's me, your friend Lu-C. Hey Alicia, I don't know if I ever thanked you properly for those yummy pork chops. You're the best.

I was wondering if you ever had the time to start those custody papers? I know you're busy and all that, but Cathy is trying hard to cut into your action.

Not that you have anything much to worry about. No, from where I stand, I think she has some kind of personality flaw. Take for instance instead of getting me a real pork chop, what does she do? Well, first she sends me a picture of one. What am I supposed to do with that? Next, a plastic mutant looking chop that squeaked and has the odor of stale milk bones. Scary. She tried harder on Valentine's Day to butter me up. I received a card with some doggy heart throbs and little words of endearment, like I woof you, poochy, poo. Lame, but then she ruins it all with an article about a dog beauty show. I got so excited thinking it was my ticket to Dog Dis only to have my dreams and aspirations shot down. How? It was a show for purebreds. Purebreds! Like I'm chopped liver or something.

I tell you Alish; I can call you that, right? As I was saying, Alish, I cried for days. Thank goodness I had my cousin, 'the Codester', here to commiserate with me. He's a Cook-a-Poo too, but insists he's not a mutt; he's a hybrid. The pain is wearing off, but don't you think she has some kind of sadistic personality flaw? She was even mean to you at book club. What about those dreadful questions she made you read? No, Alish Baby, I'm all yours. So as you lawyer types say, time is of the essence.

I can't wait for more pork chops and that cushy queen sized bed is just calling me.

I bet you're asking what's in it for you, besides my warm and affectionate self.

To sweeten the pot, I figured you could be my manager/agent for when I become the next dog super star. You can accompany me to Dog Dis, bring the kids of course and you can all enjoy basking in my glow. You could even give up that ordinary day job and go on tour with me. How's that for incentive?

Don't you go worrying about Yia Yia; she'll be fine. She's getting too old to handle all the stress that will come with my celebrity. I'll write to her often and you can take me to book club so she can visit with me.

It will be great. So rev up that paper work and get my room ready. I have a couple of posters that I'll bring, so a nice corkboard or empty wall opposite my bed will do to hang them.

Oh and by the way, those Girl Scout cookies you sent to me, Yia Yia refused to give me any. Said they were bad for me. So not only is she standing in my way for success, I also have to endure deprivation and canine abuse.

Gotta get me outta here Alish, The sooner the better.

Your new best friend,

Lu-C

P.S. Oh, just one more thing Alish, let's keep this between ourselves till it's a done deal. Don't want to upset anyone and you never know, maybe Cathy with reform and up the ante.

Mea Culpa Letter to Cathy

March 12, 2010

Hi Cathy,

I don't know how to tell you, but I'm mad that Yia Yia sent out my letter to lots of people. That was a private missive to Alish. Not that I have any reason to hide my doings, but it was a big invasion of my canine privacy.

There, that being said, I want to explain to you a few simple facts.

Being the educated, super smart and savvy individual that you are, I'm sure you saw right through my scheme. It's imperative that I get good old Alish motivated ASAP to get me out of my dastardly living conditions. A little competition is always good. With me so far?

I know you didn't set her up with difficult questions at book club. No, she was just frustrated at sitting in that corner so far away from the cashews. Having to watch Jo and Fran monopolize the nuts from their front row advantage, plus the stress of the competition over me and what do you expect? She went right over the edge.

Though, you have to admit, she certainly offers me more perks than you. However, that could easily be corrected. I could be swayed by a trip to Dog Disney to see my dream dog hunks. Not a bad deal when you think about all the benefits you will receive with me being your pet.

Forget whatever I said about your sadistic side, that was just a sympathy ploy. You have however been a little, what's the word I'm looking for? Insensitive? No. Ignorant? No, that's not the one either. Let me think. Oh yeah, got it, oblivious to my feelings. A creative artist like me needs special handling. A sensitivity course for you might come in handy.

There are some items, should you decide to do the Dog Dis trip and claim me for yourself, that you have to promise before it's a done deal. My needs are few, I don't expect a queen size bed, a full with lots of cushy quits and pillows will do. Don't forget my dream dog posters. I'll have Yia Yia pack them. Pork chops at least three times a week, bone in preferably and grilled medium. Pet grooming every six weeks that includes pawdicures however, absolutely no silly tail pom poms. Frequent walks so I can pick up messages from my many admirers. Anyplace that has fire hydrants and trees is good. Tummy rubs on demand and lots of chew toys.

And under no conditions, am I to be stuck on a toilet seat while you sing in the shower. No way. The last time that happen I was almost a real hot Hot Dog. I'm still traumatized by that. Maybe I need counseling, put that on the list.

All right then, get the tickets and let me know when I can move in. I have to let the neighborhood dogs know so they can throw me a going away party.

Glad we had this little chat, Cathy. With a little training you'll do fine. Tell Mario I'm coming, I'm sure he'll be thrilled.

See Ya Soon,

Ciao,

Lu-C

Lunch Disaster

March 13, 2010

Hi Kids,

Another horrific day, this winter has been forever and difficult. I swear it feels like it's been snowing since August. I can't tell you how many times I lost Lucey in the monumental snowdrifts.

Boring, boring, and boring. I was in need of some new adventure. Ever since I had that tragedy with my electric guitar, life has been dreary. All my aspirations of a senior rock band shot down in flames. Literally! Sitting around moping, I decided I should go over and visit Shirley. She's been in that sanatorium for a while now.

Hopefully her chicken obsession is over and we can do some fun things. Off I went, optimistic and full of hope. Ah yes, I could feel the surge of excitement in my clogged arteries. Well, maybe it's the new medication. Whatever.

I arrived and started to sign in at the front desk. Some smart aleck guard came over and wanted to chat. "So looky, looky, looky what we have here. My, my, cute cow has come back for a visit. Seen any good MOOOvies lately?"

"Actually, I did. It was about a rent-a- cop that was full of bull. Sort of reminded me of you a lot," I said. "Really? You think I could be in a movie?" He was glowing. "Yeah, Sherlock, you'd be type cast, " was all I could mutter.

Brother, where do I find these people? And they tried to lock me up?

Anyway, I asked him where I could find Shirley. "Probably in the dining hall," he said. I got my pass and went to find her. I spied her sitting at a table in the corner, by herself. "Hey, Shirl, Hi, it's me Yia Yia. How are you? You look great! What's happening?"

I guess it was too many questions all at once because she just kind of stared at me for a while. Finally the light went on and the elevator reached the top floor. "Oh my goodness. Yia Yia! Great to see you, I've missed you. No hard feelings right?" "Heck, no Shirl. You just were having a rough patch but you seem fine now. How's that Chicken thing doing?"

"Oh, Yia Yia, I'm fine. How silly was that? Me, a chicken? Geez, I've got great legs and bigger boobs, why would I want to be a chicken? I'm a lot more glamorous than an ordinary chicken. No, I'm more like a gazelle or a beautiful swan. Don't you think?" "Well, sure Shirl, if you had to be an animal go for the rare and exotic."

I was starting to get a little concerned here, but at least her chicken obsession seemed cured.

She asked me to join her for lunch. "Okay, what are they having?" I asked. "Oh, I don't know, they just serve whatever the chef decides. Sort of potluck," she said.

We sat there chatting for a bit, when the server came over with our lunch, a nice salad and a piece of quiche.

"Hey, Shirl, this looks good, let's dig in." "Wait one second," she called the server over. "Excuse me, excuse me. Can you tell me what's in this?" "Oh, the quiche? Let's see. Today's quiche is asparagus and ham," the server replied.

"No," Shirley asked, "what's this other stuff in it? How is it made?" "Oh, it's got cheese and cream and eggs," was the answer.

"EGGS? EGGS?" Shirley went ballistic. "What do you think? You think I'm cannibalistic? That I eat my young? What kind of people are you? Feeding my little ones to all these people." With that, she got up and started collecting everyone plates. She was on a rampage. "Do you think I sit on all those eggs so my children can be sacrificed to the chef god? I'm going to give these quiches a decent burial," and off she went down the hall with her arms full of plates.

I tried to stop her, but she was totally on a mission. She flew down the hall to a side door. Nurses, orderlies, aides were in hot pursuit, but she outran them all. I saw her reach an emergency exit door and barreled through it. Now alarms started ringing and clanging. All out pandemonium was at hand.

The exit led to a walled garden where patients with their family and friends were visiting. The sight of Shirley bursting in with her arms full have broken dishes and covered in food drippings scared the socks right off them. Also, I should add, she was giving off blood curdling clucks.

Everyone scattered, some tried climbing trees, and they weren't even the patients. No, the patients were climbing over the garden walls.

Shirley found a patch of ground where she started scratching and pecking. She was depositing the remains of the quiche when I caught up to her. "Come on Shirl, calm down, and let's go back in," I pleaded. "NO, no, I need to give the little ones a decent burial, "she was hysterical.

I figured I play along to get her to co-operate. Grabbing a spoon, I started digging. That's when Sherlock the security guard got to the scene. "What have we got here? Henrietta hen and Elsie the cow at it again," he chuckled.

"No, Sherlock, you don't understand. I was just pacifying her to get her to go back inside," I tried to explain. "Sure, sure, let's go tell the good Doc all about it," he snickered as he led us away.

Now what? No good deed goes unpunished. I'll have to see that twitchy Doctor again, this all because I was trying to be a Good Samaritan.

Okay kids. This might take a while. Do me a favor and hide my cow suit. Thanks.

Love ya,

Yia

Waiting Room Entertainment

March 21, 2010

Hey Kids,

Here I am, sitting in the Doctor's waiting room at the sanatorium. It's pretty dreary. Lots of old furniture plus the paint needs to be brightened up. How do they expect anyone to get happy in such a depressed atmosphere? I'll have to tell that to the Doc when I see him. The guard, Sherlock said he wanted to talk to me. I guess he needs more of Yia Yia's expert advice on Shirley's treatment. I'm always glad to help.

A few other people are waiting here with me. Let's see. There's a prim woman, could be a church lady. She's sitting very straight, sort of at attention. She's dressed in a very somber suit, clutching her handbag tightly on her lap. Her feet in sensible shoes, of course, are firmly planted and her knees are so fused together, I think they must be gorilla glued. Then there's a bookish looking man. He's sitting opposite her. His attire is more casual; it resembles that of a college prof's; sweater vest, tweed jacket with suede elbow patches and corduroy slacks. He's wearing a pair of round wire rim framed glasses to finish his outfit. He's eyeing the Primster. Off to the side is a pair of what could be over aged biker boys. Scruffy looking duo with beat up boots, old jeans, wearing tight black tee-shirts that cover the torsos of steroid addictions gone bad. They are eyeing each other.

I'm getting bored. I'm in a beat up red vinyl chair that squeaks when I move. There's no TV, the only thing on the wall is a security camera scanning the room. I don't know why, nothing here to steal except year old magazines. I'll have to do something to make the time pass.

Let me think. Okay, I'll do my rabbit imitation. I pull up my top lip, tuck in my chin and move my nose up and down. A few minutes of that brought little reaction. The Prof and the Primster gave bemused smiles and the Biker Boys didn't notice. Moving on, next is the fish face. Pursing my lips together then opening them in a wide circle and making underwater sounds. Next, I open my eyes as wide as possible, and then rotate my head side to side as if I was inside a goldfish bowl, searching for the cat.

More bemused smiles and this time the biker boys nudged each other. Now I'm getting somewhere. Okay, having their attention, I pull out all the stops. I put my fingers in my ears and rotate them counter clockwise, slowly sticking out my tongue with every turn. When fully extended, I then turn my fingers clockwise retracting my tongue with each spin.

The Primster looks aghast, Prof appears baffled and Biker Boys give toothless smiles. I'm telling you kids, I missed my calling. I should have been in show biz.

Pleased with my accomplishment, I sit back in the chair. It gives off a sounds like a whoopee cushion. The Primster snaps her head around stares at the Bikers expecting to see a mushroom cloud over their heads. The Prof does a poor imitation of my rabbit face and I give a cold hard look at the Bikers also. The Bikers, well, they are oblivious to all of this.

All righty, I'm on to something here. I wait a little while, and then I move to my right, making believe I'm going for a magazine.

Another loud fart sound goes off. This time, Miss Manners reaches into her purse and takes out a hankie to fan over her nose. The Prof tries to appear debonair and, the boys, well finally they look bemused. I, of course, look all around as if I can see farts. I'm ready to do it again, when the nurse calls me. I get up and make the loudest, Mack Daddy fart stinger sound of all. Primster now dives her nose into her purse, the Prof suddenly needs to look inside his jacket armpit and the Bikers nod in approval and give me a thumbs up.

As I approach the office door, The Primster, recovering her composure complains that she was there before me; in fact she admonishes the nurse that everyone in the room was before me. I inform her in my best authorial tones, that I, Yia Yia am not a patient, that I am a consultant, here to confer with the Doctor on patient treatment. "You? You? What?" she stutters?

The Prof now opened his mouth; I think he was trying my fish impression. No sounds came out but he had that bugged fish eye stare down perfect.

Suddenly, Miss Prim's knees become unglued, she looks over to the Prof and they get up and leave together. Once again, I succeed in bringing people together. Maybe they'll invite me to the wedding.

The Biker Boys smile and wave at me on their way out arm in arm. Well, now the Doc will have extra time to hear my advice.

Catch cha later.

Love,

Yia

Doctor Interview

April 02,2010

Hi Kids,

Guess you're wondering how I made out with the grouchy Doctor. He took me in his office before I finished my last missive to you. He's the same one I saw when I had to impersonate a cow to get Shirley, aka Henrietta the Hen back to the sanatorium. He really values my insight and advice.

Doctor: Hi Yia Yia, please take a seat.

Me: Hi Doc. How's it going? How's that twitching thing?

Doc: Haven't had any since last I saw you.

Me: Great, you had me worried for a while there. Say, where's your pad and pen today, Doc?

Doc: I've switched to a recorder. That's very observant Yia Yia.

Me: Just part of my charm. So, Sherlock said you wanted to see me.

Doc: Sherlock? Oh, you mean the guard, why do you call him Sherlock?

Me: That's just a play on words; I really mean to call him the reverse.

Doc: The reverse?

Me: Yeah, Sherlock spelt backwards is Doofus. Get it?

Doc: Yia Yia, do I detect a problem with authority?

Me: Heavens no! My best buddy is that cute cop you have here. They still won't let me see him. According to his nurse he has to avoid any type of stimulus. He saved my life a couple of times, so now I really belong to him. I told him that right before they admitted him here. I hope he gets better soon.

Doc: Oh yes, we need to keep you away from him. You're eh, too stimulating. Besides him, any other authority figures that you may have had dealings with?

Me: Let's see. There is that cranky older policeman who always takes me downtown. He gets even crankier when I ask why we never go uptown. He could use some daily fiber. I don't know if this counts, but a manager threw me out of his restaurant for having patrons do, Jump, Jump, Shake your booty on his chairs. I told him he needs looser shirt collars, his eyes were bulging right out of his head. Plus, maybe Scout Master Bob...

Doc: Enough, I see a pattern emerging. Let's get back to Sher, eh, the guard. He said he found you digging and pecking at the dirt with Shirley, burying the quiche. He said it appeared you were behaving like a chicken too.

Me: Nah Doc. That was just pretend. I was trying to quiet her down to get her back inside.

Doc: Just like a while ago you were just pretending to be a cow?

Me: Of course. Geez Louise, Doc. Do you have any idea how hard it is to be a cow? Those udders got stuck in my steering wheel and my hooves kept slipping of the pedals. No one in her right mind would want to be a cow.

Doc: Exactly. So what were you pretending to be in my waiting room? I saw your performance on my monitor.

Me: Great! What do you think? Do I have a shot at getting in show biz? Hey Doc, do you have something in your eye? Your left eyelid seems like it's fluttering.

Doc: No, I haven't noticed. About show biz, I have no idea what constitutes talent these days, but I would say you are off to a late start.

Me: Well, I was very busy when I was younger, now I have the time. Besides my Rocket Ship friends think I have latent possibilities.

Doc: Your Rocket Ship friends. Are they pretend too?

Me: No Siree. Remember Doc? I already told you about them. They are a great group of gals. Let's see, my main crew is Cathy, the co-pilot, Jo, our navigator and Linda, our cadet -in-training. Actually she's up for a promotion. I think I'll make her mission co-coordinator. We have others in my book club that are possible recruits, but we have to vet them out first.

Doc: Vet?

Me: You know, security clearance. We have a couple of candidates that might be E. T. sleeper cells. Say Doc, you should check your eye. It seems to be getting worse.

Doc: Not right now. Let's continue. What makes you think you have aliens among you?

Me: Nothing overt. There are two of them that exhibit inhuman like rapid hair growth, nails too. One gal, Fran, she has a serenity about her that's unworldly, and Sharon is the opposite, bright and perky all the time. Besides the hair and nails, these gals are extraordinarily organized.

Doc: Yes, I can see where you would have concerns. Are there any other people in your group behaving strangely?

Me: Not strange, but Cathy and Alicia are trying to woo my Lucey away from me. They're making all kind of promises to her to entice her to live with them. Of course, she's manipulating them both. She's wants to get to Dog Disney in the worst way and is being shameful about it.

Doc: Why does Lucey want to go to Dog Disney? Is there such a place?

Me: Hey, Doc? Did you just wink at me? You old goat, you're flirting with me.

Doc: I assure you Yia Yia, that it would be very inappropriate for me to flirt with a patient, no matter how tempting. No, I think I'm having tics.

Me: Oh ticks. I give Lucey medication for that. Keeps the fleas off her too. Would you like some?

Doc: TICS, NOT TICKS! It's an involuntary spasm.

Me: Oh, you mean you're having twitches.

Doc: Yeah, twitches. Why do you give Lucey dog medication?

Me: Duh, Doc, you forget? Cause she's a dog.

Doc: A dog that manipulates your friends. Wait a second, Yia Yia. Oh Jane, would you step in here a moment?

Jane: Yes, Doctor?

Doc: Jane, please cancel the rest of my appointments today. (Big wink) and take me home.

Jane: Of course Doctor. (Winking herself) I've been waiting twenty years for you to ask me.

Doc: No, no Jane, (another big wink) that's not what I mean.

Jane: (Winking back) Oh, I understand. Not in front of your patient. Not to worry. All the other patients are gone. Those two big fellows left a while ago holding hands, so we are free to go you, Honey Bunch, you.

Doc: Jane, Jane I have to tell you I have tics.

Jane: Don't worry Doc; I'll be gentle.

Me: Well, Doc, you have to go. I'll come back at a later time to discuss Shirley. Meanwhile, why don't you lift that visitor ban on my cutey patootie policeman so I can cheer him up?

Doc: Never!

Me: Man, he's still cranky. He could use some fiber too!

So I left the sanatorium, I'll go fire up the rocket ship and take Lucey for an orbit around town. Sure hope the Doc and Jane have a nice afternoon. He was having tics in both eyes when I left. Jane didn't seem to mind. She was dragging him out of there as fast as she could. Spring is in the air; love in bloom. Ah, yes.

That's all for now, kids.

Love,

Yia Yia

Doctor Interview X's 2

April 04,2010

Hi All,

As expected, I got a call to see that quirky doctor at the sanatorium. I knew he would be calling to ask my input on how best to treat Shirley. It was only a matter of time.

I arrived early and spent some time chatting with Jane. You know? His loyal nurse? Anyway, Jane says he's doing fine and today; she only had to double his medication twice in anticipation of my visit.

I asked if there was any chance of seeing my cutey patootie policeman. Unfortunately, she said, he got so excited and out of control when he heard I was in the building that they had to transfer him over to another facility.

Can you imagine that? I still have it guys. I don't know how, but I'm magic. Sorry I missed him. I'll make it up to him next time we meet. I bet he can't wait. As for Shirley, they still have her in quarantine, something about bird flu or another contagious disease. Anyway, she's not available either.

As I chatted with Jane, Dr. Grouchy poked his head out his door and invited me into his office.

Doc: Hi Yia Yia, glad you were able to come. How are you?

Me: Great, Doc. You look a lot better than last time I saw you. How are things going with you and Jane?

Doc: Now Yia Yia, you know a gentleman shouldn't talk. However, let's just say I'm happy.

Me: Hey Doc, that's what I do. I go through life trying to make people happy.

Doc: So I've noticed. Okay, let's get started. Tell me about your book club.

Me: Hold on! I thought you wanted to see me to discuss Shirley's progress and of course, her treatment. You know, I'm well versed in her problems.

Doc: Yes, we'll get to that later. Let's just say you have become somewhat of a professional challenge. I need to clear up some things that I didn't get to last time we met. Okay?

Me: Certainly Doc, always glad to help out a colleague.

Doc: I knew you would understand.

Me: Sure, let's get started. What do you want to know?

Doc: Well, there are some open-ended items. Like the aliens in your Book Club, your talking dog and the Rocket Ship adventures with your crew.

Me: No prob, Doc. It sort of all revolves around the club, so I guess we should start there. My rocket ship crew consists of the Book Club members, and we go on various adventures together. We travel to places such as museums and ethnic restaurants in search of sub rosa groups.

Doc: Just a second. What exactly do you mean, sub rosa groups?

Me: You know, Doc. Secret, ancient societies, other worldly types. We found Eyetrailians at the museum; a questionable aging Vietnam veteran stuck in a time warp, driving a cab, a few transgender servers at local eateries. Believe me they are all out there.

Doc: Yes, there are a few in here too! Sorry, please continue.

Me: Regarding Lucey, everybody encourages her, and in fact two members are vying to adopt her. And as for the aliens, it's not carved in concrete but there is certain phenomenon that embraces two of our ladies.

Doc: Hmm, very well. Give me a little back ground on your members. A mini bio, if you will.

Me: First, let me say they are all very intelligent and caring individuals. There is a great deal of camaraderie in the group. It's composed of mature women. Some more mature than others, chronologically and in temperament. Mostly, they all live within close proximity of each other. Let me think, some have careers in education, others in the legal system, a few in business and the medical field.

Doc: And how do you fit in that grouping?

Me: Let's say I'm a jack-of-all-trades. I started out in the medical profession, became a businessperson, now I'm trying to break into show biz. I guess I am an all around Renaissance woman.

Doc: Interesting. And how did you come to join this Club, do you live nearby?

Me: No, I live a few miles away. When I moved to Fairfield, my daughter introduced me to all the club members at a meeting. I was welcomed warmly and as they say, the rest is history.

Doc: I'm just trying to understand how you influence the mass delusions that they all seem to have.

Me: What delusions? Why do you think that? Everything I told you is a reality.

Doc: Oh, come on now Yia Yia, a talking dog? Really?

Me: Guess you never had a dog, Doc. If you did, you would know that they could communicate. Not necessarily by words. No, it's more like telepathy.

Doc: You say you communicate with your dog through brainwaves?

Me: That, plus her dog speak and her pointing.

Doc: So, she thinks about going to? What is that again? Dog Disney? And you understand?

Me: No, actually, that's the pointing part. Whenever a commercial for Disneyland is on, she runs to the TV, barks and points at it then at herself. Clear as a bell to me.

Doc: And what about some club members wanting to adopt her?

Me: Now Doc, wouldn't you like a smart dog like that?

Doc: I guess. Wait a minute. I'm getting off base here. So, you are saying that the club members all think Lucey can communicate and they all are on board with that?

Me: I really don't know why you can't get it, Doc. Twelve smart, educated women can't be wrong.

Doc: I would love to sit in on one of your meetings to catch the dynamics. I might even get a paper out of it. What do you say? Is it possible, Yia Yia?

Me: Of course, it's up to the girls. It might be possible, but Doc, there is one stipulation; you have to come in drag.

Doc: Drag, whatever for?

Me: We have a no men allowed rule. So, if you want to observe you have to come in drag. Actually the girls are used to it.

Doc: I'm afraid to ask. How so?

Me: Oh, Cathy and Jo's husbands do drag every Tuesday night.

Doc: And the women all know and are okay with it?

Me: Sure, saves them some money. A restaurant in town has Ladies Night on Tuesday and the guys go in drag to get the discount.

Doc: And there's no problem?

Me: Well, sometime when the girls go with them and they hold hands or smooch, they get strange looks, but other than that, it's cool.

Doc: I'll have to consider it. I think our time is up today. Thanks for coming in.

Me: Whoa! Not so fast, what about Shirley? We were supposed to discuss her

Doc: With the talking dog, aliens, rocket ship stories and now this stuff about drag, I'm on overload. Okay, just a few more minutes. What do you suggest?

Me: It's really simple. You know she wants to be a chicken because of her obsession with Frank Perdue? All you have to do is get her another love interest and bingo, case solved.

Doc: Actually, transference might work. Good insight, Yia Yia. Now you'll have to leave. On your way out, ask Jane to come in here with my pills.

Geez, I've been thrown out of better places. Can't wait to see him in drag.

"Hey Jane you better get in there, his twitches are starting."

Later,

Love,

Yia

Neighborhood Review

May 05, 2010

Hi All,

Sorry I haven't written in a while. My computer privileges were cut. Yia Yia found me writing to some friends and narcing about her so she cut me off. It's time for me to get my own PC anyway; I'm in the process of starting a foundation, a non-profit for writers such as moi. It's El Lu-c Dough for My Own Computer.com. Anyone wanting to donate money just send it directly to me. Okay?

Recently, Yia Yia has been this side of boring. No wild excursions. No crazy schemes. Nada. Actually, I miss the excitement. She has been working on a plan to get Shirley out of the institution. Had some ideas, but has fallen short of the execution. Pardon the word.

So, I've been bored. More than that, B-O-R-E-D! The only thing I have going is the messages I pick up on my walks. I feel like I'm voyeur, living life through other canines, dreadfully sad, n'cest pas?

However, there are bright spots, I have some interesting things to report. First, there is Bruno. You know, that superior German Shepard with the propensity to bite? He left a spritz telling about what is going on in his house. I think he is living with a bunch of white supremacist. Seems they have all sorts of opinions about us canines. They think Fifi was a French collaborator in a former life. That Roscoe the Boxer is mentally deficient, a real box of rocks. Actually, they said his owners should have named him Rocky. As for moi, that I am cute but a Mutt. A Mutt, a genetic freak! How dare they? I am scientifically engineered to bring out the best of my ancestors and look at how successfully that turned out, all modesty aside.

They never mentioned Chi Chi, that little Mexican whatever. Guess they never saw her. Speaking of whom, Chi Chi and her walker passed our open garage door last week and paid a visit. Yia Yia was blabbing to her walker while Chi Chi ran rampart all over my house. She even went over to my dog dish for the few morsels I was saving for a snack and helped herself. Boy, I couldn't wait for her to leave. Just came in and made herself at home. How rude!

Later the walker called Yia Yia all frazzled to tell her that poor Chi Chi got sick. In fact, she got sick all over her owners house. They were terribly upset. What could she have possibly gotten into? What a shame! That'll teach her to invade someone's territory and eat my munchies.

Fortunately, Yia Yia managed to straighten that out. Next day, I picked up a message from my aforementioned nemeses, Fifi. Seems her owners had quite a row. Her Mistress was fighting with her husband because he was refusing to pay for anymore Botox treatments. He said she was staring to look like the Cheshire cat in a permanent state of fright.

She retaliated by switching liniment for his hemorrhoid ointment. The poor man's backside was on fire for hours.

As for Roscoe, a supposing tough dog, remember he's the Boxer? He's really a whuss. He overheard his master saying how he put down some guy at work and he had it coming to him. Wifey agreed and said it was about time. Roscoe remembered a couple of his four legged friends getting put down and never seeing them again. He thought it was illegal to do that to humans and now he's terrified they'll do it to him. Frankly, they seem like really nice people. You never know.

Then there's a new pup on the block name's Skippy. Can't tell yet what he is, I think they said he was a rescue dog. I can't imagine him rescuing anyone. He's very small and acts wired. His owner was complaining to Yia Yia how he chews up their shoes and tears the newspaper to shreds before they even read it. Boy oh boy, I sure hope they never speak to Roscoe's family.

That about sums up the extent of my existence, living on the fringe when I used to be the main attraction. So, please, please, please send in the moola so I can get back in touch with all my buddies. Alicia, if you get this, what's keeping you with the custody papers? I'm getting stale here and you should get me while I'm still in my prime. And oh, yeah, Cathy, jump in anytime. I'm flexible.

See ya,

El Lu-C

Cat Attack

July 28, 2010

Hi All,

I have to tell you that I've been pondering and I am sure there's something amiss about that cock-a-mamie Doctor at the sanatorium. After my last visit, I left with an ominous feeling of foreboding.

Let me tell you my reasoning. He calls wanting to confer about Shirley's case and treatment. Does he? No. He gave me one brief minute to discuss her and then threw me out. Curious, don't you think?

What did he really want? Going back, I realized he had an abnormal interest in the Book Club. Oh, yeah. He pumped me for a mini bio of the members and info about their interest in the Rocket Ship. He was concerned about Lucey's telepathic ability and most importantly; he concentrated most of his attention to our possible sleeper cells. Then he asks to sit in on a meeting under the guise of writing a paper about mass delusions.

What hooey! I suspect that he maybe a sleeper cell himself. Or even scarier, he might be a trigger. You know, the one who wakes up the cells. No wonder he gets all anxious and twitchy when I speak of my suspicions of ET's in our group. It's all becoming clear. To think I almost had him come to one of our meetings.

How could I have exposed him to my Book Buddies? I could have put them in danger. Good thing I figured that out in time. Phew!

My biggest concern now focuses on Shirley. She's locked up in that place with that sadist guard and the ET psychiatrist. Somehow, I have to manage to get her out.

What to do? What to do?

To start with, I'll have to go see her and convince her she's not a chicken. I called the hospital and asked if she was out of quarantine yet?

Oh yes, they told me. I said great, I'd be coming to visit. I was put on hold and when they got back on, they asked who I was. "Her good friend, Yia Yia, of course." "Please hold again." Geez! When they finally picked up, they informed me that Shirley had a restricted visitor list and I was not on it.

Uh oh. Something's wrong. It's that creepy Doctor keeping me away from her. My worries were getting stronger. What did I tell you? CODE RED!

I managed to have them tell me who could visit. The answer floored me. Just about anyone but ME! Well, I'll see to that. This means war! No more Miss Nice Guy!

Straining my brain, I came up with a plan. I'll go incognito to get past security and then save poor old Shirl. Don't worry Shirl, Yia Yia's on her way; now to decide on my disguise.

In a moment of genius, I decided to change myself into a Greek seaman. Yeah, I'll be Nick, Shirley's long lost friend. First, I'll need some sailor clothes. What do those guys wear anyway? Let's see. I guess a pair of baggy jeans, a fisherman's sweater, a pea coat and a Greek fishing cap. Some dock shoes to complete the outfit.

Okay, I'm getting into the swing of this. Next, I need to morph into a guy. A black wig or should I be bald? Hard call. I guess I'll go with bald and get one of the skinhead rubber thingies. Hope it doesn't give me a headache. A beard and moustache should be all I need to finish off the look. Er, you know what, maybe some bushy eyebrows, a unibrow.

Extra sweatshirts layered under the sweater to bulk me up. Yep, it's all coming together. Good thing I watched all those Gordon Fisherman's commercials. Who knew they would come in so handy?

Next, I'll cab it to the sanatorium, just in case they know my car, one can never be too careful.

Well, the big day arrived. I called the cab, stuck some old fish in my pockets for the authentic sea air aroma and was off. The cabbie started sniffing his armpits, then the air as soon as I got in. He turned, wrinkled his nose and asked if I might have stepped in something? I checked my shoes, "Nope, all clear here," I told him. He went back to his driving but not before he cranked down his window. Maybe, I should have only used one fish.

When we got to the sanatorium, I asked him if he would wait or come back for me. He said he was off duty and needed to get the cab fumigated.

Slowly, I walked up to the front door, keeping an eye out for that doofus guard and Dr. ET. No signs of them. Good! A couple of stray cats followed me, meowing loudly for attention. I bent down to pet them and they attacked my jacket pocket. I gave them a couple of fish to quiet them down. No need to draw any unnecessary notice to my mission. Making my way to the information desk, I must have looked impressive, I was getting lots of stares and nods. I just tipped my Greek Sailor's cap and smiled. See, there are plenty of friendly people out there. Can I help it if I'm just a people magnet?

Suddenly, as I approached the desk, a thought struck me. I was supposed to be Greek. Should I speak with an accent? I could try to fake one, I don't know. This is tricky. Well, I can't stop now. Oh, I got it, I got it! Good thing I think so fast on my feet. I'll make believe I can't talk at all. Yep, that's the ticket. I'll pretend I have a bad cold. No, no cold, they won't let me in the place, contagious and all that. Okay, I'll be a mute.

The receptionist's head was down as I neared the desk; she looked up, sniffed the air and gave a little startled look when she saw me. "Aren't you a bit over dressed for July, Grandpa?" she asked. I wanted to say, "That's Popou, to you Toots." but I remembered I shouldn't speak. I gave her a little smile and wrote, See Shirley, on a slip of paper and handed it to her.

"Shirley who?" she asked. Oops. Could there be more than one Shirley? I never knew Shirley's last name. I always referred to her as Chicken Shirley. Think, Yia Yia, think. Got it. I started doing a little Chicken dance around the rotunda, strutting and flapping my make believe wings.

Unfortunately, that attracted quite a crowd and with them, that doofus guard. "Hey, what have we here?" he asked. "You look somewhat familiar, Gramps. How about showing me some ID?" "It's not Gramps, its Popou," I yelled, forgetting to be mute, I blew my cover. Rats!

"Com'on now, what's yer name there, Pops?" he shouted. "I'm, ah, I'm Nick Seagapopoulis,"I replied and started backing up to the door.

"Wait, just one minute," he shouted to me. Next, he turned to the receptionist, told her to call Dr. Smith, and that he was needed immediately.

Oh no, I had to make a getaway. If Dr. Twitchy gets near me, I'll be doomed.

The crowd got bigger and closer, Guard Doofus yelled again for me to stop. That's when I reached into my pocket and brought out the biggest fish. "Get back all of you, "I said, and wiggled the fish at them.

Doofus looked at me and said, "Whadda you got there, Pops? A secret weapon?" "I told you before, it's Popou and yes, this here is a bomb, so out of my way before it goes off." "Looks like an ordinary old fish to me, Pops, Popou, whoever you are. Why don't you calm down and let me have it, before you kill us all with the stink."

"You'll get it alright," I waved it at him. "You have to ask yourself, Sonny. Am I bluffing, or is this really what I say it is? A very clever bomb, designed to get through the toughest security. Oh yes, who would suspect a dead fish? So again, I'm asking you. Do you feel lucky today? Are you willing to risk all these nice people's future? Well, do you?"

Out of the corner of my eye I saw Dr. Twitchy coming down the hall, I had to make my move right away. Doofus was still trying to figure out what to do when I was able to reach to door and get out.

Waiting outside was an even bigger bunch of stray cats. They started following me down the sidewalk, all meowing and hissing, vying for the fish. Looking back, I saw the guard and Doctor in hot pursuit. I stopped, turned and threw the remainder of the fish right at them, one hit Doofus dead on, the rest scattered. Wild, fierce cats all raced to get their meals, surrounding Doofus and the Doc.

In the confusion, I managed to high tail it out of there. The screeching and screaming was ear shattering and that was just the guard and Dr. Twitch. The cats were hissing loudly too!

I ran looking for a spot to get rid of my disguise. There are no more phone booths around. I wonder where Clark Kent changes now? That's probably why we don't see Superman anymore. Luckily, fortune was smiling on me that day, because when I turned a corner, there was a construction site with a Port-a Potty. I dashed in and shed my pea coat, my sweaters, my moustache and beard and skullcap and hat. I shoved all the stuff into the Port-a-Potty hole. Whew, if you thought the fish smelled bad, this place was worse. Toxic almost. They'll never try to dig these things out. No way.

I re-entered the street and walked back to the sanatorium. Curiosity was getting the better of me. As I approached, I saw a large crowd assembled and two vans from the ASPCA. The Doctor and the guard were trying to get the cats off them with the help of the animal wardens. Boy, did they look bad, all disheveled and dirty. The cats however, looked fine. Maybe they'll be adopted from the shelter to a nice home and get fed regularly. Just another by product of my good deeds.

As I stood watching, a stranger came up to me. "Lady, you sure missed all the action. I never saw a cat attack before. It was something else." he said. "Yeah, sorry I missed it, what happened?" He told me some crazy guy dressed up in seaman's clothes was throwing fish around and when they tried to capture him he sicced the cats on them. I asked him how he knew the fisherman was crazy. He answered by telling me the seaman was wearing heavy clothes in the middle of July, doing a weird chicken dance. He had a cult of feral cats with him, plus he was shouting terroristic threats. "You're right, that sounds pretty crazy. One never knows does one?" I chuckled.

Just as I started to leave, he called out to me, "Hey Lady, you have a big, black caterpillar on your head." OMG, my unibrow. I forgot it. "Thanks Mister."

Trudging home, my mind was spinning trying to devise a new scheme to get to see Shirley. Not to worry, I'll come up with something.

Later,

Love you,

Yia

Cousin Elly Mae

August 01, 2010

Hi Guys,

All I can say is drats and cats; I'm pretty bummed out about my failure to visit Shirley. I thought for certain my seaman's disguise was perfect. That doofus guard got me so rattled I dropped my cover. Thank goodness for those cats. They sure helped me get away.

I'm still left with the dilemma of getting in to see Shirley, but first I have to get her last name. I'm straining whatever brain tissue is left, trying to come up with a foolproof plan. I guess I'll start with patient information. Yeah, I'll call and just ask for it. How hard could that be?

Okay, here I go.

Operator: Hell-o. Feel Good Sanitarium. If you know your party's number you may call it now.

Yia Yia: If I knew the number, I wouldn't be calling you.

Operator: All others stay on the line. Listen carefully to the following menu.

Yia Yia: Menu? Is this a takeout place? How about a cheeseburger?

Operator: Press one for the Emergency Room.

Yia Yia: If this were an emergency, I'd push a panic button.

Operator: Press two for Medical Records.

Yia Yia: Hey, how about some Disco Music?

Operator: Press three for the dietary department.

Yia Yia: So, where's my cheeseburger?

Operator: Press four for the Billing Department.

Yia Yia: You're billing me for the cheeseburger I didn't get yet?

Operator: Press five for directions to the hospital.

Yia Yia: What? You're not going to deliver my cheeseburger?

Operator: Press six for Patient Information.

Yia Yia: Finally, I'm pressing. I'm pressing.

One ringy dingy, two ringy dingy, three ringy dingy, four ringy dingy, five ringy dingy, six ringy dingy…eighty-seven ringy dingys…. at long last…

Information desk: Please stay on the line. Someone will be right with you. Calls are answer in the order we receive them. Thank you for your patience.

Yia Yia: What patience? I'm frazzled and now I'm actually craving a cheeseburger.

One ringy dingy, two ringy dingy, three ringy dingy, four ringy dingy, five ringy dingy… seventeen ringy dingys…

Information desk: Good Morning. How may I assist you?

Yia Yia: First, I have to ask, do you deliver cheeseburgers?

Information desk: Sorry, I don't have that information, but I'll connect you with the Dietary Department. Perhaps they can help you.

Yia Yia: NO!! NO!! Don't connect me. I'll call them later. I'm calling for information on my cousin.

Information Desk: What's her name?

Yia Yia: Shirley, (I'll have to make one up) Shirley Brown, but she might have changed it.

Information desk: We don't show a Shirley Brown on our patient list.

Yia Yia: Well, like I said she might have changed it. Perhaps you might know her as Chicken Shirley. You see she has this chicken obsession and…

Information Desk: Please hold the line; I'll try to get someone to help you.

One ringy dingy, two ringy dingy three ringy dingys..

Yia Yia: Oh No! I can't go back on hold. Now I'll never get my cheeseburger.

"Officer Joe here. Who were you looking for?"

Yia Yia: Officer Joe? Are you a policeman?

Officer: No Ma'am. I'm a Security Guard.

(Oh my gosh! Could this possibly be that doofus guard again? How can lightning three times? Once when I was in my cow suit, next when I was Nick the Seaman and now on the phone? What luck! I wish I could hit the lottery like this. I'll have to use a phony voice. Okay, I'll be Miss Elly Mae from Georgia. Yeah, that should do it. Talk nice and slow with a Southern drawl. At least a South Jersey drawl)

Elly Mae aka Yia Yia: Officer Joe, Well, I just love a man in uniform. I bet you are just about the cutest thing ever.

Officer Joe: Ah shucks Ma'am. I don't want to brag but I've been told I could be in the movies.

(Yeah, I bet… horror movies… That's him, Doofus. Has to be.)

Elly Mae: Maybe I could come and feel your big muscles when I visit my cousin. Do you know her?

Officer Joe: What's her name again?

Elly Mae: Shirley Brown, but I think she might have changed it. She's the gal with the chicken obsession. Do you know who I mean, Big Boy?

Officer Joe: I might. Give me a little more information. When have you seen her last? How long do you know her? Things like that so I can figure it out. Okay?

(He couldn't figure how to get out of the rain. I think he's trying to stall me.)

Elly Mae: Oh, we were young'ums together. Shirley lived on her Daddy's chicken farm, an only child. All she had was the chickens to play with; she used to try and dress them up and push them around in her dolly stroller. I would visit now and then and we'd play house with the chicks. Shirley sure did love those birds! I saw her last about ten years ago when she ran off with a chicken salesman and came North. I haven't seen her since and we y'all are fretting mightily over her. Got her poor Daddy all down in the mouth. Her old Mammy just rocks and smokes her pipe all day, waiting for their girl's return. So if you can help me find her, we y'all would be soo appreciative, Sugar.

Officer Joe: Well, Miss, why don't you come down to the hospital and see if you can identify her? I'll be happy to show you around.

Elly Mae: I guess I could do that. I just wanted to be sure she was there before I visited. I don't have a lot of time, you know. What's her name in case I come and you're not on duty?

Officer Joe: Unfortunately, the patient I'm thinking about is a security risk and has her visitors screened.

Elly Mae: You mean she's violent? Could she hurt someone?

Officer Joe: Oh no. She's fine except for a few minor episodes. No, there have been some incidents here involving her. She's just under my protective custody. Just keeping her safe, Ma'am. That's what I do.

(I want to throw up!)

Elly Mae: Oh my goodness. Are you in any danger Big Joe? Do you at least carry a weapon?

Officer Joe: Now don't you go worrying about me, Little Lady. I don't need anything but my strong self. I don't want to blow my own horn, but just last week I single-handedly foiled a bomb threat. Some people called me a hero, but like I said, just doing my job.

(Now I'm really going to throw up. Stood up to a dead fish and was beaten up by a bunch of stray cats. Some hero!)

Elly Mae: You're amazing. Hope to see you when I visit. What's Shirley's last name again? I forgot what you told me.

Officer Joe: Oh Purdue, Ma'am, Shirley Purdue. What's yours, Sweet thing?

Elly Mae: Elly Mae Clampert. So nice speaking with y'all, take care of yourself now. Bye-bye.

Officer Joe: Bye, yourself. Can't wait to meet cha.

(*Where's that barf bag?*)

I should have guessed. Of course, Shirley would give Frank Purdue's name. I hope it's not a bluff. Nah. Doofus can't be that clever. Now I'll have to hatch my next plan. Obviously, they are going to watch Shirley's visitors more closely. At least I've been warned about that. I couldn't get Doofus to tell me his day off. I'll have to call each day for him and pretend I'm his friend. Yuck!!

Perhaps I'll go as Elly Mae's Grannie; maybe I should be a Nun, two good possibilities. Now that I know her last name it should be easy. The hard part will be to convince Shirley that being a chicken isn't cool. Who wants to kiss a chicken, beaks and all that, and what about the feathers? What if you're allergic?

It certainly narrows down the available men out there. If that doesn't do it, I'll just mention the fact that Frank Purdue is actually a mass murderer. Where do all those chicken dinners come from anyway? No, I better not go there. She might not be ready for that truth yet. I'll save it for an emergency break through.

Hang on Shirley, hang on! Help is on the way!

Wish me luck, Kids.

Love and Kisses,

Yia

A Nun's Story

August 11, 2010

Hell-o, All My Little Pals,

Finally decided how I'm going to get in to see Shirley. I settled on being a Nun, a Sister of the Church. Who could ever question a Nun? Not even Doofus would be that bold. It has to be the perfect cover. I even amaze myself, sometime. Pure genius.

Okay. Where do I start? Of course, I have to get a nun uniform or whatever they call it. I'll go to the costume store; I bet it has a whole bunch of them there. I can hardly wait to get this plan in action. Let's see, what else does a Nun wear? Wish I paid more attention in Church. The Sisters used to scare the stuffing out of my brothers and if I remember right, they all had these gigantic Crosses on their chest.

I got a big wooden cross and drilled an eyehook on the top and looped a rope through it. How's that for originality? Has to be the most pious Cross-ever! I bet I could market those. No time now, have to focus on the job at hand.

Off I went to the costume store. Good thing they're revving up for Halloween, they probably will have a bigger selection. Uh oh, not open yet. Now I'll have to go to that dingy rental place up the block. Hope he has one. Here I go.

"Hi, Mister. Do you happen to have any Nun costumes available," I asked? "Heh, heh, Grannie, getting closer to your Maker and need some extra Brownie points?" he snickered. "Don't you Grannie me, I'm Yia Yia and you're the one that's going to need help soon." "Oh, feisty are we? Let's see what I have for a feisty old timer like you, heh, heh," he replied, again with that snicker. The indignities I suffer on Shirley's behalf. Guess that'll make up for tying her to the back of the bus.

Into the back room he went, shuffling around in racks and cartons. Finally, he came out all dusty and wheezing. "Must be years since anyone wanted one of these," he said. "I found the perfect one for you, Gran, Oh right, Yia Yia."

"Let's see what you got," I was anxious to get out of that rat hole. He put down a box covered with 2 inches of grime. He opened it with a flourish and said, "It's an original, one of a kind. It's the Flying Nun outfit!"

"What? Flying Nun? Are you out of your kazoo? Do I look like a Flying Nun? I want to look Holy and serene. How am I going to do that airborne? You Ninny, I'm leaving," I said and headed for the door. "Wait, wait a minute," he yelled after me. "You don't have to use the flying apparatus. Just a little extra if you need it, great for parties. Come on back and take a look." I hesitated and managed to simmer down. " Okay, alright, might as well take a look while I'm here. Show me what you got," I told him and went back in.

He pulls out a scratchy looking black robe dress with a stiff white bib and collar. Next was the habit that completely covers the head and hair, pretty much what I had in mind. "How are you supposed to fly in this thing," I asked?

He turned the dress part around and in the back were two pockets for air containers, converting it into a jet pack. Hmm, interesting. Not that I would use them, but you never know.

I took the outfit, gave him a hefty deposit and hurried on home. Now I had to fine-tune the plan.

I called the Sanatorium daily; suffered through the eternal ringy dingys to inquire if Officer Joe was on duty, pretending to be Elly Mae. The guy never takes a day off. Then one Monday, he wasn't there when I called, so I decided today's the day. I donned my disguise, put on a pair of wire-rimmed glasses, sandals on my feet. Whoops, better get rid of the blue nail polish on my toes, not very Sister like. Hung my Cross around my neck and took a look in the mirror. Wow, I even fooled myself. Just for the heck of it, I stuck the jet packs on the back and called for a cab.

The taxi came and pulled up slowly. I realized it was the same driver as before that took me to the Sanatorium. He said as I made myself comfortable, "Sure glad it's you Sister. The other day I picked up some smelly Seaman from this house and he stunk out my cab. It took me three days to get it back to normal. Where to?"

When I told him the Sanatorium, he turned and gave me a peculiar look. He also took a good whiff of the air. Satisfied, he drove on. Guess I passed my first test.

I arrived, paid the cabbie and went to the reception desk. The gal behind the desk said, "Good Morning Sister. How may I help you today?" Got her fooled too, I thought. "I'm here to see one of my flock, (Bad choice of words) Shirley Purdue," I answered. "Shirley Purdue, Shirley Purdue, are you sure that's her name?" she asked.

"Uh oh…now what? "Well it was when she was in my care, thought of herself married to that Frank Purdue fella. Poor soul has a chicken obsession. I pray for her daily," I said, looking as holy as I could.

"Oh yes, that Shirley. She's on a restricted visitor's list. We have to screen anyone who comes to see her," she said. "My dear Lord. Is the poor child violent? I'll have to pray harder." Now I was really laying it on. "No, no, she's not violent although there have been incidents with her visitors that have been troubling," she told me.

"Surely, I could see her and give her some spiritual comfort. Actually, I am proficient in exorcism; perhaps I could be of help to rid her of her demons. I'm only here to lighten her pain. A few minutes can't be much to ask for," I begged. "Well, Sister, it's against regulations, but a few minutes might do her some good. She's in the day room. It's down the hall to your right. What's your name?" "Sister Angelina Julie," I replied, "but you can call me Sister Angel." She looked up with an appraising stare and handed me the pass. "Don't stay too long now," she reminded me. "Oh Bless you my child, There's a special place in Heaven all mapped out for kind people like yourself," giving her my most benevolent smile.

Great, I'm in, now to find Shirl. I went down the corridor to the Day Room. People I passed all said, "Good Morning Sister, How are you Sister? Good to see you Sister." I blessed them and they all smiled. Boy, I could really get into this Sister thing. Everyone likes me.

I finally made it to the Day Room. It was a big open space with a gigantic TV on one wall playing mutely, while all around patients sat in various positions of lethargy. I spotted Shirley in one corner and started to make my way to her.

"Sister, Sister so glad you made it." I turned as a young nurse approached. "Excuse me?" I asked. "Oh Sister, we have been waiting for you. Some of patients have given up hope. I'm so relieved to see you," she answered.

"Oh sorry," I said, "I don't think you are waiting for me. I'm here to see Shirley and I have very little time."

"What a shame, everyone is so despondent. They have been waiting for Sister Beatrice for hours and have sunk to a low despair. Can't you please give them some words of comfort while you're here?" she pleaded.

"You poor child, I would if I could, but the receptionist put me on a restricted list and my time is limited." (I was trying my best to get out of this.)"Not to worry Sister. I'll see to the front desk. Just do your thing with my patients; they could really use some encouragement."

Oh drat's! Now what? "Of course, of course. You see what you can do to get me a little more time to visit and I'll be happy to spread some cheer." She said, "Great!" and left.

Looking around, I realized that I had to put some zip into this crowd. They're all stuporish. Time to snap them out of it so I can get to Shirley. I scanned the room and decided to blast the volume of the TV to get their attention. It worked for most. When they roused and spotted me, most gave me a weak smile. Shirley, I could see seemed a little skeptical. I said, "Gather round my children, time to hear the Word and get well. It's all done with the power of self. Believe it and you can do it. Like my Momma said, put on your big girl or boy underpants, or for some of you, your Depends and deal with it. Your faith will show you the way."

Some wise guy piped up and said." "Yeah, well the only WAY I need is a WAY out of here. Some chance of that."

Ahh, my golden chance, I told him that's why he required faith. "I'll have faith when I see pigs fly," was his retort. I needed to make them believers. So I said, "Maybe not pigs, but would you believe if you saw a Nun fly?" "Com'on Sister who are you kidding?" he growled.

"Lock that door and I'll show you a miracle, but you all have to help." I made them stand in a circle and hold hands. I stood in the middle. I told them, everyone has to start believing they have the power of change, if you trust in yourself anything can happen. "Ready? Close your eyes and start believing now."

I opened the jet packs and started levitating about two feet from the floor. "Okay now, open your eyes!" They all ooh'ed and aah'ed, except for that cynic. He said, "Yeah, but that's not flying." This isn't going to be easy, I needed to face the challenge.

"Okay, now just continue to keep the faith," and with that I opened the valve a little more. I started ascending to the ceiling and before I crashed into it, I spread my arms and started flying around the room. Boy, was it fun. I zoomed did swoops and loops and even a 180. Finally, I made a hard landing to the floor. All were astonished, even Mr. Skeptic. "Oh God has sent us an Angel," they cried.

"No, my children, that's the power of self. You must believe in yourself and you can do anything." I saw Shirley out of the corner of my eyes. She was scratching her head and smiling broadly. Perhaps she got the message, or maybe she knew it was me. Am I something or what?

I made them all swear not to tell a soul what they witnessed, just a little miracle among friends. Agreeing, they unlocked the door and were in a state of euphoria when the nurse returned.

"Sister, what have you done? Everyone seems so much better, so contented. What's your secret?" she asked. Some smart aleck perked up, "Oh we can't tell, it's our little secret. Wild horses won't get it out of us. Right guys?" Everyone said, "Yes, we'll never tell, but it was awesome. A miracle. You shoulda been here." Even Mr. Skeptic joined in.

By now the nurse's curiosity got the better of her and she told them to let her in on it and she would get them extra dessert at dinner. Well, that did it. They all caved. What a bunch of quislings. I was sold out for Jell-O.

Right before they spilled the beans, the door open and in came, my nemeses, Dr. Twitch, Oh no! He surveyed the room and turned to the nurse. "Miss Nightingale, have you doubled these patients' happy pills, they all seem so ecstatic?" he asked.

"No, Doctor," she replied. "They were just getting ready to tell me their big secret, a miracle right before you came in." "I would love to hear it, perhaps, you could tell me," he told the group. All of them clamored for his attention and tried to speak at once. "Hold on, hold on." he said, "one at a time." He turned to the skeptic and said, "Thomas, how about you go first? What's this all about?"

I tried in the confusion to make it to the exit; I had to make my escape. As I neared the door, someone from the group grabbed me and said, "She's our miracle, she's an angel! She can fly!"

Dr. Twitch lowered his gun sights on me, and asked, "You all saw this little Nun fly? Are you sure?"

"Yes, yes, yes! She had us empower her with our positive thoughts and she took off flying around the room. It was awesome." With that a rousing cheer went up. "Sister Angel, Sister Angel!"

Dr. Twitch turned to the nurse and I heard him say, "A case of mass hysteria or delusion. There's only one person I know that can accomplish that." Next, he said, "Dear Sister, a moment please. I like to ask you some questions."

"I'm already late for a prayer meeting," I told him." Some other time I have to run along now. Bless you all," and made my way to the door.

He reached out and grabbed my arm to stop me. "Release me, Sir!" I demanded. "You will be sent to the first ring in Hell for assaulting a Woman of the Cloth." He was stunned for a second and backed off. "Of course, sorry," he said, "but this is important. Surely, you can spare me a few seconds, then you can be on your way."

I didn't want to create a scene; I could see Shirley looking at me. I had to get out of there before she gave me away. "Alright, but my time is limited. Lead the way." I was stalling, thinking how to scram.

As we were walking down the hall to the elevators, I spotted the Ladies Room. "Excuse me Doctor, but I need to use the facilities. Go along now and I will join you in your office in a couple of minutes." "That's okay, good Sister. I'll just wait for you here," he replied.

Where's St Jude when you need him? I went into the bathroom, hoping there might be other way out, which, of course, there wasn't. Foiled!

Back into the hall I went and followed the Doctor up to his office. He was humming, all smug and full of himself. I wanted to tell him pride goeth before a fall, but decided he's on his own.

His waiting room was empty and he proceeded to take me into his private office. "Wait a second, Doctor. I can't be alone with a man. It's not allowed, I'm a Bride of the Church and have to be chaperoned. You wouldn't want to be responsible for me breaking my vows would you?" I asked.

"Ahem, very well, have a seat and wait here. I'll find Nurse Jane to join us and then we can talk. I wouldn't want you to take any chances, Sister," he said with that smirk. He left and I heard him lock the door. I was trapped, but not necessarily. I looked around for a way out, and there it was, a window, my escape route. I opened it a wide as I could and looked below. Not that far to the ground, only about two stories. Time to use the jet packs to make my get away. Who knew they would come in so handy?

I removed my Cross and placed it on his desk. I proceeded to write a note. Simply it said, HAD TO LEAVE, WAS BEAMED UP! I turned on the jets, breezed out the window, turned around and shut it. Next, I gently floated to the ground.

I hailed a cab and got home ASAP. I removed my costume and took it back to the store. The owner asked, "How'd it go? Do the job for you?" I told him it was uplifting, paid and left.

Thinking I covered all my bases, I headed back home. I promptly painted my toenails blue again to ward off any suspicion. Now, I need to devise another strategy to reach Shirl. I can't believe both my genius plans were thwarted.

I turned on the TV to relax a bit and saw the news. A reporter was standing in front of the sanatorium. She said earlier today a psychiatrist went berserk and tried to get his patients to make him fly. Something about mind control. When it didn't work, he ran around screaming to be beamed up. The poor man was subdued and sedated but not before 10 inmates made an escape.

The police were looking for them and anyone with information should call 911.

Immediately, I got into my Rocket Ship and drove back to the hospital. I pulled up just as they were putting the Doctor into a waiting ambulance. "That's her!! That's her," he yelled when he spotted me. "That's the flying Nun and the Smelly Seaman and the one who makes fart faces, it's HER! Get her!" "There, there," they told him trying to calm him down." She looks like a harmless little old lady, nothing to be frightened about. Let's go now, Doc," they told him.

Boy, you should have seen all that twitching; he outdid himself while they were strapping him down. .

Gotta run now, hopefully Shirl is still inside and I'll get to see her.

Later, be good.

Love ya,

Yia

Chaos

August 12,2010

Hi All,

Figured I give you the up to the minute report on the sanatorium crisis. As I told you, when I saw the news and the info on the inmates escaping, I hurried back to the hospital. I had to check the where abouts of Shirley. If she weren't there I would start looking in the Shop-Rites to see if she was sitting on eggs in the dairy case.

I arrived just in time to see the good Dr. Twitch taken away and in the chaos I managed to sneak back inside. I had to elbow my way to the reception desk and the same gal was there that I spoke to earlier. Boy, was she frazzled. The phones were ringing off the hook, people throwing questions at her, reporters asking for facts. Total pandemonium.

She looked up and gave me a faint hint of recognition. "Weren't you here earlier?" she asked? "Oh, no I just came to see if my good friend is alright," I replied. "What's the name?" she started to ask, but was interrupted by someone handing her a note. She gave it a quick look, and then turned to me. "We have been told not to give out any information. They are asking all visitors to leave the building. Family members will be contacted. You can check with them. Sorry."

Great. Now what? I started to go and saw a reporter on his cell phone. He was quite animated, so I moved closer to overhear. He was telling someone on the other end, "They have managed to round up eight of the missing patients, so far. The two that are missing are men ages about 30 to 40. They're not considered dangerous, but are on medication and need to be found." But, then he said, "That's not the most interesting part. They have issued an All Points Bulletin for an older Nun who seems to have visited earlier today. She is a person of interest that they need to question and seems to be at the root of all this commotion. The receptionist tells me there has been some crazy things on here lately and that doesn't include the patients."

Good news, bad news. Shirley's still there, but now they're looking for ME!

I could be arrested for terroristic bomb threats, for assault with a deadly fish, for impersonation of a nun, for flying without a license. I'll be locked up and they'll throw away the key. My freedom will be taken away. No more rides in my Rocket Ship, no more adventures with my crew. I'll have to give up Lucey...well there's always that bright side. What a mess. I'm going to have to lay low for a while. Maybe this will blow over.

I got home, pulled down all the blinds, screened my calls and glued myself to the TV. Some news shows were making this story the flavor of the day. It was a human interest, a mystery with a hint of danger and a whodunit all wrapped up in one. The search for the kind and compassionate Nun with supernatural charm and powers was turning her into a folk hero. Multitudes of celebrity seekers were claiming responsibility. Appears, the police were overwhelmed by the response.

Someone found the visitor's log from that fateful day and saw that the good Sister signed in as Sister Angelina Julie. That set off a media storm with speculation. It wasn't long before Angelina Jolie herself admitted that she was the person in question.

She said she was doing research for a movie and wanted to get the feel of the character. Claimed she underwent a transformation when she stepped into the part and was moved and inspired. When asked about the flying, she said it was a special effect and to go see the movie. She was milking it all the free publicity she could.

People who weren't even there got on the bandwagon. Saying how kind and caring Angelina was, how she lifted everyone spirits. How she gave heartwarming encouragement to the sad and downtrodden. A regular Sister Teresa. What a faker! I should show her up for once and for all. I bet there isn't even a movie, not yet at least. The woman's a thief. First she steals my Brad and now she's stealing my thunder. There ought to be a law.

Can you imagine Angelina Jolie is trying to be me? In her dreams. Eat your heart out, Angie. I should threaten her; make her give me her pouty lips secret.

At least one good thing came out of her deception. The APB got lifted and it's safe for me to stop myself imposed exile.

I was trying to decide my next step when my phone rang, I checked the caller I D. Uh oh, it was the sanatorium. They must be on to me. Now what? Reluctantly, I pick up the receiver. The voice on the other end was yelling, "Yia Yia, Yia Yia."

"Shirley, is that you?" " Yes, I'm allowed to make a phone call to tell my family I'm okay. Of course, I had to call you, Yia Yia," she said.

"I'm sorry I haven't been to see you Shirl, they banned me. I tried to sneak in but I didn't know your last name and got stopped. By the way, what is your last name?" "Temple, my name is Shirley Temple."

Why doesn't that surprise me?

She told me she has a new doctor now and he said if she keeps making progress, she'd be eligible for a weekend pass soon.

I hesitated for a second before I asked, "Shirl, how's that chicken thing going?" "Oh Yia Yia, I'm completely over that. I was a fool to fall in love with Frank Purdue. Why he only has eyes for something with feathers. He never gave me a tumble after all I did for him. No, I have me a real man now."

This is news. "Someone you met at the hospital? What's his name?" I asked? "Oh, Yia Yia, it's so romantic. It's Nick, Nick the Greek seaman. He was here fighting to see me. He took on the whole security department. He must be madly in love with me to be so daring, so courageous. It must be my Nick I left behind in Greece. He never got over me and now he's back to claim as his own."

"I have to go now Yia Yia, my phone time is up. I'll call you soon when I get that pass. We have so much to catch up on. I'm going to start eating feta cheese again. Maybe I'll get to like it. Bye for now." And with that she signed off.

Talk about getting from the pan into the fire, I've managed to do that in spades. Hopefully, Shirl will get over this infatuation soon.

Yeah, when pigs fly. Say wasn't that what started this whole thing?

Later, be good, and boycott Angelina movies.

Love ya

Yia

Friday the Thirteenth

August 13, 2010

Hi Guys,

It's Friday the 13th. Some people have triskaidekaphobia, that is the fear of anything thirteen. I, of course don't believe in that stuff, but just as a precaution I make it a point never to walk under a black cat. Just for today, I think I'll wear my clothes backward to ward off any evil spirits that might be lurking.

All set, I'm leashing Lucey for her mid morning stroll when the phone rings. It's the hospital; I pick up to hear an excited Shirley. "Yia Yia, come get me, I have a weekend pass. Let's go do something fun. Yia Yia are you there?"

"Hi Shirley, didn't expect to hear from you so soon. That's great. I don't know about today Shirl, Friday the thirteenth and all. Might be a bad omen," I told her. "Oh com'on Yia Yia, you're not superstitious. It's looking like a beautiful day, beach weather. What do you say? "How can I turn her down? "All right Shirl, I'll be there in an hour. First we have to set some ground rules, Okay?"

"Sure, sure Yia Yia, just get me out of here. What are they?" she asked. "For starters, no more chaining me to a fence, no more trying to throw me off a bridge and no more sabotaging my car."

"No problems Yia, as long as you don't tie me to the back of any buses, drag me around on an ironing board and don't you throw ME off any bridges, we have a deal."

With that out of the way, I went to pick up Shirl. Walking into the reception area was none other than officer Doofus on duty, already, a bad sign. "Well, well, well, if it isn't little OLD Yia Yia. Say do you know you have your clothes on backward? Boy, do you look silly," he remarked.

"Yeah, well your clothes are on straight and you still look ridiculous," I shot back. "You might think so, but I'll have you know that there are plenty of women out there that think I'm very attractive and virile."

I couldn't help myself, I knew I shouldn't, but I was weak. "Y'all not talking about that southern belle, Miss Elly Mae Clampert are you, big strong Officer Joe? Could I feel your muscles?" I purred. "Oh no! How did you get hold of my private conversations? You're speaking about the woman I love. I'll get you arrested for unauthorized wire tapping." His eyes were starting to bulge.

"Go ahead Sherlock, knock yourself out. Oh yeah and while you're at it, there's a few stray cats outside looking for you too. "I left him red in the face and sputtering. I should take it easy on him; he can't help it if he's a doofus. Can he?

I went to the front desk and said I was there to pick up Shirley Temple. "Oh, she's waiting for you, but first you have to fill out some forms," the receptionist said. "Look," I told her," I'm not adopting her, just taking her out for the weekend." "She only has a day pass. She's not ready for a weekend pass yet," was her reply. "My mistake, I thought she said weekend. (I got a creepy feeling all of a sudden) Where do I sign?"

All set, she called for Shirley. Out the door she bounded, all smiles. She was wearing a raincoat over, what was that? Couldn't be, oh yes it could. It was that blue spandex wet suit. The one with the lightning bolts on the front.

"Shirl, I think you should change, you only have a day pass. Let's do lunch and a movie, Okay?" "No Yia Yia, we have time just a couple of hours at the beach. The summer will be gone and I want to go swimming before it does. PLEASE, PLEASE!" She begged.

"Fine, I'll have to go home and get my stuff then we'll take a fast trip to the shore. No shenanigans Shirl," I warned her. On the way Shirley told me she wants to do this new thing she saw on the sports channel. Tube skiing. "What the heck is that?" I wanted to know. She told me it's so safe and so easy. "You wear a life jacket and then instead of regular water skis you get into a gigantic truck inner tube and a boat pulls you all around. Let's try it, Ok?"

Here we go. "I don't think so Shirl. Not today. You said swimming, remember?" "Oh Yia Yia you know I can't swim. This is a no brainer, besides, it looks like you could use some exercise."

"Don't put this on me Shirley. I'll tell you what. You can go and I'll watch," I said. I thought I'd defuse whatever plan she was hatching. To my surprise she agreed. "I won't take long, just a couple of runs. Oh, I can't wait. Thanks Yia Yia."

We got to the marina, Shirley signed up for a ride; got some instructions and was off. She was sporting a grin from ear to ear. Maybe I was being too hard on her. I should give her the benefit of the doubt, don't you think?

From the shore, I could see her being pulled behind the boat at a pretty fast speed. She was waving towards land, though I doubted she could make me out. She was having a grand old time. On the next pass, I saw the boat but then I didn't see the tube behind it. I figured they probably hauled her in and was headed back to the dock.

A few minutes passed and the boat just kept circling. That old feeling of angst crept up my neck. Something's amiss, I knew it. Next thing I saw was a number of other boats in the same region and I realized they were searching for something or someone. Soon a couple of helicopters arrived at the scene and then I saw them hovering over an area. I just knew in my bones that Shirley was at the center of all this commotion. At least, she didn't have a chicken suit on this time.

It seemed like forever, but then the boats started to disperse, the copters left and the towboat was heading back with a Coast Guard escort.

Sure enough, Shirley was what the fuss was all about. I waited on the pier and I saw her on the deck all wrapped in blankets, she was talking to one of the sailors. I think I was never so glad to see her.

When they got her off the boat and into the marina's office, I manage to catch up to her. "What happened Shirl? Are you okay?" "I'm fine Yia Yia, I was having a great time but I dropped the tow rope and slipped out of the tube. I was bobbing around in the swells before they found me. I want to go home now."

Poor thing looked scared to death. "Just let me check with these gentlemen here Shirl and see what's up, "I told her. They said she was fine, just a little worse for the wear. After they filled out some paper work, I could take her home. I didn't mention where 'home' was. Might muddy the waters, so to speak.

At last, after some hot soup and a final check-up she was free to go. We returned to the car and began the journey back. She was very quiet and I kept asking if she was all right. It had to frightening to be in the middle of that big ocean.

Eventually, she turned and said to me, "Yia Yia, I failed, I had it all planned but I couldn't pull it off." "What the heck are you talking about," I screamed, "you had what planned, Shirl? You weren't trying to hurt yourself, were you?" With a look of confusion, she asked, "You think I was trying to kill myself?" At that she started to laugh. "Really Yia Yia, of course not, why would I do that? No, I thought if I could get out on the ocean and cut myself loose from the boat, I would be carried into the shipping lanes by the Gulf Stream."

"The Gulf Stream? The shipping lanes, whatever for?" Now I was totally confused. "To get to Greece, why else? To go meet up with my man, Nick. You must have heard how hard he tried to see me; the least I could do is go to him. I know he's waiting for me there on the beautiful shores of the Aegean. Now, I've let him down. I can only pray he won't give up and forget me." "No chance of that, Shirl. You're unforgettable," I told her.

Oh my, what have I done? I realized that she transferred her chicken obsession from Frank Purdue to Nick, the seaman. How could I tell her he was just another fantasy? This can't be happening. I've got to find a way to make it right. All the way back, I searched my brain for a solution. If she transferred her feelings once, could she do it again? Worth a shot.

"Hey Shirley, I know you want to see Nick. But he might not be around for a while. Sea duty and all that," I told her. "I'm sure there are plenty of guys out there that would love your company. Why not play the field?"

"Oh Yia Yia," she said with a note of despair, "who am I going to meet at the sanatorium? Everybody there is nuts." "Not necessarily, Shirl I know someone who would love some attention from you. He's a big strong virile guy, just aching for a girlfriend." With that she perked right up. "Really, at the hospital, someone who may be my type?" She took the bait. "Oh, he's your type, no doubt about it... A man in uniform (I can't believe I'm doing this) a sucker for sweet talk."

"Perhaps he'll be able to mend my broken heart Yia Yia. What's his name," she asked? "Officer Joe, Shirl, Officer Joe."

Yep, Friday the 13th. My lucky day!

Later kids,

Love ya bunches,

Yia Yia

Vet Visit

November 14,2010

Hi All,

Sorry it's been a while since my last communiqué, I've been R & R-ing with various canine and family members. Needed it for my mental health, just so much living with Yia Yia I can take before I snap. Unfortunately, all good things eventually come to an end and now I'm back in the war zone.

Last week was going to the Vet day. I figured it out on our walk, because Yia Yia usually collects my deposits and puts them in a flowerpot. Not so that morning. No, that one was wrapped in a special little container then put in a brown paper sack and labeled from Lucey. She always gives my little gift to the snooty nurse at the vet's office. Why? I don't know, the woman is never pleasant.

We arrived and Yia Yia gave Miss Snoot my offering. Typically, she took it with scorn and told us to have a seat. The waiting room was pretty empty, just a few of my fellow patients anticipating their fate.

One giant St Bernard was shaking and shivering in his boots. He tried to crawl up on his owners lap and he was bigger than she was. Another, I think some kind of Mexican dog, was pulling and tugging on her leash, heading towards the door, trying to escape. She would have made the Clydesdale Horses proud, what strength! Then there were the crybabies. A Basset Hound, who just sat and brayed and brayed. It was pathetic. He was only outdone by a sissy German Shepherd that was yapping and whining, making a complete disgrace of her breed. But Moi, El Lu-C was brave and endured the cacophony surrounding me.

Finally, my turned came and Miss Snoot led us into the exam room. Of course, we had to wait in there too, but at least I was away from the pathos in the waiting area. Yia Yia pranced around the room, checking out the posters and the equipment, as if she knew what she was looking at.

Then she gave me my instructions. "Remember be nice to the Doctor, and don't piddle if you get nervous, it embarrasses me." Embarrass you? What about me when you walk me around the neighborhood dressed as a cow? Am I not embarrassed? No wait, I take that back. No, I'm completely mortified. Embarrassed, my paw!

Eventually, the Doctor entered, he's not such a bad guy. He's pretty nice to me and thinks I'm cute. He checked my heart, my teeth, my ears and asked YiaYia how I was doing and if she had any concerns.

What followed next blew me away. Can you believe she asks the Doctor if he could give me some tranquillizers? Tells him I'm so high strung and hyper, she thought I'd get calmer as I got older. Are you kidding me? She's the reason I'm a nervous wreck, I never know what's coming next, I live in sheer terror.

Just take for instance the trip over here and every trip I'm forced to take in her so called, Rocket Ship. The car door opens and I'm thrown into the back seat, no safety belt, no doggie harness, nada for my protection. Then we're off. Sometimes she makes it out of the garage without hitting the mirrors, sometimes not. She revs that thing into warp speed and takes the corners on two wheels. That's when I'm sliding back and forth across the seat trying to hold on for dear life. Actually, it's not the worst. No, that happens when she makes those sudden stops. I'm propelled into the back of the front seat where I smash my head and fall to the floor. She usually turns around and coos, "Are you alright, Lucey?" I hear birds chirping in my ears and my eyes are seeing stars. I'm fine, if you don't count the three concussions I've had so far this month. This woman could give lessons to Kamikaze pilots.

I tried to tell the Doc, "Listen to me, if the driving wasn't enough; just think of how I live in fear, never knowing what's happening next. Did I tell you about being in a locked bathroom with her? She gussied up in some outrageous costume practicing on her electric guitar so she can become an octogenarian rock star. The guitar shorts out, the room turns black and a fire breaks out. I was lucky I made it out of there before I became a real hot, hot dog. Then there are all those mysterious costumes she goes out in, a cow, a stinky Greek fisherman, a flying nun just to say a few. In fact, a while back I think she was in trouble with the police. She went out in one of those get ups, came back in a hurry, changed, then ran out again. When she came back she proceeded to lock down the house. It was like going to the mattresses on the Mafia shows. She locked all the doors, closed the blinds, drew the curtains, put the TV on mute and wouldn't let me bark. She was definitely hiding from someone. Later, whatever crisis it was passed and the house arrest was over."

Reliving those events now gave me a panic attack. I tried to jump into the Doc's arms attempting to crawl up his shirt to make him to pick me up. I was frightened out of my fur.

He was very sweet. "There, there Lucey, what can we do to calm you down?" he asks. How about a full frontal lobotomy for Yia Yia? That should help. He just put me back on the exam table and told Yia Yia to give me a little more time. Traitor, I used to like you. Anyway, he tells us to stay put; his nurse has something for me.

Yes, she finally appreciates all my little packages and wants to reciprocate. In she came still looking grouchy, came over to me and stuck me with two needles. I take it she didn't like my gift.

Next Vet visit, I'm going to be the one that howls the loudest. Meanwhile, I'm going to need some more R&R real soon.

Love,

Lucey

2011

Rent-a-Guy

April 08,2011

HI All,

Yeah, yeah, I know you haven't heard from me in a while. I had the winter doldrums but more than that, life got almost normal, actually, almost boring. I thought Yia Yia's disaster with the guitar and that near run in with the police calmed her down. She was turning into a regular old lady. No more wild schemes, no more acting like twenty-five again. Now she was paying lots more attention to me and I even got an occasional pork chop. Life was good.

Too good to last it seems. It was the calm before the storm. For a few weeks now she has become obsessed with that show, Dancing With The Stars. She's been doing some quirky moves around the house with the music blaring. Has herself one of the dance CD's on the big screen TV downstairs. She goes down every morning and pops it in and turns it on. Next, she starts making these inhuman moves trying out the routine on the tube. It's more like Dancing with St Vitas. A grand mal seizure if ever there was one. What happens if she falls and breaks a hip? Who's gonna walk me? Who's gonna make my meals?

Then I came to realize that there is more to this than just her thinking she's some kind of Rockette. Oh no, there's a whole lot more. Since Shirley finally got out of the sanatorium, they're back to their old tricks. A cruise is on their agenda and all that dancing stuff is part of it. You'll never believe the plan they're hatching.

Ready for this? They intend to rent a guy, someone to dance with that they have all to themselves. You see, on cruises there are dance hosts that dance with the single ladies. Unfortunately, there are not hosts enough to go around, so Yia Yia and Shirley decided to take matters into their own hands. Now as a result they want to Rent- A-Guy, but just not any guy! Well, I'm going to let you in on the conversation I just happened to overhear.

Yia Yia: So Shirley, we have to agree on the requirements for our guy.

Shirley: Oh Yia Yia, don't be so fussy. A guy, you know any nice guy will do.

Yia Yia: Not, if we're paying for him, we should get what we like. You know, a dream rent –a –guy.

Shirley: I guess. What exactly are you talking about?

Yia Yia: Things like age, height, hair, body piercing, stuff like that.

Shirley: Oh yeah. Okay let's start with age. I want someone young, maybe 35 to 45. Let me think.

Yia Yia: No way. I don't want to rob the cradle. No boy toys, I think the 55 to 75 year old range should be the way to go.

Shirley: Well. Ok, but he has to be able to move, no old codger. I need someone who can move, who can Boogie. I just love to Boogie.

Yia Yia: I've seen you Boogie. There's not a person alive that can Boogie quite the way you do Shirl. Defies all laws of physics.

Shirley: What do you mean? I go regular every day.

Yia Yia: Not the laxative. Physics the law of.... oh, forget it. A guy 55 to whatever, that can Boogie. Got it. Next, height.

Shirley: Nobody too tall. I'm short and I don't like talking into someone's belly button while I'm dancing.

Yia Yia: Don't be ridiculous. He'll be wearing a shirt. Let's see, how about a range of 5'9" to 6'. If he's a little tall you can wear those funky platform shoes you have.

Shirley: But I can't Boogie in them. Who knew this would be so hard?

Yia Yia: Stop with the Boogie already. Take off your shoes if you have to Boogie, Okay?

Shirley: Guess that'll work. Next?

Yia Yia: What about ethnicity?

Shirley: Isn't there a vaccine for that?

Yia Yia: Ethnicity, Ethnicity! What should he be?

Shirley: Alive?

Yia Yia: His race! What about his race?

Shirley: Race? Oh right. I knew that. Let's see. Not an Asian, they're too precise and probably can't Boogie...

Yia Yia: AARGH!! All right, no Asian. How about Native American?

Shirley: No! No! No! That's a really bad idea. What if he starts one of his specialty dances and it starts raining in the ballroom or worse yet, a war breaks out? You're just asking for trouble there.

Yia Yia: Never thought of that. So it leaves Hispanics, Blacks and Whites.

Shirley: I don't know too much about Spanish guys, just that they do that cockroach dance. So, I'll pass on them.

Yia Yia: Actually Shirley, there a lot of beautiful Latin dances. Rumba, Samba, Cha Cha, Tango…

Shirley: Yeah, but can they Boogie?

Yia Yia: I DON"T KNOW! Let's move on. What about a Black guy?

Shirley: Oh My Gosh! Yes, they can Boogie the night away. Yes! Yes!

Yia Yia: Not so fast. It's not all about you and the Boogie, Shirl. We're sharing. Get it? Sharing. I want to do more than the Boogie. How about a White or Black fellow that can Boogie and do other dances?

Shirley: Fine. Well, all right. Just don't get your pantyhose in a bunch. Geez. Didn't you have any fiber today?

Yia Yia: Leave my fiber out of this. Next on the agenda; tattoos and body piercings.

Shirley: I kinda like tattoos, my Greek boyfriend Nick; he had a tattoo of the Acropolis across his entire back. When he moved it looked like an earthquake in progress. You should have seen it. It was awesome.

Yia Yia: Shirley, he's not going to be dancing naked so don't make that a requirement. I say any tattoos that are covered up are acceptable. Deal?

Shirley: Ok. So do you like body piercing? My boyfriend…

Yia Yia: Please don't tell me, I vote for no piercings other than an earring.

Shirley: You really should check your fiber intake Yia Yia. You're getting very testy. Where were we? Right, earrings, what kind? Hoop, Stud, Chandelier?"

Yia Yia: This is my last word on this. No Hoops. No Chandeliers. A Stud, only.

Shirley: At last we agree on something. I want a stud too!

Yia Yia: Shirley, this is taking way too long and getting too difficult. How about I ask you a question and you answer yes or no?

Shirley: Maybe.

Yia Yia: Maybe?

Shirley: What if I need an explanation?

Yia Yia: I'll keep it simple.

Shirley: Okay. So what's left?

Yia Yia: Hair.

Shirley: Yes. On his head?

Yia Yia Where else?

Shirley: Gee, I don't know, his knuckles?

Yia Yia: Hair on his head, and not on his knuckles or creeping up out his collar like your boyfriend Nick. ON HIS HEAD!

Shirley: His own?

Yia Yia: Preferably.

Shirley: Ok, but I like bald guys too. So, you see that's a maybe.

Yia Yia: Let me summarize. We're up to a fifty-five year old or more, white or black guy with no noticeable tattoos or body piercings other than a stud earring, with or without hair on his head that can dance and do the Boogie. With me so far? So that leaves the matter of teeth and facial hair.

Shirley: Oh, I love facial hair, teeth, too for that matter.

Yia Yia: I've seen the facial hair you love. It usually sticks out of his nose and his ears also come to think of it. And when I say teeth I mean a matched set. No missing pieces. I say a trimmed beard or clean-shaven and all his teeth.

Shirley: His own or store-bought?

Yia Yia: I don't care, as long as they don't fall out. OK?

Shirley: I guess, anyway, there's always Gorilla Glue. Hey, Yia Yia, where are you going? Are we done yet? When do we advertise? Do I get to pick my favorite? Wait Yia, are you drinking so early in the day? You know it's not 5PM yet. Oh well, can I have one of those?

Lucey: So you do realize what's going on here. I think someone should step in before it gets violent. I'll keep you posted once things calm down. Meanwhile, could you get out those adoption papers?

Love ya,

Lucey

Decisions, Decisions

April 12, 2011

Dear Everyone, Anyone,

Somebody come rescue me! I can't take anymore. My life has been changed from ennui to total chaos. The tension here is palpable. There is a cacophony of screams and yelling every minute with no end in sight. I think I'm witnessing the end of days. My fragile nervous system is on overload. I'm suffering severe panic attacks all day long and then I night I am subject to night terrors. How long could I possibly survive this torture? Remember that I have a shortened life span compared to humans anyway so my clock is ticking on overdrive. Please if you have an ounce of compassion or mercy, deliver me from this agony.

I know what you think, you think I'm exaggerating, but if anything its even worse. Yia Yia and Shirley are at each other all the time, every waking minute of the day. It was bad enough when they were deciding on their "Guy," but it got worse after that, much worse.

Yia Yia was ready to advertise and then thought about how to place the ad; she didn't want to get in trouble with any group. What group? According to her she couldn't put in age, age discrimination. Couldn't put in race for fear of being called a racist. Any reference to body art or piercing might make her seem prudish. Heaven forbid she doesn't seem cool. So in order not to offend anyone the ad read as follows; Wanted a mature gentleman to escort two ladies on an all expense paid vacation dance cruise. Please send picture and resume.

Shirley questioned why they made their wish list and not put it in the ad? Yia Yia said she didn't want to hurt anyone's feelings and they would just sort out the candidates when the responses arrived.

The ad was placed in the local papers and then sent out over the internet into cyberspace. That's when all this pandemonium began. Letters and e-mails came in by the hundreds. Yes hundreds maybe even thousands. The response was overwhelming.

You wouldn't believe all the replies. Seemed everybody and their brother answered the ad. Cranky postmen, complaining about their backs, were delivering mail sacks. The e-mail overloaded the computer and it crashed a couple of times.

Yia Yia decided to divvy up the selection process. She open the mail and sort out the candidates according to their guidelines. Yeah! Right! Like that might happen. Shirley took the Internet responses, She took one look at all the replies and bemoaned that they would never finish. "By the time we get through all of this, our cruise ship will be a broken down rusty hulk sinking in the New York harbor," she wailed.

"Don't be such a cry baby and get on with it," she was told by an equally frazzled Yia Yia. As you can tell their nerves and tempers were becoming undone. That's when all the screeching and sparing began and I ran for cover.

First salvo was when Shirley interrupted Yia Yia enthusiastically proclaiming she found the 'guy'. Actually she referred to him as 'my man.' That lit a spark from Yia Yia who quickly and loudly reminded her about the sharing. “Let’s see OUR GUY, what have you got, she growled. “Oh Yia Yia, I think this is the one, his name is Felix Perez and isn’t he just adorable?” “Perez? I thought we ruled out Hispanics because you said they didn’t Boogie,” she reminded Shirley. “But, he’s so cute, I can teach him, look at him, he’s just so cuddly.” Obviously Shirley was smitten already after opening the first e-mail.

“What’s that big black thing going across his face,” was Yia Yia initial question? “It looks like a caterpillar. “That’s his unibrow Yia Yia, isn’t it sweet?” Yia’s face turned beet red, she shrieked, “Sweet my feet!! He’s out! No unibrows! Get back to work.” Then began15 minutes of begging and pleading for mercy and that was just me. Shirley finally relented and sulked away.

This went on all day. Shirley finding her dream guy and Yia Yia shooting her down. Anyone was fine for Shirl and Yia Yia was extra picky. It was two worlds colliding. They worked late into the night and called it quits about 2AM with plans to start first thing in the morning.

I tried my best to sleep but visions of unibrows kept creeping into my head and I wondered how I could get one. I thought they were adorable too! I wondered if Felix had a dog with a unibrow. I’ll have to try to find that letter.

Next AM, bright and early the hostilities began anew, the eagerness of Shirley and the rejections of Yia Yia. The too youngs, the too olds, the too skinny, the too hairy, the toos, the toos, the toos. This went on for nearly a week but the breaking point arrived yesterday.

About ten minutes into the day, Shirley announced she had found the perfect man. An ultra supreme white man from California, 58 years old, 6 foot tall in fine physical condition, single, bald and no noticeable tattoos or body piercings. And best of all he loves to dance and can do the Boogie. Yia Yia looked up from the computer with a hint of interest. "Really, Shirl? He seems like a possibility."

"Okay Yia Yia, but first I have to tell you he need a letter from us stating he is being offered a job, so he can get out. "Wait a minute Shirley; just where in California is he from? Let me see the message."

That's when the nuclear bomb detonated.

"It's from San Quentin! This guy is a convict. He's supreme all right! He's a white supremist! Are you insane? Wait a minute, that's a rhetorical question!" Shirley fought back; "There you go again with the big, fancy words, rhe, rhe, rhetorical! Arrgh! You think you're pretty special don't you? You and that fancy Cock-a -Mamie dog of yours."

"Leave my dog out of this and for your information she's a Cock-a-Poo!" Yia Yia shot back. "Cock-a-Poo, Cock-a Mamie, Cock-a-Roach. Who cares? I want this guy, you hear me Yia Yia? This is the one! He just needs a break in life, a chance. What's wrong with that? He has all the requirements you picked. PLEASE! I think I'm in love." And with that she rolled herself into a ball and plopped on the couch.

Yia Yia calmed herself down and went over to Shirley saying they would work it out. "What do you know about him Shirl?" "Oh, Yia Yia I've been e-mailing him for the past few days and he seems perfect."

Yia Yia fought to control herself, " Ok, Shirl, what is he in for? Why does he need a letter? Did he tell you?" "Of course he did. The letter is for the parole board. He swears he was framed, said he's innocent and I believe him. Can you imagine being locked up for 15 years for something you didn't do? Your best years taken from you? It's an American tragedy. He touched my heart strings, he truly did," Shirley lamented.

"Oh Shirl, anything in pants touches your heart strings. What is he innocent of?" "Well Yia, he was framed by his vindictive girlfriend; she set him up for the fall, that's what he said."

"Er, what exactly did she do to frame him, Shirl?" "She committed suicide and made it look like he did it. So there, check it out for yourself, here's his e-mail address," Shirley offered. "Better yet Shirl, I'll check with the California Board of Corrections." With that Yia went on-line. Armed with information, she confronted Shirl.

"Ah Shirley, I think it might have been difficult for that girlfriend to commit suicide. According to the police report she was found in a locked freezer with an axe in her head. Do you realize you are interested in a real true axe murderer? What do you say to that?"

"Boy she was really determined. I wonder what could have made her so mad? Poor guy. So what do you say? Let's send him that letter so he can get out on parole and come on our cruise with us," Shirley pleaded with Yia.

So it began again, more screaming, more yelling plus crying and shouting. I'm begging, you have to get me out of here. What happens if that axe murderer finds me? I'm too young to die, I have places to go, people to jump on, and pork chops to eat. I'm in my prime and all this stress is giving me wrinkles I'm starting to look like a Shar-Pei.

Save me,

Lucey

Official Visit

April 25, 2011

Hell-o anybody, somebody,

Where are you guys? What part of save me, help me, come get me, didn't you understand? I've been waiting anxiously for you. Every time the doorbell rang, I rushed to the door expecting my deliverer and who's there? The frumpy, grumpy mailman with another sack of letters, that's who!

I know that I may have exaggerated my problems before and might have called out a little prematurely. You must be aware that life with Yia Yia is erratic. But this time it was crisis maximus! My two worlds were colliding.

It finally reached a crescendo and when the cataclysm was over there was just a few smoldering embers and an occasional sharp barb left, but mostly it was hurt feelings and disappointment. Yia Yia and Shirley realized that their vision of dream guy were too far apart and agreed to disagree. I felt terrible for both of them.

Shirley is my bestest human friend. She's the tops; we always have so much fun together. She's so excited to see me and whenever I jump up at her she always catches me, spins me around and gives me the best hugs ever. I lick her face and then she licks mine and then we romp throughout the house. Sometimes we go for a walk and she lets me off my leash so I can explore and get messages. Whenever I stay over at her house, she rents a dog movie (Beethoven's my Fav) and we sit in her bed watching it and eating chocolate. At lights out, she lets me sleep with her under the covers and she doesn't even do that hiney burp thing like you know who.

Yia Yia is ok, not as cool. She has all these rules, "Lucey, dogs don't walk on the kitchen table, get off now. Lucey stop chewing on that wire, Lucey come over here and get your leach on, dogs can't run around amok, Lucey, dogs can't have chocolate." And on and on, my life is filled with frustrating stops. Stop jumping, stop barking, stop scratching, stop digging, and stop rubbing your butt on my clean carpets, stop, stop and stop.

Is that any way for a free spirit like me to live? I know she means well. She does her best to take good care of me. I guess it's because she's just a Mom. So you see it was painful to see them at odds. That's why I needed you.

Eventually Yia Yia and Shirl had to decide what to do with all these letters. Finally, Yia came up with an idea. She told Shirley even though they couldn't see eye to eye on their guy; they might find a use for all those applications. How about starting a Rent-a-Guy business?

Now they were off and running. Opening letters, cataloging and dreaming of the riches their success was going to bring them. Yia Yia took to organizing and Shirley took over the computer end.

Things were humming along splendidly; it was great to see them getting along so well. Of course nothing ever runs that smooth for long. Sure enough, one morning as they were processing yet another batch of mail, the doorbell rang. I'm thinking it's that haggard mailman again and didn't even get up to bark.

I raised my head as Yia opened the door. Uh oh. Trouble, I put myself on alert.

There on the doorstep is a group of dour looking men in dark, cheap suits. I recognized one of them. It was that cranky old policeman that's always driving Yia Yia either uptown or downtown, one of those.

"Well lookie here, now you're a den leader and you brought all your little cubs scouts with you. Selling cookies today?" Yia Yia asks. "C'mon Yia Yia, you know it's the Girl Scouts who do that," he retorts. "Exactly, what kind you got?" she snapped back

"No need to get smart Yia Yia, I'm here on official business", he replied as the redness started creeping up his collar into his neck and face. "Now what kind of official business could you have with me? Am I aging over the speed limit or are my creaky knees disturbing the peace?" Yia wanted to know.

"Yia Yia, this is serious. These men are a task force put together for special OPS and we're here to ask you and Shirley a few questions. By the way, where is your friend, Shirley anyway?" Yia Yia looked around but Shirley was nowhere in sight. "She's probably in the basement or in the yard, she's got to be someplace," she told him.

"Well, can we come in or do I need to get a court order?" Mr. Crank was getting mean. "Hold on a sec there, Flatfoot, (oh boy, Yia Yia was digging her heels in) who are all these bozos you have riding shotgun?"

"Let me introduce them, Yia Yia and then we'll precede with our investigation. First, this is Detective Eeinystein from the F.B.I., next is Lt. Meenywitz with Homeland Security, then Inspector Mineyburg with the Federal Prison System and Moe."

"Moe, who's Moe?" Yia asks. "Oh Moe, he's a cookie salesman. Now can we come in?"

"First let me see their ID," she insisted. With that Eeinie, Meeny and Miney pulled out their badges, Moe whipped out a box of chocolate chunk and an oatmeal raisin.

Yia Yia reluctantly let them enter and started getting a little concerned about Shirley's disappearance. Where could she be? I did my best to greet all of them. I wanted to stay on the good side of the law, plus Yia hasn't renewed my dog license in two years.

Detective Eeinystein took the lead, first he asked YiaYia to sign a waiver that she was talking voluntarily. From the look on her face I knew there was no way she would. "I only agreed to let you in; I don't plan to talk to you. Why don't you do all the talking and let me know why you here and why you're hassling me?" she wanted to know.

"Alright, that's Yia Yia right? Okay, Yia Yia here's the situation. There has been an extraordinary amount of chatter between the white supremist groups in prison and some known terror cells. It all revolves around your Rent-a-Guy business and how they mean to use it to their advantage. Now you are either involved in this scheme or you are completely noncompliant. That's one of the reasons we are here, the others we'll tell you if you co-operate," he explained.

"What if I don't co-operate, what then," Yia wanted to know. "Well, then Officer Cranky, sorry I mean Officer Newman will have to take you downtown or uptown, one of those," was the answer.

I knew that wasn't going to happen. Yia Yia always tells me after one of their rides together how much the man could use some fiber and definitely a good dose of happy juice. Oh yeah, she was gonna crack.

She told them how she and Shirley thought up the idea and how they got an amazing response. How they couldn't see eye to eye on a choice for themselves, but turned their disagreement into a business venture. Making lemonade out of lemons. Blah. Blah. Blah.

"Well, Yia Yia,"the detective said, "unfortunately the majority of these replies are from inmates looking for a way for an early parole. Your promise of employment gives them an edge to get out early. That's bad enough but the real problem is the supremists joining up with terrorist groups and having you insert them into places they probably wouldn't have access to before."

Yia wanted to know what he meant. "Places they would take your lady clients, like cruises, fancy restaurants, special parties, vacations. They could weave themselves in and cause serious damage."

Inspector Mineyburg took over. He went on to say that they traced all the internet messages between the prisons to Yia Yia's computer. What they found out was the leader and chief organizer of the plan was a white supremist who was in constant contact with Yia Yia.

"Oh no, can't be me, I don't do the computer that would be," and then she shut up. Insp. Mineyburg read between the lines and said, "I think it's time to ask Shirley a few questions. Could you please ask her to join us?"

Yia called out, "Hey Shirl, where are you, what are you doing?" "I'm in the kitchen," came the answer. "Doing what?" "I'm sharpening a few knives."

With that all the cops stuck their hands in their jackets and pulled out guns. Moe did the same and whipped out a package of Oreos. I think I'm going to like Moe.

"Oh, for crying out loud, Shirl put them away and come out here. And you fellas do the same, Shirl is harmless," Yia explained. I could see Officer Cranky in the corner vigorously shaking his head no. But the guys all calmed down and Shirley finally joined the party.

"Shirley these gentlemen have some questions about our new business. They want some information about the computer. Tell them what they want to know. Okay?" Yia relayed strongly to her.

Inspector Mineyburg started, "Shirley we have intercepted a lot of messages between you and San Quentin prison. Could you tell us with whom you spoke and the nature of your conversation?" Shirley gave him and everyone a blank stare and the said in her most authoritative voice, "I can't speak to you."

Yia Yia said, "Sure you can, we have nothing to hide. What's the problem?" "It's called spousal privilege and I don't have to incriminate myself or my husband," Shirley told her. "What husband," Yia Yia screamed, "when did you get married?"

"Oh Yia Yia, it's been in the works, my sweetie Dolfy set it all up with the warden and while you were narcing your guts out to these coppers, I was getting married on the computer to the love of my life. I am now Mrs. Adolph Hiller."

Everyone fell silent except for Officer Cranky who gave out a long, low whistle trying to hide the hiney burp he just made. All eyes looked at him as he was holding his nose and pointing at me. What a guy!!

Lt. Meenywitz got up and said, "Let's go guys, round up all this correspondence and the computer and give YiaYia a receipt. Ladies, you will be hearing from us. Meanwhile don't make any travel plans." Shirley cried out, "I'm going to California for my honeymoon. I can't stick around."

Yia Yia quickly interceded, "Oh Shirley, it's for the best. Give you time to realize what you've done." "What exactly would that be Yia?" Shirley snarled. "You know, you married an axe murderer, Shirl."

"Sez you, he was framed, "I told you. "You always criticize my men. I think you're jealous. Admit it! If you're lucky maybe Dolfy has a friend. He'll fix you up maybe then you'll leave us alone."

It was getting ugly again. The cops all stood watching and ready to take them downtown or uptown, one of those. I reacted quickly and jumped up at Shirley and started to lick her face. She was startled but couldn't help herself. She licked me back. A lot of yucks and gee whizzes came from the group. But I managed to break the tension. Did I ever tell how smart I am? Beethoven, eat your heart out.

The guys were finishing up and started leaving. Moe came over to Shirley and offered his congratulations. He gave Shirl two big boxes of cookies as a wedding present and told her to be sure to share them with her new hubby. Shirley was overwhelmed and said she would. Yia just stood there shaking her head.

I followed the men outside while they were packing up. One of them asked Moe if Shirley accepted the cookies and how sure was he they would get to San Quentin to her Dolfy? "Pretty sure," said Moe. Insp. Mineyburg looked at him and winked. "Now we will just have to sit back and wait for him to eat a few and start transmitting. We'll break that ring yet. Good work Moe, or should I say Agent Bond?"

I ran after them as they were getting into the squad car, trying to get their attention. Hey guys, let me join you. I could be your K-9 unit. I'm great at disguises. I was a Rottweiler for Buzz and I bark in three languages. French, English and Cocker. Wait up… Rats...Oh well, I'm sure they'll be back. TTYL

Lucey

Sarge and the Cookie Man

July 18, 2011

Hey, hey, hey all of you,

Happy to let you know that things are finally settling down around here. Shirley is still in California; most of the police and G-men are gone. The mailman is cheerful because he doesn't have sacks full of mail to haul to the house and at last I'm getting the attention I deserve.

One thing however, I suggest one or more of you should keep a bail bond's number on your speed dial. If not now but sooner or later Yia Yia is going to be thrown in the clink. Let's face it, she's always running amok skirting the fringes of the law one-way or the other. Just take her latest toy, a new rocket ship, she calls, 'Big Red.' The woman drives that thing like she just stole it. It's just a matter of time. Then what? What about me? Who is going to make my meals, walk me, and get me to the groomer? What about my belly massages and oh yeah, my occasional pork chop? She's still an owner in training but right now she's all I got till something better comes along.

Come to think about, I bet she's hiding all adoption applications I ....wait a second. There's someone at the door; I heard the bell. Okay, here I go, attack dog mode, Arf, Arf (hard to do while you're jumping three feet in the air) Arf, who goes there? Oh, I see them; it's that farty Officer Cranky with Moe the cookie guy. I wonder what they want so early?

Oh boy, this should be good. Yia Yia is having her usual slow start morning. No eyeballs in yet (contacts), a bed head that defies gravity and her favorite baby doll pajamas that date back to the 60's.Gouge my eyes out. Maybe she won't hear the commotions. No luck, here she comes. "Who's here Luce?"

She opens the door and stares at them. "Now what?" That's her greeting. Officer Cranky speaks up. "Good morning Yia Yia." "It was till I saw you," she replies.

"Mind if we come in?" he asks. "Yes I do." With that she closes the door in his face. Again with the bell, this guy is asking for trouble. Reluctantly, she opens the door again, "What do you want now?"

Moe, cookie guy takes over. "Yia Yia we have some good news for you. I think you'll be happy to hear it." "Unless you both are getting transferred to traffic duty in downtown Baghdad, I doubt it." Man, she's really grumpy this morning.

"Okay, come in, I have to go make myself presentable." Off she goes leaving them in the living room with me. Well, you better get a load off guys; this is 'presentable,' is going to take some time.

They plop themselves down on the couch and I manage to wiggle in between them. Never know when a good petting comes along, plus I want to eavesdrop.

Moe: So Al, (aka Officer C) I hear you made Sergeant, I thought you were retiring.

Officer C.: I was but then they offered me a promotion and more pay. All this terrorism stuff going on, they need more men. My wife passed away a couple of years ago so I figured why not? I'll hang in for a few more years. Not as lonely when you're working. Besides, I have to keep the public safe from Yia Yia and her friend Shirley.

Moe: They're really a pair. How long do you know them?

O.C.: More years than I want to admit. You wouldn't believe some of the situations they get themselves into. This last one was mild in comparison. No one would ever believe these two harmless looking grandmothers could wreak such havoc.

Lucey: *(You're telling me!)*

Moe: Well, we should wrap this one up soon with a little help from my friends. How about you Lucey? Are you a friend?

Lucey *:(You got a pork chop and I'm yours.)*

Moe: Ok Lucey, let me see what I have here. How about a nice big cookie? A chocolate chip, this one is made special for you.

Lucey: *(Oh, Boy!! Didn't I tell you I like this guy? Next to pork chops, chocolate is my favorite. Okay, let me have it!)*

Moe: Hold on a minute, Lucey, let me get it open. Here you go, eat it all up.

O C: Say Moe, isn't that the same kind of cookie you gave Shirley as a wedding present? And while I'm asking, are you really a cookie salesman and if so how come you get to tag along in an investigation? What's up with that?

Moe: Can't fool you Big Guy. Actually, I am a cookie man but not the usual kind. I specialize in chips, Nanochips. I'm assigned to a super secret branch of Home Land Security. The cookies I gave Shirley contained those special chips. That's how we infiltrated all those suspects and got loads of info on them.

O C: And now you fed them to Lucey? Who is she supposed to spy on? Oh no! You're going to check out Yia Yia? How does it work? I don't think I like this at all Moe. What if Lucey gets sick? What if Yia Yia finds out? How come I wasn't told earlier?

Moe: Take it easy. Slow down. I'll explain. You see these chips are very small almost invisible. They're extremely specialized. Once the chips are absorbed into the blood stream they go to their particular receptor cell and.

O C: Wait a second; speak English. Receptor what?

Moe: Cells. Okay? The simple version, these mini-micro chips are programmed like this. The eye cells go to the eyes. The ear cells go to the ear. The heart cell goes to the heart. Got it now? After they are in place they start transmitting data to a computer that interprets the information in real time. So when Lucey is looking at Yia Yia we can see and hear what Lucey hears and sees; that's how we're able to keep an eye on Yia Yia. Someday this will revolutionize the medical community. No more invasive tests, no cath scans or x-rays. Just swallow a particular chip and we can see right inside the body. Fantastic, right?

Lucey *:(Excuse me, I'm gonna try to throw up.)*

O C: I don't know... is it legal? I sure don't think it's ethical. How can you have Yia Yia's own mutt spy on her?

Lucey: *(Mutt? Did he just say mutt? Hey Flatfoot I'll have you know I'm an expensive hybrid. Mutt my paw!)*

Mo: It's definitely legal. Ever since they passed the Patriot Act there is a lot of leeway in information gathering even when it might interfere with a person's privacy. As for ethical, who better to keep an eye on Yia Yia? It's much cheaper than Hi Tech surveillance and just involves Lucey and an agent checking the computer. Pretty clever eh?

O C: I still don't like it. Why are you spying on her?

Moe: We're concerned that some of the guys we nabbed might trace it back to Rent-a-Guy and she might be in danger. There were some pretty nasty threats made when we arrested them.

O C: What about Shirley then? Is she in any trouble?

Moe: Actually, she ate some of the cookies and we have her being watched right now. So far she's safe. Don't worry Al, nothing will go wrong.

OC: Obviously, you underestimate these two. I hope you're right. Shirley's not all that stable to begin with and Yia Yia is always hatching bizarre schemes. Together they can send your little program back to the dark ages.

Moe: Stop worrying. It'll be fine. Come here Lucey. Let me give you a belly rub.

Lucey: *(Trying to butter me up, heh? Well, I'll think about it. Long enough. Actually, I'm overdue. Okay, here I come.)*

Moe: Hey little lady now you are a real watchdog. Be sure to stick close to Yia Yia and there will be extra special treats for you later.

Lucey: *(Oh, you smooth talker you, I guess I can do this. What the heck, maybe I'll get that trip to Dog Disney after all. Lucey, the dog's world super spy. Who knew?)*

Without anyone realizing it, Yia Yia was standing there. How much she overheard, I don't know. However, she looked calm and that was a good sign. As for presentable, that's another story. She was in her workout clothes, sequin leggings and a New York Yankee tee shirt, 4 sizes too big. Orthopedic sneakers with pink pompoms and a matching pink sweatband. I sure hope these guys had their morning coffee. If not, this is sure to jolt them awake.

"Okay, guys, let's get this over with I need to do my morning exercises. Have to keep my girlish figure." With that she sat down on the adjoining chair and snarled at them. Incidentally, if she's keeping her girlish figure, it must be kept hidden someplace she can't find it, cause it's been missing for a very long time. Please forgive me I digress.

Moe led off, brave soul that he is, "Yia Yia we have some really good news for you. First, I want you to know for all his hard work on this case, our Officer Al here has been promoted to Sergeant and is staying on the force. He'll be around to watch over you and the neighborhood."

With that Yia Yia snarled louder and her face got beet red. I thought her head was going to burst into flames. Moe continued, "and with all you help and information we have broken the terrorist ring in San Quentin and arrested some of their outside members. We also uncovered some crooked prison guards and they have been suspended and are awaiting prosecution. That's all that because of your Rent-a-Guy data. Your country owes you and Shirley a big load of gratitude. I have been told to tell you that you will be awarded a Medal of Freedom from the President. Of course, we can't go public with this right yet. There are concerns about reprisals and you might not be safe if we identify you. Sort of have to keep this below the radar. Understand?"

For once Yia Yia was speechless. When she recovered she asked if Shirley was going to get a medal too. Moe told her that unfortunately with Shirley running off and marrying Dolfy the convict, it wasn't possible to include her. On the surface it was as if she changed camps and was aiding the enemy.

Then Yia Yia asked if Shirley was in any danger, what about Dolfy, was he getting out? No, Moe answered, "She's fine and actually Dolfy has retracted his petition for parole. Seems after meeting Shirley he prefers to stay in prison." Yia Yia nodded her head in agreement but said she was concerned it might break Shirley's heart.

"No chance of that Yia Yia," Moe said, "Shirley has already set her sights on the Greek prison chef. She got to know him on her visits to Dolfy and they have hit it off. For what we can tell, it appears she already over Dolfy and is moving on."

"Yeah, she's fickle that way, I hope she gets over that chef fast, I'd like her to come back. It gets boring around here without her. We have our cruise coming up and still we need a dance partner," she sighed.

"Oh, I can dance," the new Sergeant Al piped up, "and I could keep an eye on you two. When's the cruise?" "On the Twelfth on Never," was Yia Yia's sharp remark, crushing his newly inflated ego. So much for being Sergeant, the guy still doesn't get any respect around here.

Yia Yia got up, opened the front door and hurried them out. "Time for my workout guys, go catch some crooks and leave us old people alone." With that she slammed the door behind them. She was pretty bugged. I don't know why. Shirley is okay, she's getting an award from the President and Sergeant Cranky offered to go on the cruise and dance with her. What's the problem?

So now I got to go do my spy stuff. I feel okay; I wonder if these things are really working? I'll let you know how this goes. Lucey, the new James Bond maybe I need a code name, a real spy moniker. Yeah, I'll think about it.

Later,

Lucey

The Prodigal Friend Returns

August 06, 2011

Greetings all, from Lu-C the super sleuth,

Oh yeah, I'm really getting into this spy stuff. All I have to do is just follow Yia Yia around and be cool. I'm a real live video recorder with these nano-chips inside me.

I'm thinking of enlisting in the CIA when this gig is over. I could go to the Middle East and infiltrate terrorist groups. Nah, they don't treat their dogs and women all that well. Okay, maybe become a drug dealer's dog and get the scoop on them. I don't know. Could be a tad dangerous with all those other Pit Bulls in their employ. I think I have it. I'll become a Mafia Don's girlfriend's pooch. I'll live in the lap of luxury and still be doing my civic duty. Best of both worlds, if only Yia Yia would let me go.

Speaking of which, she doesn't make my job easy. No, I'm being cool, just tagging along wherever she goes. What do I get? "Will you quit dogging me? Go lay down! You're always underfoot. What's wrong with you? Do you have to go out? If you don't stop I'm throwing you in the laundry room! Get out of here... let me pee in peace for crying out loud!"

See what I'm up against. You would imagine she'd appreciate all the attention I give her. But NO!! The other morning I went into the bathroom after she showered to make sure she was okay.

She had some water dripping down her legs and I decided to be helpful and lick it dry. Man, you should have heard her then, jumping around hooting and hollering. You would think I took a chunk out of her calf or something.

I just hope the guy recording all of this, sees what I have to put up with. No respect for all my efforts. Talk about a dog's life. So, I guess I'll be a little more covert. Hang loose. Back down. I'll stare at her from a distance. Ok, Cool Hand Luce, that's me.

Now what? There's the doorbell. Might be danger. Don't worry Yia, I'm on the job. I run over to the door as fast as I can with Yia Yia a few steps behind me. Oh my goodness, it's Shirley. She came back. Hi Shirl! Hi Shirl! She reached down, picked me up and gave me one of her best smooches. Wow, she's a sight for sore eyes. Now maybe I'll get some consideration around here.

Yia Yia welcomed her in and they began talking at once to one another. Hold on there ladies. I'm trying to transmit. Speak slower, sure hope they can ungarble this on the other end. Sounds like they're conversing in tongues. "So, Shirl, how are you? What brings you back? What's up with Dolfy? I heard you have a new love interest already." Yia Yia was rapidly firing questions at her.

"Slow Down, Yia. I'll explain everything. I don't know where to start. Let's see. I guess I'll begin with Dolfy. You should have seen him Yia Yia. He was a fine specimen of a man; in really great shape with most of his hair and all of his teeth. He was pretty smart too. I felt like a very lucky woman. But then after a while I came to realize he was lying to me."

"What do you mean, Shirl? You found out he was really an axe murderer?" "Oh no, not that Yia. I found out he couldn't bogie. I married him and went all the way out there, under false pretenses. And to make it worse I gave him most of the cookies we got as a wedding present. I asked for them back. Told him he didn't deserve them. He just laughed, said he and his convict friends ate them up already. Didn't even think to share them with me. Good thing I kept a few for myself. No, I recognized him for what he was, a lying, selfish, no goodnik that can't dance. I'm cutting him loose ASAP."

"Good for you Shirl, I didn't like him from the start. What about the new man in your life," Yia asked? "Unfortunately, Yia that relationship went down in flames. Actually, I'm pretty bummed about it."

"How so, Shirl? Care to share?" "Well, Yia, I met this chef at the visitor's cafeteria at the prison. We started talking and I told him all about my troubles with Dolfy. He was very sympathetic and we got to be friends. Did I tell you he was Greek?"

"Uh Oh Shirl, not another Nick?" "No, his name is George. He said his Popou was George, his grandson is George, he has six cousins named George and his brother has twins, George and Georgia, but no Nick in his family. He said most Nicks came from a different island. Anyway, one day when I was especially down, he asked me to come over to his condo and he would make me a nice dinner. He was going to create this fabulous Greek meal. Greek salad, Greek Kota and finish with homemade Greek baklava. Sounded yummy and I accepted."

"During the time I was in California I didn't renew my pills and now I realize I was feeling blue because I was off my meds. I must have had a flashback. All went well during the salad course; I even managed to enjoy the feta cheese. George excused himself and went into the kitchen. When he returned he put a giant roast chicken on the table. I freaked out. Called George a murderer, then I grabbed the chicken and ran fast as I could downstairs to the yard. I was trying to give it a decent burial when George caught up to me." "Why didn't you just tell me you don't like chicken?" he said, he was very confused.

"You said you were making Kota, how was I supposed to know it was chicken? You slayed this poor creature." I hissed at him. "Take it easy, Kukla, it was already dead when I got it. Why don't you come back upstairs, I give you a nice glass of Ouzo. You feel better." He was being so kind.

"Don't you Kukla me, you cannibal, I bet you even eat eggs too! I can't see a man that has total disregard for poultry." With that I walked away, still holding on to the roast. Not too far away, I crossed a bridge over the river and gave the ill-fated bird a burial at sea. So that was the end of George.

"Anyway Yia, what's going on here? Are the cops done with investigating our Rent-a-Guy business?" "A few interesting things, Shirl. They took out all our data, and the computer. Then a few days ago Officer Cranky and your friend, the cookie guy, Moe show up. They tell me that with our information they were able to break up some terror cells, stop a prison break and put away some crooked guards. Pretty awesome right?"

"Next came the news that officer Cranky was promoted and is staying on the force a little longer. Just when I thought I was getting rid of him he's still around. And guess what? This really set me off! Can you imagine what nerve he has? He said he could dance and would come with us on our cruise and be our Rent-a-Guy. What hubris. All the man ever does is grumble about having to respond to whatever predicament that befalls me, complains about having to drive me downtown, never even offers me a cup of coffee and now he wants to horn in on a free vacation."

"Hey Yia Yia, I think maybe you might like him," Shirley noted. "What are you out of your mind? Wait forget I said that. Rhetorical, I'd rather have a root canal than dance with him and don't you go thinking about it. No way Jose."

"There you go again with the rhetorical, Yia Yia. Don't think for one minute I don't know what you mean. Using those big fancy words again!"

Well, gang, things are returning to normal around here, Yia Yia and Shirl are back at it. Maybe the powers that be will take some pity on me and remove me from my torture. I need some peace and quiet. A trip to Dog Disney should work wonders. After all they can't expect me to work for free. There are laws about that. I'm going to call my ASPCA representative now.

All righty, I'll write later and hopefully it will be a postcard from Disney.

Lucey, aka 008

Lucey's Evaluation

August 08, 2011

Hell-o Again,

I'm not at Dog Disney yet, still working on it. Yia Yia and Shirley are their old selves again. Shirley stayed over last night and this morning they're back at bickering and hatching new hare brained schemes. Oh yeah! The new one is to forget the cruise, buy a convertible and drive to Canada. Of course, their opinions differ to what kind, what year, what color, whose driving and on and on. So this might take a while. Yep, things are returning to normal. Their normal, that is.

As they were discussing the plans, I was at my post, keeping Yia Yia under observation. All of a sudden the conversation changed. Yia Yia looked down and saw me staring at her. Then she started telling Shirl how I'm driving her crazy. Said I was following her around incessantly, always underfoot, never gave her a minute's peace. She complained I even followed her into the bathroom, that there was no escaping me. How true, I'm just doing my job.

And get this, she even recounted to Shirl about the other morning. Said she must have left the bathroom door ajar and was toweling off when she felt a big creepy bug on her leg. How it scared her and she started hopping around trying to swat it only to realize it was me again, licking her leg. I was only trying to be useful, and that's the thanks I get. Geez, Louise!

Shirley thought that maybe I needed some of her tranquilizers. Even mentioned that I was always high strung. What nerve, talk about the kettle calling the pot black. I'm offended. High strung my paw. I'm just energetic.

Yia Yia thinks that I am just going through some sort of separation anxiety. Can't bear to be out of her sight. Well, yeah! I'm supposed to keep 24/7 surveillance on you, you ingrate.

I was working myself into a snit, when the bell saved me, literally. That blasted doorbell again. It's not like I haven't enough to do, I have to guard the door too. I need a raise. Double pork chops for starters.

Uh oh, more trouble. It's that Sergeant Cranky standing outside. You remember how well he was treated last time. I think I'll run under the couch for cover. Here it comes; Yia opens the door and snorts, "What now?"

"Yia Yia, I'm here to pick up Lucey and take her downtown," he answered." "Why? Is she under arrest for stealing milk bones or something?" She asked in her most surly voice.

" No, nothing like that Yia Yia, I don't know if you are aware of it, but you haven't renewed her license in 3 years. I was instructed to bring her in for an examination to make sure she not a danger to the community. Actually, it's usually the dog warden's job but being I know the dog myself, I figure I would pick her up on my way to work. I personally vouched for her and I promise to try and get her back by this afternoon. Okay?"

She was flabbergasted. "I never heard of such a thing. Must be some kind of bureaucratic screw-up. I think you are just harassing me and using my pooch to do it," she protested. "Not at all. Why would I want to get on your bad side, Yia Yia? Just give me a chance to straighten it out for you. I'll take Lucey, show the vet she's healthy and get her a new license. Okay?"

Boy, was he trying to butter her up. I sense some intrigue here. I think Yia Yia's suspicious too. "You're just stopping by and doing me a favor? Trying to soften me up so you can be our Rent-a-Guy and get a free cruise? Is that it, Flatfoot?" she asked.

"I wish you would stop calling me that Yia, I'm really very nice once you get to know me." He was laying it on thick now. "All I know is that you're usually cranky and you fart a lot. Let me talk this over with Shirley. Stay here, I'll be right back," she told him.

Shirley was in the kitchen listening to what was going on. "I think you should let him take her Yia Yia. Could give you the break you need and it wouldn't hurt to have the vet check her out. Maybe she has an overactive thyroid or something."

Yia Yia was convinced, but she wasn't going to make it easy on Sergeant C. "Okay, you can have her, but I want her back by 4 PM sharp. Got It? Also, no smoking or farting in her presence, I don't want her coming back here all smelly. Oh and one more thing. Tell the vet she seems overly attached to me lately. It's annoying," she ordered.

Sergeant C. leashed me and walked me to his patrol car. He put me in the back, closed the door and proceeded to get into the driver side and off we went. I tried communicating with him with telepathy "Hey Sarge, how about I sit in front with you? You could let me flash the lights and sound the siren. Com'on, it's not nice back here, not even a cushion on this plastic seat. I'm sliding all over and what's with metal screen? How am I supposed to jump into the front seat? The rocket ship much nicer than this hunk of junk, I've been tricked."

Finally, we got to wherever it was we were going. I couldn't wait to get out. That back seat is hard; I got bashed from end to the other and talk about smelly. Whew! I looked around expecting to see a lot of policemen, but no, he must be taking me to the vet. Sure didn't look like a vet office. Then I saw Moe walking down the steps of a drab gray building with bars on all its windows. Oh no! He was taking me to jail! "Whatever I did, I didn't do it! I'm innocent, IN- NO- CENT, I tell ya!"

Moe came over, bent down and gave me a big pet. I would have bitten his hand off but I'd probably get put in solitary. Woe is me. He asked the Sarge if he had any problems with Yia Yia. Sarge said it was a piece of cake, she didn't suspect a thing.

"Come on Lucey, I've got something to show you," he was pretty cheerful. Sure probably wants to show me my cell. I want to go home. I reluctantly followed them inside to a big open room with lots and lots of different kinds of equipment. Mostly computer stuff like we have at home. I got it! I was at spy headquarters. For a minute I thought they got me for stealing the hot dog out of that little kid's bun. That was close.

"Hey Dudley," Moe yelled, "come meet Lucey, our little web cam spy. How's it going? Everything working OK?" Dudley looked up; he was what Yia Yia would describe as nerdy. Young, longish dishelved hair, skimpy beard, wire rimmed glasses and clothes that looked like he threw them on and missed.

"So you're Lucey? You sure are a busy little bee. I can't believe all the things you get into. I think you're amazing," he cooed. Finally, someone who knows my true value; I think I'm going to like Dudley too! Those nerds sure are super smart. I wonder if he has any pork chops.

"So Dud", Moe interrupted, "what's the latest?" "Well, Moe the visual is coming in fine, but I can't get any audio. Couple of bizarre transmissions that I think you should see. Without the audio, it's hard to get a clear understanding."

Moe called over Sarge and told him to join us at Dud's computer. Dud said he was going to run a few tapes and see what they thought and if I had any reaction. Okay Dud. Let her rip. I was all set sitting on Moe's lap. This super spy stuff is the real me.

"First item, remember we see everything from about a foot off the floor and occasionally Lucey's ears flop over her eyes." Hey, watch what you say about my ears, Dud. I can still remove you from my list of favorites.

He continued, "I processed this tape yesterday morning and I'm having a bit of trouble identifying the object. Let me roll it and see what you think." On the screen came a picture of something that looked like a pole or a log, it was pinkish, with a bunch of blue squiggles and had what seemed like porcupine quills sticking out all over. I could see myself licking it when it suddenly moved away and I ran out of focus. They all were wondering what it could be. Hey fellows, don't sweat it. That was Yia Yia's unshaven leg. I was trying to dry before she freaked out.

Next scene they showed was taken in the family room in the basement. Dud said, "Here are two subjects; one is Yia Yia and another unknown female. Watch carefully. I don't know what to make of this. They are wearing bizarre outfits that are inappropriate for their age. They are making all kinds of jerky, spastic, unnatural movements. It looks like they have some kind of demonic possession going on. Scary." I recognized that one right away. It was Yia Yia and Shirley doing their morning dance routine to the tape on the big TV.

Moe, Dudley and Sarge C. all turned and looked to me. I was cool, just another day in Paradise. They all agreed that because I didn't show any response to the tape that it was nothing to be concerned about. Well, easy for them to say, they don't have to live there.

Next Sarge C. said he was going to bring me over to the vet and return me to Yia Yia. "Not so fast, Sarge, she needs another cookie. I think the others are running out of power. They have a limited time period and need to be renewed," Moe told him.

Sarge was reluctant, "I don't know Moe, and I think we should stop this now. Yia Yia seems to be fine and now Shirley's back they'll be ok." Moe was not convinced. "No, Sarge, I think they are in even more danger. Dolfy's sure the bust up of his little operation all began with Rent-a-Guy and Shirley's visit to him. I say we keep them under surveillance a while longer. Come on Lucey, cookie time."

So down to Moe's office and his stash of spy cookies. I guess I'll have to do my duty a little while longer. Sure hope they appreciate this and I get that trip to Dog Disney. I wolfed down some chocolate chips and then Moe took me back to Dudley for a sound check. There I could see myself on his monitor and he could hear what I did. I was all set to be super spy again.

Sarge gathered me up and then took me to the vet. I hate the vet. I tugged and pulled and tried not to go in. Sarge just dragged me, picked me up and put me on the exam table. I hate you Sarge! I got the once over, every opening checked and probed and then got stuck with two needles. The Vet said I was a fine specimen, which is more than I could say about him. I got my new license and was free to go. I hate you too, Doc!

More insult added, I had to endure another ride in that smelly slippery back seat of the patrol car. I sure hope none of my dog pals see me. It's embarrassing. I'm getting treated like a perp. It'll ruin my all-American hybrid dog image.

Sarge C. Got me back before 4PM, Yia Yia opened the door, scooped me inside and waved Sage off without as much as a Thank you. She's still mad at him, that's obvious. If she really knew what was going on, I think his days would be numbered.

So I'm back on patrol. Never heard from my ASPCA representative. Maybe I should call PETA. Anyway, I need to get some sleep before my next watch. This spy stuff is exhausting. Catch ya later

Lu-C aka 008

Shades of Thelma and Louise

September 29, 2011

Hi to all my two legged friends,

I guess by now you are all back at school and hopefully settled in and doing your thing. Sure hope you're having a good time. I'm doing my thing too and let me tell you, I'm not having a happy time.

I'm still on surveillance and have become the ultimate watchdog. That's me. I watch and watch and watch some more. I watch Yia Yia cooking, eating, talking, reading, sewing, walking and on and on and on. The most painful of all is watching Yia Yia do her Zumba routines. Then I want to put needles in my eyes. The only break I get is when I sleep, but then I dream about watching Yia Yia.

I don't know how much more of this I can take. I haven't seen Moe the cookie guy, I guess I'm on duty until he tells me it's over. There better be a year's supply of pork chops from him. No more of his hi-tech cookies. He owes me big time. My only bright spot is when Shirley comes over for a visit. She's up to something, I can tell, a lot of humming and trips to the computer, definitely a scheme in the works.

Oh, here she is now. Hi, Shirl, Hi Shirl, got a pork chop for me? Com'on how about a belly rub? Hey, what's your hurry? Off she goes to tell Yia something. Maybe it's important. I'd better hurry and keep my eye chip on both of them.

Shirley: Hi Yia, what's up? Got any plans today?

Yia: Not yet Shirl. What do you have in mind?

Shirley: Well, you know Yia; it's been pretty boring around here. I'm getting restless for some new adventure before the winter sets in. I've been thinking.

Lucey: *(That's impossible.)*

Yia: Shirl, am I going to like this? I'm still bummed out about what happened with the Rent-A-Guy project that went bad. You ran off and left me with all the fall out, remember?

Shirl: Don't get your pantyhose in a bunch, Yia. Love called and I had to answer. It's my nature; I'm a fool for love.

Lucey: *(Should I add to that?)*

Yia: Okay, I guess I'm also getting bored. Just let's not do anything too extreme, we still have Sgt. Cranky hovering around.

Shirl: You're gonna like this Yia. In fact, I got the idea from you. Sort of a different take on one of your goals. Yep, it's pure genius on my part.

Lucy: *(Shirl and genius, - Hell-o.)*

Yia: Lay it on me and it better not include any men or chickens.

Shirl: Well Yia, you know how you're always talking about getting a convertible and taking to the open road? How you want to feel the rush of air in your hair and go cruising the highways and byways? How you'd travel with the radio blasting 50's tunes and wear big sunglasses and a colorful kerchief and

Yia: Shirl, snap out of it. I think you OD'ed on the Thelma and Louise flick!

Shirl: Geez Yia, I'm doing a presentation, building the scene, and establishing the ambience, putting you in the mood…

Yia: AARGH! Get to the point Shirley! In case you haven't noticed, I'm not getting any younger. In fact, I don't even buy green bananas anymore. Hurry it up.

Shirl: Don't bite my head off Yia. What's eating you? Why are you so frazzled?

Yia: Oh, I'm sorry Shirl. My nerves are shot. It's Lucey. All she does all day, every day, every night, and every moment is stare at me. She stares and stares and stares some more. The only break I get is when I'm sleeping and then I dream about her staring at me. I don't know how much more I can take.

Shirl: Did you call the Vet?

Yia: Yes, she said Lucey was going through some kind of separation anxiety. I tell you Shirl, It's giving me the heebie jeebies.

Lucey: *(Heebie Jeebies, that's the thanks I get for being diligent. I'm ready to run away to the Bide-a-Wee home. Heebie Jeebies!)*

Shirl: Then I have the perfect solution Yia. You'll gonna love it. A sense of freedom, of adventure, of exploration, of…

Yia: SHIRLEY! ENOUGH! SPIT IT OUT!

Shirl: Okay, I say we get two motorcycles and take to the open road.

Yia: That's it? A motorcycle? A motorcycle, you say? Hmm, I love it Shirl! Yeah, let's do it. Where do we get one? What do we wear? What colors do they come in? Oh, I can't wait. Let's go right now.

Immediately, it was decided to get motorcycles. Of course, they had to dress for the occasion. Yia Yia told Shirley about a previous motorcycle adventure she had, so she was the fashion guru. Knew that helmets were required, the hunt for them resulted in finding a bicycle and a football one. Adding to the list of must haves were boots. To protect the legs you know.

Out of the closet came a pair of knee high, fleece lined Ughs and a pair of lime green rubber rain boots. They both settled for jeans and topped them off with long sleeved polos, finishing the outfits were stylish vests. One, a green sequin number, to match the boots, and the other a puffy, down filled white one that looked like it was stolen from the Michelin man. Next we all piled into the rocket ship and took off at warp speed.

I sure hope Dudley is watching all this on his computer and notifies Sgt Cranky. These two are out of control. Motorcycles. Where am I supposed to ride? Does Yia expect me to run alongside? And what if there is room for me on her bike? Do I have to wear a helmet and those funky outfits too? And I give her the Heebie Jeebies?

The chatter in the car between the two of them had my ears burning, first my eyes now my ears. I'm aging faster than normal with all this stress. Finally, we arrived at a lot filled with all kinds of motorbikes and a whole lot of strange looking guys hanging around them. Most of them had tattoos all over their exposed body parts. Many were wearing doo rags on heads not covered with menacing looking helmets. Black clothes, ankle high ratty work boots and lots of leather were the outfits du jour. Actually, Yia Yia and Shirley didn't look that much out of place in this environment. Nope, they fit right in.

We parked and got out. Shirl and Yia checked out the bikes and pretended to know all about them. Yia Yia did a lot of head shaking and a bunch of, "Oh Yeahs,"trying to be cool. I tried to act as if I didn't know them; hard to do when you're on a leash.

A scary looking guy broke away from the group and approached. He was dressed like the rest of the gang except he had a lot of body piercing that seemed to impress Shirley. She was batting her eyes at him trying to look seductive; actually she looked like she was just coming out of a coma. Her head bobbled and she was grinning uncontrollably. Yia Yia elbowed her a few times to no avail. He introduced himself as Killer. Yia asked if that was his nickname and he replied "NO, my profession." Shirley giggled and got elbowed again. I hid behind a bike.

He asked what he could do for us and was stunned when the "Girls" said they were interested in buying a couple of these contraptions. His reaction spoke volumes. "Really? You're thinking of buying a bike?" he managed with a straight face. "Have you ever had one or had a ridden one?" was the next question.

Yia was quick in answering, "Not exactly driven one, but a few nice fellows took me for a ride in a sidecar once, and I had a great time until it got loose. I went across the highway into golf green, I was okay but I never saw or heard from those fine boys again. Sure hope they made it to that farm of theirs."

A glimmer of recognition came over his face. "You wouldn't be Yia Yia would you?" he asked kind of strangely. "Yes, that's me, do I know you?" she asked the same way. "No, but you're kind of a legend around here. Wait here a minute, I'll be right back." With that he ran off to the gang of bikers at the other end of the lot. Shirley was intrigued and wanted to know what was going on. Yia said it was nothing. Just being her old famous self as usual.

Almost instantly Killer was back, said a few of the guys were coming over to talk to Yia. Meanwhile was there anything she wanted to know about the bike. "Why, yes Killer, does it come with air-conditioning?" cool Yia asked. "Only when you're driving, sort of an air-cooled system," he answered with a snicker.

Yia shook her head knowingly. "What about a CD changer? Oh yeah, blue tooth and nav?"Killer said that those options weren't yet available but something could be worked out. He was trying to be patient but didn't know if Yia Yia was pulling his leg.

He was saved by a group of bikers that came over and surrounded us. One big guy approached Yia Yia and picked her up and gave her a hug that could have crushed a bear. "Yia Yia, is that really you? Don't you recognize me? I'm Turk." "Oh my goodness Turk, is that the rest of your boys too?"

"Sure are, we've been laying low for a while, you know what I mean?" He said with a wink. "Of course Turk, I gotcha," Yia was trying to act hip.

Turk turned to Killer and told him to take Shirley and a demonstration ride. He didn't have to say it twice. Shirley was already on a bike waiting for Killer. He jumped on and she grabbed hold and nearly squeezed the life out of him. Shirley was wearing the biggest smile ever as they popped a wheelie and sped off.

Now Turk turned to Yia and said how grateful he was that she didn't rat him out. After all, he thought she might have been mad after that little incident with the sidecar getting free. "Heavens no, Turk, those things happen. How's the rest of your gang? What have you been doing? Still belong to that church group of yours?" she wanted to know. "Church group? Oh, you mean the Hell's Angels? Oh sure, we go to services all the time," and with that he gave a big wink to his group.

"Hey guys gather round and let me tell you about this fine lady. A few years ago, me and some of the boys, took this here Doll for a ride. Some of the Bros asked us to do them a little favor. You get what I mean? Well, anyway on the way to buy her the farm, we made a few stops and we had Yia, that's her right here, Yia, we had her pass a note to a few tellers requesting some withdrawals. Get the picture? She was aces, got the cash and off we raced to Route 80 making our departure. Right so far, Yia?"

"Oh right. Those girls were so sweet, I don't know why you never hooked up with them, you big shy guy you," Yia answered, glowing in the spotlight.

Turk continued, "Unfortunately, on our ride west, the side car got loose (wink, wink) and we lost Yia. She was okay, not a scratch on her, but instead of being upset with us, she managed to intimidate those lovely tellers into keeping their traps shut. How'd you do it Yia?"

"I don't know Turk, I told them you still had your eye on them and somehow in that brief space of time they forgot who I was. Must have been a bunch of dummies. I guess you're better off without them, Turk." "See Guys, isn't she great, and to think we almost lost you, Yia. You ready to do some more jobs for us?"

Yia was about to answer when a bunch of squad cars with sirens blasting and lights flashing pulled into the yard. Turk turned to Yia and snarled, "You're wired aren't you? You waited all these years to trap us. Don't think we'll forget this Yia, there's another ride in your future."

Yia Yia was totally confused. Not that it's unusual, but she hadn't a clue why Turk suddenly got mean.

Cops rounded up all the gang and one by one cuffed them and put them in the patrol cars. Sergeant Cranky came over and said to Yia that they have been waiting for years to break up this bunch of bank robbers and now they had the evidence to put them away for good.

Yia Yia was still confused, but then I realized that it was me. MOI! I was transmitting what I was seeing and hearing and Dudley must have notified the police. Oh yeah! Dog Disney here I come!

Sarge looked around and asked where was Shirley? Right, Shirley, she was off some place with Killer. Uh oh! This might mean trouble. Yikes!

Yia Yia was totally puzzled with the turn of events. When the fog lifted she had a gazillion questions. "How did anyone know where she was? What's this about a wire? Why is Turk mad at her? Did Sarge like her outfit? He didn't answer that but said he was going to take us downtown again and offered to tell Yia all about it.

"Oh no. Not that downtown stuff again, besides I can't go anywhere until Shirley's back. She has my car keys," with that she dug in her Ugh boots. "Listen Yia, leave your car here and I'll send out some of my men to look for Shirley and bring her in. We want to talk to Killer, too. What is she wearing?"

"She has on a green sequin vest and matching boots. I told her to put her football helmet on, but I'm not sure she did when she left. She's obviously not thinking to clearly right now." "I take it she's in love again, Yia," he asked? "Looks that way. Okay let's get this over with," she sighed. We got in that hard back seat of the Police car and made out way downtown again.

Moe was waiting for us when we got to the station house. Dudley was with him. Together, they explained how they fed me a special computer chip in some cookies and had me watch over her. "Now I know why she's been acting so weird. She had me nuts with all that staring. So, I have you guys to blame? And you Sgt. Cranky, you're in on this too?"

"Isn't this against some kind of law of privacy or something? You mean you saw me with my bed head and all my personal moments. I'm incensed! Incensed! I'm calling my lawyer now," Yia yelled and threw a hissy fit.

"Calm down Yia Yia, it's all legal. We got a court order of protection on you. We were nervous about the supremacy group in prison making a move on you and Shirley, never expecting you to break up a bank robbing operation. You and your trusty dog Lucey are heroes. Couldn't do it without you," Moe said stroking her.

Yia Yia was quiet and after a minute or two wanted to know if everything was over now. No more observing her, no more feeding me spy cookies. And where's Shirley? Have they found her yet?

The Sarge and Moe said that they felt that Yia could use a little more watching but they would do it the old fashion way; sort of her own bodyguard team for a while. They promised not to give me anymore spy cookies and I should go back to normal. Told her they last saw Shirley and Killer speeding down the Garden State Parkway, this time with Shirley driving. Hopefully, they would have them in custody before dark.

Me, the real star of this thing was being completely ignored. No pork chop, no promise of Dog Disney, nada. As usual, underappreciated and no respect. At least I am relieved of duty, an unsung hero. So, tonight I'm dreaming of Roscoe and of chasing rabbits. Tomorrow I'll hide at Zumba dancing time and look for the couple of milk bones I hid. Should keep me busy for a while.

I wish Shirley got back soon. I hope she doesn't fall for that Killer guy. He had a tat of a mean looking bulldog on his arm. Under it was the name, Killer 2.

I'll keep you posted with this latest dilemma. There's never a dull moment around here. Motorcycles, Rent-a-Guy, Zumba dancing, how much can one dog take?

Later,

Lucey

2012

The Chase

February 07,2012

Hi All,

In crisis mode here, FYI (For Your Information) Shirley and Killer are still MIA (Missing in Action). Sgt. Cranky has issued an APB (All Points Bulletin) to capture them as POI (Persons of Interest). If they don't surrender ASAP (As Soon as Possible) they are going to be in DDD (Deep Doo Doo).

Last seen Shirley, in her shimmering green sequin vest was speeding down the Garden State Parkway with Killer stuck to her like gorilla glue. Car chase by the State Troopers was hampered due to heavy traffic and Shirley's ability to weave between traffic and blow through tolls. Pictures taken at the toll plazas show her with a broad happy grin; having the time of her life and Killer looking terrified.

Sgt Cranky confirmed that killer is indeed a killer. His last job was for a pest exterminating company where the biggest kill he made was a family of cockroaches. He also ran his rap sheet that showed he was part of the White Supremist gang in San Quentin. This could be serious.

Yia Yia was just as cranky as the Sarge because he appointed himself her bodyguard due to all the excitement of the day. He thought she was in danger and she thought he was a big fat jerk.

Anything he said or did just annoyed her no end and she was letting him know.

He casually remarked to Yia how much he was impressed with Shirley's ability to drive that motorcycle so well and how she is out maneuvering the State Troopers. She snapped back that if he had done his detecting work instead of trying to weasel a free cruise out of her, he would have known that Shirley used to be a stunt woman.

That certainly got his attention. Now he was pestering Yia Yia to tell him more. "Find out for yourself, Mr. Smarty Pants, I'm not doing your job for you," and off she stormed. I almost felt sorry for him, but then I remembered how he was one of the guys that fed me those special cookies and reneged on any kind of reward when I saved the day. Yeah, I'm holding on to this grudge. I may even bite him in the ankle just for fun. And to think of all the eyestrain I had to endure. Yep, this grudge is forever.

Just then the Sarge's cell phone started ringing and vibrating at the same time. He fumbled around trying to get it out of his jacket pocket and managed to drop it on the floor next to me. Butter Fingers! Ah! Here was my chance! I grabbed it before he could and ran behind the couch with it still ringing and vibrating. Wow! That was some weird feeling. I'll have to leave a few messages on my next walk and tell the gang to try it. Better than those stupid squeaky toys.

The Sarge realized I took the phone and began trying to get it back.

Sgt: Come on out, Lucey and give me back my phone.

Moi: Er. No.

Sgt: Please Lucey, the call could be important.

Moi: Er.No.

Sgt: Oh Lucey, look at what I have. Come and get it.

Moi: What's that? Oh, a smelly old sock? I don't think so.

Sgt: Hey Lucey, look I have your ball. Want to play fetch?

Moi: Ah. Maybe later.

Sgt: Guess what I have Luce? I have a pork chop.

Moi: A pork chop? I better look. Oh, that mutant plastic thing? Get me a real one with a bone and no squeaky gizmo and I'll consider it.

Sgt: Lucey, how about we go for a walk? I have your leash; I'm headed for the door. Come on out.

Moi: Nah, Flatfoot. I'm tired. Think I'll hang out back here for a while.

Sgt: Oh, I know, a ride in my Police car. You love going for rides. Let's go.

Moi: What in that hunk of junk? The back seat has no cushions, I slid from one end to the other last time I was I in it. It smells of assorted farts and cigars. You wouldn't let me play with the sirens or lights. And to top it off you finished my ride with a trip to the Vet who stuck me with two needles. No way, Jose.

Sgt: This isn't funny anymore Lucey. I want that phone NOW!

Moi: Let's see…asking, begging, bribery, and threats, what's left? Ultimatum?

Sgt: Lucey! Give me that phone, OR ELSE!

Moi: Yep, that's it.

Sgt: No more fooling, I'm coming to get it now.

With that, he reached under the couch with those big mitts of his trying to get me. I saw my chance and ran out before he could straighten up. I took off like Big Bird, zigging and zagging to avoid getting caught when I saw Yia Yia's bedroom door open a crack. She was in there taking a nap. I ran through the door and right under her old four-poster bed. Sgt. Cranky was hot on my trail and rushed in right behind me. The clumsy oaf didn't see Yia's big fluffy slippers on the floor, tripped over then and did a nosedive right onto the bed, right onto Yia.

She woke up with a fright and started whacking him with a pillow and screaming that he was some kind of pervert. Said she knew it all along and was going to call his superior to get him locked up. He tried to explain it was me he was after and with that he got whacked some more. She now accused him of being even a worse pervert.

Luckily, that phone continued to ring and Yia took a breather from beating him. She called me and I appeared with that contraption still in my mouth. I tell you, that tongue massage was something else. The Sarge reached over and grabbed it with Yia still glaring at him.

He walked away saying, "Yes Sir, No Sir, Okay Sir, Right away Sir, I'm on it." "Well, what have you got to say for yourself?" she wanted to know. "Like I told you, I was trying to retrieve my phone from your dog because she grabbed it and took off. I didn't even know you were in here," he said in self-defense.

"Yeah, all the same, you better keep your distance, I know karate and could do you some serious damage. So was that phone call about Shirley?"

"Yes."

"Yes? That's it? Yes? Nothing you're going to let me know?"

she asked. "Why should I share, Yia? Tell you what. Give me some info on Shirley and I'll fill you in on the latest news."

Guys, this could be bad, Yia's ticked off already and he's trying to blackmail her. I'm hiding behind the couch before the war breaks out.

Yia was outraged. She started to sputter, "Why that's nothing short of blackmail. What kind of person are you exactly? Oh, I know a perverted blackmailer!" "Hold on there a sec, Yia, it's sort of a, Quid pro quo deal."

"Quid, now you're talking fish?" she asked. "Not squid, quid. You know, an exchange. I have info, you have info, I want info, you want info, we exchange. Nothing nefarious about it," he explained.

Yia began calming down. Seems she realized she would have to co-operate to get what she wanted. I got out from behind the couch. If this keeps up, I'm gonna need a bomb shelter soon.

"Okay, Yia you go first."

"Not on your life, do you think I don't know what you're up to? You go first. "

"Com'on Yia, don't you trust me?"

Here we go again. I'm headed back behind the couch.

"Tell you what, we go in stages. That way we don't give out all the information at once and can stop anytime. OK with that Yia?" "Guess I'll have to be. Ok you start," she agreed and sat back to listen.

"There have been some developments. Seems that the bike they took wasn't for sale. It was actually in for service. Also Turk and Killer don't work there. They were just hanging out and Turk had no authority to tell Killer to take the bike."

"So you're telling me, that the bike is actually stolen?" Yia was surprised. "They seemed so business like, like they really worked there. Oh my, I can't believe it. I was totally fooled."

"Yep, and what's more, I think Shirley didn't know, but Killer had to. And something else, neither Killer nor Shirley has a valid driver's license. There are a lot of charges adding up Yia. Maybe it's time for you to tell me what you know."

Geez, the Sarge sounded almost nice. I got out from behind the couch again.

Yia Yia was worried now. It wasn't unlike Shirley to take off and do a wild thing, but breaking the law, in fact a lot of laws were a different story. "Okay," she began, "Shirley used to be a stunt woman for the movies and some TV shows. Pretty much anything that reeked of danger was her thing, but high speed car chases and motorcycle stunts were her specialties."

"What happened Yia? Why isn't she still working?" The Sarge was getting more puzzled.

"It's like this; you know how Shirley gets infatuated very easily. Sometimes to get attention you might say she goes over the top. On one of her jobs, she fell hard for the leading man. He didn't return the interest and Shirley became more and more obsessed. She took more chances and did riskier stunts just to impress him. Still he ignored her."

Now the Sarge was at full attention. "Go on, this is amazing." "Not so fast, we have a deal, you tell me what's happening now?" Yia dug her heels in.

"My Chief told me that in addition to driving without a license, there are other charges of reckless driving, resisting capture, and not wearing a helmet. Also we're not sure if kidnapping is involved and if it is, we don't know who kidnapped who."

Yia corrected him, "It's whom."

"Whom?"

"Yes, Whom kidnapped whom, not who. Didn't you go to school?"

"Com'on Yia. Don't give me a hard time here. I had enough with your dog. She dog slimed my phone real good. Let's get back to Shirley." Yia continued, "Alright, anyway, the insurance company took notice of Shirley's behavior and pulled her policy. The director had no choice but to let her go. She was a little despondent for a while, still pining for her object of affection, but she moved on."

"And what else, Yia?"

"Nope, your turn," she insisted.

"This is torture, here's the rest of what my chief said. If Shirley turns herself in, he will consider dropping her charges if you agree to testify at the motorcycle gang's trial. We will continue to give you protection until it's over and if you want put you in witness protection. You and Shirley."

Poor Yia was flabbergasted. "I can't believe this. I can't leave here. I have to help raise my grandchildren. What about my friends? My home? My Book Club? I'm too old to start a new life. I like the one I have now, except for you."

"Can't you cut me a break? All you do is gripe. You're no picnic to be around either. I should have retired when I got the chance. No thanks for the scrapes I pulled you out of." The Sarge was really losing it. Me thinks its couch time again.

Sarge offered, "Just for now, let's call a truce until Shirl gets back, Okay? Tell me the rest of the story and don't hold back. I need to call the Chief."

"Nothing much left to tell. After Shirl lost the movie job she joined a circus. She drove her motorcycle around in one of those cages. She was doing fine until she fell hard for a Portuguese tightrope walker and he was into her too. Unfortunately, he had a girl partner who threatened to grease the rope and cut the net if he didn't break up with Shirl. So, she was heartbroken once more. This time her despondency turned into depression and that's why she was in the sanatorium. She hasn't got a license because she just never renewed it. So that's it. End of story."

"Wow, Yia that's quite a tale. Doesn't quite explain everything but I can understand a little better." Then his cell phone started ringing. I was hoping he would drop it again; I loved having him squirm. Revenge is so sweet.

He talked fast and when he hung up he told Yia Yia that Killer surrendered at a rest stop on the Parkway. Seems they stopped for gas and he got off and locked himself in the men's room until Shirley left without him. He then had the attendant call the Troopers. When they arrived he begged them to take him to jail. Said he found religion and was never, ever going to do anything bad again. It was a deal he made with Lord if he ever got off the bike.

Shirley was headed towards the Delaware Memorial Bridge, still having a grand old time and still eluding the cops. They had decided to set up a road block on the bridge, that way she would be forced to stop with nowhere to go.

Yia Yia got hysterical. "That's the worst idea. Don't you remember what happened on the GW Bridge not that long ago? Shirley went over the railing and you guys dredged the river for weeks. Meanwhile she was on an oil tanker headed for the Middle East. We're talking Shirl here, extraordinary stuntwoman and daredevil. You have to tell them to let her pass. She'll get tired soon. If they don't chase her the fun will be over and she'll come back."

"Okay, Yia I'll try my best. That's really good advice. I just hope they listen to me." So I came out from behind the couch again, Yia & the Sarge are on the same wavelength now and maybe I can get some rest.

I'll let you know what happens.

Lucey,

Ride's Over

February 08,2012

Hi All,

Happy News! Shirley's back! Came back last night safe and sound. Safe at least, sound is questionable when we're talking about Shirley.

Remember when I last wrote? I told you that Shirley was racing down the Garden State Parkway headed for the Delaware Memorial Bridge. Initially the Fuzz was going to set up a roadblock there to apprehend her. Somehow the Sarge got someone to listen and he convinced him to just stop chasing her. Said she would get tired and turn around if she thought the pursuit was over.

Actually, that's exactly what happened. When Shirley realized that no one was after her, she slowed down and headed back home. Of course, she was kept under surveillance the whole way. Chalk one up for the Sarge. Who knew he was so smart?

Back at Yia Yia's he still wasn't getting any respect. As news reached here that Shirley was returning and seemed to be driving reasonably, Yia Yia told him to leave. He promptly said absolutely not. "I'm not here at your behest, Woman; I'm here because I have been assigned to keep you in protective custody. I don't take orders from you."

“Oh yeah,” she shot back, “Go tell your boss that I don’t need a baby sitter and especially not YOU!” “Well for you information I’m no sitter and you are definitely no baby, Granny!” “Ha, ha, ha, that’s a joke, next time you decide to do a battle of wits with me Flatfoot, don’t come half prepared,” she yelled back.

And on and on the verbal barrage continued until Yia Yia said, “Enough, I’m going to get some rest now before Shirley gets back. Don’t be making any moves towards my room. Remember I know Karate and I have a brand new can of mace.” “Right, and don’t you be coming in here making any moves on me either, remember I have a gun with real bullets,” he let her know.

Yikes! Karate, mace, real guns and bullets! I’m in a war zone, me a noncombatant! I gotta get out of here! I looked all around and finally found a corner out of the line of fire. I tried to settle down and get some sleep, but every time I fell off I had visions of my puppyhood and my misspent youth pass before my eyes. I’m too fragile for all this stress; I need a pork chop.

Finally, sleep over took me and I was snoozing peacefully when in the recesses of my brain I began to hear (via my super sensitive canine ears) the roar of an engine. It was getting louder and louder and then I realized it was the same sound as when Shirley took off on that two-wheeled contraption earlier today.

I woke up and ran to the front door all excited. I was barking and jumping and willing the door to open so I could go out and greet her. Come on Sarge, get up and open the door, Shirley’s back my man.

He finally, slowly came around; he must have been out like a light, at the same time Yia Yia stumbled out of her room. There she stood sporting her infamous bed head, her 50’s pink baby doll pajamas and her orthopedic slippers. She doesn't need mace. One look at her and your eyes starts stinging.

Sarge finally opened the door and I ran out to greet my pal Shirley. She sat very still on the bike basking in the light of at least 10 pair headlights. Seems every municipality in which Shirley committed an offense sent an officer to arrest her.

There were the New Jersey State Troopers, the Delaware State Troopers, and several Sheriffs from the small local towns she blew through. County cops and local cops, I even thought I saw a dog warden, maybe not, my guilty conscience at work.

Shirley just sat there, quiet as a statue. Actually if you didn't recognize her goofy grin and know about her head bobs, she would be hard to identify. Her green sequin vest was all cover with black soot, as were her lime green rain boots. As a matter of fact, she was just about cover from head to toe with a mixture of soot and dead leaves. And talk about smell, she stank of exhaust and gasoline plus other obnoxious odors I'm too polite to mention. The image of the creature from the black lagoon seemed to be an apt description.

Somehow, all the commotion didn't seem to faze her. She just sat there grinning and bobbing. Good old Shirl.

The Sarge took charge, waved his badge around and told all the law enforcement people he would bring Shirley downtown in the morning for questioning. Although none of them seemed too pleased, they insisted they impound the bike if they couldn't take Shirley. Just in case she went for another ride, they all agreed. Sarge then went over and tried to get Shirl off the bike. She didn't budge; it was like she was frozen in place. Another officer came over to help and he and Sarge lifted Shirley up beneath her arms and rolled the bike out from under her.

Poor Shirl's legs were petrified. She couldn't move them. I guess being in one position for so long made her paralyzed. Didn't seem to bother her. She just kept grinning away; maybe her brain got paralyzed too. It's hard to tell with her.

There she stood all barrel legged. She looked lost. I ran over to her "Hey Shirl! Hey Shirl! It's me Lucey!" I was leaping up and down trying my best to get her attention. I did a few figure eights around and in-between her legs, rolled over to show her my belly, anything to get a response. Nada. I tried jumping up and down again. "Hey Shirl, What's the word, huh Shirl? What's the word?"

"Knock it of, Lucey!"

"Nope, that's not it."

"Knock it off NOW, LUCEY!"

Uh, oh. That was Yia Yia and she was using her mean voice. Drats. I unwillingly walked to the side of the driveway and sat down. Shirl was still transfixed in the same position. What happened to her?

Yia Yia had combed her bed head and put a robe over her baby dolls. She proceeded to Sarge and gave him some orders. "Tell all the drivers to kill their headlights when I yell, CUT," she told him. He started to disagree but she held firm and gave him her iciest look ever.

With that he went over and repeated the request to all the cops and asked them to play along as a favor to him. Reluctantly, one by one they nodded their heads, yes.

Yia Yia went right close to Shirley; she had what looked like a megaphone in her hands. She waited until everyone was in position and then she yelled loud and clear, "That's a wrap. CUT! Put that in a can. Great job, Shirley!"

All the headlights went out and only the street lantern illuminated Shirley. She started to straighten up very slowly, looked around and finally she gave the best goofiest grin ever. Clearly, she was very proud of herself.

The Sarge was pretty impressed too. "How in the world did you know to do that Yia?" "Simple. Shirley was delusional. She thought she was doing stunts in a movie. I snapped her out of her stupor by letting her think the picture was over. See you're not the only one that can use psychology, Flatfoot."

"I sure wish you would stop calling me, Flatfoot. I have a name you know," he wined. "I have plenty of names but Flatfoot is the nicest." Yia was still being mean.

They were at it again. Shirley interrupted them when she walked over and declared, "Geez, I really am home. Can we go inside?"

Yia Yia and Sarge both looked a little embarrassed and snapped out of their squabble. "Oh my goodness, of course. The Sarge will say 'Goodnight' to all the crew and you come on in with me. Let's get you out of those clothes and into a nice hot bath. Then how about a big bowl of my famous chicken soup? Okay?"

Shirl agreed and told Yia that she was tired she had a very busy day but couldn't wait to tell her all about it. Said she had the best time ever. With that she headed upstairs and Yia headed for the kitchen. The Sarge was still outside talking to all the policemen.

When they all left he came in and joined Yia in the kitchen. "Well, now that Shirley's back, I guess you can leave," she said ever so sweetly.

"Not so fast, Yia Yia, Shirley is in my custody, I have to take her downtown tomorrow to answer a litany of charge. And remember you are still in my protective care," he shot back, not ever so sweetly.

"Downtown, downtown, when are you ever going to go uptown?" she snarled. "In case you have noticed, that's where Police headquarters is Smarty Pants."

Oh boy, here we go again. I think I'll go see if Shirley needs any help and let these two duke it out. Hey Shirl, hold on, I'm gonna find my rubber ducky for you.

Talk to you later kids; I need to get away from the clash of the Titans.

Your pal,

Lucey

Yeronna?

February 09,2012

Hi All,

Took some time finding my rubber ducky. I think Layla hid it the last time she was here. My poor sister doesn't have any toys, best she gets is a ratty old sock and she even has to steal that. Once I found ducky, I raced up the stairs and into the bathroom, there I saw huge mountains of bubbles. Hell-o, anybody in there, I barked. Suddenly this thing, this claw came out of the suds. It was ghastly. All shriveled up and wrinkled. I could only vision the creature from the Black Lagoon lurking beneath the bubbles.

I dropped Ducky as fast as I could and high tailed it under the bed. I had to lower my heart rate. It was finally happening. Shirley was morphing into the Swamp Thing.

While I was deciding what to do, I heard Yia Yia's shrill voice yelling, "Shirley, come on down, your soup is ready." "Be right there Yia, give a me a sec to get out of the tub."

Okay, I had to make a run for it. I dashed out from under the bed and flew down the stairs. Racing into the kitchen, I hid behind a chair. I heard Shirley come into the kitchen and covered my eyes with my paws. I couldn't bear to see the transformation.

“Oh Shirley, look at you. You must have stayed in that tub too long; your hands are all waterlogged and pruned. Sarge, doesn’t it look funny?” Yia Yia was chuckling.

Wait a minute. What? I did a slow peek and Shirley was fine, a lot cleaner and if it wasn’t for her wrinkly fingers, she was the Shirley of old. So that’s the story, if you stay in the bathtub too long you get all wrinkled. No wonder I hate baths. No more baths for me, I’ll look like a Shar-Pei. Yuck.

Shirley was scarfing down her soup while the Sarge was explaining what they had to do in the morning. She was barely listening. When she finished eating she turned to Yia and said she was very tired and was going to bed.

She asked if I could stay with her and Yia agreed. “Just be sure to lock your door so Lucey can’t get out and the Sarge can’t get in." that comment got a 'Harrumph' from Sarge.

So off to bed we went. I was expecting to watch a movie, get some belly rubs, maybe some chocolate but no, Shirl was really pooped and it was lights out. It wasn't long before Shirley was making little snoring noises. Nothing like that lumberjack Yia, whose snores peel the paint off the wall. No, these were just little squeaks.

I settled in too and was just falling off when Shirley started shouting. At first I thought she was awake, but actually she was talking in her sleep.

"Watch out!.... Get out of my way!.....If you can drive, get off the road! ....Stop screaming, Killer!.... Oops, that was close!.... Stop praying Killer, it's distracting!....Wow, we're doing 95!.... Killer, quit your crying!....Hang on, I'm gonna jump this wall!.... Killer, what's wrong with you? God won't let you off, I'm the one driving...Duh!" I guess she was reliving her day. Finally she quieted down and became still.

As morning was beginning to peek through the window, I had to use the great outdoors, if you know what I mean. I needed to wake Shirley, but I had to be subtle about it. I learned my lesson when I was first allowed to sleep in bed with Yia Yia.

It was horrible. One morning when she was sleeping hard, I went to wake her up. I gently licked her face, but she just shooed me away. Then I tried shaking and scratching and for that I got, "Cut that out!" Finally, as a last resort, I did a flying leap and gave her a full body slam. Well, that did it all right. She bolted upright, grabbed me by the scruff of the neck and carried me to the laundry room. There she threw me in and slammed the door. I still had to go out, so I started scratching furiously on the door. Then the most frightening thing of all happened. The door opened and there she stood, face scarlet, neck veins popping, eyes bulging and at the top of her voice, she hissed, "NEVER, EVER wake me up unless you plan to live the rest of your life in a crate, in the laundry room! GOT IT?" With that the door slammed again and I cowered in the corner for two hours.

I tell you kids, don't dare wake up your Grandmother; her reaction will scar you for the rest of your life and stunt your growth.

I proceeded cautiously with Shirl. First, I did the jump on and off the bed a few times to soften her up. Then I got close to her and wiggled around. When I felt her stirring, I pulled out the coup de grace. The dog stare, I went as close to her face without touching and proceeded to stare at her intensely. Sometimes this takes a while but ultimately I see an eyelid flutter, open a little and then I got them. Oh yeah, it never fails, well hardly ever.

Unfortunately, Shirley wasn't waking so I started my routine over again. A couple of jumps, a few wiggles, I even added a scratching segment, all to no response. This was a challenge. I thought at one point I detected some progress. Shirl's shoulders moved a little and her one leg uncurled. I moved in for the stare but then she pulled a pillow over her head.

No good. She will probably be asphyxiated breathing that gruesome morning breath. I had to save her. All that was left was the body slam. Hopefully, she is a better sport than that meanie, Yia Yia. I jumped off the bed, went to the farthest corner of the room, ran at top speed, jumped on the bed and leaped high into the air and straight down onto Shirl.

I didn't give her time to know it was me, I was hoping she thought she had some kind of spasm. I heard a loud OOF and she sat straight up.

Of course, I was already off the bed and under it. She never knew what hit her. "Lucey are you in here? Where are you?" I slowly came out, stretched like I just woke up too. Then I wagged my stump of a tail and greeted her. Pretty cool, eh?

"Good Morning Lucey, do you have to go out?" she asked. Isn't she a doll? No yelling at me, no threats. That's why she's my BFF.

The Sarge and Yia Yia were already in the kitchen when I got downstairs. They were mapping out the strategy for the visit with the judge. Sarge looked all rumpled and tired, guess he didn't get too much sleep on that couch. He told Yia Yia he was going to talk to Shirley again about what was going to happen today, and then he was going home to change. He said he another Officer would safeguard them and bring them Downtown. "Oh no," squawked Yia, "I'm not riding in a smelly police car. I'll drive myself and Shirley." "Fine, have it your way," he said. Boy, he must really be tired out to give up so easily.

Shirley came in and Yia Yia asked her if she had a good sleep. "Not so good Yia, I think you need a new mattress, my back is killing me. I feel like I got hit by a truck."

Er, I think that would be me, I tried not to look guilty when Yia glanced my way. "Oh Shirl, it was probably your long ride, you might have overdone it yesterday," Yia replied.

The Sarge was trying to tell Shirl what to expect but all he got was head bobs and grins. Nothing much was getting through. Finally he told her, "If nothing else just to remember to call the judge, Your Honor when you speak to him."

"Yeranna? What kind of name is that?" she wanted to know. "That's his legal name, Shirl and that's what you call him in court. Okay?" Sarge was starting to do head bobs too." Sure, Sarge, no prob." Under her breath she said, "probably Mexican or Italian, something like that, maybe Turkish."

The Sarge left and Shirley and Yia got ready to go. I was looking forward to having the house to myself for a long day of rest and relaxation. I was already day dreaming about Dog Disney when I was brought back to reality with Yia Yia telling me, "Let's go." I pretended I didn't hear her, but she just called again and was hunting me down with a leash. Why do I have to go to court, I didn't do anything. Maybe she found out about the body slam and I'm going to be charged with assault.

Nah, I'm a dog, besides Shirley thinks it was the mattress.

"Come on, Lucey you need to be a Therapy dog today, let's go." Therapy dog? I'm the one who needs therapy living with this bunch of Wackos and I'm the Therapy dog? Where's the justice? I reluctantly came out from behind the couch and submitted to my fate, Therapy dog, my paw.

When we got to the courthouse downtown another policeman who asked where we were going stopped us. Shirley told him we had to see Yeronna. "Yerronna?" he asked. "You know, Yeronna the judge," she told him. "Oh, you mean, 'His Honor,' the judge." "Hosanna? The Sarge said his name was Yeronna," Shirl was getting more confused as if that was possible. "No," he told her, "it's His Honor." "Oh, I guess Yeronna's his brother, anyway where is he?" she said, happy that the fog lifted.

"Upstairs, in the big court room, you can't miss it." He was shaking his head too and I detected a few bobs. "Wait a minute, you can't bring a dog up there," he shouted. " It's alright, she's a Therapy dog," Yia Yia told him and off we went.

Sarge was already there when we entered. If he was surprised to see me he didn't show it. I think he's becoming immune to surprises from these two. He gave Shirl a little pep talk. "I spoke to the judge about dropping these charges citing special circumstances. He is considering it but he wants to talk to you. So remember, Shirl be polite and don't forget to call him 'Your Honor'."

"Yeronna? The cop downstairs said his name was Hosanna." Uh oh, the fog returns. Sarge hesitated for a moment, then said, "It is sometimes, but for today you call him 'Your Honor', Okay?" Sarge was pulling out all the stops here. "Okay, okay Sarge." Geez. The guy doesn't know what name to use and they call me confused, she mumbled.

The judge came out and took his seat. He looked pretty pleasant; he was smiling at least, a little old, a little chubby and not much hair. He had his glasses perched on the bottom of his nose and he peered over the top of them. He was wearing a big black dress. I couldn't see his shoes, I wonder if he had on heels. He should be right at home with this strange bunch.

Somebody yelled for us all to be quiet, and then His Honor started to speak. "Miss Shirley, will you please approach the bench?" Shirley looked puzzled, "Where's the bench?" she wanted to know. The Sarge whispered to her it was in front of the judge and just go stand in front of it.

"I don't see it", she said, "but I'll take your word for it." With that she ambled over and stood practically right on top of it. The judge got up, looked over and asked her to please back up to where he could see her.

He began," This is a most unusual case and I need some more information before I decide what to do with these charges. Let me start by asking you your last name Miss Shirley, it seems all these tickets are only made out to Shirley. So please state your full name for the record."

"I'm making a record? I can't sing."

"Don't try to be funny, Miss Shirley, just tell me your last name."

"Oh, I'm Shirley Temple."

"Shirley Temple? Miss Shirley Temple? Are you trying to be cute?"

"No, I don't have to try, it just comes naturally," was her reply.

He hesitated for a moment, next he said, "I'll let that pass for now. Let's continue. You state for the record that your name is Shirley Temple, is that correct?" "Yes, that's my name but I already told you I can't sing. Oh, I forgot.... Yeronna."

The judge continued, "I was told by Sergeant Newman that the motorcycle that you were driving was originally in the possession of a person called Killer. That this Mr. Killer took you for a test drive and you lost him somehow. As a result you a drove the vehicle yourself; do I have that right so far, Miss Temple?"

"Something like that, Yeronna."

"So tell me, what happened to Mr. Killer? How did you lose him?"

"Well, I really can't say what happened to him. He got this religious conversion all of a sudden. One minute we're having a grand old time and the second we switched and I started driving he started calling on the Lord. It was spooky," Shirley told him.

"I'm beginning to understand. I think I'll need the Lord's help soon myself, Miss Temple. Anyway where did you leave Mr. Killer?" Shirley told him, "Oh, I tried not to leave him, he just wouldn't come out of the restroom. He was in there just praying and thanking the Lord for saving him. I asked him when he intended come out and he told me when Hell freezes over. I couldn't wait that long so I left......Yeronna"

The Judge asked if anyone knew the whereabouts of Killer now and someone told him he took refuge in a monastery.

"Okay, Miss Temple, moving on, you do know that you broke a considerable amount of laws. You look old enough to know better. Actually, do you mind telling me exactly how old you are?"

"No, Yeronna."

"No what, Miss Temple?"

"No, I don't mind, Yeronna."

"Miss Temple, I'm trying very hard to have patience with you. Frankly, your cuteness is wearing very thin right now. What do you think of that?"

"Well, for someone who can't decide what his name is and wears a dress and doesn't know one piece of furniture from another, I think you shouldn't be a Judge," she shot back.

A big groan came over the courtroom. The Sarge was almost crying and Yia Yia was holding my leash so tight I was almost strangling. The judge got all red face and stood up and said to Shirley, "I asked you a a simple question, how old are you and you take the opportunity to embarrass the court. Frankly I don't care how old you are. It is obvious that you are certainly no spring chicken."

Uh oh. Did he just say Chicken?

Shirley stood there; slowly a glazed look came over her. She stretched her head from one side to the other. Little by little her left hand rolled into a fist, she lifted her arm up the bent it inward and tucked her fist under her armpit. She did the same thing with her right one. When she had both arms in place, she began flapping them like wings and then the strutting started. While strutting her buc, buc, buc, buccing rang out loud and clear.

Shirley was in full fledge chicken mode again.

The Judge was transfixed. I don't think he knew what to make of it.

Finally, he called the Sarge over and they had their heads together for a while. I ran over to Shirl but she just tried to peck at me.

Yia Yia asked the Judge and Sarge if she could take Shirley home. At first the Judge said no, he thought she need professional care. Yia Yia told him she went through this before with Shirl and if she didn't soon snap out of it, she would take her to the sanatorium.

He agreed to that and said he was going to dismiss the charges. It was obvious that Shirley is delusional and she was probably that way when she went for her joy ride. A good lawyer would get her off so why waste the court's time.

Yia Yia got Shirley out of the court, down the stairs and into the car with promises of fresh worms. Riding home she turned to Shirley and said, "Poor Shirl, don't worry you'll be okay." Shirl piped up, "I'm fine now Yia, how'd you like my chicken act?"

"Shirley, it was awesome!"

Later,

Lucey

Lucey the Therapy Dog

February 10,2012

Hi All,

Sorry I haven't written in a while. Things have been a-popping around here like mad. Let's see, where should I start? Okay, the car ride home. That was something else.

I almost felt like I was driving home in a chicken coop with all the clucking that was going on around me. Yia Yia was gushing about how clever Shirley was to confuse the judge with her chicken transformation. She ranted on and on about what a genius old Shirley had become. Shirley of course, was basking in the compliments. Head nodding and bobbing and her big silly grin plastered all over her face. She was relishing the moment. Then out of nowhere a big gloomy cloud descended over Shirl. The smile was gone, the head bobs continued but in a sad, slow way. She grew quiet and remorseful.

"Shirley, what's the matter? Are you okay?" Yia Yia was getting concerned. "Oh Yia, I have a confession to make. I know you think I pretended to morph into my chicken alter ego but the truth is not all of it was pretend," Shirley admitted.

"Whatever are you talking about Shirl? You're fine, your old self, more or less." " Yeah, Yia, but actually I wasn't pretending the whole time. I actually did change back into Henny Penny. I was so stressed out with Hissonna or Yeronna, whoever he was yelling at me. First he kept insisting I do something for a record. I told him I couldn't sing but he wouldn't listen. Then he kept drilling me about Killer. Can I help that he decides to have a religious conversion and lock himself in a gas station bathroom praying? It wasn't like I abandoned a two year old, Geez. Hissonna just kept peering down at me with those glasses perched on the tip of his nose, intimidating me. Next he wanted me to tell the whole court how old I am. It wasn't any of their business. Did I ask how old he was? Or why he wore that silly dress? Or why he couldn't decide on his name, or….or.."

"Shirley, calm down, I understand. Try to get a grip on yourself; it's over. You won. Don't get your feathers ruffled. Oops! Sorry, wrong choice of words." Yia Yia was getting pretty flustered herself. "Let's get back to what you're trying to tell me, what's this stuff about not really faking your chicken conversion, Shirl?"

"Oh right, sorry I lost it for a while. Let's see. I was doing okay but like I said I was nervous and getting more and more stressed. Then suddenly I felt this inner peace come over me then everything got quiet in the courtroom. I could still see Hissonna's eyes bugging out and his lips moving but it was like a mute button got pushed. I became all calm and then I felt my wings, sorry, arms flapping and I had overwhelming desire to find some worms."

Oh my gosh, Shirl, that's amazing, but how did you snap out of it so fast? It usually takes months of treatments and some strong meds to bring you back to your Shirley self."

"Yeah, Yia, I don't really understand what happened. It was when Lucey ran over to me. I remember seeing her and thinking she was going to go after my eggs and so I bent down and started pecking at her. She gave me the saddest look and yelped so loud that somehow it snapped me back to the present. I realized what was going on but by that time Sarge and some other people were talking to the judge."

"There was a lot of heads shaking up and down and side to side. While I was strutting around I overheard the judge say he couldn't lock up a chicken. That's when I decided to keep the chicken persona going. I'm glad they let me go home with you. I really didn't want to go back to the sanatorium. They serve a lot of omelets there and it freaks me out."

Wow, did you hear that Kids? Me, Lucey the wonder dog did it again. I must really be a Therapy Dog. Who knew? I'm always amazing myself. Maybe this time I'll get appreciated and there will be some pork chops, maybe even a steak, coming my way. Now Yia Yia has to show me some respect. It's about time.

The rest of the ride home was uneventful. No more revelations except Shirley was talking about getting her driver's license back. She had so much fun riding that motorcycle that now she wants to go out and buy one ASAP. Wasn't that how all this started? She was trying to convince Yia Yia they both should take to the open road when she took off joy riding with Killer. Yia told her that she should lay low for a while; lot's of cops still not happy with her last adventure.

In fact, Yia Yia wasn't too sure about what to tell Sarge. Shirley wanted to tell him she was fine and have him help her get her driver's license. Yia thought that she would wait a couple of days so Sarge wouldn't think Shirley was just trying to fool the judge; which if you think about it, she did.

Anyway, the Sarge arrived right after we all got home. Yia Yia as usual wasn't too please to see him. He told her that the judge had dismissed the charges due to all of Shirley's hard work in helping break up the white supremist group and also there weren't any coops in the county jail. However, the judge suspended Shirley's driving privileges for a year. He also imposed 300 community service hours of beautifying the local roadways when she recovered. That was to make the law enforcement people happy. All in all, he said Shirley got off very lightly.

Then Sarge announced he would be right back after he went home to get some clothes. "What are you talking about? I thought you were going to leave after you took Shirley to court." Yia was shrieking, all red in the face.

"Surely you don't expect me to go now, do you?' he shrieked right back. "That was the plan but I can't go now with Shirley in this condition. I either stay here until she comes around or she has to go back to the sanatorium. Your call, Sweetie."

Yia Yia snorted, and then said, "Hopefully she will recover quickly and then I can get rid of you for good." Then Sarge backed down, he told her they would have to make the best of it and offered to pick up some take out for dinner as a peace offering. Yia agreed reluctantly and he left.

Shirley hadn't said a word the whole time they were arguing. She sat the table making believe she was pecking at her food. Or was it a pretense? She had that wild stare to her eyes and then suddenly got up, went to the refrigerator. She opened the door and let out a squawk and next thing I saw was her reaching in and grabbing a carton of eggs. She took them into the living room where she piled the eggs on a couch cushion and proceeded to sit on them.

Then I heard, "What in Heaven's name are you doing? Why are you sitting on eggs? Have you lost your mind? Shirley? Shirley? Shirley? Oh no! Lucey come quick I need you!" Yia was screaming form help.

Oh yeah. Time again for Lucey the Therapy Dog. I still didn't even get a reward for my last rescue, now I'm getting called into service again. Well, I took my sweet old time. I could pretend too. I'm sleeping. Had a rough day at the office, Yia Yia. Maybe the scent of a pork chop will wake me up. I'm hanging a Do Not Disturb sign on my collar. Sometimes you have to play hard to get to be appreciated.

"Lucey get in here this minute before I take you to the Bide-a-Wee home! Lucey! NOW!"

Yeow, nap over, keep your support hose on, will ya? I never get any rest. Watch dog, therapy dog, companion dog, and under cover dog, how many duties does one small dog have to do?

When I got to the living room I heard Yia Yia talking calmly to Shirl. Shirl was perched on the couch, sitting Indian style not seeming to hear.

"Come here Lucey, go see what Shirley has, I think she's sitting on your favorite toy. Your little monkey, go fetch it. Go on. Go get it."

Nah, I don't want to. I'm tired. I'll go finish my nap.

"Lucey, get back here. Go fetch that toy or else!" With that Yia picked me up and threw on the couch next to Shirley. Shirley stared at me for a moment and then flapped her arms and bent down and bit me. That's right, she bit me. Do chickens get rabies shots?

Yia Yia started yelling at Shirley, "Look at what you've done. You bit your best friend Lucey, what do you have to say for yourself?" "Buc, buc, buc." was the answer. So Shirley's Henny Penny again and we should have little chicks running around the house soon.

But Yia Yia wasn't defeated that easily. Next thing I know she goes and gets a magazine with a big picture of George Clooney on the cover. She sits facing Shirl and opens it. She begins to read out loud that George is scheduled to present an outstanding citizen award to a Miss Shirley Temple for her undercover work in breaking up a terrorist gang.

No response so far. Then she continued to read, "Along with the medal goes an all expense paid vacation to Greece. Hosted by (here she pauses for dramatic effect) Nick Seagapopoulos. Wait a minute, isn't that you're old flame Shirl?"

That got Shirl's attention. She got up very gingerly, went over and snatched the magazine out of Yia Yia's hands. "Where does it say that? I can't find it."

"Sorry Shirl, I just said it to snap you out of chicken mode. You were slipping back into it. What happened?" "Oh Yia, I guess I can't take any more stress. When Sarge said I couldn't drive for a year and then I had to clean up roadways, well I just reverted to a more comfortable place."

"It's understandable. You are very fragile right now but let's tell Sarge that you are back to normal. That way I can get him to home and we can relieve all this stress. Then you and I can have some fun. Okay?" Yia Yia was almost giddy at the thought of getting rid of poor old Sarge.

"He's not so bad, Yia. He sure does try to take care of us. I think he especially likes you." "Shirley, I'll forget you said that. After all you get confused sometimes and take a lot of medication. Your judgment can be skewed."

"If you say so, well I better put these eggs back in the fridge."

With that the doorbell rang and Yia opened the door. Sarge stood there with his suitcase in one hand and a bag of food in the other.

"Com' on in, Yia said, smells delicious, what did you get?"

"Oh, I just picked up some Kentucky Fried Chicken. I hope you like it."

Yia grabbed the bag from him and pushed him out the door. But it was too late. Shirley started flapping and running around like a chicken without a head. Then she jumped back on the couch and nestled onto the eggs.

Last I heard as I ran under the bed was Shirley clucking and Yia Yia screaming at Sarge. Will this nightmare never end? Can dogs enter contests? Maybe I can go to Greece.

Later,

Lucey

Cry for Help

February 12,2012

Hi All.

I'm back, but barely. I don't know what the heck is going on around here. First Shirley's a chicken, and then she's not a chicken. Then she's my best bud and then she bites me. Sarge is supposed to leave and now he's not. It's way too confusing for a little pooch like me. I'm of a delicate nature. A designer dog, you know.

Anyway I'm going to stay under the bed for a while. I have a whole bunch of naps to catch up on. Yep, that's my plan. Let's see, a spot near the top of the bed, high up. Yia Yia can't bend down far enough to see me there. A couple of scratches to smooth out the rug and I'm good to go. Time to get my beauty rest.

Ah, yes, this is just what I needed. Maybe later when I'm hungry I'll venture out and check on what's happening. Everything will have settled down by then, I hope.

Wait a minute. What? What? Lucey? She's calling me? Fergettah bout it Yia, I'm off duty. I'll just ignore her. She'll never find me.

"Lucey, Lucey where are you? Come here, I have treat for you."

Oh no, Yia is looking for me. I'll have to be extra quiet. I know something is up. She's doing the bribe card early. I'll have to dig in deeper. "OH Lucey, I know you got scared, come on out and I'll give you some petting and make you feel better."

Are you serious? The only way I'll feel better is if I had a pork chop in both paws on a plane going to Dog Disney. Yeah, that would do it. So, I'm staying put. Good Night, Yia.

"Oh Lucey, Sarge is here, he's looking for you too. Come say Hell-o to him."

Say what? Last I saw was Yia Yia throwing him a body block that would make Eli Manning proud and now he's in the house dying to see moi? Do they think I'm another dumb dog? Try again Yia. There's trickery afoot, I feel it in my dog bones.

"Lucey, I have your favorite, cheese. Oh, wait a minute. Sarge has a special treat for you too. Right Sarge? Oh my, Lucey. It's a... no, can't be... Lucey. It's a pork chop, an honest to goodness pork chop. Yummy, I think I'll eat it myself. It looks so delicious."

Er...A pork chop? You think they're trying to fool me? Yeah, probably, but what if they're not? I mean a pork chop. Geez, this is hard. I'm sniffing I really don't smell a pork chop. Maybe he has it wrapped up or something. I would hate to miss getting a pork chop. You know, I could just go get it and bring it back here under the bed and have a snack in my little hideout. Let me think. I mean, why not? Yia seems to be nicer now, she let the Sarge in the house and there is no yelling going on.

I think I just go and scope it out, you know, play it cool. No racing in all excited over a dumb pork chop. Yeah, that's the ticket. Okay, here I go. Very quietly, I slithered out from under the bed and did a belly crawl towards the kitchen. With my extra canine hearing I made out what the Sarge and Yia was talking about. Yia was telling him I was Shirley's last hope. That she connected to me somehow in a human way that broke her chicken spell. Unfortunately, she said to Sarge, Shirley had pecked and had bitten me so now I was afraid to go near her.

What? Me afraid? Never. Where did she get that idea? Yia said if that didn't work, they would have to take Shirley back to the sanatorium in the morning.

Oh, so that's it. What if what doesn't work? They're scheming up a plan that endangers me. No thanks, I don't think so, I just didn't like gotten bitten or pecked.

I inched passed the doorway and crawled into the living room. Checking out what's happening. There was Shirley, or Henny Penny sitting Indian style on the couch. She looked very contented. She moved her head side-to-side and stretched a little. But other than that she was serenely quiet.

I decided to go over and see if she would let me sit next to her. You know, maybe give me a belly rub. If she got upset, I would leave. I just wanted to be her friend. Shirley or chicken, made no difference to me. What's the harm in being a chicken? Just think if we were all chickens we wouldn't have any wars.

Nobody would be bullied and a rooster would be President. Maybe not, I might have gotten carried away with that one. Anyway, I gently walked over and looked up at her. At first she gave me a wild-eyed stare, but it soon passed. Then she smiled. I jumped on the couch and wiggled next to her. Before I knew it, she reached over and started petting me. I laid my head in her lap and she played with my ears. Oh, my best bud.

I stayed with her for a while and kept hearing Yia and the Sarge making more and more promises if only I would come out. I looked up at Shirley only to see a tear fall from her eyes. I stood up and tried to lick her face but she brushed me aside. Next I knew she got up and went into the kitchen.

Yia and the Sarge were amazed to see her. She told them she realized she needed to go back to the hospital to get cured. She couldn't live her life being part chicken. Also, she said after her motorcycle experience, it was what she wanted to do again. To be able to ride and be a stuntwoman while she still could.

One thing though, she asked if I could come along. That I comforted her so much she thought she could get better faster if I was with her.

Geez now what? Yia said that probably she could convince the hospital that I was a therapy dog and they might allow it. Yia admitted that she would miss me but it would be for a little while. Then she said that Sarge could go home too.

So that's it. Sacrifice me to get rid of the Sarge.

Fine with me Yia, with me, Shirley and Sarge gone, who you gonna yell at? Heh? Well, I'm game so you can count me in. As long as I get my own blankie, belly rubs and a lot of treats, otherwise I'm outta there.

So kids I'm of, therapy dog Lucey at your service; Lassie eat your heart out.

I'm the new wonder dog.

Later,

Lucey

Back Again

February 13,2012

Hi Again,

Finally, we all got in the car headed to the sanatorium. That would be the three Musketeers and Moi. The ride was pretty quiet, Yia Yia wasn't griping at the Sarge and Shirley was hanging on to me for dear life.

Once we got there, Sarge pulled into the circular driveway and dropped us off. Then he said he was going to park the car and be back in a jiffy. Yia Yia carried Shirley's little suitcase and Shirley carried little me. We went to check in at the reception desk. I could tell Shirley was a bit nervous. Actually this was the first time she ever went voluntarily.

Seated behind the desk was a woman with the bushiest blonde hair I've ever seen, dressed in a style that went out in the 60's. She was sporting big gold dangling earrings and rings on each of her fingers. She busied herself filing her nails and chewing her big wad of gum, which she did open mouth and making loud smacking noises. I would love for her to teach me how to do that; it looked pretty cool.

We stood there for a while. I don't think she noticed us. Yia Yia made a few ahem noises that got louder with each ahem. Finally, Yia couldn't stand it any longer and she said in a very loud voice, "Excuse me Miss, are we invisible?"

Miss Blondie looked up and replied, "Gee, I don't think so," and continued to file her nails and smack her gum. Not to be deterred, Yia asked, "Where's the lady that usually works here? I'd like to speak to her."

"Oh you mean the little old lady with the white hair and pink smock?"

"Yes, that's her, Mrs. Parker, I believe, is she here today?"

"No Sweetie, she's out getting her pace maker recharged, I'm a temp, just filling in."

"Well," Yia replied sarcastically, "you sure are on the ball, Sweetie."

Shirley was getting even tenser. She was squeezing the life out of me. I hope this doesn't get too stressful. I may need my eyeballs popped back in soon.

"Gee, thanks, Grannie, nice of you to notice," Blondie replied.

Yia Yia stood there staring at her and said in her frostiest voice ever, "I was joking, you, you." Then she shut up; I think she didn't want to get Shirley more upset.

After a deep breath, she said pleasantly, "Miss, we want to check in, could you please page the Doctor and tell him we are here, if you're not too busy that is." "Oh, why didn't cha say so? Sure thing, Gran, I'm on it. Both of you?" "No," Shirley answered meekly," just me."

"So what's cha name, Sweetie?"

"Shirley."

"Shirley what? Sweetie"

"I'm Shirley Temple."

"Go 'on, yeah, right and I'm Marilyn Monroe. I swear there

are some really strange people around here." Yia started to fume, "Her name is really Shirley Temple and if you're Marilyn Monroe, I'm the Queen of Sheba."

"Whatever you say, Grannie, personally you look like old Mother Hubbard, but hey, that's just me."

Yia Yia started to sputter and Shirley got a wild stare in her eyes. Uh oh! Things were heating up. Someone had to defuse this situation; Lucey the Wonder Dog was called to action. I jumped out of Shirley's strangle hold and ran around the desk and growled in the meanest voice I could conger up. I don't think it was mean enough because Blondie didn't notice me. Next, I gave her my most ferocious bark, no response. I had to pull out all the stops. I jumped up as far as I could and tried to pull her hair. I managed to reach it and gave it a good yank. Instead of crying out in pain, as was my intention, her hair came off her head. I didn't know what it was or what to do, so I just took it and ran around the waiting room growling and shaking the snot out of it.

I heard some people yelling behind me and Blondie, who wasn't blond anymore, was shrieking. On one of my laps around I spotted Yia Yia's and Shirley's old nemesis, Doofus the security guard running over just as Sarge was walking in the door. Good, if I need any help, I'll get old Sarge to shoot my prey.

Meanwhile, I just kept running and shaking the hairy creature trying my best to kill it. For all I knew it might have been a dangerous cat or rabbit. A crowd was gathering, some people were cheering me on; some were trying to have me come to them. They all would have to wait while I finished this mission. Soon I saw a solution. There at the entrance was a big indoor garden complete with a little fishpond. Perfect. I decided that I should bury whatever this thing was and then go back and take care of Shirl.

I ran over as fast as I could, jumped into the flower area and started digging, I almost had it buried but Doofus was hot on my trail. I did the next best thing I could think of, I drowned it. I was so proud of myself; I didn't understand all the fuss. Instead of yelling at me I should be getting a reward. Couple of pork chops, minimum.

Miss Blondie was stomping up and down. Actually, she should have been the first to thank me for saving her from that beast; it was covering up her pretty pink Mohawk. Don't ask, I'm cool, I watch MTV.

She gathered up her nail files, stuck another piece of gum in her mouth and marched out. Before she left she said she couldn't take anymore Whack a Dos. Some thought they were invisible, some thought they were Shirley Temple, the old one had delusions of being the Queen of Sheba, and then to top it all off, Toto the rabid dog attacked her. Enough was enough and she was quitting and started to leave. As she reached the door, two nurses grabbed her and told her they were taking her back to her room. One of the nurses yelled to Doofus to try finding out what happened to Mrs. Parker, the real receptionist.

Yia Yia took Shirley to a sofa in the corner of the room. I went over and jumped up and joined them. Shirley was smiling; I think she was proud of me. Sarge walked over, shaking his head. He asked Yia Yia why she couldn't stay out of trouble? In the short time he was gone she managed to cause a commotion.

Before she could answer, Doofus showed up and said, "Well, well, well, if it isn't my old friends, Miss Chicken and Miss Cow, who'd ja bring with cha? Mr. Rooster or Mr. Bull?"

"Neither one Sherlock, meet Sergeant Newman. Hey Sarge, why don't you show this genius here your badge and your gun?" Yia replied.

"Whoa, take it easy, I'm just trying to be friendly. No need to get testy," he stammered. "I take it that the dog belongs to one of you?'

Sarge spoke up, "Is there a problem Officer? That dog is Lucey and she's a Therapy dog. She is here to help Shirley." "What's that? Some kinda new breed, one of those fancy designer mutts? Don't matter, pets aren't allowed here. She has to go especially after the chaos she just caused."

Yia couldn't stand much more of him. "No, she's a working dog, for your information. The chaos she created defused a very tense situation. She's here to give Shirley love and comfort, so she's staying."

"Really, Yia? Love and comfort? Can't you Ladies get yourself a real boyfriend?" He started chuckling at his own humor just as the Sarge grabbed his elbow and nudged him towards a corner. We couldn't hear what they were talking about but the Sarge was in his face and Doofus was doing a lot of head bobbing up and down. When it was over Sarge walked back to us and Yia was all over him wanting to know what happened. He blew her off saying he took care of it and leave it alone. Wow, he sure is brave talking like that to her. Who knew?

While we were waiting, we saw Mrs. Parker come back to the reception desk. Story was that Blondie had approached her and told her she was her relief. Mrs. Parker was needed in the library to count each page in War and Peace. She was to make sure none were missing. She was finishing up when the search party found her.

Presently, a nice Doctor showed up, talked to Shirley and Yia. Said I could stay but had to be on probation because of the earlier incident. Geez Louise, I was only doing my job. Again, no respect, no pork chops.

The Doctor told us that Shirley was going to room with a very nice lady who loved dogs, that I would be very welcomed. I wanted to ask if she might have a? Oh forget it. Wishful thinking.

So the three Musketeers and moi walked upstairs. Shirley's little suitcase was covered with stickers of all the places she went while in the circus. She was so excited; all she could talk about was getting over her chicken obsession and getting her driver's license back. After that maybe she would join the circus again.

I sure hope she's not expecting me to go with her. I'm not cut out for a vagabond life. No, I'm more of the pampered pooch type. Well, first things first.

We reached her room and there sitting in a chair looking out the window was a short black woman. She got up and greeted us warmly and then she gushed over me. I really didn't understand her too well. She was talking fast and with some kind of drawl. Introductions were made all around and she told us her name was Betty. Yep, she was called Betty and her friends and family called her Betty Bam Be Lam.

Sarge and Yia said their Good-byes and left, leaving me with Shirl and my new friend Betty Bam Be Lam. Betty is going to be a lot of fun. She already sneaked me a cookie and said I could sleep on her bed. I think Shirley's a little jealous. But hey, I have to get my treats somewhere. Right?

Have to catch you later kids, on duty now with my therapy stuff. Oh, by the way, if you get a chance could you send some care packages? Doesn't hurt for me to have my own stash, for emergencies, of course.

Later,

Lucey

Bette Bam Be Lam

March 1, 2012

Hi Kids,

I'm here at the sanatorium with Shirley and her roommate Bette. I've been having a grand old time. Everyone here just loves me and I've been getting lots of belly rubs and even some extra treats. When Shirley took me down to the Community room, she told them I was a Therapy dog and I became much in demand, a sort of celebrity.

I jumped from person to person, giving them licks and getting lots of petting .One little old man in a chair slipped me a piece of his beef jerky. It was a tough as some of the shoes I chewed but it tasted real good. He told me not to tell anyone, seems he wasn't supposed to have it either.

There were some really strange things going on, I thought it must be me because nobody else seemed to notice. Lots of patients talking to nobody I could see. At first I thought they were on their phones, but no, just chatting with their invisible friends.

Later in the afternoon, Shirley and my new best friend Bette were hanging out together in our room. It was supposed to be quiet time. Shirley asked Bette why she was here; did she have a chicken problem too? Well, Bette got herself into a snit. She got all excited and started yelling, "Whadda ja mean? I ain't got no problem! What wrong with youse? You think I'm as daffy as some of these folk here?Here I am thinking you're my friend! Bah!"

"Hold on a minute, Bette no need to get all excited, I just thought you..." Before Shirley could finish, Bette snorted and left the room. She stomped and mumbled her way down the long hallway. Geez, everybody's so touchy. Between Bette and Shirley, I had a good thing going. I get lots of treats, belly rubs and an occasional leftover pork chop, sort of double dipping. Now what?

Shirley was all sad and confused. I thought I'd go and try to find Bette but I didn't want to leave poor old Shirl. So we just sat there on her bed, in the gloom and waited. I tried cheering her up by licking her face, rolling over and even tugging at her slippers. But no, nothing worked. Shirley was sad and no amount of my abundant charm was changing that, I must be losing my touch.

Time passed then quietly Bette slipped back into the room. She wasn't talking and quit her stomping. I think she saw how sad and upset Shirley was and felt bad. Me, I was just happy to see her, double treat days were back, maybe.

She mumbled something real low and Shirley asked, "What did you say?" Again the mumble followed by, "What did you say?" That went on for a while until couldn't stand it anymore and began barking and jumping on and off the bed. Both Shirley and Bette stopped and stared at me, and then they began laughing followed by crying. Crying?

Crying and laughing and talking over each other; sorrys and sorrys and more sorrys going round and round. Hey, what about me? Are you two pals again? Where's my afternoon treat? I waited a while for this love fest to be over then gave them my best cute look. You know, the one where I cock my head from one side to the other and give the sweetest whimper I can. Gets them every time. It took a couple of tries but finally they noticed me. Did they run over and give me a pet or a hug? No! They started laughing again and doing that sorry stuff all over again.

When they did get a hold of themselves, they turned to me and then back to themselves and declared that I was the greatest therapy dog ever! Yep ever, Moi, who knew? It's just one my natural talents. Now I was a super star again and they both took turns grabbing and petting me and slobbering all over me. Enough already, quit it why don't you, it's getting annoying. Where are the darn treats?

They finally calmed down and got a grip. I was showered with lots of treats that I deserved. All I could say was it was about time. I really worked hard for a few biscuits, some cheese and yucky carrot stick. As you can see, not one pork chop in the mix. Maybe later.

All went well the rest of the day, no dramas. Came nighttime and I was having a hard time deciding who I was going to sleep with, Bette or Shirley, Shirley or Bette? I couldn't decide. Guess it would depend on who gave me the best bedtime snack. Yeah, that would be fair. While I waited, Bette started talking to Shirl. Quietly at first, then in her usual fashion all excited and animated.

"Slow down Bette, I can't understand a word you say when you talk so fast," Shirley told her. "Sorry, I can't help myself. It's a touchy subject for me and I get all embarrassed or something. Everyone here is free to go if they want, but I's can't. No Siree, I's stuck," Bette lamented.

"Why Bette, did your family sign you in or something?" Shirley asked." "Heavens no!" Bette yelped. "Theys don't even know I's is here. Golly!" Shirley was all confused at this point,

I could tell by the twitching she began making. "It's okay Bette, we're all here to get better."

Bette yelled at her, "What wrong with youse? Didn't I tell you already that there's nothing wrong with me? Something wrong with your hearing, Girl?"

Uh oh, here we go again. I think I'll sleep in the hall tonight.

"No Bette, don't be getting your pantyhose in a bunch, I'm just trying to understand, that's all. Why don't you tell me what's got you in such a twist?" Shirley suggested. "Ok," said Bette, "maybe then you'll get it and we can get us some sleep."

And so the tale began:

It seems that Bette worked for a nice family as their housekeeper for a number of years. They had a nice relationship and treated her well, like one of their own. As the years went by, the children grew, went off to school, got married and started families. Bette was included in of all the events. She loved all the family very much as they did her.

Sadly, the dad became ill and passed away, the mom sold the house and moved away. That left Bette even in spite of having her own family; with a big empty hole in life.

Not one to brood, she decided it was time for her to do something different. Something she always wanted to do. This was her time and she was going for it. Oh yeah!

Reading the want ads in the papers, she set her sites on the job of her dreams. Morning found her all geared up, the stuff she needed packed in her little suitcase, and ad in hand and off she went. Taking the New York City subway downtown she got off at her stop and walked the remaining blocks to the advertised establishment.

At first it didn't appear open. She rang the buzzer and waited. What seemed to take forever, the door opened and a person asked what she wanted. Bette replied she was there for the job, was shown in and escorted down a narrow hall. The way was illuminated by little lights in clear tubes running down both sides of the carpeted path.

Eventually, they reached a cavernous room with lots of different size tables dotting the area, all facing an elevated stage. There were giant mirrors and fancy chandeliers all around. Bette was overwhelmed but felt this was it, the place she was destined for, and it was where she belonged.

The woman told her to take a seat and wait for the boss. As the minutes passed, Bette took in the surroundings, picturing herself there. She heard someone and when she looked up she saw a rather young gentleman. He walked over and shook her hand and introduced himself. He was dressed in a real fancy suit, his shirt open showing lots of thick gold chains hanging around his neck. His hair was dark, slicked back and tied into a scrawny ponytail. A big diamond stud shone in his ear and completed his ensemble.

He asked what he could do for her and she replied by telling him she was there answering the ad. "Of course, let me tell you a little about the position," he began. Bette was all excited until he explained the maintenance and housekeeping duties. "No, no, no," Bette cried, "I'm here for the dancer's spot!"

"The dancer's spot? Really? Surely, you are pulling me leg." he replied rather brusquely. "See here Mister, this here ad asks for an exotic pole dance and that's me," Bette informed him. "Surely Miss, oh sorry, what's your name again?" he asked. "Bette, Bette Bam Be Lam! That's who, Mr. Smarty Pants; I ain't here for no cleaning job. I's an experienced dancer. Best your sorry eyes ever saw!"

"I am sure you are Ms. Be Lam, but maybe your day has passed, you certainly are a bit over your prime and I might add a little thick across the beam too," he answered. "Say what? Are you saying I'm old and fat? Is that what cha saying? Cuz if it is I'd be suing you for age and weight discrimation.as fast as I can walk out those doors."

He told her to calm down saying she sure had a lot of fire. Next he asked her if she had any costumes. The position called for the dancer to supply her own. "Sure do Sonny, right here in my suitcase. Do you want me to change?" she asked. "I can show you all my moves, guaranteed you ain't seen nothing like it."

"Well, I'm sure I haven't, but don't change yet, I have some more questions. Let's move on. Do you have any experience with pole dancing?" he asked. "Are you serious? I can dance with any pole youse got. May pole, flagpole, beanpole, telephone pole, theys all the same to me. I can dance myself around those suckers like crazy," she answered.

"Unfortunately Ms. Be Lam, those aren't the kind of pole we have here, so I think this interview is over. Allow me to walk you to the door." With that he went over and took Bette's arm to show her out. Bette wasn't ready to go and told him to take his hand off her. He didn't and tried to pry her out of the chair. Bette jumped up and in a flash took her suitcase and whacked him upside his head with it.

"Passed my prime am I, Pretty Boy? 'Bout time youse got smacked long side your big head." Just for good measure, she yanked on his ponytail as he was slumping to the floor. "And don't you'd be thinking I don't know what broad in the beam means. Youse saying I have a big butt, well so does J-Lo and she gets plenty of jobs. How do you like that, Mr. Smarty pants?"

Meanwhile, the person who admitted Bette heard the commotion and called the police. They arrived just as Bette was leaving and took her downtown, kicking and screaming.

When the judge heard all the evidence he decided to have Bette committed for observation. That's why she's here and believes she unfairly confined.

"Wow, that's a heck of a story Bette, but I think that the judge was trying to do you a favor," she told her. "What cha saying? You think I's daft? Is that what cha think?" Bette was getting all worked up again. "No Bette, listen to me. I know a little about this stuff." Shirley tried to tell her. "I think the judge was trying to keep you from going to jail; giving you a reason for your outburst. Maybe letting a little time pass so tempers can calm down. Do you understand what I'm saying?"

"Come again, the judge did me s a favor by sticking me in here? You sure 'bout that?" Bette was puzzled. "Not 100% Bette, but you did assault the guy and he could press charges." " I was acting in self defense, that fancy Pants done put his hands on me, ain't nobody touch this body without my permission. Nobody! Youse knows what I's thinking Girl? I's thinking I should sue his sorry behind for sexual harassment. Yeah, that's what I's gonna do."

"Slow down a bit Bette, what proof do you have? Might be hard to prove," Shirley tried to explain. "Are you saying that I's not irresistible? Cuz I am you know," Bette said seeming defeated. "Not at all, Bette, I would just be he said, she said. Plus, you knocking him out gives him more sympathy with the judge," Shirley tried to reason with her.

Bette was pretty clever too. "I wouldn't of had to hit him if he kept his big mitts offa me." "You're right about that, Bette can't argue that point. I can only tell you that I got some serious charges against me and the judge cut me a break. Maybe he did that for you too, that's all."

Well, I was getting pretty exhausted with all this stress and free-floating emotions swirling all around me. I jumped on Bette's bed and gave a big stretch and doggie yawn. Bette and Shirley stopped their yammering and finally paid some attention to Moi. It was about time, Geez.

"Guess Lucey's ready for bed," said Shirley. Bette gave a little chuckle and agreed it was a tiring day. "Best we turn in a see what tomorrow brings," she replied.

So that was it, lights out and before you knew it, they were both asleep and snoring loudly. I tried covering my ears with my paws but the racket still got in, keeping me awake.

There's no justice kid; I'm telling you, just no justice in a dog's life at all.

Later,

Lucey

Lucey's Nightmares

March 2,2012

Hi All,

Finally, some rays of light sneaking through the windows on what seemed to be an endless night. Try as I may, I couldn't block out the synchronized snoring of my roommates, Shirley and Bette. If it were an Olympic event these two would win a gold medal.

Whatever happened to Shirley? She used to give out little purring sounds when she slept, nowhere near the ten-decibel racket she and Betty were making.

At 3 AM I decided to take a walk and check out the night nurse. Sometimes she saves some of her dinner for me. As I approached I could see that all the lights were dimmed and her feet perched on the desk. Next, I heard her before I saw her. Her head was laid back on the chair and she was snoring loudly. I think I have entered the third ring of hell. What a night!

I need to get in some power naps in today, no socializing with the gang in the Community Room for me. No siree, making myself some quality Lucey time under the covers.

Hold on, my dog walker is here to begin my morning routine, a nice long refreshing walk, next my breakfast and then my therapy routine Well, they can just forget about the last part. It's my day off!

Okay, I'm back, time to get started on the naps.

Uh oh, Shirley and Bette are at it again. I think. I hear their raised voices as I head back to our room. As I return, I realize they didn't even miss me. No, they are busy laying some sort of plan.

This is trouble, I mean, REALLY! Remember when Yia Yia and Shirley hatched their wild ideas? Do you remember the results? I do! That's why I'm locked up with this bunch. Maybe one of you should come and rescue me before it gets out of control. How much can one little hybrid dog do? I'm only canine, you know. I slip in quietly and go under Shirley's bed. I'm trying to block out their conversation, but some of it gets through and I'm hooked.

You should get ready for the following it's a doozy.

Shirley: You can do it Bette I know you can. Why not give it a go?

Bette: Oh, I's don't know, you really think it'll work? Maybe the Doctors won't let us.

Shirley: Of course they will: just think, it will liven up this dreary, depressing place. You'll be a hero.

Bette: Ok, tell me your, I mean our plan again.

Shirley: We are going to put on a show. Can't you see yourself doing your pole dance routine and wowing the audience? I'll try and get a motorcycle and do some bike tricks. Maybe we can get some of the other patients to join us. I bet there is some latent talent out there waiting to be heard

Lucey: *Are you guys getting this? Hope you're sitting down. Pole Dancing? Motorcycle? Next, they'll think of a dog act.*

Shirley: Oh Bette, I just thought of something. How about we get Lucey to do some kind of dog tricks?

Lucey: *Yikes! What did I tell you? It's time for you to rescue me!*

Bette: Great Idea. Everybody here loves her. What do you think she can do?

Lucey: *Escape!*

Shirley: We'll think of something. Now let's get a plan in action. I'll canvass the patients and see who wants to participate. You get Leroy to bring you your costumes and print up some invitations for our families and friends. This is going to be so much fun. Let's get started at breakfast. Hey, have you seen Lucey? I bet she's entertaining the group already. I wonder where I can get a motorcycle? How about a pole? Where can we get a pole? OH, my mind is racing a hundred miles an hour. Let's go Betty, times a wasting.

You all do realize that this is a stick of dynamite waiting to off. These things never go the way they're planned. And me, I'm stuck in the middle. Dog tricks! If I knew any tricks I would have joined the circus long ago. I'm starting on that nap now.

I drift off and then the nightmares begin. The first one I find myself on a high wire, way above the roaring crowd below. I'm in the middle and can't see either end; I'm suspended in air. The wire starts vibrating and swaying back and forth. It begins going in bigger and bigger arcs causing me to lose my balance. I have all four legs holding on tight, but it is no use. I start falling head over paws. Down and down and tumbling in circles and just as I'm about to crash, I wake up. I'm in a cold sweat and shaking all over. Terrifying!

I settle down and drift off again. This time I am on stage with a magician. He has a girl Friday with him all decked out in some sequined outfit. At first I thought it was Yia Yia, but his helper was at least 50 years younger. There is much ooh's and aahs from the audience and occasional applause. The magician is doing his disappearing acts with the rabbits. I'm watching on the sidelines with Miss Shiny Outfit and when she brings me on stage, I get a big ovation. Hey, this ain't so bad.

The trick is being set up. A large box is wheeled on stage and opened, oh, I know what this is, it's the saw in half trick. The audience is shown how it's all one-piece, no hidden passages. The Magician takes my leash and walks me around the box a few times. Before I know it, he picks me up and sticks me into the box and straps me in. The lid is closed and locked.

Desperately I try to get loose when I hear the sound of something. Oh Yeah! An electric saw…it starts cutting into the wood above me inches from my perfect body. I wake up in a cold sweat again, trembling. Horrifying!

I'm not too sure I even want to sleep at this point, but how can I have an even worse nightmare than the ones I just had?

Bravely, I try again and doze off. All is going well and I am wandering around a carnival ground. It's so real I can hear the calliope music and smell the funnel cakes and cotton candy. Everyone is having fun and heading to the big sideshow. I follow along and when the Emcee asks for a volunteer, I decide why not?

I raise my paw and again the mob gives me a big round of applause. I go to the center of the ring and given a small helmet and a colorful cape. This is going to be so much fun. It's about time I have a decent dream. Some cute He-man, a Mr. Clean look alike, comes over, takes me and holds me above his head for all the adoring crowd to see. He struts me around the edges of the ring and I acknowledge all the good wishes that sing out, "Good Luck, What a Brave Dog, How Cute and Happy Landing." What a nice bunch. They love me! I'm elated.

Then just when I thought it was over, and he was going to put me down, I look up and there is the most enormous cannon that I ever saw. What the heck is that doing in my dream? This can't be good. I wiggle to get out of the He-man's clutches but it's to late. Now he's shoving me down the mouth of the cannon and pushing me further and further back with a padded plunger.

I reach the bottom and realize that a silence overcame the audience. What seems like forever, I hear a count down begin. Ten, nine, eight, seven, six, five, four, three, two, one.... Ker-BOOM!

I'm startled awake and feel for my body parts. I'm still in one piece and swear, no more sleeping for me, ever!

Shirley and Bette come back into the room, still excited and making all kinds of plans and schedules. I can't even feign any sort of interest. I am so wiped. They look over at me and think that maybe I should see a Vet. Yeah, maybe. Some of their tranquilizers could erase the terror that I have just endured. When they say it was time for lunch, I realize that not much time has passed. What seemed lie an eternity was really only a few hours, if that.

You know, I am going to go with them. I can't face falling asleep again. There are ghosts and vampires and witches and who knows what lurking beneath my eyelids.

So kids, I need your help. Hurry and form a posse and if you can't rescue me, please bring me some pork chops.

Thanks,

Lucey

PS: Some chocolate couldn't hurt too!

The Burglar

March 10,2012

Hi All,

I'm home at Yia Yia's for a while, having a much needed break from my dog therapy job. Seems Shirley called Yia and told her I was acting peculiarly. I mean, how could she tell? Everyone there acts peculiarly.

Anyway, Yia showed up while Shirley and Bette were in the middle of planning the big Talent Show event at the sanatorium. Immediately Yia volunteers to get an electric guitar and do her, "Wake up little Susie," number. That's when Shirley told her it was patients only and she couldn't participate. Yia Yia took the news pretty well, said she was disappointed but she understood. Yeah. Right.

In the car on the way home, you should have heard her. Actually, I'm glad you didn't. She was ranting and raving and saying some pretty unpleasant things she was going to do to Shirley and Bette. If she goes through with those threats, she's looking at some serious jail time. Then what happens to me? I had a hard enough time breaking her in and she's not even 100% there yet. It's always the innocent that suffer. Moi!

And talk about suffering, we made a stop at the Veterinarian en route home. You know how much I hate that place and especially the quack doctor.

A bit of luck shone on me that day because the big sadist who always sticks me with needles wasn't there. No, instead a nice lady Vet saw me. She gushed about how cute I was, although a tad over weight. Hey, can I help it if I got paid in snacks for all my therapy treatments?

Anyway, Yia told her I was more high-strung than usual and that I was suffering from insomnia. Darn straight I am, it's scary enough just being awake among the patients but in my sleep I'm falling from high wires, getting sawed in half and shot out of cannons.

The Vet asked if I had any recent traumas, Yia didn't know, and asked why? The Vet said that she thought that I had some sort of posttraumatic stress syndrome, rare but not impossible in canines. Hey, that was it. Wow, who knew? Of course I would get something rare. No ordinary pooch am I, I keep trying to tell folk that but now it's documented. I'm rare.

Yia was told to take me home and keep me in a quiet environment with not too much stimuli for a couple of weeks. That's impossible. Obviously the Vet had no idea about the frenetic household I call home. Additionally, that I get shipped off as a therapy dog to a sanatorium full of zany patients. My stress meter blew long time ago; I'm surviving on reserve power.

So I spent a few days at home with Yia Yia trying her best to be calm and caring. She's reverted back to calling me by my pet name, Hemorrhoid.

I think it's German for Cutey or Sweetie, something like that. I was sleeping better and getting my self-confidence back. Seeing all my doggie friends and getting lots of new messages wiped out the terrors that lurked behind my eyelids. I was on the mend, starting to be my old self. Watch out world, Le Luc is Back! Geez that felt good.

Yia realized the old Lucey had returned and resumed doing whatever it is that she does. Zipping around in Big Red, taking Zumba lessons and totally interfering in the raising of her Grands. Oh, Blessed Normalcy.

One bright morning, after a walk, I was quickly ushered back inside. Yia was on the move; she gave me a pet on the head and rushed out the door. Time to look for some dog biscuits I stashed for days like this.

While I was sniffing and hunting, I heard someone at the door. First the bell rang a few times and the doorknob jiggled. I did my sentry bark and went to investigate. Standing outside was a man, peering through the windowpanes along side to the door. He was covered with a ski mask with only his eyes peering out. He had a bunch of sacks with him so I figured he must have been looking for donations. Before I knew it he had out a tool, which he stuck in the door lock and opened the door.

Hey, Hi! Yia's not home right now, but you can play with me if you want. I greeted him with my usual exuberance. Hi, Hi, Hi, Hi, Hi! What' cha looking for? I can help. Why don't you take off your coat and hat it's warm in here. Let me get the hat. Oops, almost reached it. Bet you never saw a dog jump so high. Should have seen me as a pup, springs for legs. Getting…hey wait, I'm not done showing off. Where you going now?

Oh, the dining room. Are you putting the silver ware in that sack? That's good, Yia needs someone to clean it; she's always complaining how much work it is.

Done already? Where ya going now? Only bedrooms and Yia's office upstairs. Ok, I'll go with you. What are you doing in Yia's office? No silverware in there. You must be the computer guys she's been waiting for. She's always breaking something. Are you going under the desk? It's really tight in there. I've hidden a few cookies back there. Let me get in there with you and take them out. Say, be careful with that extension cord thingy, I got a few buzzes when I chewed on them. Cozy aren't we?

You know you have some food stuck on you chin, it smells like Ketchup. I'll lick it off for you. Watch it, did you just bump you head? Almost got me too. So, what are you doing? Now I see it. You unplugged her desktop. Oh did you just get a shock? I told you to be careful, that thing is dangerous. Are you taking the computer for repair? Better leave a receipt. Watch out going down the stairs, I'll go first. Geez, how'd you trip over me, you big oaf? I could have gotten hurt. Look at the computer now, so many little pieces. Yia isn't gonna be happy. Why are you putting me behind the gate? Don't you want any more help?

Did you just take all those sacks into Yia's bedroom? She sure has a lot of clothes she can donate. Let me get over this gate and

I'll show you. Wow, look at all the mess you made. You have her stuff-strewn all over.

Why don't you put it in your sacks? I see you found the safe, hard to find with all these clothes hanging in front. Yia sits on the floor to so she can open it. Yeah, that's the way. A gun's in there you know, I heard her tell the Sarge. You look so frazzled, let me wiggle in there and lay on your lap. Now why don't you give me a few belly rubs, it's very relaxing; it's what I do at the sanatorium, give it a try. So, start petting. Now where are you going? No petting for me? How rude.

Back in the dining room already? Oh, yeah, the sacks let me get them for you. Oops, sorry grabbed wrong end. You'll just have to put all the silverware back in.

Why you going already? What about all the stuff? Say, are you crying? Why don't you give the belly rubbing therapy a shot? Here, let me lie down in front of you. Oh, Geez, why'd you trip over me again? You sure are clumsy.

You better return later and help Yia put back this stuff. She's scary when she's mad. You should have shut the door when you left. Boy, no manners. See ya.

I strolled around outside for while, it was still a bit cold and damp. I was getting bored just when Yia Yia arrived. She took one look at the house, then another at me. Hey, she can't think I made this mess. I knew she'd be mad. Actually, what she did next surprised me. She came over and hugged me and checked to see if I was okay? Man, she must have really missed me.

Before long the Sarge shows up with a couple of his guys. He's asking Yia why she didn't have the alarm on, like he told her. She gets all flustered and yells at him for asking. They're back to normal.

After they establish that nothing was taken, Sarge remarks that something must have scared the burglar off. Burglar? That oaf? No way.

The Sarge stayed behind when the other cops left. Said he had a few more questions. Then as Yia calmed down, he began talking about Shirley.

He was happy to hear that she was progressing so well. He wanted to know why I came home. Yia told him about my stress disorder and the Sarge got a big chuckle out of that. Really? I was overworked and under paid. How would he like a nip in the ankle?

Anyway, Yia made some coffee and said after the coffee break she had to clean up the mess. Sarge volunteered to help. Instead of throwing him out like she always did, she accepted. Something's going on here. She must be getting old. Older that is, wearing out. Where's the spunk? The insults? The attitude? Maybe she needs a belly rub.

After everything was back in order, the Sarge told Yia to make sure she kept the alarm on and not to forget. Sometimes he asserts himself. Not always, but now and then. Yia agreed and said she would. Now definitely, something's amiss. How long have I been gone?

At the door saying, 'Goodbye', Sarge asked if Yia would go to the Patient's Talent Show with him. Said he had a big surprise for Bette and wanted Yia to be with him when he told her. Yia wanted to know what it was immediately but when the Sarge wouldn't cave. Yia finally accepted after he told her to go with him to find out.

So that's the up to the minute, kids. You have any ideas about what's going on here? Should I be worried? Just when I was getting stress free, now this develops. Where's the justice?

Please ask your folks if you can go to the show too. You know there's safety in numbers, especially mine.

Later,

Lucey

Dance Lessons

March 15,2012

Hi, Hi, Hi,

I'm back in demand. Yep, they need little old Lucey. Maybe I should use my stage name, El Lu-c. This might be the break I've been waiting for, my big discovery.

Yesterday, Shirley called and asked Yia to bring me back to the hospital. Yia thought Shirley was despondent again, but no, Shirley's fine. Said she never felt better and was making great progress.

She spoke to Yia about the Talent Show and said she needed me for a special part of the program. Yep, Moi! They need MOI!

Yia was hesitant, reminded Shirley that the show was supposed to be for patients only. Shirl countered by saying that I was listed in the patient rolls with her, making me eligible. Seems Yia is still smoldering about being excluded. Get over it Yia, it's my time to shine.

Shirley asked Yia for another favor, if she could of course. She wanted Yia to sign her and Bette out for a few evenings. They wanted to go down to the local dance studio to take some lessons. Need to punch up Bette's pole dance routine, maybe add some extra moves. Shirley said it would be great fun and Yia should join in, just for the heck of it. Yia said she would look into it and talk about it when she dropped me off.

After lunch, Big Red was fired up, my gear all packed and off we went. Upon my arrival, I was greeted like the celebrity I'm about to become. All rushed over to see me, said how much they all missed me and was so happy I returned. Enough with the adoration, where are my treats?

Shirl and Bette brought Yia Yia up to date with the preparations for the big night. I squeezed in the middle of them to hear what was happening and what was planned for me.

First, they got permission from the head doctor and hospital administrator, who gave them the green light for the project with a few exceptions. Only patient participation allowed, (Yia sulked at that one) no strobe lights, (sets some patients off) and nothing with motors. Last show, they had a juggler using chain saws with disastrous results. Put some patients back months in therapy and it took three weeks to clean up the blood.

Shirley said she was disappointed she couldn't use a motorcycle but said she would do her routine with a bike or a unicycle. Bette was beside herself with glee. I couldn't understand a word she said, she was bubbling over so fast.

The line up included a comedian, a trio of girl singers, ala The Supremes, Shirley's bike tricks, and a baritone that does Sinatra songs, a violinist, Bette's dance number and a ragtime piano player. So where did I fit in? They saved me for last; I was to be a ventriloquist dummy.

Heh?

I'm no dummy! How rude! Shirl explained that the ventriloquist plans to have Lucey be a talking dog. That he can throw his voice so it sounds like Lucey is talking and maybe even singing.

Said it would be amazing. He needs to rehearse with Lucey and teach her how to move her mouth when he gives her the silent commands.

I don't know? Thought of myself in some other venue. I'm a fantastic jumper, I can climb ladders, and I can roll over. And don't forget about my artistic side, I'm also a great painter. Of course, a talking dog could be the ticket to Dog Disney, cute and can talk, Hmm, has possibilities. Ok, I'm in.

Group rehearsal starts next week, meanwhile all the cast is polishing their acts in the day room. Bette has been hampered by a lack of a pole. Does her routine but really needs to practice with a pole, that's where Yia comes in. Yia agreed to drive them with the stipulation that she's the understudy for one of the Supremes. With a little negotiation, it was worked out. I just hope Yia Yia doesn't do something drastic to one of the singers.

Next evening, Yia comes to pick us all up. She decided to take a few lessons. Couldn't hurt, just in case Bette needed an understudy too. She was wearing a raincoat and I was dreading what was under it. I remembered the other outfits she used to wear when planning her Nursing Home tour.

Bette and Shirley were raring to go, so we all piled in Big Red and hit the road. The dance studio was on the Avenue right in the middle of town. Yia parked and cracked the car windows, and then she told me to stay in the car and behave myself. Yeah, like I have a choice. The three of them jumped out, ran for the door and disappeared in a second. Talk about excited.

As I kept watch guarding the car, I perused the area. My eyes focus on the second story of the studio. It had floor to ceiling windows and the dancers were doing their routine for the all world to see. How neat. OH, hold on. Not so good, I started getting a bad feeling. I didn't have to wait long to know what my gut already knew.

There standing right in front were the three amigos. Shirley had on her electric blue body surfer suit with the lightening bolt, Bette had on a shimmering gold leotard with black tights accenting her J Lo backside on steroids. The next vision had me wanting to gouge my eyes out. There stood in all her glory was Yia Yia, resplendent in a neon pink unitard and matching tutu.

While I stared in disbelief, I saw the Ballet Master instructing the students in exercises, warming them up. Sure hope he has blinds or shades for those windows. Bette was pretty limber, Shirl was keeping up but poor Yia was struggling. Looked like she had a few too many vinos at supper.

As I watched I became aware of a small group of gawkers assembling and pointing up at the windows. Oh no! I prayed for a blackout, a downpour, and a meteor to streak by, anything to divert the mounting interest in the images above. No such luck, now the trio moved on to bar exercises. The bar was brought over closer to the window. Has this instructor no shame? He can't want the world to see this catastrophe in progress. All three got their hands on the bar, big goofy smiles on their faces and started doing plies. You know, squats. Bette and Shirl weren't bad; the Tutu lady needed help getting up.

By this time the gawkers turned into a crowd, the crowd this side of a mob. Someone said it was a comedy routine. Yeah, hold that thought.

As I looked around, I noticed that the traffic was at a stand still; nobody was moving; sounds of horns beeping and the raised voices of frustrated drivers. The Avenue and cross streets were all stopped and backing up. A gazillion eyes were focused on the spectacle on the second floor.

Time passed and now the girls were doing some stretches on the bar. Their one leg was extended and they were trying to bend down to touch their knee with their head.

Shirl was amazing; I could see her being very flexible. Bette, on the other hand was a bit stubby, plus the big payload on her back end had her off center. She was floundering like a fish being reeled in. But the hardest part to watch was poor Yia Yia who was frozen in place; she had to be pried off the bar.

Off in the distance, were the sounds of sirens. Looking I could see a number of flashing lights on the vehicles trying to get to this scene. Please, will this nightmare ever end? To think I thought being shot out of a cannon was terrifying.

The mob was starting to get restless. Some were sure it was a made for TV video, others thought it a promo for the school; the rest said it was a bunch of old ladies being ridiculous. Hey watch that, they're my old ladies, you nincompoop. If I get out of this car, I'll bite off your attitude.

The sirens got closer and soon the Calvary arrived. Police took control of the traffic and tried to untangle the jam that stretched for blocks. The crowd was told to disperse. Some of the insolent ones had some smart comments, once they were told they would be arrested for unlawful assembly, they eventually left.

Looking out I could see Sarge. He was in charge and directing some of the other cops. He found the car with me in it and I could see the moment when he realized that this had to be the work of Yia Yia. By the time he looked up at the window the trio were finished and gone.

Yia Yia, Shirley and Bette emerged from the studio all excited and unaware of the commotion they caused. Yia was surprised to see the Sarge and asked if he was following them. He answered by saying there was a traffic mishap in the area and he was called to clear it up.

What? Is this the same guy? Now I know he must have a terminal disease or something. A complete personality change, next thing you know he'll stop farting. The group got back in the car and we returned to the sanatorium. Last I saw Sarge he was headed up to the studio. I think he is telling them to use shades. At least I hope so.

Yia, Shirley and Bette were scheduled to go back for more lessons in two days and then some more the following week. Fortunately, I had started my lessons with Bob the ventriloquist, so I couldn't witness any more chaos.

I sure hope the Sarge warned the dance instructor about the danger he was putting the public in by exposing the three amigos in his window.

Sleeping is still a problem, no the nightmares have ceased but the snores continue. I've managed to block them out pretty much with borrowed earplugs. Now however, Shirley and Bette are slathering themselves in with Ben-gay or some other foul smelling liniment for their aches and pains. The stuff has my eyes stinging and nose running. Is there no mercy?

I'm going to visit the night nurse. She can't possibly be taking a nap with the odors swirling around here. Actually, the smell has made me hungry and it's time she ponies over some of her sandwich. I'll keep her company and hope the fumes won't make the smoke alarms to go off.

So kids, I'm going to get Yia to send you some tickets so you can see me in action. The show is only open to staff and patients and their friends and family. You'll have to tell them we are related. Okay?

Later,

El Luc

(Using my stage name now)

Rehearsal

April 16,2012

Greetings Fans,

Tis moi, El Luc, on the brink of my stage debut and my long awaited stardom. This is my moment, the one with destiny and I want all of you to bask in my glow. Make sure you get your tickets and mention you can't wait to see my performance.

It can't hurt to build up enthusiasm for what promises to be the highlight of the production. All modesty aside, I'm great. This will launch my fervent quest, Dog Disney at last!

A little inside info for my best fans, Bob my second banana is firming up the act and making good use of my multiple talents. He's been here for a few months and just about ready to go back home.

As I might have mentioned, he's a ventriloquist and has a condition call automatonophobia. Whew, hope they don't expect me to say that! Anyway, that is the fear of puppets or dummies.

Bob was doing the circuit, that's show biz lingo for tours, when he began thinking his dummy was alive and was terrorized by it. The dummy took on an intimidating persona that Bob had no control over. What could he do? He decided to murder it.

At first he stabbed it multiple times, but the dummy just laughed at him. Next came drowning, but again the dummy just mocked Bob's efforts when he took him out of the tub, then came hanging, which too was met by scorn. In public the dummy cried out for help and ridiculed poor Bob. Finally, Bob thought of a solution. He decided to smother the dummy into silence. First he duct taped its mouth and then held a pillow of its head until all his sounds were silenced. Bob finally found peace.

However, it was short lived. Now the dummy was haunting him from its make shift grave in the closet. Bob went over the brink, flipped out and it is now his good fortune to be working with the consummate professional, Moi.

As for the rest of the group, Yia has been taking Bette and Shirley to the studio without me. That's my rehearsal time with old Bob. She's still bemoaning the fact she's not included in the cast. She has been stalking the Supreme singers, humming their tunes and trying to follow their dance moves. I'm worried that she might become desperate and do something rash.

Shirley has been awesome. She has this routine with her bike where she does hand stands on the handlebars. In addition she does wheelies, jumps over obstacles and various other feats that astonish everyone. Who knew she had so much talent?

And Bette, well, that's another story. You know that I told you she has a giant booty. (Butt, hiney, rear-end, back side, tookus.) Take your pick. Anyway, while she's doing her dance number she has been shaking that equipment so fast and so hard that she has been setting off the seismograms at the earthquake center. Seems they have picked up activity measuring between 3 and 4 on the Richter scale. When they traced the source of the epicenter it led to sanatorium and directly to the rehearsal hall.

Bette was asked to tone her act down for the safety of the public. After a bit of protests about her art she reluctantly agreed to a less vigorous shaking of her aforementioned apparatus.

After supper, in the evening when all becomes quiet, I snuggle with either Bette or Shirley. Depends on who gives me the best treat.

On a night not too long ago, Bette was asking Shirl about her friendship with Yia Yia. Shirley traced it back to here where it all began in the hospital garden. They knew each other a little before that but it blossomed the day Yia befriended her and signed her out to the beginning of their many adventures.

Shirley had Bette in stitches when she recounted the time that Yia and she went to a Broadway Show. After it was over and they were exiting, Shirl convinced Yia to take a rickshaw ride back to their hotel to avoid the crowd waiting for cabs. Yia was dubious, disinclined until Shirl hopped right into the one at the curb. When Yia got in the driver took off and started dodging traffic immediately. There were sounds of horns beeping, brakes screeching and cabbies yelling obscenities. Yia was screaming at the driver and telling him to slow down, be careful, watch out only to realize that he didn't speak a word of English, except when it got time to get paid. Yia continued to shriek the whole way hanging on for dear life. She made death threats to the driver and Shirley if she ever got out alive. Shirl meanwhile was loving life. She lived for the adrenaline rush that came with the danger.

Another time Shirl said was the cruise they took together. Everything was going fine until Shirl disappeared. Yia got herself in a twist looking for her. She was convinced that Shirl had fallen overboard. It began when Shirley didn't show up for breakfast, as was their routine. Yia waited a while and then returned to her cabin. She phoned Shirl's room a few times and then went to look for her. Her door was closed and she didn't answer the knock. Yia found a steward and convinced him to open Shirl's door. Upon entry Yia saw the tumble of bed linens and the general upheaval in the room. A quick look around convinced Yia that something terrible must have befallen Shirley.

Yia roamed the ship from top to bottom searching everywhere, to no avail. Outside on the decks she checked every chair and looked in every cranny. No Shirl.

Panic was overtaking Yia. She decided to report a possible man overboard to the ship's crew. On her way through the hall, she heard a knocking. Curiosity grabbed her and she stopped to hear where it came from. It was the handicap bathroom. Yia was torn, who to help first, she decided to get an officer to get assistance for the person trapped in the bathroom and report the missing Shirley at the same time.

The muffled voice was still yelling and frantically pounding on the door as the officer went to retrieve a key. Yia was telling her fears to the officer as he stood unlocking the door, when lo and behold as it opened there was Shirley.

Shirley was grateful, Yia was relieved and the Officer wanted to know why Shirley just didn't use the phone on the bathroom wall if she needed help.

Shirl said she never saw it. This is the same cruise that gave birth to the idea of "Rent-a-Guy'. Shirl began telling Bette all about that when my eyelids got heavy and I fell off to sleep. Hey, I need my beauty rest, plus I lived that episode for real.

So now, everything is just about ready, today is the dress rehearsal. The patients and staff are seated for a preview. I'm starting to get some jitters but I am assured all great performers are subject to them What can I say, I was born for show biz.

I met Bob behind the curtain; he had a pocketful of treats for me. Part of the secret way he gets me to look like I am speaking.

We're up next; he grabs hold of my leash, gives me a treat and leads me on stage. On the way to the chairs set up on the set, he trips. I call out, '"Watch out you big oaf!" and the cast and the audience laugh and cheer. We are on our way.

Our act was a big hit and Bob was very proud of himself and me. How could he miss as me as his partner?

There were a few glitches that needed to be worked out, but nothing major. Excitement was mounting as the reality became palpable. A little extra medication was given for the more tense ones among us. I settled for extra treats and belly rubs for comfort,

Meanwhile, my concerns about Yia Yia were increasing. I have my dog antennae up and sense something afoot. Could it be because she's sneaked into the wardrobe area and tried to squeeze herself into the Supremes' costume? Said she got lost backstage and was admiring it when she was found hanging it back. Uh oh!

Betty is so excited I haven't understood a word she has said in two days. It was something about a big surprise from Leroy, her old beau. Then Yia told her that Sarge had a surprise for her too, now there is no possible way to slow her down. I hope she doesn't forget to shake her booty gently or all of the area will be a risk.

So guys, don't bring me flowers, some grilled pork chops instead. Okay? Also take lots of pictures. I'm going to need them for my portfolio. I need an agent, so maybe one of you can investigate a talent agency specializing in dog acts. Want to cover all my bases before the rush. As for an attorney, I think my pal Alicia will handle my legal matters. She's been waiting for years to adopt me. Yia has stood in the way.

Speaking about Yia, perhaps you should think about getting her another dog or maybe a cat. With me gone, she will have a lonely existence. She will be so sad without me. She has become so dependent on my company. I know that's why she's hanging out here as much as possible. Actually, it's making me sad, who will watch out for her? Oh, the cross I must bear for my art.

I know Shirley will be fine, in fact for the past few weeks she has hardly paid me any mind. Her crying sessions and staring all but stopped. Her outlook has been great and I heard her ask Yia if the Sarge can help her find a way to do her community service.

Well, have to run along now, time to get my fur trim so I can be my gorgeous self tomorrow.

Don't forget the chops.

You can say you knew me when,

Bye Bye My Darlings,

El Luc

Show Time for Lucey

April 20,2012

Hell-o All—It's SHOW TIME!

Yes, the big day has arrived. Tonight I make my stage debut. Please remember to bring your cameras for your pictures with a celebrity. Of course, that would be me.

Bob and I have been honing up the act and we have the timing down to a science. Bob taught me lots of tricks and a couple special effects. I'm not sure if I can give away one of Bob's secrets: but, okay you pulled it out of me.

You know what Bob does to make me look like I'm talking? Give up? He slips me a treat that has peanut butter in it and when I try to lick it off my teeth, it makes my mouth move and it gives the illusion that I am speaking. Cool, right? Don't tell Bob I narced, just a little show biz info.

I'm still a little worried about what Yia is up to, she still stalking the Supremes. She told Shirley that Sarge is coming to the show and asked her to go with him. Maybe he can keep her under control. Doubtful.

As for Shirley, she has blossomed. She has helped all the patients with their acts; all her previous experience has really given her a lot of self-confidence. I think this time she is going to be all right. No more chicken delusions, she's doesn't need that crutch anymore.

And Bette, wait until you see her; just hold on to your seats while she's performing. The room begins to shake when she does. She so anxious to see Leroy, her boyfriend, he said he had a surprise for her and it has her curiosity meter running overtime.

Have to run now, time for my beauty bath and paw-de-cure. Oh, the life of a star, however will I go back to my old existence? Maybe I will go with Shirley if she decides to go back to the circus. Maybe Bob and I can be the opening act for Celine in Vegas. Maybe Dog Disney will want me for their next Dog feature film. The list is endless.

You can tell your children how you knew me when. My head is spinning, so much to do, so little time.

See ya later.

El Luc

The Show

April 24,2012

Hi All My Grands,

The show was awesome and so glad some of you could be there. It was amazing: what a great production the patients delivered.

The Emcee, Dr. Feelgood, praised all the cast and singled out Shirley and Betty in particular. Said Shirley and Bette were the driving force of the whole thing, recruiting the talents and working with the hospital staff around appointments. He added that Shirley's previous show business experience made this project very professional.

I tell you kids, I was never so proud of someone. I had tears in my eyes thinking of all the progress she made these past few months. I am still a little disappointed I didn't get to show case my talents.

Earlier in the day I went to visit Shirley and check up on Lucey. I wandered around with Lucey, wishing everyone 'Good Luck' and 'Break a Leg.' I found the 'Supremes' getting their hair and nails done in the Patients Beauty Salon. Remember I was the understudy of the group, just in case one of them had to back out? The one who was doing the Diana Ross role, (her voice sounds like nails on the blackboard) was having a cup of tea.

I could out sing her any day, but rules are rules. While I was chatting with the group, the wanna be Diana started to cough, said she had a tickle in her throat. I reached in my purse to give her some mints to soothe her throat. As I handed them to her, Lucey freaked out, jumped up and knocked the candy out of my hand and tried to bury them. She became all frantic and tugged on her leash trying to pull me out of there. I have no idea what came over her, just nerves I guess.

Once we left, she calmed down and I brought her back to Shirley who was busy giving last minute instructions to a group.

I went home to get ready for the big night and felt a little happy that Lucey would be coming home soon. The place is quiet without her; please don't ever tell her that. Okay? Her ego is big enough now.

Sarge was picking me up in his own car; I never realized he had one. He is always driving around in that stinky police vehicle that smells of stale cigars and old farts. He rang the bell and when I opened it he stood there sheepishly and presented me with a bouquet of flowers. I immediately asked him what he wanted, why was he trying to butter me up? He told me if I didn't like them I could throw them away.

How rude! But I felt better that the old Sarge was acting true to form so I relaxed.

I put the flowers in a vase, got my coat and we left. As Sarge held open the car door for me, I could see two more bouquets lying across the back seat. When he got into the car, I asked him who the flowers were for? "Shirley and Bette, of course. Who else?" he replied.

Wow! How thoughtful, who knew he had this soft side? I couldn't say anything; I was thinking maybe I misjudged him.... Nah!

What I did pester him about was what was the surprise he had planned for Bette. He held his ground and said he wanted to tell her first. I was welcomed to be there when he did. Now he was acting more normal again.

We arrived and parked then joined others in the Hospital's auditorium. As we entered, Sarge waved over a younger man and introduced me. "Yia Yia, oh, I'm sorry, I mean Patricia, this is Mario Corleone, he will be joining us this evening."

As I checked Mr. Corleone out, I realized that this had to be the man that owned the nightclub. I wondered what the heck was he doing here? Betty is not going to be happy to see him. I tugged on the Sarge's sleeve to get his attention, but at that moment, the lights dimmed and the show began.

A ragtime piano player was the first act. He pounded the piano with enthusiasm belting out hits like, 'The Entertainer, Proud Mary, and finished his act with a rousing edition of 'Good Golly Miss Molly.' The audience were hooting and clapping and everyone was put in an upbeat mood.

Next came the Sinatra impersonator. He was skinny like Old Blue Eyes, and he had on one of the signature hats he used to wear. That's where the similarity ended. The man tried hard but it was more croaking than singing. He got an A for effort and went off the stage a happy camper.

Then it was Shirley's turn. Oh My Gosh! Was she ever something else? The tricks she did with the bike and then the unicycle, some of them defied gravity. I was glad she had on a different costume then the regular blue body suit with the orange lightening bolts. Actually, this one was a bit more subdued. It had patriotic theme: a blue top with red and white striped pants. She really wowed the audience.

Some more acts then the 'Supremes' turn. I couldn't believe my ears; they were bolting out 'Baby Love, You Can't Hurry Love and Stop, in the Name of Love.' It took a moment until I realized they were lip-synching. That's why no one worried about how they sounded. I felt better that those cat skinners didn't out do me. (You know, I sing so much better.)

On the program next was Bette. The curtained opened and there she stood. She was resplendent in a blue and gold costume of harem pants and blousy top, She had on all sorts of jangling bracelets and anklets that rang out with her every move. A small veil covered face and her hair was braided with ribbons of gold through out. She looked gorgeous, like someone out of Arabian Nights. I took a peek at Mr. Corleone and the Sarge finding them transfixed.

Bette started with a low slow beat as she twirled gracefully around her pole. She stepped off a few time to do a partial belly dance and to shake the booty around. As the music intensified, Bette increased her twirling and shaking. The auditorium seemed to be vibrating with her every move.

At her conclusion, she spun around the pole a few times and then gracefully descended to its base with her head bowed as the lights lowered. She brought down the house with the ovation and had three curtain calls. How great for her. She really could dance.

Finally, the last act, it was the ventriloquist and Lucey. As Bob, the ventriloquist, walked on stage, he tripped. Lucey trotting behind him said, "Watch where you're going, you big oaf." Everyone started laughing. Bob sat in a chair in the middle of the stage and Lucey jumped up to a hassock that was along side him.

Bob slipped Lucey a treat and then asked her how was life treating her? Lucey looked around and moving her mouth complained, "Would you believe me if I said I lead a dog's life?"

Bob asked. "Is that so bad? Doesn't seems all that terrible to me." To which Lucey replied, "Yeah, but you've never been fixed." The audience howled at that.

Bob: So Lucey, they tell me you are a Cock-A-Poo. What exactly is that?

Lucey: I'm a genetically engineered hybrid: half Cocker and half Poodle.

Bob: Impressive. So can you speak French?

Lucey: Oh, Oui, Oui!

Bob: Not now Lucey, you have to hold it for a while

Lucey: Not wee wee you Numbskull, Oui Oui means yes in French.

And so the act went on like that with Lucey mocking poor Bob and having the audience in the palm of her paw. At the finish of their act, Bob and Lucey had the pleasure Lucey of inviting the cast members out for their final bow.

As the curtain descended, the cast dispersed to greet family and friends in the audience. Leroy was a glow with Bette's triumph and said he had a big surprise for her.

"Me too", offered Sarge. "Who should go first?" Leroy gave Mario a skeptical once over and then told Sarge that he should. Said he wanted a little privacy, if we didn't mind.

Uh oh, I thought that there might be something serious going on here. Bette and Shirley found us and came running over, dragging Lucey with them. Lucey was stopped to receive all kinds of compliments and praise. Great. As if her head isn't big enough!

When they got closer, Bette recognized Mario and she got an

attitude immediately. Then she spotted Leroy and just got plain confused. Sarge went over handed her the bouquet and spoke to her quietly, and then he told her Mario had something he wanted to tell her.

Mario in front of all of us told Bette he owed her an apology. He explained he was insensitive and never gave her a chance. He said he dropped the charges and would pay any expenses she accrued because of the incident. Next he offered her a job at the club. Said she was amazing and would she consider it.

Leroy jumped in at that. Said his woman wasn't going to dance for anybody but him. That's when he got down on one knee and asked Betty to be his wife, so much for privacy.

All Bette could think of saying was, "Golly!" Followed by, "YES! YES! YES!"

Shirley and I were holding on to each other blubbering. Lucey was looking around to see who would give her a treat. But the Sarge still had more to say, after giving Shirley her flowers he told her that he had worked it out with the judge, that when Shirley was released she could do her community service as a crossing guard. She still had to wait for 6 more months to reapply for a driver's license but everything looked good.

What a night. Bette gathered up her belongings, kissed everyone goodbye and left with Leroy. She invited us all to the wedding and Mario offered the club for the reception. He based the offer on the condition that Bette does her dance one more time. Bette looked over to Leroy who nodded his approval.

Shirley and Lucey returned to patient floor for a few more days until Shirley got transferred to outpatient care. Sarge drove me home and I was still going on and on about the night's events.

I'm stilled amazed how Sarge orchestrated the whole thing. I tried to get more information out of him, but he insisted he was just doing his job.

He walked me to the door, gave me a peck on the cheek and left. I wondered if I was ever going to see him again. Maybe I can get arrested or something. No, he ain't going far. Who is going to keep me out of trouble?

Good night for now.

Love you all,

Yia

Moving On

October01, 2012

Hi All,

I can't believe how quickly the time has passed, summer is over already and fall has begun. There is so much that has happened since the big night at the sanatorium.

The best event was Bette's and Leroy's wedding. Shirley and I were attendants and Bette's daughter was her maid of honor. Lucey was the flower dog and almost stole the show from Bette. The whole thing was remarkable; not a dry eye to be seen anywhere in the church. Bette and Leroy were glowing and as usual, you couldn't understand a word Bette said when she was reciting her vows. She was excited and spoke too fast but Leroy and the Pastor seemed to know what she said, so that's what counts.

However, the entire Church did managed to hear what she said as they were pronounced man and wife, she blurted out, "Golly!"

Mario Corleone kept true to his word and held the reception at his nightclub. No detail was overlooked. The food, the flowers, the music, just everything was first rate. Towards the end of the evening, Mario asked us all to stand and to raise a glass to the happy couple. Then after the toast, he told everyone to be seated and announced, "I want to introduce the best dancer in NYC and the toughest lady I ever met. She taught me a lot about perseverance and being human.

Ladies and Gentlemen, I present Miss Bette Bam Be Lam!"

The curtain open and there was Bette; she repeated her performance that she did at the sanatorium. A hush came over the guests at they watched in awe. At the conclusion of her number it took a while for the group to react, then they all clapped and hollered as Bette basked in their response.

Meanwhile, Mario was seen chatting up Leroy and then he took the mike again and declared that with permission from her new husband, (here he interjected that he didn't think Bette needed it) that Bette would be appearing on weekends at the club.

A loud round of applause rocked the place and Bette was over heard saying, "Golly" again.

As for Shirley, upon her release from the hospital, Sarge got her a job as a school crossing guard. She got some training and was issued a bright yellow jacket and a big hand paddle that said Stop on one side and Go on the other. After a few days of shadowing a fellow guard, learning the ropes, she was assigned her corner.

The first week went well with no incidents. The kids all got to know her and she them. As the weeks progressed, Shirley would spend time talking with the children waiting to cross. As more kids arrived and joined conversation, there were several occasions when the students were tardy. Shirley was told to confine her discussions to after school hours.

One particular damp and dreary morning, Shirley was at her post, crossing her students. It was getting close to the bell and kids were rushing not to be late. A little second grade girl was hurrying across the road, wearing her backpack and carrying a small sack. As she got to the middle near Shirley, she tripped and fell. Her little package dropped and rolled a few feet from her.

Shirley kept the traffic stopped and rushed over to help her. First she checked to make sure she was okay, but the child was crying and worrying about her sack. Shirley looked around and at first didn't see it.

The little girl told Shirley through her tears that she had to find it, it was for Show and Tell, and she was bringing in her baby chick for the class to see.

In the mean time, the cars were backing up in all directions, motorist were getting annoyed at the delayed and some honked their horns and got out of their cars to see what was the hold up.

Time was suspended for Shirley as she now frantically searched the area for the chick. Other students gathered at the corner waiting to cross and witnessed Shirley looking under stopped vehicles and in sewer drains. The little girl remained in the sitting in the middle of the street, bawling.

The gridlock spread out in all directions, a couple of drivers at the front of the jam got out to see if they could help. They saw the little girl still crying, the growing group of students yelling on the corner and Shirley's legs sticking out from under the front of another vehicle.

It was obvious; the car struck the Crossing guard. They called 911 and reported the accident and the need for an ambulance.

As the chaos continued, a larger group of drivers abandoned their vehicles and joined the scene. One of the drivers went to aid the child in the street and saw the paddle lying next to her. She decided to try to unsnarl the traffic jam but gave up the thought as she turned and saw the magnitude of vehicles. Another wanted to pull Shirley out from the car she was under but was stopped by somebody else who thought it may injure her more. Nobody had a clue what to do.

Looking down at Shirley's legs, someone saw that they were moving, actually going further under the car. In the meantime, the ambulance and police car sirens were wailing in the distance.

Finally, Shirley's legs all but disappeared; her whole body was now under the car. The driver was accused of moving his car, but the car had been turned off and in park.

The haunting sounds of sirens just added to the cacophony that filled the area. Help was near but struggling to get through the maze of traffic. Then when some of the motorists comforted the crying child and others tried to cross the waiting students, an amazing thing happened. Shirley's legs reappeared and she was inching her way out from underneath the car.

She struggled to get out and stand up. The startled crowd was shocked into silence until the little girl cried out, “You found it!” There stood Shirley, all covered in road soot and bedraggled, holding on to a fluffy yellow stuffed chick.

Shock registered on the faces of the group, relief that she was all right, followed by anger that all this caused an inconvenience in their daily routine. The mob almost turned ugly except that help in the way of Sarge arrived and took charge. He checked Shirley and the girl and upon knowing they were not hurt, he cancelled the ambulance. Next he told everyone to return to his or her cars. He cleared the walkway and crossed the remaining students.

Shirley and the little girl, her name was Susie was told to wait on the sidewalk for Susie’s mother.

Traffic control unsnarled the gridlock eventually and the Sarge, Shirley, Susie and her Mom all went downtown to fill out a report on the incident.

Sarge was concerned that the stuffed chick may have had an effect on Shirley, but she seemed fine. She said she just was doing her job and had no idea what the fuss was all about. Susie's Mom was grateful the Shirley had such compassion for her child to even endanger herself. The school asked that Shirley be reassigned. It was obvious that Shirley had great rapport with the students, but she was easily detracted.

Luckily, an opportunity in the PAL program was available and Shirley was given a new job. It was the best of two worlds, she taught riding safety and how to do minor repairs on bikes to keep them in safe and good condition. A job made in Heaven for her.

At the end of her community service, she stayed on for a while, but she had other plans for her future. For a while she was in touch with George, the chef in California. He never understood why she didn't like his cooking and left so fast. They started communication via phone and E-mail and George invited her out for a visit, a long visit.

Lucey is thoroughly bored at home; she is sulking all around. She was reluctant to get off the stage when her act was over with Bob. She had to be dragged. She perked up at Bette's wedding when she got lots of attention. She's such a people friendly dog. I'm planning on taking her a couple times a week to the sanatorium where she can do her therapy shtick.

The other day when I was at the sanatorium making arrangements for our schedule of therapy visits, I had an opportunity to go relax in the garden. You know, the one where I met Shirley. Anyway, you'll never guess what happened. There in the shadow of a big old tree, sitting on a bench, chattering away like a chipmunk sat a lonely woman. I went over an introduced myself. I asked if she was ok and she told me she was just a little bored. She wasn't haven't any fun lately. I told her I had a cure for that and would she like to join me in some adventures. She said sure!

Oh, by the way, her name is Marsha.

Off again,

Love,

Yia

Encore

A little extra in the way of Yia Yia letters; these were sent as Thank You notes. I was going to include my Book Club records, however that started a bit of a controversy.

The most recent is my letter to my New York friends who invited me into the city to enjoy the day with them. They had just recently relocated to a beautiful East Side apartment and proudly gave me the tour. I expanded a tad in my enthusiasm to show my gratitude for their efforts. Perhaps going a bit out there in a way.

The other, a few letters to the Audi manager in response to a form letter that I am sure is sent to all new customers. I decided, why not invite him to join our clan as a polite gesture. Maybe even round up a few more buyers.

Needless to say, neither of them ever called or wrote me back. I reached out to my friends in the city but their number has been changed and my mail came back, return to sender. Do you think they may have moved already?

As for Audi, I stopped in the showroom but the sweet gentleman to whom I wrote was transferred out of state, by his own request.

Onto my Book Club buddies, they said they loved the written notes of our literary meetings and the extra stories of the rocket ship adventures. However, when I told them my intentions to publish some of the letters, they all threw a hissy fit, stomped around and in unison shouted, "NO WAY!" Next thing I knew I was dismembered. Figuratively not literally.

As Lucey says, all great artists suffer for their art. Well, when I am famous, I'll try to understand and forgive. Fortunately for me, the family sticks with me. In fact just the other day they were altogether and told me that it wouldn't be long until they find me a nice new place to live. Said as soon as the commitment papers were ready, I was good to go. Aren't they something?

So here some of Yia Yia's personal letters, just a little extra to fill out more pages. The first, my Thank You letter to my dear friends. The others were sent to the Audi dealerships with hopes they had a sense of humor.

I've changed their names just in case they don't.

May 12,2014

Dear Ned and Rosa,

Many thanks for your generous and warm hospitality. I had a lovely day and discovered that I like Vietnamese food and enjoy the more modern style of the ballet. The Joyce will be in my future for more performances.

When I got home, I couldn't wait to tell the children and the grands about my great day in the city and about your beautiful apartment. As I described what wonderful hosts you were and the ambience of your gorgeous home, they all decided right then to make you honorary members of the Linaris clan.

From now on you will be Uncle Ned and Aunt Rosa in our family. Please tell Rocco and Marla they have a whole bunch of new cousins. I'm sure they will be as thrilled as you must be too.

We have all coordinated and decided that the last month of July would fit our schedule to come in and spend a week with you. The little ones can't wait to ride that super sonic elevator, which should keep them busy for a while. The others are excited to see the weather fronts that arrive at your spectacular 27th floor western views.

The fussy ones were worried about sleeping space. I assured them that there was plenty of room. Last place we visited only had one bedroom for the 12 grands and they were a little squished. They can really spread out in your digs.

And Aunt Rosa, don't worry about meals. We'll be fine with any take out you can order, pizza or Chinese are the favorites. I would suggest not using your best china though, it might get broken during their food fights. Just be sure to have plenty of soft drinks available for the young'ums. Us, older bunch look forward to the five o'clock hour with some hard stuff. (Actually the son-in-laws get a meaner than rattlesnakes without some real libation, if you know what I mean.)

Also the grands wanted to know if the building had a pool. I told them I didn't know but that big Jacuzzi should be able to hold at least 3 or 4 of them for some water fun.

So thank you once again and I can't wait for our family vay-kay with you in July.

Warmest regards,

Your new cuz,

Pat

PS: Please tell cousin Marla that when the group found out their new cousins lived in Virginia, they immediately began planning a visit to her and her family to get acquainted. I figured I give her a heads up.

A Message from Amici Audi Dealership

September 22,2011

Yia Yia Linaris

Fairfield, NJ 07004

Dear Mrs. Linaris,

In today's automotive market place, there are many fine automobiles to choose from and many excellent dealerships eager for your business. So I am especially please that you have chose to purchase your 2009 Audi from Amici Audi. You are joining a family of thousands of satisfied customers that has been growing for many years.

I hope your purchase experience met your expectations and that you are extremely satisfied with your Audi. Our team of automotive professionals stands ready to ensure that your ownership experience remains a source of driving joy and your vehicle stays in top form.

I will be sending you a customer Satisfaction Survey. If for any reason you cannot score us EXTREMELY SATISFIED, please contact me immediately, so I may resolve whatever the issue may be. If there is anything else I can do to ensure your ownership experience continues to be excellent, please do not hesitate to contact me directly.

Congratulations and thank you again,

Sincerely,

James Rocco

General Manager

Amici Audi

September 24,2011

Amici Audi

Attention: James Rocco

General Manager

Dear Mr. Rocco,

Thank you so much for that lovely letter. You all make me feel so much like family. You won't mind if I call you Jim, will you? I seem to know you already with you making me feel so welcomed.

I didn't realize that purchasing an Audi would have brought me so many nice people into my life. I should have bought one years ago, by golly.

I'm going to return the favor and extend the hospitality to you and all those lovely people at your dealership. You are all now honorary members of the Linaris clan. Let's see, there are four of my children and their spouses and of course, all those 12 grand-babies. Lot's of extra nieces and nephews and numerous hanger-oners. We don't know them all, but they are family just the same. No need to thank me.

Talking family to family now, I was wondering if you have any openings in that place of yours? A couple of the grand babies are having a rough time landing a job. They are due out next week and need letter of employment for their parole officer. Any job will do, but Charlie is awful good at stripping cars, and Jeb can jump start just about any make or model. So you see they have lots of experience.

Well, I got to be going now, taking that Audi for another spin. Just leave me an e-mail where you all are having Thanksgiving dinner. I'll be sure to tell the rest of the clan. You're gonna love

Billy-Bob's moonshine. I had to convince him to share. His supply is getting low because he blew up his still and the back of his house last week. He's being a good sport about it, just be sure to give him the drumstick.

Your new kiss'n cousin,

Yia

Wednesday, October 12,2011

Amici Audi

Attn: Cousin Jim Rocco

Hi again Jim,

I was wondering why I haven't heard from you about our Thanksgiving get together. I know you must be very busy being a big executive and all, probably a little shy too. But then it dawned on me. Thanksgiving is not a good day to spring all your new extended family on you. Of course not! Whatever was I thinking? You'd never have time trying to get the turkey and all the fixin's on the table and all.

So to break the ice and speed things up, I decided to have what you people in the business call, a Meet and Greet session. I've rented a school bus for all the young'uns and told the elders to follow in their pick-ups. We're all coming to your dealerships on Halloween. You'll love the kiddies in their costumes. (Be sure to have a few treats for them, some can get meaner than Tasmanian devils when they need a sugar fix.) Their folks will be fine with that there Quarto Café. A little real libation wouldn't hurt to loosen up some of the more bashful ones.

And this is not just a social call, heck no. My niece Gertie is in the market for a mini- bus. With eight kids and one on the way, it's pretty tight in their old Subaru hatchback. Please throw that deal Benito's way. I'm trying to round up some customers for that sweetie so he doesn't have to the Santa gig at the mall.

As usual, no need to thank me. Whatever is family for? See you at Halloween. You're gonna love my costume.

Cousin Yia

October 16, 2011

Dear Cousin Jim,

Benito has e-mailed me and told me how much you love hearing from me. He also told me that you haven't time to respond because you are the head honcho of two of those big dealerships. You are really something. When I told the rest of the family, they just about popped their buttons with pride knowing there was such a big executive in the clan.

Word got out to our hanger-oners and they want to get in on the introductions. They rented themselves a bus and are coming to our get together on Halloween. Just a little suggestion, make sure the Café is stocked with some hard stuff. These guys are heavy hitters, if you know what I mean.

No need to worry about the food. The Church ladies and I are planning a real feast that we'll bring along. Oh, they're coming in the Church van. This little Meet and Greet is turning into a real big old fashion shindig. I can hardly wait.

In order to ease your load, I copied your masthead info from that nice letter you sent me. I wrote a letter of employment to the parole board for those two Grands of mine. Honestly, they are so anxious to get out and start working on cars again. Simply one thing you don't have to do. Happy to help.

And here's the best part Jimmy, I've been saving it for last. Remember I told you my niece Gertie was in the family way? Well, she just had herself twins. Everyone was surprised. I don't know why. The woman was the size of an airplane hangar. Forgive me, I digress. In honor of you, she named the girl Jaime Lin. Lin after the family name. And that little boy, she named him James Rocco Jr. No explanation needed. I'm bummed out she didn't have triplets. Then we could have called that extra one Benito after my Sweetie Pie.

Have to run along now, got to blow the dust off that Audi!

Big cousin kiss,

Yia

October 24, 2011

Dear Jim,

Hope you are sitting down because this will knock your socks off.

The most amazing things are happening. My nephew Lionel, he's Floyd's boy, he's a reporter for a large local newspaper. He's been asking me a lot of questions about our Halloween gala and mostly about you.

Of course, I told him about your wonderful and heartwarming letter when you invited me into your Audi family. Then I told him about your help in getting Jeb and Charlie out of jail with a promise of employment. How you're hosting the Halloween party and having all of us over for a Thanksgiving feast. I let him know that our family admires you so much that they are even naming their children after you.

He was astounded that a big captain of the automobile industry has taken the time to be so warm and generous to our big extended family. He informed his editor all about it and guess what? They are going to do a human-interest article featuring you. That's right! How in this day and age of antibusiness sentiment and corporate greed you are throwing open the doors of your dealership and feting a needy family.

However, that's not the best part. Oh no! He contacted a major TV network and they will be there too, doing a live report from right in the dealership. Can you believe? Maybe even a docudrama would come out of this.

I hope you don't mind but I embellished it a little, just to give it an extra zip. I casually mentioned that you were going to name me, 'Customer of the Year' and that you are donating one of those

Audi SUV's to a needy member of the clan. Be sure to make it Gertie. She's jamming poor little Jimmy and Jaime into that hatchback with the rest of her brood. There's hardly any room left for the dogs.

Sorry, but I have to run along now. With all this media coverage I have to tone down my Halloween costume. I was going to be a Dallas Cheer leader. Might be to risqué for the evening news. I'm considering a pregnant Nun or Girl Scout now. What do you think?

One little favor. Please have that cutie Rob in finance at the party. I told my cousin Lola about him and she can't wait to get her she-devil claws into him.

Just to think, this all started when my sweetie Benito charmed me into buying that Audi. Be sure to thank him and maybe give him a little bonus. I wouldn't want him to have to moonlight at the mall.

Bye for now,

CousinYia

October 26, 2011

Dear Cousin Jim,

I have sad news for you and I hope you don't get too upset. Unfortunately, I had to call off our party. That's right. No Halloween bash and no Thanksgiving visit either for that matter.

Remember I was going to tone down my costume from cheerleader to pregnant Nun or Girl Scout? Well, I picked pregnant Nun and the family was outraged. Called me blasphemous. Jimmy, can you imagine? What a bunch of prudes.

Well, any family that hasn't got a sense of humor is no family of mine, so I canceled all our get togethers. They didn't deserve you.

And don't you go fretting about Jeb and Charlie. While working in the prison garage, they decided to hot wire the warden's car and take it for a little joy ride. They won't be getting released anytime soon.

As for Thanksgiving, Billie Bob repaired the back of his house and has a new still. The clan is going there to help him break it in on turkey day.

I'm disappointed too, but then again there's always Christmas. Maybe the feud will be over by then. Actually with Benito doing his Santa gig, it might be just the thing to bring us back together. I'm going to try to get them to go visit him at the mall.

Don't tell him, I want to surprise him.

Be well and thanks again for all your help.

Cousin Yia

Author Acknowledgements

What started as a fun way to communicate with my grandchildren at camp has become the effort you have read here. It began with my granddaughter Danielle's letter relating how she and her bunkmates cheered themselves when they were homesick. My responses became a popular read at camp and mushroomed over the years.

My family and friends encouraged me to put the stories in book form to hand down to the generations to come. (I think they just wanted to prove that insanity was a part of the family's genetic makeup.)

It has not been a solitary endeavor. I have had the help of my daughter Marilyse Sclafani with the editing, a daunting job. Also, the gifts of art work from my talented daughter-in-law, Sara Linaris and my stepson Michael.

Sara helped in organizing the images and designed the book cover. Michael drew the interior illustrations, bringing to life the zany characters.

A great deal of thanks goes to Terri Abstein and Colleen Goulet who have guided me throughout this process. I could have never done this without them.

My special cheering section came from the Dirty Dozen who have made me amaze myself with this undertaking. Thanks Kids!

Finally, heartfelt gratitude goes to my BFF, Marsha Diamond, on whom I fashioned my muse Shirley. Marsha has managed to keep my inner child alive and kicking.

Oops! Just a last item I almost forgot, Lucey. Actually, Lucey is a better writer than me and never lets me forget it.

CPSIA information can be obtained
at www.ICGtesting.com
Printed in the USA
BVHW032219300320
576390BV00001B/3/J